Godmother Night

Also by Rachel Pollack

Fiction

Golden Vanity (1980)
Alqua Dreams (1987)
Unquenchable Fire (1988)
Temporary Agency (1994)
Burning Sky (forthcoming)

Nonfiction

78 Degrees of Wisdom, Part 1 (1980)
78 Degrees of Wisdom, Part 2 (1983)
Salvador Dali's Tarot (1985)
Teach Yourself Fortune Telling (1986)
The Open Labyrinth (1986)
The New Tarot (1989)
The Haindl Tarot, Part 1 (1990)
The Haindl Tarot, Part 2 (1990)
Le Jeu Divinatoire (1991)
Shining Woman Tarot Deck (1992)

As Editor

Tarot Tales (with Caitlín Mathews) (1989)

RACHEL POLLACK

ABACUS

An *Abacus* Book

First published in the United States of America by St Martin's Press 1996
First published in Great Britain by Abacus 1996

*All characters in this publication are fictitious
and any resemblance to real persons, living or dead,
is purely coincidental.*

Note: Kate Cohen's healing potion, *Phytolacca Americana*, is an actual plant. This plant is poisonous and should not be taken as described in the story. It works for Kate only because Kate's godmother made it work.

A CIP catalogue record for this book
is available from the British Library.

ISBN 0 349 10836 6

Printed and bound in Great Britain by
Clays Ltd, St Ives plc

Abacus
A Division of
Little, Brown and Company (UK)
Brettenham House
Lancaster Place
London WC2E 7EN

for FARA SHAW KELSEY

in gratitude for

Wise Woman knowledge of babies and magical potions

and so much more

and

for ISABEL MILLER

Godmother of us all

Madrone Tree, red as blood
that once my mother was, be my rod
Death came when I was born
And from the Earth now you are grown
My father's a shadow, the wind is my god

ROBERT DUNCAN

Part One

The Woman Without a Name

One

The Toad Queen

There were once two women who lived on the back of a turtle. Their home lay on the edge of a city at the end of a river, where saltwater surged in from the sea. Far away, by other towns and rivers, the rocks and trees and black roads of the land ended by a second sea, so that the country where the women lived rose up out of the water like a turtle drawn to memories of the sun. A great variety of people had come to live in this land. Most of them thought of the country as somehow the same as the laws and committees pasted like artificial mushrooms on the surface of the Earth. But the people who had lived there first, who may have come across a bridge from somewhere else, or may have woken up in darkness and emerged through holes into the light, or may have followed a lizard or a fish or a bird or even a turtle through tunnels up to the sun, these people who had lived there so long understood that the land is nothing else but itself. And they understood the way it lay between waters, with its hard shell hiding a soft, slow belly and a mind dull and tender and patient.

The women who lived on the turtle were named by their separate parents Lauren and Jacqueline. As a child Lauren allowed common agreement to change her name to Laurie. At the age of thirteen, however, she gathered up her childhood coloring books, her diary, and several other bits of paper with the name "Laurie" on them and burned them all in her parents' backyard. For several years she allowed only her grandmother to call her Laurie, a curious exception, since it was this grandmother who'd originally named her Lauren. Lauren, formerly Laurie, née Lauren, insisted that "diminutives diminish" and that "Lauren" sounded like an ancient bird, whereas "Laur-ie" sounded like some small animal poked with a stick.

Late one spring evening several years later, she once again abandoned "Lauren" and returned to the "-ie" of her childhood. She did not do this casually, or simply to annoy people, or to demonstrate she could train and retrain them "like dogs in the circus," as her father said. She made the change because of a special event that happened that night in the last half of her senior year of college.

Jacqueline bore the same name for eighteen years, including brief periods in which she thought of variations, such as Jac-qué-line, or Jacque-lien, or even Jack, none of which she mentioned to anyone, even to those people she thought of as her best friends. She never believed in the name Jacqueline. Sometimes, in school or at family parties, people would have to call her two or three times before she realized that "Jacqueline" meant her. People accused her of dreaminess, or arrogance, or stupidity, despite her high marks and carefully written compositions. Jacqueline accepted whatever version they created of her, never explaining that the name was wrong, that it could never refer to *her.*

It sometimes seemed to her that her real name lay just out of reach, just past memory. She tried playing tricks on herself, like writing down everything that happened in her dreams, thinking she would automatically catch some dream person calling her Helen or Sophie or Rachel or Gretel. But nothing ever came. She tried studying lists from books, such as *Lives of the Great Storytellers,* or *What to Name Your New Baby.* She would say each name aloud and slowly, waiting for some flash of recognition. Or she would read the names very fast, hoping to stumble over one in particular. Again, nothing. She began to think her real name didn't exist, that God, or the angel in charge of such things, had forgotten to give it to her.

Throughout her childhood she cohabited with this name that had nothing to do with her, thankful at least that only doctors insisted on calling her Jackie. On her sixteenth birthday, when her parents insisted on a party, and ordered a cake with "Jacqueline" written in pink across it, and even gave her a gold bracelet with a name tag attached to it, the birthday girl decided to accept the emptiness created by a body and mind without a name. For another two years and four months, she tried not to think of this emptiness, until a single event changed both her name and her life forever.

The event that broke open the names of Lauren and Jacqueline began as a dance on the campus of their college, in that city in the eastern part of the turtle, not far from the sea. The school announced the dance to celebrate a victory in a yearly contest among a league of colleges. The contest was a quest sponsored by a foundation that had been created by an archaeologist who had won a government lottery. The goal of the quest was the same each year, a large porcelain toad, with black stones for eyes and a dark red circle on the top of its head.

In recent years, as the quest gained more and more status for the school that found the toad, more and more resources went into it, with plans and analyses coming from the departments of computer science, physics, psychology, cultural anthropology, and even comparative literature. Lauren and Jacqueline's school, however, won that year by the efforts of an unusual champion, a woman who washed dormitory sheets and lab coats in the school laundry.

Fed up by all the shouting and the demonstrations (for the different departments had taken to attacking each other), the laundress, Gertrude, was sitting by her washing machines when the sheets spinning round and round reminded her of something. That night, she dreamed about a time when she was very little and her mother had taken her to hear a storyteller at a shopping mall near their home. The storyteller had sat outside, before a giant lottery wheel, which appeared in Gertrude's dream as a rack of wet sheets turning and flapping in the wind. On her next day off, Gertrude took the bus back to her hometown and the shopping mall. The wheel was still there, and at the back of it she found a small door with a brass ring. Gertrude pulled, and pulled again, while a group of teenage girls in leather jackets and tight skirts stood around laughing. The door jerked open; inside, Gertrude found something cool and smooth. The dark eyes of the toad stared at her as she held it up to the sun.

So the toad came to Jacqueline's college. In the week of the dance—with banners going up around the gym, and posters appearing on walls, and flags flying from dormitory windows, and men and women in toad masks and overalls building a giant replica of the trophy out of balsa wood and papier-mâché—in this week of spectacles, Jacqueline thought over and over of attending the dance, and every time, she decided it was not for her, not for a woman without a name.

In high school she had never participated much in teenage culture. Her friendships always seemed apart from the various groups that clustered around sports or honor societies or gangs or intellectual pretension. And the people she considered friends always seemed to put the group first, spending time with her mostly at her invitation, when nothing of greater interest summoned them. Jacqueline did not think of herself as very interesting. Without a name, even her body seemed half out of existence, a little like the holograms displayed at science fairs. She went to a few dances but didn't stay long. The other girls always seemed to know what to do—how to stand, or make jokes, or dance with each other if there were no boys available. Jacqueline would sip punch, or try dancing or talking to people, but after a while her legs and shoulders would hurt from the strain of trying to appear relaxed, and she'd leave.

Sometimes boys asked her to dance, just as boys sometimes asked her for a date. Usually she agreed. She'd move around the floor, or she'd go to whatever horror movie the boy had chosen, and do her best to work out the correct responses of a girl with a name to anchor her in the world. Her parents never understood why their daughter wasn't more popular. She was certainly pretty, they reassured her. And smart, they added, as if they'd forgotten. Maybe she should join more clubs. Her mother suggested different hairstyles or brighter makeup. Her father gave her money for clothes. Their daughter never paid much attention. They kept saying that name that had nothing to do with her. "Jacqueline, would you like a party?" or "Jacqueline, do you need a new dress?"

For a while in high school Jacqueline went out regularly with a boy named Dan Reynolds. Dan was a science student who frequently angered his teachers by demonstrating ways to cheat on lab experiments. Dan planned to open a computer business after college. At other times he talked of gathering a squad of renegade hackers and sabotaging the armed forces of several nations. He was handsome, or could be in a few years, when his face cleared and his body filled out. He never seemed to know how to behave in groups of people, sometimes talking too loudly, other times saying nothing at all. A couple of times Jacqueline overheard girls talking about Dan, calling him "weird" or "slimy." Jacqueline guessed they knew she was listening.

Dan's mother drank, Dan told Jacqueline one night after he himself had drunk several beers stolen from home. Because his mother was drunk so often, he and his father had to do all the cleaning and shopping. Dan and Jacqueline were sitting in Dan's car, in the parking lot of a golf course. He kept his hands on the steering wheel while he talked, and though he didn't look at her he clearly expected some reaction. Jacqueline said, "There's nothing wrong with men doing the cleaning."

Dan said, "Shit," and started the engine. To both their surprise Jacqueline insisted on driving, even grabbing the keys from the ignition. For a moment it looked like Dan might hit her, but she just sat there, with the keys closed in her fist, saying, "You're drunk, you can't drive," until at last he got out and came around to the passenger side.

As Jacqueline drove onto the highway a red sports car passed her. Inside, a woman with long hair and shiny teeth waved at her. "Did you see that?" Jacqueline started to say, but Dan was staring at the trees along the road. When Jacqueline looked again, the red car was gone.

That night, Jacqueline lay in bed, thinking not of Dan but of the woman in the car. The woman had waved to her, she was sure of it. Jacqueline thought she knew her, but couldn't think from where. A long time ago: Very young. Her mother had left her in the stroller, outside a store. There was a park or something—she remembered trees and a group of people, women with short red hair, running or dancing. With her eyes and fists shut, she tried to bring it back. Someone came up to the stroller, a woman, bending over her, long hair . . . No use. If it actually had happened she'd been too young to remember it. Except—she remembered a sound, which when she thought about it now might have been sirens. And people crying, and her mother wheeling her away very fast. She sighed. Maybe Dan could hypnotize her. The idea made her laugh. Jacqueline did her best to relax; after a while she fell asleep.

The next morning, Dan called while she was having breakfast. Very calmly, he told her his mother had died during the night. An accident, he said. She'd fallen asleep at the wheel of her car and smashed it into a tree. Would Jacqueline please tell his homeroom teacher what had happened, and explain that Dan would be out of school for a few days? Perhaps she could bring him his assignments.

At the funeral, Dan stood very stiffly in a gray suit, thanking everyone for coming, including Jacqueline and his own relatives. For a week afterward, Jacqueline attempted to persuade Dan to talk about what had happened, to tell her the details of the accident, to describe how he felt. "I'm okay," he told her, and "Life goes on, with or without us," and "There's no sense crying over spilt milk." He then went on to describe his project for the science fair, a method of decoding cosmic radio signals for signs of UFOs.

Jacqueline's relationship with Dan ended one evening on the floor of her parents' house. She and Dan were alone, her parents having gone to a party. "Fate's sending us a message," Dan told her, kissing and rubbing her. Lately he'd been pressing for an "affirmation" of their love, saying that virginity was old-fashioned even in their parents' time, or else describing ancient rituals to celebrate nature. Just as it looked like she might give in—they were half undressed, and Dan had his hand somewhere inside her panties—he breathed to her, "Jacqueline, I love you, Jacqueline. Oh, Jacqueline." Suddenly he stopped. She wasn't looking at him. When she turned she said, "What?" in a confused sort of way, as if he'd been talking to someone else. Dan yanked out his hand from her crotch. He slammed the door as he left.

In her first year of college now, in the week of the toad, Jacqueline couldn't see much point in going to another dance. It would be just like high school. And it was a costume dance, too, which meant trying to think of something, spending money, feeling dumb.

Her roommate, Louise, was going. She'd already gotten a black shirt and tight black pants, a black polyester cape with a plastic sword, and a mask to cover her eyes. Sometimes Louise would wave the sword and leap onto her bed, until she fell over laughing. Louise had recently joined the Lesbian Student Union. She was "in love with all womankind," Louise told her roommate. Jacqueline thought how wonderful it must be to belong somewhere.

On the night of the dance Louise tried once more to convince Jacqueline to come with her. "Everybody's going," she said. "This is really special. It'll probably never happen again."

"I don't have a costume."

"We can make you one." She began searching through Jacqueline's clothes.

"Stop it," Jacqueline said. "I'm just not going. I won't have anyone to dance with."

"Dance with me." Louise grabbed Jacqueline and whirled her around. "You can toad-hop with the LSU. We'd love to have you."

Jacqueline laughed but pulled loose. "I can't do that."

"Why? Because people will think you're a dyke?"

"I don't care what people will think. I just wouldn't belong. I'd feel like a fake."

At nine o'clock Louise tied on her mask, gave her sword one last twirl at the air, and leaped out the door. Jacqueline listened to the thump of her boots as she strode to the elevator. At nine-thirty Jacqueline decided it was too hot to study and went down to the lounge to see what she could find on television. Two boys sat there, slumped on the couch watching a baseball game. Jacqueline walked outside.

She could hear the music before she even saw the gym. When she rounded the corner of the library, she saw that the gym was hung with banners and a huge drawing of a toad lit by a floodlamp. Inside, the band played "The Toad Hop," a record from a few years back. Over the music sounded the thump of people squatting down and then leaping into the air. Jacqueline stood about fifty yards from the building, watching the people who were hanging around outside, some kissing, some taking quick drinks or puffs of officially forbidden substances.

Just as Jacqueline was about to leave, a black limousine rolled up on the narrow road in front of the gym. A woman stepped out wearing a long patchwork dress made of scraps of velvet and hung with beads, pearls, feathers, and ordinary rocks. A wide-brimmed hat with a soft crown was tilted back on her head. Her red hair hung in three long braids down her back. Five more women came out of the car; they all had short hair, and long white scarves, silk probably, fluttered down their backs. Despite the heat, all five wore red leather jackets, tight red pants, and black sandals. Gold stitching on the backs of their jackets formed a small labyrinth, and below it, in graceful script, the words "Mother Night." When they turned slightly to glance about the building, Jacqueline saw sharp lines running across their cheeks.

The limousine moved softly away. At the door of the gym the woman in the patchwork dress turned and raised her head slightly. It was the smile Jacqueline recognized. The clothes were different, and the woman had given up her red sports car, but Jacqueline knew that smile. She ran forward as the woman and her gang disappeared into the crowd and noise.

A skinny boy in a cowboy suit and a cardboard toad mask blocked Jacqueline from going inside. "Gotta have a costume," he said.

"I just want to speak to someone," Jacqueline said, and tried to shove him aside. A few people laughed as the boy pushed her back. Half running, Jacqueline rushed out the campus gates and down to the local shopping street where an all-purpose store stayed open late. She found a bunch of colored ribbons and a dark red lipstick.

Back in her room Jacqueline put on a green sleeveless top—she'd decided not to wear a bra—and a long black skirt, and no shoes. She taped the ribbons all up and down her arms, then tied one around her neck so that the ends hung down over her breasts. With Louise's kohl eyeliner she drew a mask around her eyes, with lines drawn back to her ears for the strings. She used her own mascara to create dark streaks in her blond hair, then put on the lipstick in thick strokes, laughing at the way it lit up her face. She was about to leave when she ran back to the mirror and used an indigo eye pencil to draw a crude labyrinth on her chest, just above the cleavage revealed by the green top.

The cowboy let her in without comment. Inside, she pushed her way through the thick crowd, ignoring the loud music and the dancers banging into her. Near the front of the room, not far from the giant toad on its platform, a group of women were dancing together. For a moment Jacqueline thought she saw one of the red leather people, but when she came closer it was only one of Louise's friends in a devil suit. Standing on tiptoe to see over the crowd, Louise herself waved excitedly at Jacqueline, who waved back and went on searching.

It was so confusing. Everyone had become a knight or a princess or a witch or a toad—there were lots of toads, some with whole costumes, including elaborate helmetlike heads, others with nothing more than the same cardboard face worn by the bouncer at the door. Jacqueline didn't know who had manufactured the toad masks, but she remembered seeing stacks of them for sale around the campus during the past week. People had worn them at rallies, or working on the dance preparations—she remembered a crew of bare-chested toads hammering the platform together in the unusual spring heat—or even while just walking along campus or sitting in the dorm lounge or cafeteria. As Jacqueline looked through the crowd, the band started playing "The Toad Hop" again and people rushed to grab each other's hips, hopping up and down in long lines until the building shook. Jacqueline did her best to shove past them or look over them when they fell laughing to the floor.

She found the redhaired woman standing by someone near a makeshift table with bowls of peanuts, potato chips, and some sort of creamy salad. The other person wore a top hat and tails, and black patent-leather shoes, like an old-fashioned tap dancer. She stood with her back to Jacqueline, with her weight resting on her left leg and her hands in the pockets of her striped pants. Jacqueline knew it was a she, despite the short hair, the wide shoulders (exaggerated by the cut of the jacket) and narrow hips.

Next to her, the woman in the velvet dress looked very small, much smaller than she'd seemed standing by her limousine. She smiled at Jacqueline. Very fine sparkles dotted her face, and when she smiled the sparkles danced in the light like fireflies. She looked up at the woman in the top hat. "Laurie," she said, "I want you to meet someone." Her voice had a curious accent, or rather lilt, that gave it a half-foreign quality, like someone who's lived for years in another country and now has returned to her home.

When the tall woman turned her head, Jacqueline stepped back. The woman had whitened her face, then darkened her eyes and mouth to make a skull. When she took her hands from her pockets she was wearing black gloves, with skeleton bones painted down the backs and fingers. She looked like an old drawing—Death in a top hat and tails. Ignoring Jacqueline, the tall woman said to the other woman, "How do you know my name? Anyway, you're wrong. It's not Laurie, it's Lauren."

The red-haired woman said nothing, only sipped from a plastic cup she held in both hands. "Laurie," the tall woman repeated. "Lauren. Laurie." She laughed loudly, drowning out the music, at least in that corner of the room. "Well, why not?" she said. "Let's make it Laurie again." She clapped her hands. Now she turned and looked at Jacqueline. There was something predatory in that look; not malicious, just a hunter sizing up a prey. But then she softened, and became a little confused. Jacqueline just stood there. She'd come looking for the woman with the red hair, but there was something about the other one. She had flat cheekbones, a sharp chin, and a thin straight nose. Her large eyes shone with excitement, ruining the skull effect.

Looking at the tall woman, Jacqueline became conscious of her own body as a kind of awkward assemblage. Her breasts were too large and floppy in her too-thin green top. How could she ever have been so stupid as to go without a bra? She felt sweaty as well. She was standing awkwardly. When she tried to correct her posture, she realized—too late—that the gesture pushed her breasts forward. The tall woman grinned, and grinned wider when Jacqueline caved in her chest again.

"Laurie," the woman in the velvet dress said, "I want you to meet an old friend of mine." She took Jacqueline's hand and drew her closer. "This is Jaqe," she said.

She pronounced it "Jake," but Jacqueline—Jaqe—knew how to spell it from that first moment. She stood shaking, unaware of the tears surging from her eyes. *It's so simple,* she thought. It was there, it was always there, all those years. Jaqe! Her name was Jaqe! She grabbed the tall woman—Laurie—and spun around with her. "Congratulate me," she said. "Don't ask why. Just congratulate me." When Jaqe let her go, Laurie bowed. "Congratulations," she said, and made a swooping gesture with her top hat. Jaqe curtsied. Standing up, she felt a little dizzy, and wondered if that's what books meant when they said the heroine felt faint.

Laurie smiled, and Jaqe couldn't help but laugh. It looked so incongruous, Death smiling at her just when she felt so alive, so in focus, as if she'd clicked into place. She had a name, she'd stepped into the world. Laurie said, "What's your costume, Jaqe?"

Jaqe laughed again. "I don't know."

Laurie moved her fingers through the ribbons. She said, "I thought you might be a spider." One gloved finger lightly traced the pattern Jaqe had drawn on her chest. Jaqe imagined that finger moving down, grazing the sides of her breasts. Jaqe shook her head. "It's so hot in here," she said.

The woman in the velvet dress held out a plastic cup. "Drink some punch," she said. "It'll cool you off."

The first swallow sent a shiver through Jaqe, but after that she felt a relaxation spread through her muscles. Everything in the room became softer, the music not so aggressive, the lights on the gym walls less glaring. She looked again at the red-haired woman. The face was small, almost delicate under the wide hat. The eyes were black, large, without makeup. They shone like the sparkles dusting her skin. Jaqe said, "Who are you?"

The woman waved a hand. It seemed to move on its own, like a bird. "I have so many names," the woman said, "I can hardly remember them myself."

Jaqe turned to Laurie. "Is she a friend of yours?"

Death shrugged. "I just met her. I thought she was your friend."

Jaqe looked again at the woman, who slowly raised her head so that a red spotlight, previously blocked by the edge of the hat, fell upon her face. The woman said, "Call me Mother Night." When she smiled, her teeth gleamed within the red of her skin.

Without thinking, Jaqe grabbed Laurie's hand. At that moment, she heard a whistle and turned just in time to see Louise's arms coming around her for a hug. "Wow," Louise said. "You've really been keeping a secret, haven't you?"

"A secret?"

Louise struck a pose, one hand on her hip next to the dangling sword, the other flinging back her hair. "You don't just join the DCC like the rest of us. You go right to the boss."

Laurie said, "For Goddess's sake, Louise."

"DCC?" Jaqe asked. "Boss? What is she talking about?"

"DCC is kind of a joke," Laurie explained. "It's what we call the Lesbian Student Union. It means Dyke Central Committee."

Jaqe looked at Louise again, then grinned at Laurie. "Are you the boss?"

Laurie stared at the floor. "Well, I'm the president. But it's just a title. It doesn't mean anything."

Louise said, "You've always been a great roomie, Jacqueline, but you really should have—"

Jaqe stopped her with a hand held up like a traffic cop. "Not Jacqueline," she said. "Jaqe. Don't forget."

Louise laughed and hugged her again. "Wow," she said. "When you come out, you go all the way."

Before Jaqe could answer, the band struck up a loud and slightly off-key fanfare. A moment later a whistle of feedback accompanied a man's voice in the loudspeakers. "May I have your attention!" he said. When Jaqe turned to the front she saw a group of men in various costumes, each with a toad mask over his head. The one who spoke into the microphone wore a bird outfit, a one-piece suit hung all over with polyester feathers. From inside his toad face he announced that a great moment had come, when the committee would choose the Toad Queen to officially present the trophy to the university. The committee, he said, had studied all the lovely women in their beautiful costumes, and had chosen the one "whose radiant costume lights up our glorious Toad Castle." Three men walked into the crowd.

As they came near her, Jaqe looked around for some woman in a shiny bikini or diaphanous gown. As they came closer, she looked in surprise at Laurie, then Mother Night. When they took her hands she pulled away in amazement. Mother Night said, "They want you to go with them." Jaqe looked at her friends. Laurie tipped her top hat and kissed her on the cheek. Louise waved her sword.

"But this is nothing," Jaqe said. "It's not even a costume." Yet when she looked at the indigo labyrinth it seemed to glow where Laurie's finger had touched the skin. And when she moved her arms, the ribbons flowed like streams of light. She walked through applause and whistles to stand on the platform before the wood-and-papier-mâché toad with its glass eyes, and the school insignia painted on its puffed chest. Next to her a man in a black dinner jacket with a cardboard toad mask over his face stuck out his hand. Jaqe shook it. Only when he began to speak did she realize he was Samuel Benson, the school's president.

Jaqe paid little attention to the speeches and the cheering. When they gave her the trophy she passed it right to President Benson, who had to give it back so she could hold it for everyone to see. "And now," the man in the bird suit said, "the Queen will choose her king." The band began an old-fashioned slow song. The spotlights made it hard for her to see, but she still knew just where to point her open arms. From out of the crowd Laurie strode forth, Death emerging from the mob.

Like sounds across a lake, the noise drifted past Jaqe and Laurie as they swirled about the floor. There was talk of going too far, and a few stamps and boos, along with scattered cheers from the DCC, and above it all one amazed voice proclaiming, as if no one else had noticed, "Hey, that's another girl!"

Jaqe laid her head on Laurie's shoulder. She felt the soft weight of her own body in the spiral of Laurie's arms. A moment later other couples began to emerge onto the dance floor.

"Come back to my apartment," Laurie whispered. Jaqe nodded, then remembered all the questions she'd wanted to ask Mother Night. She glanced back to where she'd seen her, but all she spotted was Louise leading a march of women to congratulate the royal couple. Jaqe grabbed Laurie's hand and rushed her to the door.

In the street, Jaqe wondered what in God's—Goddess's—name she was doing. She wasn't Louise, after all; she'd never thought of herself as . . . as gay, if that was even the right word. She'd just found out her name; shouldn't she find out more about herself? But then she looked at Laurie, who was grinning under her Death's-head makeup like a small child on her birthday, and Jaqe's nervousness softened.

Laurie's apartment was the messiest place Jaqe had ever seen. Plates and glasses and even frying pans perched on piles of books. Papers, crumpled or flat, covered the floors, even in the bathroom. Jeans and tank tops and T-shirts and underwear obscured the bed, the chairs, the desk. Jaqe thought about the flow of chaos in Louise's half of their dorm room and wondered if being gay made you sloppy.

When Jaqe laughed, Laurie blushed—Jaqe could see it through the makeup—and began shoving things together, as if to clear a space for the two of them to stand. "Sorry about this mess," she said. "It's usually not this bad." She blushed again, as if she knew what an obvious lie that was. When Laurie began scooping things off the bed, Jaqe saw that the sheets were freshly washed. She grinned, just in time for Laurie to see and become embarrassed all over again.

"It's okay," Jaqe told her, and held out her hands. She felt a chill when Laurie took them. To herself she said, "It's okay." But she kept thinking, *This is crazy. I don't belong here.*

"Jaqe," Laurie said, and the sound of her name washed over Jaqe with a flood of joy. She squeezed Laurie's hands as if to keep from floating right through the ceiling. She laughed as she realized that Laurie had called her. She said, "What?"

Laurie repeated, "What?" and then both of them were laughing.

Jaqe reminded her, "You said my name." *My name*, she thought.

"I just like the sound of it."

"So do I. Laurie. I like that one too." Jaqe wondered what someone might think of them. Two women standing in a sloppy room holding hands and saying each other's names. To her own surprise—after all, Laurie was the boss of the DCC—it was Jaqe who pulled Laurie closer, who lifted her face for Laurie to kiss her. *The kiss of death*, she thought, and nearly started laughing again, but didn't.

Not dying, she thought, *dissolving*. The touch of Laurie's breasts against hers—even through their shirts—the softness of Laurie's face, the pressure of her arms, of her lips . . . Death kissed the front of her shoulder, the slight indentation between her shoulder and her breast, and then the top of her breast, the sides, even underneath, before coming up to around the nipples and finally the nipples themselves. "Oh God," Jaqe said, "Oh my God."

"Goddess," Laurie mumbled, and the two of them laughed and hugged each other. While she and Laurie were taking off their clothes, Jaqe thought, for just a moment, that she saw Mother Night standing in the doorway, still drinking her cup of punch.

"What is it?" Laurie said. "What's wrong?"

Jaqe shook her head. "Nothing." Then, "Say my name. Please."

"Jaqe. Jaqe, Jaqe, Jaqe."

Jaqe put her head against Laurie's shoulder and hugged her. Then Laurie kissed her, and the hand at the top of Jaqe's back moved down her spine until it came below, between Jaqe's legs, and somehow lifted Jaqe off the littered floor and onto the summer fields of the bed.

Late that night, Jaqe woke up and looked happily at Laurie's face, just visible in the streetlight coming through the tree outside the bedroom window. As softly as possible, she let one finger stroke Laurie's cheek. Laurie slept with her mouth open, and Jaqe played for a moment at seeing how far her finger could go in without actually touching the tongue and waking Laurie up. She lay back on the pillow, wide awake. Finally, she got up and dressed, borrowing Laurie's dinner jacket and sandals, and went out, taking Laurie's keys. She headed back to campus, wondering if there'd still be anything going on at the gym, if other people were wandering around inflated with joy in the middle of the night. But the gym was dark, and the only person she saw was a security guard. All over the ground lay cups and cigarette butts and cardboard toad masks.

She was about to turn back when she heard a low noise somewhere to the left. When she followed it she noticed a red light near the end of the campus. She came just close enough to see the police car, the ambulance, the few people standing by the open door of a large private home. A woman appeared in the doorway. She wore a paramedic's jacket and pants. Her red hair was short and spiky. In her arms she carried a man in blue silk pajamas and a toad mask. Jaqe turned and headed back to Laurie's apartment. The next day, in art class, someone told her that President Benson had died of a heart attack during the night.

Two
Snakes and Cakes

At that time in the land of the turtle people did not know what to think of women who had sex with other women. Previous generations knew exactly what to think: that it was physically, morally, and spiritually repugnant. In Jaqe's time many people stayed with this old-fashioned view; others, however, insisted that the practice did no harm to anyone, while still others considered it a superior approach to life, even commanded by God, whom they pictured as a woman with an axe on a white horse.

Unsure of what to think, some people became unsure of what to say. The first time Jaqe went with Laurie and Louise to an LSU meeting several women debated what to call themselves, insisting that "women-loving women" was a better term than the nationality of a small island thousands of miles away. While Jaqe sympathized with anyone who wanted to discover her real name, she found the discussion tedious, except when Louise suggested that all the women-loving women go to the small island and claim citizenship under the Right of Return.

Jaqe wondered if she really could call herself a woman-loving woman. What would she do, what would she look for, if the universe shifted and Laurie vanished? She had found her name and desire and love all at the same time, so that when Louise talked of coming out, Jaqe knew she had never been in. She tried once to tell Louise that she had not really existed until that night of the Toad Dance, but Louise didn't seem to understand. "You were just repressed," she told Jaqe. "The patriarchy buried you so far in the closet you couldn't even see the door."

Sometimes Jaqe looked at women in the street to see if she desired them. And sometimes she found herself filled with love, or simply fascinated, like a scientist of femaleness, by breasts and hips and hair. But desire? None of them was Laurie, so how could they excite her?

Laurie had known she desired women since junior high school, when she and a girl named Carol Hamet had cut afternoon classes to imitate the poses found in dirty pictures hidden by Carol's father in the attic of Carol's house. Carol had wanted only to create "tableaux"; Laurie, however, had wanted to improvise and experiment, until finally Carol declared her "sick" and kicked her out. For several days Laurie tried to speak to Carol at school and phone her at night, always without an answer. At the end of the week, Carol announced to her friends in the cafeteria that she and a boy named Bryan Forbes were going steady. With a superior effort of will Laurie managed to finish her lunch without crying or even looking up as Carol kissed Bryan and ran her hands up and down his back. Two days later Laurie opened Carol's locker at school—they had traded combinations—

and left a pink rose and a note. "You have found normality," the note read, "but I have found my life's work." She made sure to change her own lock before Carol would have a chance to reply.

In high school Laurie pursued her vocation with ambiguous defiance. She cut her hair short and wore jeans and a leather jacket, but so did many other girls. A classmate took her aside once and warned her that she looked "a little bit like a lesbian," and maybe she should wear makeup or something. "Maybe I want to look this way," was all Laurie could say, an equivocation that disgusted her whenever she thought about it. She wore a pinkie ring, a tribal sign, but only to those in the tribe, or those who had read the same books as Laurie. In her senior year she sometimes wore a green scarf to school on Thursdays, for high school a more open declaration, but she usually left the scarf in her locker during classes.

All this changed several months before graduation, with the arrival in Laurie's school of a girl named Anne Lewison. Anne looked like no one Laurie had ever seen—long straight black skirts, a black blazer, hair pulled back and held with a filigreed clip, pale makeup and red lipstick, eyebrows plucked to a thin arch. Anne's father was a violinist recently hired by the local orchestra. Anne herself played the cello, though she refused to join the school orchestra, despite a speech by the school principal denouncing "those with God-given talents who isolate themselves in pathetic arrogance." During this lecture, Anne sat motionless, with a slight smile and single finger extended along her left cheek. Sitting half a row away, Laurie couldn't take her eyes off her.

It did not occur to Laurie that Anne Lewison might have noticed her, or that Anne—who wore makeup and skirts—might be a woman-loving woman. One Friday afternoon, between classes, Laurie saw Anne coming toward her outside the gym. She was concentrating so hard on not staring that she almost didn't see Anne standing in front of her. "You're Lauren Cohen," Anne said. Laurie nodded. Anne said, "There's a woman's bar across the river. They have dancing every Friday night. Would you like to go with me?"

Laurie found herself shivering. She was afraid her teeth would chatter. She said, "I don't have a car."

Anne smiled. "I do."

For the rest of that year Anne instructed Laurie in the theory and practice of her life's work. After they graduated, and Laurie went to college on the East Coast, and Anne to an experimental communal school out West, they promised to send each other copies of their diaries and to long for their school breaks when they could "fulfill the longing of our isolated bodies"—as Anne wrote inside the cover of a book of women's poetry she gave to Laurie for Valentine's Day. Despite Anne's promises, Laurie was terrified the day she saw Anne to the airport. Anne would find some poet or sculptor and forget Laurie had ever existed. Or worse, she would lie in her sculptor's arms and joke about the small-town girl she'd left behind.

In the end it was Laurie who first stopped writing, telling herself that classes took up all her time, but knowing that if she wrote she would have to leave out what really mattered—the women in the cafés and small theaters, the muscles on a particular woman in a bowling alley, the way a certain woman looked in a sleeveless T-shirt as she held up a banner during a women's antiviolence march. Just before the spring break of their freshman year, Anne wrote that she was staying at school to rehearse with a string quartet. That night Laurie went to an all-night reading of the works of a lesbian novelist. During the break after a book about pioneer women, Laurie left with an Englishwoman whose skin Laurie would later describe as "legendary."

With great diligence, Laurie began creating her own legend. With a small group of women she organized theatrical, and successful, protests against heterosexism and the university's refusal to allow a lesbian student union. She picked up women in bars and brought them to lectures in literary history. She sent roses to women professors. And she seduced a string of students, many of whom had confessed they might be gay, and could she advise them?

Yet in her final year she began to long for graduation as much as she feared it. "Lauren Cohen" had become a performance, with a bored star and no new routines. When Toad Fever took over the school Laurie had no plans to go to the dance, until the LSU pleaded with her that they needed their leader to help them remind the heterosexists that women-loving women would not be driven back into hiding. For several days, Laurie tried to think of a costume, until, the afternoon before the dance, she saw something thin and white lying on the grass outside the library. When she picked it up, it took her a moment to recognize the bleached bone of a bird's claw.

When Laurie and Jaqe had been together a month, a couple of women at an LSU meeting accused Laurie of neglect. "You're thinking with your cunt," one of them told her, and the other said it was a wonder she didn't stay at home all day baking cookies. Laurie told them to go to hell and resigned the presidency.

That night, in bed, Jaqe asked, "Am I bad for you?" Laurie tried to kiss her, but Jaqe turned away. "I've got to know," she said. "I don't want to ever be bad for you."

Laurie sat up. With her left hand on her heart and her right arm flung out, she declared, "You saved my life."

"Be serious. You had a wonderful life. You're important. Louise just about worships you. Or she did, until I stole you away."

Laurie kissed her shoulder. "I was dead."

Jaqe twisted away. "Don't say that. Not even as a joke."

"It's no joke," Laurie said, but she was grinning. "I was just too stupid to lie down, like the mummy in one of those old black-and-white horror movies. You revived me. You and Mother Night." Jaqe scrambled up and started to get dressed. Laurie said, "What are you doing?"

"I told you not to say that." When Laurie tried to grab her arm she jerked loose. She was already putting on her shorts when Laurie said, "I'm sorry. I'll never do it again. I promise. Do you want me to bake some cookies?"

Jaqe sat down on the edge of the bed. "You don't know how."

"I could learn. I could make special Goddess cookies. Shaped like a pregnant woman."

Jaqe let Laurie unzip her shorts. "I just wanted to know if I was good for you."

Laurie kissed her belly button, then slid her face down to rub against Jaqe's pubic hair. She said, "You did for me what no one else could ever do. You got me to clean my apartment." Jaqe laughed and finished taking off her clothes.

Laurie's apartment was in a once-grand building in the poor neighborhood down the hill from the university. There were three rooms (counting the small kitchen) and very little furniture—a foam mattress on a bed made from a door, a wobbly desk Laurie had made herself, a pair of chairs Laurie and a friend had found on the street. Next door lived a woman, her small daughter whose face was always smeared with chocolate and jam, and sometimes the woman's boyfriend, who came late at night and played loud music till dawn.

On those nights, Laurie tried pounding on the walls until the plaster fell in small piles on the rug she'd bought at the Salvation Army. At other times she played her own music or sang very loudly.

Jaqe got Laurie to paint the walls, throw out the rug, pile the books and papers on the desk or against the wall, and buy new sheets when the old ones revealed stains left by earlier lovers. Together they scraped the grease off the kitchen. For their first month's anniversary Jaqe gave Laurie a set of kitchen curtains. To Jaqe's surprise Laurie gave her a pair of plants, tall and leafy like small trees, to stand on either side of the living room window like guardians against the world beyond the freshly cleaned glass.

Jaqe told her parents her new name before she told them about Laurie. "Jake?" her mother said on the phone. "That's a boy's name. Look, Jacqueline—"

"Jaqe," Jaqe corrected her. The discussion lasted five minutes, during which Jaqe corrected her mother, and then her father, a combined total of eight times. "People will think you're a lesbian," her father said.

"It's not a man's name," Jaqe said. "It's my name, and I'm a woman."

Jaqe knew she'd have to tell them soon about her new life. Summer was coming, and her parents would expect her home. They would expect her to get a summer job, and lie by the lake on weekends, and pull weeds from the garden, and talk about boys. And Laurie was graduating, with an acceptance to a graduate program in women's studies from a school hundreds of miles away.

Jaqe found out about this last problem by accident, for Laurie had neglected to mention it, saying only that she "wasn't sure" what she was doing after graduation.

"Shouldn't we make some kind of plans?" Jaqe would say, and Laurie would kiss her and promise to talk about it. One afternoon while Laurie was in class, Jaqe found the graduate school acceptance letter lying on the floor by Laurie's desk. Until that moment, Jaqe had thought they would never fight, that nothing Laurie could do could ever make her angry. "What am I supposed to do when you go to your seminars?" she screamed.

"I don't know that I'm going," Laurie said.

"What do you mean you don't know? What did you tell the school? Did you write them you were coming?"

Laurie shrugged her beautiful shoulders, wide and delicate all at once. Her loose rayon shirt rippled over her body. "Well, yeah," she said. "But I can change it. I can write and tell them I've changed my mind."

"I don't want you to change your mind. If you want to study women, go and do it."

Laurie grinned. "I could just study you."

Jaqe was having trouble breathing. She felt like she would die if she stayed angry a moment longer. She just looked at Laurie but her face must have shown something, because Laurie's grin vanished and she looked scared as she held out her arms for Jaqe to come home.

Jaqe knew she had to tell her parents before the summer, before Laurie's graduation. "What am I going to do?" she asked Louise one night. "They can't even accept my name."

Louise sat back and crossed her arms. "Now you know what it's like," she said.

Three weeks before exams Jaqe called her parents to say she was coming home for a long weekend. "To rest up for the big push," she said lightly, and then added, "And I'd like to bring a friend with me."

"A boy?" her mother asked.

"No, a girl—a woman."

When Jaqe and Laurie arrived in the train station late Thursday evening, Jaqe's mother wrapped her arms around her while her father shook hands with Laurie. In the car, Jaqe's mother talked all the way home, telling Jaqe about scandals in the neighborhood, problems at work, and pregnancies in the family. At home she continued her report while setting out cheese and bread and filling the coffeepot. She finally paused after they'd eaten. "Well," she said after a moment, "I guess you're tired. Come on, Laurie, I'll show you your room."

"She's staying with me," Jaqe said. All three of them stared at her, Laurie as surprised as Jaqe's parents. On the train Jaqe had asked Laurie not to make a fuss about the bedrooms. The spare was upstairs, Jaqe explained, next to hers, and Laurie could just slip next door after Jaqe's parents had gone to sleep. Laurie had said, "We'd better not forget to rumple the sheets in the guest room."

"I don't understand," Mrs. Lang said. "There's plenty of room. It's no trouble really. I've already put fresh sheets on the bed."

"That's not what she means," Mr. Lang said. He took a step toward

Laurie, who crossed her arms and shifted her weight onto one foot. "Who the hell do you think you are?" he said.

Laurie said, "Your daughter's lover."

"Jesus Mary," Mr. Lang said.

"Please, Allan," Mrs. Lang said. "Do we have to fight?"

"You know what she's saying, don't you?"

"Can't we all talk about it in the morning?"

"In the morning it'll be too late!"

Laurie said, "It's already too late."

"I want you out of here," Mr. Lang told her.

Jaqe said, "If she goes, I'm going with her." Horrified as she was, she still wanted to giggle at hearing those words coming out of her.

"This is ridiculous," Mrs. Lang said. She asked her husband, "Where do you want them to go? A motel?" She turned to Laurie. "You're sure you won't use the guest room? It really is very nice." Her face quivered with suppressed tears. Jaqe half expected her to say, "Pretty please."

Laurie glanced at Jaqe, who stared at the rug. "Sure," she told Jaqe's mother. "I'd be delighted."

The next day, with Jaqe's father at work, Jaqe's mother took Jaqe and Laurie to two supermarkets, a wholesale beer and soda outlet, three malls, a diner for lunch, and a chain ice cream parlor for an afternoon snack. The moment they got home she said, "Look at the time. Your father will be home and we haven't even started dinner."

Laurie whispered to Jaqe, "Glory be."

During dinner, Jaqe's parents filled the air with questions about life as a college girl, more stories about neighbors and descriptions of local politics, and the outrageous plans for a garbage processing plant only a half mile from the Langs' housing development. Laurie expressed great interest in anything Jaqe's parents said, asking questions and sympathizing with family problems, expressing shock and outrage at the corruption of the town council. After dinner, Jaqe's mother promised ice cream if everyone would gather in the family room to watch television.

Jaqe said, "I'm going for a walk." When Laurie followed her toward the door Jaqe whispered that she wanted a few minutes alone.

"I have to stay and watch TV with your parents?" Laurie asked. Jaqe suggested she go upstairs. "Say you have to study. You do, don't you?"

Outside, Jaqe told herself she should think, make some decision, though she wasn't sure about what. Instead, she just walked up and down the gentle hills of the development, her head down, her hands in the pockets of her father's golf jacket.

On the way back, she found a stone. It was flat, elliptical, and crossed on both sides with scores of lines. Jaqe squinted at it. If she looked at the lines a certain way they formed pictures—on one side a kind of tree with a wavy central trunk, branches like arms out to either side, and a tangle of lines at the bottom like packed roots. The roots themselves seemed to form an image, though Jaqe could not decide what they reminded her of. At the top, an oval shape made Jaqe think of an egg in the uppermost branches. The other side was even clearer. A white column up the middle with a line underneath it looked like a ghostly ferryman standing in a boat. The ferryman even held a pole, a diagonal line that ran from one corner of the stone to the other. Jaqe put the stone in her jeans and headed home.

She woke up sometime in the middle of the night. She and Laurie were sleeping in the guest room. "After all," Laurie had said cheerfully, "I promised not to sleep in your room; you didn't promise not to sleep in mine." For a few minutes Jaqe lay there thinking she could just fall back asleep, but she couldn't seem to get comfortable. Every time Jaqe turned on her side or back, Laurie groaned and tugged the blanket.

After a while she slid carefully out of bed and went to the window. What had happened to the lights? The windows of the guest room looked out across the houses and down the hill so that Jaqe could see glimpses of homes through half the development. There were no windows lit. She knew from her childhood, when she sometimes would wake up from a bad dream and go look out the window, that there was always somebody awake, somewhere. And when she looked to the left, at the street, all the lamps were out. Power failure, she thought, and switched on the desk lamp, only to switch it off instantly when the light hit her eyes. Laurie groaned again but stayed asleep.

Quickly Jaqe pulled on jeans, Laurie's sweatshirt, and sandals. Downstairs she opened the door as softly as possible, afraid her mother, who had always been such a light sleeper, would wake up and investigate. When Jaqe got outside she half expected to find the street empty, but no, there were women there, a whole group of women—

five, seven, nine of them—nine women weaving in and out among one another in something like a dance.

Jaqe did her best to hide behind the oak tree on the front lawn. A few houses down, by Terry Santorini's house, the women moved in a rough circle in the road, making a funny noise and shaking their hands. No, it was rattles, they were shaking rattles at the road, baby rattles; she could see the plastic clowns' heads. Jaqe tried to make out the women's faces, see if she recognized any of them, but they were too far away. One of them looked a little like Mrs. Bennet from across the street, and another looked like Jackie Lee, the one who used to give all those Tupperware parties. Maybe she'd supplied the rattles, Jaqe thought, and had to hold in a laugh. She wished she could get closer, but didn't dare, in case they saw her and ran away.

The women were dressed up, she saw, like proper ladies going to town. They wore straight or pleated skirts, some with little suit jackets, others with ruffled blouses. They all carried shiny black purses with metal clasps. And—though it was hard to tell without any streetlights—Jaqe thought they were wearing gloves, white gloves climbing into their sleeves.

Something was happening in the street. The sewer was backing up—but how could it back up without any rain? No, it wasn't water coming out of the grate, it was snakes! Masses of snakes were slithering out of the sewer into the street, coming up to the sound of the rattles. Jaqe had to shove her hand in her mouth to keep from screaming. A moment later she wanted to laugh. She remembered her father's complaints years ago about extra taxes, and then later his civic pride when the county put in the sewer system to replace the old septic tanks. She almost wanted to run in and wake up Daddy and drag him outside.

There weren't so many snakes as she'd first thought. A dozen? Twenty? The way they moved together made it hard to tell. Snakes are so clannish, she thought, and had to fight not to giggle. She was giddy, she knew. Fear or excitement. The snakes were all in the center of the road now, with the women around them. The women did a kind of side shuffle with their bottoms out—Jaqe wondered if they were wearing girdles. When all the snakes had come together the women stopped their rattling. They stood still for a moment, with only a slight sway of the hips and shoulders. And then they opened their purses and took out . . . cardboard statues? No, they were cakes. Small cakes shaped like people with their arms and legs out, just like the pictures of the gingerbread cookies in that children's story about the witch and her giant oven.

The snakes caught the cakes in their mouths and headed back to the sewer. Jaqe wondered what snakes did with cake. Did they break it into crumbs with their fangs, or swallow it whole? When all the snakes had gone, two of the women took out pieces of chalk and began drawing on the road the way little girls draw a hopscotch pattern—a line down the center of the road and a lot of short lines crossing it. When the women with the chalk finished, two others sprinkled something on the ground around the outer circle. Pebbles, Jaqe thought, or maybe rock salt. Before the women could do anything else, a noise came from down the block, and then lights as a police car came around the corner of Mapleleaf Drive. The women all looked at each other, clearly surprised. Something had gone wrong, Jaqe realized. No one was supposed to bother them. That was why all the lights had gone out. But it was too late now for corrections. Before the lights of the police car could catch them, the women ran across Terry Santorini's lawn and up the hill to Ashgrove Road. Jaqe was so busy staring after them she didn't notice the patrol car slowing down behind her. Only when it stopped did she realize how peculiar she must look, crouched behind a tree in the middle of the night. She hurried inside and closed the door. Her heart beat very hard and she didn't move, afraid the cops would come and knock on the door. At last she heard them drive away.

Upstairs, Jaqe touched Laurie's shoulder. She whispered her name. "Wake up," she said.

"Sweetheart?" Laurie mumbled, "I love you too," and rolled over.

Jaqe reached out with her hand again, hesitated, then let it drop. She realized she didn't want to tell Laurie, though she wasn't sure why. Maybe she thought Laurie wouldn't believe her. Or maybe she wanted it for herself. Or maybe she was supposed to keep it secret.

She crossed the hall to her own room, where she sat down on the bed. She looked at her books, made a face. The last thing she wanted to do was study. Near the foot of the bed lay a photo album, pictures of Jaqe as a child. Jaqe smiled, remembering how Laurie had laughed and then kissed her when they came to the picture of Jaqe in a tutu with her feet crossed and her arms over her head. She opened the book and saw herself on her side in a pink crib, with a pacifier stuck in her mouth and her hand on the bottom of a white walrus.

I want a child, Jaqe thought. Startled, she looked up at the window, as if someone had slipped inside to put the strange notion inside her head. A child. The idea was ridiculous. She hadn't even finished her first year of college. What the hell would she do with a child? Bounce it on her knee in French Lit? And where the hell would she get a child? Women-loving women didn't get pregnant. "Safest method of birth control ever invented," Louise had once proclaimed. Well, there were some who had children, but usually from before they'd begun their women-loving careers. "This is ridiculous," Jaqe said out loud and closed the photo book. When she put it down, she felt a great desire to cry. She was overemotional. Something about those strange women. She jumped up and looked out the window. Lights. The streetlights had come back on, and she could even see one or two houselights somewhere up the hill. More people up late with crazy thoughts.

Jaqe went back to the guest room, where she stripped down, and slid into bed. Gently she put an arm around her lover's shoulders and pressed her front against Laurie's back. *I love you*, she thought. *I love you so much*. And yet, just before she fell asleep, the other thought came again and with it the astonishment. *A child. A baby.*

In the morning Jaqe slipped outside before breakfast. There it was—the childlike drawing. It looked faded, as if it had lain there for weeks instead of just a few hours. For a moment she wondered if she'd seen it earlier in the weekend and then dreamed the rest. She squatted down. It looked like a tree, about a yard long, with a central trunk and nine crossing branches. At the top, the trunk forked, somehow suggesting a head or a face. Suddenly Jaqe jammed her hand in her pocket to find the stone she'd picked up in the street the day before. She wasn't sure, maybe her imagination was jumping too many gaps, but the picture in the street looked a lot like the tree she'd seen in the stone. She looked again at the rock, at the tangle of roots at the bottom. When she looked back at the pavement, she saw that a car must have driven over the roots, for she could hardly see them. She bent down to look closer. They looked like circles or a spiral. Only when her finger traced the pattern did she recognize the in-and-out route of a labyrinth. Her hand leaped away like a toad. "Mother Night," she whispered.

Breakfast was pancakes, something Jaqe's mother hadn't made in years. After breakfast, Mr. Lang offered Laurie the keys to Mrs. Lang's minicompact and suggested a couple of historical sites Laurie might want to visit. "The point is," he said, "we'd like to talk to our daughter," and Mrs. Lang added, "And we don't feel you should have to just walk around the block."

"Gee, thanks," Laurie said, and flipped the keys in the air. To Jaqe she said, "Well?"

"I don't mind," Jaqe said, "if you don't."

"In that case—" Laurie put the keys in her pocket. She whistled "Oh Susannah" on her way out the door.

"Oh," Mrs. Lang said, "can you handle a stick?"

"For God's sake," her husband told her, "of course she can handle a stick." He blushed. "I just mean, if you can—"

"No problem," Laurie said. Halfway out the door, she turned. "Jaqe," she said, "I love you." She waved a salute at Jaqe's parents and went out the door.

The talk came mostly from Jaqe's parents, who told her about unnatural acts, the perfect fit of male and female parts, danger to their standing in the community, the availability of psychiatric and religious assistance, dangers to Jaqe's future career, dangers to her marriage prospects, dangers to her health, including breast and cervical cancer (Jaqe remembered Louise at a student debate shouting "Cancer comes from penises"), Laurie's niceness and how Jaqe's parents wished her well, how Jaqe wasn't helping Laurie, the pathos of those who cannot help themselves compared with the hope of those who can, and finally various great villains of history who were men-loving men. Jaqe said very little because she could think of very little to say. Laurie, or Louise, would have matched them point for point (or else slammed the door), but Jaqe knew that none of these calamities had anything to do with her. She broke in only now and then to explain that she and Laurie loved each other with a certainty beyond the need for professional consultation, and that her name was not Jacqueline but Jaqe. Otherwise she felt like someone standing on the grass and watching a high-speed merry-go-round. Only once did one of the horses brush against her. "You know we've always wanted grandchildren," her mother said, and took up a fresh tissue.

Jaqe looked at the floor. "I think I'm a little young," she said.

"Of course, of course," her father broke in. "We don't want you running out and getting pregnant. But if you get into bad habits now . . ." He let his voice trail off while he stared ominously at her.

Jaqe forced herself to look at him. "Do you mean when the time comes I won't be able to give them up?"

"Sometimes," her mother said, "we start something; maybe it seems like an adventure—"

"Or a rebellion," her father said.

"Or a rebellion," his wife repeated. "And then when we've made a mistake it's too late. I mean, we think it's too late. It's never really too late, but we feel . . . we feel ashamed."

"Or stubborn," Jaqe's father said.

Jaqe was thankful to get back to safer ground. "Laurie is no mistake," she said. But her parents weren't listening, for they had gone on to the theme of justifiable social anger and the difficulty of finding a man big enough to forgive the past. "Men are only human," her father assured her.

Laurie returned with a handful of flowers plucked from the garden of a famous governor's childhood home. "For you," she said, with a slight bow, to Mrs. Lang, who looked first at her husband, then took the flowers nervously, as if the bouquet might give her a rash. The moment she was rid of the flowers Laurie stepped to Jaqe and took her hands. "Are you all right?"

Jaqe smiled at her. "Of course I'm all right. They're just my parents." Looking at her lover's face Jaqe could see the emotions as clearly as if Laurie had labeled them: worry, anger that Jaqe might be hurt, desire to rescue Jaqe like some princess imprisoned on a glass mountain, shame at having left the princess alone with the wicked king and queen, fear that Jaqe's parents might have turned Jaqe against her, anger and fear at her own helplessness if Jaqe should ever decide to leave her. Jaqe wished that she and Laurie could exchange hearts, each one beating in the other's chest, proof that nothing could ever pull them apart. "I love you," she said, and took a half step into the garden of her lover's arms.

Jaqe met Laurie's parents on graduation weekend, when Mr. and Mrs. Cohen and Laurie's younger sister, Ellen, drove in for the ceremony. Jaqe was delighted at how well they all got along, especially after the fight she'd had with her own parents when she'd told them over the phone that she wasn't coming home, at least not until after Laurie's graduation. It all went so smoothly. Laurie's father shook her hand, Mrs. Cohen kissed her on the cheek, then rubbed the lipstick off with a scented tissue, and Ellen told her, "You're a lot prettier than the last one," at which Mr. Cohen laughed heartily and Mrs. Cohen scolded, "Ellen, don't embarrass your sister." After the ceremony they all stood arm in arm for photos, with Laurie and Jaqe in the middle, Ellen in front of them holding Laurie's hand, Mrs. Cohen with an arm around her daughter's waist, and Mr. Cohen with his arm over Jaqe's shoulders. The following week, when Laurie's parents sent copies of the photos, Jaqe set up the family shot in a glass frame above the refrigerator. For a long time—a year and two months—she would not understand why the picture made Laurie so furious. "What the hell is that doing there?" she shouted.

"I thought you'd like it," Jaqe said.

"Well, you thought wrong."

"But it's sweet."

Laurie was almost shaking as she pointed at the photo. "Get rid of that fucking picture." She stamped out of the room. Later, when Jaqe asked her about it, Laurie said, "I just don't like it there, okay?"

On that sunny day in June, however, Jaqe knew nothing of her lover's ambivalence toward her family. In fact, she was relieved to find them as nice as Laurie had said. After her attempts at harmony with her own parents, Jaqe had dreaded meeting the Cohens and had taken the distance of several hundred miles as a blessing arranged secretly for her by God. "My folks aren't like that," Laurie kept saying. "Wait till you meet them." And some of the members of the DCC agreed. "Laurie's parents are really special," they'd say, and talk about the time Laurie took five of them home for Christmas and they could sleep with each other or hold hands in the living room. Or the time Laurie's parents came to campus and Mrs. Cohen went along to a lesbian bar to see what it was like. "She looked great," someone said. "I mean, you could see she was straight, but she still looked really great. She danced with a couple of women too." And Laurie herself told Jaqe about the time she seduced a hometown girl, and the girl's father came to the house when the two of them were upstairs in bed together. Laurie and Gail had held each other fearfully and listened to the argument. "Do you have any idea," Gail's father had asked, "what they're doing up there while you watch TV or whatever the hell you're doing with your head stuck in the sand?"

"Having fun," Laurie's father had said.

"Fun!" the other had shouted. "Are you crazy? Your perverted daughter—"

And at that Mr. Cohen had shoved the man off the step and slammed the door.

Laurie's father was a hairdresser, the owner of three beauty parlors, one of them specializing in Black hairstyles and treatment. When she first heard of Mr. Cohen's profession, Jaqe wondered what her parents would make of this. Would they assume that Laurie had inherited his cross-gender tendencies? Or maybe that Mr. Cohen had wanted a fairy for a son and covered his disappointment by raising his daughter as a dyke? But in fact, as Beth, the LSU vice president, put it, "Bill Cohen is no faggot." When Jaqe met him at the graduation she saw a burly man with heavy shoulders, a slight potbelly, muscles that had run a little (but only a little) to fat, a rugged face that had gone a little puffy, especially around the eyes, and hands that looked too large for wrapping hair around rollers. He looked a little like a professional football player who'd retired and gone into public relations.

"Call me Bill," he told Jaqe when Laurie introduced them. "Bill and Jaqe. Sounds like a team already."

"And I'm Janet," Laurie's mother said. Janet was all suburban elegance, with her pleated permanent-press skirt and fitted blazer (pale green, to celebrate the beginning of summer), her cream-colored blouse that had never known sweat, and her medium-heeled green pumps with a strip of gold between the heel and the shoe. Molded into a gentle landscape of hills and valleys, her hair gave no clue to its natural form. Jaqe wondered if Mr. Cohen had designed it himself or, having no time, delivered her to whatever genius headed up the flagship of his small fleet. ("Marcel," he would say, "this is Mrs. Cohen, take good care of her.") Or maybe Bill kept up his old skills by practicing on his wife, just in case some young turk challenged him to show he still had the stuff. Did he set her hair before they made love? Maybe they put on special robes, like a king and queen, or priestess and slave. Maybe he wore a loincloth. *Stop it,* Jaqe warned herself. Soon she'd start to giggle, and then would have to think up some excuse when they asked her why.

Like her hair, Janet's voice gave no hint of its original shape. It was soft, pitched low, and rose and fell like a stream flowing through a formal garden. "I'm so happy to meet you," she told Jaqe. Later, when they saw Laurie's cleaned and refurnished apartment, Janet laughed and said, "Now I know you're the one for Laurie. You're sure you're not hiding a magic wand somewhere?" Jaqe discovered she liked Janet's voice, even looked forward to hearing it without much concern for what it said. And yet she found herself wondering what Janet would sound like if someone stamped on her foot.

Laurie's sister was fourteen but seemed younger. In a white dress and pink shoes with tiny heels, she tended to stand silently behind her mother. Occasionally her father would put his arm around her shoulders while he talked with Laurie and Jaqe. Sometimes Ellen looked up at him and smiled. More often she continued to look at the ground. Laurie said later that her father described Ellen as "an accident, but not a disaster."

The graduation ceremony took place on the baseball field. The platform for the speakers reminded Jaqe of the one at the Toad Dance, and in fact both the chancellor and the valedictorian referred to "the quest achieved," as one of them put it (probably the valedictorian, but Jaqe couldn't remember), as well as President Benson's "sad and untimely death." Through the two-hour ceremony Jaqe sat with Laurie's family on gray plastic chairs surrounded by hundreds of other bored and hungry people. She couldn't even see Laurie, for the graduates all sat in the first rows and all you could see were black robes and mortarboards.

On and on the speakers went. Honor students, school officials, some government undersecretary of something. There were awards, fake (honorary) doctorates, commemorations . . . Poor Laurie, Jaqe thought, stuck in that hot costume. Poor me, she thought, as she struggled to stay awake. She began to doodle in her program: circles, spirals, stick figures chasing each other up and down hills. She drew a wavy line down a blank page and then a pair of lines crossing it. At the top she drew an inverted arch, like a bowl or the bottom half of a face. At the bottom she drew a series of half circles, with lines running in between them. Only when she finished did Jaqe recognize the tree the women had chalked on her parents' road. The tree and the labyrinth. She held the program tight in both hands. Where was the stone? What had she done with it?

"Are you all right?" Janet whispered. Jaqe looked at her. "You were moaning."

"What? Oh, I'm sorry. I'm fine."

"Are you sure?" Mrs. Cohen gave Jaqe's hand a quick squeeze. "Maybe you should go find some shade."

"No, really," Jaqe said. "It's just hard to keep awake." Mrs. Cohen nodded and looked again at the current speaker. Jaqe waited a moment, then turned in her seat, as if bored and searching for something to take up her attention. She scanned the crowd, the women's faces, the clothes, searching for red hair or a wide hat. She looked in front, but it was hard to see anything, so many heads. She told herself, *She'll be in the back, it's not like her to sit in front.* It was only when she let her eyes move beyond the crowd that she saw her. There—among a row of VIP cars parked on the road that ran along the edge of the field. There was the limousine, dark blue, not black as it had seemed on the night of the dance. Dressed in red balloon trousers gathered at the ankles and a gold silk jacket with padded shoulders, Mother Night leaned against her car. She was wearing a kind of oversized pink beret; the crushed velvet flowed down, framing the left side of her face. She raised her arm and waved softly to Jaqe. As she did so, a breeze stirred her hair so that it rose off her shoulders like wings.

"Excuse me," Jaqe said to Janet, and started the climb over people's feet.

Janet grabbed her hand. "Are you all right?"

"I'm fine," Jaqe said. "I just saw an old—someone I know." Gently she pulled her hand loose and continued down the row. Why did she have to sit in the middle? Why couldn't people get out of the way? "Excuse me," she kept saying. "Sorry." Just as she reached the end of the row she saw Mother Night get into the backseat of her limousine. Softly the car slid down the road, its engine noise drowned out by the voice in the loudspeakers. "Ambition and responsibility," the voice was saying. "Necessary partners in the dance of ethical opportunity."

"No," Jaqe said. "No."

"Will you please be quiet?" a woman said. Jaqe jumped. "Sorry," she said, and began the shuffle back to her seat.

Throughout the rest of the speeches Jaqe kept trying to spot Laurie's back, the set of her shoulders, the slight leftward tilt of her head. When the school's acting president began giving out the degrees, Jaqe ran her finger down the list of names in the program, furious at how slowly they all moved, how they all had to stop and shake hands with the goddamn acting president. And then at last Laurie was there. She was all right, she was okay; look, she stood up straight, she wasn't in pain or about to faint, she was fine, she was fine.

"She looks beautiful," Janet whispered, and sniffed into a tissue.

"Hey, did you see that?" Bill said. "She winked at him. Can you believe that?"

She's okay, Jaqe thought.

For the rest of the day and the evening, Jaqe kept watching Laurie, looking for signs of illness or food poisoning. When they drove to the restaurant (where she refused to let Laurie order clams), and later the Cohens' motel, Jaqe watched every crossroad, every car, searching for drunk drivers or teenage maniacs or even broken glass that could shatter the illusion of solid tires. She didn't relax until eleven o'clock, when Laurie turned on the late news. For only then did she learn that half an hour after they had left the campus a rejected lover of the undersecretary had broken into the official dinner given by the chancellor, and then, while all the guests were drinking champagne in honor of the university, taken out a gun her lover had given her and shot the undersecretary two times in the chest and once in the face. "Thank God," Jaqe whispered, and rushed into the bathroom where no one would see her cry.

Three

The Bird Woman

Laurie went to graduate school at a university on the shore of a poisoned lake. There were many poisoned waters in Laurie's country at that time, and while some people wrote books or signed petitions demanding the water be cleaned, others continued to pour poison into the lakes and rivers, as if acting out some ancient curse. In winter the lake by Laurie's school froze and people could drive cars and trucks across it. Traditionally the local men drilled holes in the ice and built shacks where they could sit in the evenings and catch fish for their families. The state tried to forbid ice fishing, for the fish had become poisoned along with the water, but there were too many families who counted on the fish to get them through the winter when heating costs took up so much of the budget.

One afternoon in late November, Laurie's professor for Female Spirituality and the Neolithic Revolution led the class in a ritual, an "enactment" she called it, to heal the lake. "The rivers are the veins and arteries of Mother Earth," she told her class. She also told them that lakes were the Goddess's eyes, a contradiction no one dared to mention. "The Goddess loves contradictions," she once told them. The enactment consisted of performing a chant while holding (gloved) hands and walking sideways along the lakeside, drawing symbols of protection in the snow with forked branches, calling to the spirits of the winds to heal the water, and finally pleading for forgiveness from the Lady of the Lake. At the end the professor poured a bottle of distilled water onto the ice.

While the others headed for their cars Laurie stood and looked out on the lake. She'd always assumed that a frozen lake would be transparent all the way to the bottom, or maybe white and glittery. In fact, if she pushed away the snow with her foot, the ice looked almost black. She looked up at the row of shacks about two hundred yards from the shore. She saw a pickup truck parked next to one of them. When she squinted against the sun she could make out a few wisps of smoke above the roof of the shack. Someone must have a stove, she thought, or even a small campfire. She sighed. If only Jaqe were here. Jaqe would have loved this, a whole lake frozen so solid you could park a truck on it and build a fire. She smiled now. What would Jaqe have made of the ritual? Probably laugh. Sometimes—sometimes when she thought of Jaqe it became hard to breathe, and she felt all queasy inside. She made a noise. She didn't even have to think of Jaqe. Sometimes, sitting in class or the library, or waking up in the middle of the night, something would get all twisted inside her, and then her breathing would get stopped up and she'd have to pull the air into her lungs. Just the other day she'd been reading an article about parents who—

Laurie shuddered, then shook her head to clear out the memory. She hated it when she felt weird. As soon as it went away she tried not to think of it. Now she took a deep breath of the cold air, grateful that it went all the way down, that she didn't have to fight for it.

"Hey, Laurie," one of the women from her class called. "Come on, it's freezing out here."

"Go on," Laurie shouted. "I'll come back later." She wiggled her toes in their padded moon boots. They hurt a little, just like her fingers and her face, but nothing seemed in any danger of frostbite. She was glad she'd borrowed a car for the day, though she knew she'd better not stay until dark or the battery might freeze.

"What are you doing?" the woman asked.

Laurie laughed. "I'm going to walk on water."

The ice was uneven and covered in snow, which made it difficult for her to judge her steps. It took her twenty minutes and several falls to reach the shack. Inside she could hear the local radio station. The disc jockey was saying something about "serenity" and "eternal rest," and Laurie realized he was advertising a funeral parlor. She knocked on the door. No answer. She knocked again. "What the hell?" came a man's voice. "Is someone there?"

Laurie pushed open the plywood door and leaned inside. "Hello?" she said.

"Sonofabitch," the man said, and grinned. "Come in. I thought you were a ghost or something." His right hand held a fish line that disappeared down a hole in the ice about a foot across. His left hand held a bottle of beer. He sat on a stool. Next to it stood a case of beer bottles, two-thirds of them empty. By the back wall a small kerosene heater filled the prefabricated shack with warmth and the smell of oil. Above the heater a plastic window let in the sun. Near the door stood a pail of water half full of small fish. "I'm Eugene," the man said, and reached down to turn off the radio. "Want a beer? Just grab one. I gotta keep hold of this line." He jerked it up and down a couple of times to demonstrate.

Laurie took a beer from the crate. "Thanks," she said. "I'm Laurie."

"Nice to meet you, Laurie," Eugene said. His grin got wider. "Sorry I ain't got a chair to offer you. I don't get too many visitors. Tell the truth, you're the first. Ice fishermen ain't much for socializing. You from the college?" Laurie nodded as she sat down on the edge of the crate. She was suddenly conscious of her bright red boots and her padded nylon jacket. Eugene wore a checkered woolen jacket and a matching cap pushed back on his head. Though he didn't look more than thirty-five, his hair was dirty with gray. "Hey," he said, "why don't you take out all them bottles and turn that thing over. Make a real seat." As Laurie began taking out the beer bottles Eugene said, "Put the full ones on this side, okay? I'd give you a hand, but . . ." He waved the hand holding the string.

Laurie sat with Eugene for over two hours, during which time he caught six fish—smelt, he called them. For the first time since she'd left Jaqe, Laurie felt relaxed, not angry or depressed or afraid. When she told Eugene she was doing women's studies he gave the predictable answer. "Studying women, huh? Think I could sign up for that?" Somehow it didn't bother her, not like when her father said it. She thought of her course in deconstructing patriarchal discourse, and then of Eugene's wife frying the poisoned smelt Eugene brought home from the lake.

Halfway through her second bottle of beer Laurie thought she might be in trouble. Eugene asked her, "So you got a boyfriend, Laurie?" Tell him, she thought. Don't leave it open. She shook her head. "Uh-uh," she said. "Girlfriend." She took another swallow of beer.

Eugene nodded, like a doctor in a TV commercial. "Girlfriend," he repeated. The sage mask fell apart in a smile. "Women's studies, huh?" Laurie laughed. "I had a cousin once who was doing women's studies. Couldn't believe the scores she made. Pretty? You wouldn't believe some of them girls. Your girlfriend pretty?"

"Prettier than the end of winter," Laurie said.

On the next bottle of beer Eugene asked her, "You believe in past lives?"

"I don't know," Laurie said. "A lot of my friends do."

"A cousin of mine learned how to do that regression stuff. It's easy. You lie down, maybe smoke some pot, close your eyes, and suddenly you're in Egypt or someplace. Beats television anyway." He jerked the line out of the water and a fish came with it. Still talking, he put the fish in the pail, hooked another piece of bait, and dropped the line back in the water. "My favorite was a pirate. Robbing the shit out of rich people. Of course, sometimes they can turn out pretty nasty. One time I even became a lawyer. Gave me nightmares for weeks."

* * *

Sitting with Eugene, Laurie had promised herself she would study after dinner. But instead of going to the library, she wrote Jaqe a long letter. When she couldn't think of anything more to write she drew a cartoon of the two of them running through storms and flames into each other's arms. By the time she finished, the library was closing. She smoked the end of a joint she'd been saving and lay down on her narrow dorm bed. *Past life*, she thought. *Send myself into a past life*. Instead, she fell asleep. She dreamed that she was riding a snowmobile through the woods at night, weaving among the trees while birds flew in and out of her headlights, visible only in those moments they passed through the beams. Suddenly she burst out of the woods onto the lake. From either side the snow spewed into the air in great fountains. Soon other snowmobiles came to join her, a long line of women bending forward, their mouths open to the wind. In the distance she could make out something tall and shimmering, like a mirage of a tower. When she came closer she saw a woman in a loose dress that flapped against her body. Laurie and the others cut their engines to let the machines glide slowly toward the woman. Only when the others jumped onto the ice did Laurie recognize Mother Night. At her feet, dead, lay the birds of the forest.

The dream shifted and Laurie sat on a chair on the ice, fishing through a hole. Her line jerked and she pulled back on it to bring out a dark gold fish. "If you let me go," the fish said, "I will grant you three wishes."

"I want to go home," Laurie said. "I just want to go home." She found herself in her parents' house, at the dinner table, with her father beside her and his arm over her shoulders. "No," Laurie said. "I didn't mean here. I meant home. I want to change it. I want my second wish. Hurry!" But at that moment her mother brought a large iron plate to the table. On top of it lay the fish, covered in green sauce, with only the dead eyes and mouth open to the air.

The following Wednesday Laurie skipped her seminar and borrowed her friend's car to drive out to the lake. For half an hour she searched among the shacks, but Eugene must have caught his fill for the winter, for his prefabricated home was gone.

Laurie lived in a cell-like room in a residence for unmarried students. It seemed strange to be living in a dorm again, but without Jaqe there didn't seem much point in looking for her own place. Some of the male students were married and lived with their wives in three-room apartments rented by the university. Laurie wondered if they would accept a lesbian couple on the same terms. But the wives all worked, usually in office jobs for the university, and the last thing Laurie wanted was Jaqe working for her.

"I could transfer here," Jaqe told her during one of their long weekends together. "One school's the same as any other. And we'd be together."

"Sure," Laurie said. "And your parents will keep paying your tuition if you transfer just to be with me."

"I don't need their money. I could get a job. Or extend my student loan."

"I don't want you getting a job. And your loan's going to take long enough to pay back as it is." Laurie went on to point out how quickly she could finish her class time and move back to the city while she wrote her dissertation, and how they could have their summers and breaks, and how Jaqe could visit her on weekends. Only much later did she realize that she didn't want Jaqe to join her because then she could no longer dream of going home.

During the months Laurie was away Jaqe continued to live in their apartment, taking comfort in the fact that Laurie had lived there for two whole years before Jaqe had known her. Sometimes she would take a deep breath and think how Laurie had breathed the same air, how wherever she stepped she was walking where Laurie had walked. She even thought once of finding all of Laurie's ex-lovers, or at least the ones Laurie had brought home to the apartment, and giving a party. Louise had talked her out of it. "Take my word for it," Louise said. "You won't get the Queer of the Year award with ideas like this one." Officially, Jaqe still lived in the dorm with Louise, for when Jaqe had told her parents there was no point in wasting their money they insisted it was their money and they would waste it any way they liked. "Don't burn your bridges," her father told her. "If you change your mind the room will be there for you."

Jaqe found it hard not to measure her parents against Laurie's, especially when she thought how Laurie's parents were paying for the apartment—"so the two of you will always know you have your own place," Janet had said. Sometimes Jaqe called Laurie's folks in the evenings, or on weekends if she and Laurie couldn't get away to each other. She and Janet would talk of how much they missed Laurie, how they worried about her, how she was losing weight—"without your home cooking," Bill said—and sometimes looked a little green when she came home for a visit. Or they would make jokes about Laurie's rotten cooking and about all the trouble she must be giving her poor naive professors.

During the winter break Jaqe and Laurie spent half the time at their apartment and the other half at Laurie's parents' in Laurie's hometown of Thorny Woods. Janet and Jaqe cooked wondrous meals every night and Laurie sat at the table grinning at the march of turkey and baked potatoes and pumpkin pies. Twice during this three weeks Jaqe almost slammed the phone down on her parents' rage. "Jesus," Jaqe's father said. "We said you could bring her home with you. What more do you want?"

Everyone Laurie knew hated graduate school, not just the women studying women, but the women and men in philosophy or English Lit, or European history. They hated the endless work that always got worse, the private languages of academics, the attention paid to what other academics wrote on a subject in place of the subject itself, the insistence that everyone follow the school style in the way they approached their subjects, and above all the smugness of the professors, who took pride in their students' hatred. "You're not here to develop your sensibilities," the professors would tell them. "You're here to become professionals." And they would tell stories of the horrors of graduate school, such as the man who returned to his university years later to give a speech and threw up the moment he stepped through the gates.

Laurie called her program the "Ph.D. Steamroller," two years of seminars followed by oral and written exams, and then her dissertation, which the school expected her to finish in one year. "I feel like a battery hen," Laurie wrote Jaqe. "Stuck in the library and pushing out papers with a light bulb over my head."

Laurie had expected women's studies to be different. Her professors often said they were different. They proclaimed their seriousness, their dedication to the feminist revolution, or else the reclamation of the Goddess, depending on the particular prof. They sometimes enlisted the aid of their students in tenure battles with the university, and they scornfully called the male professors "the boys." It didn't take long, however, before Laurie noticed the way they attacked each other in their articles, or the way they insisted on what one of them called professional rigor.

"You know what they really want?" Laurie wrote Jaqe. "They want the boys to say, 'Hey, you guys are okay,' and take down the sign that says 'No girls allowed.' "

One professor really did seem different. Associate Professor Adrienne Beker taught women's art history, a course that seemed to Laurie a kind of rope to hang on to. Professor Beker somehow mixed a dedication to radical theory with a constant reference to what she called the "usefulness" of women's lives. Women were the first artists, she insisted, showing evidence of handprints in the prehistoric caves, and she demonstrated the way all the forms of "high" art derived originally from "the intrinsic elegance" of work done by women in tribal communities. Just as her lectures darted between centuries, she herself moved about the seminar room, sometimes with her hands in her pockets, sometimes jabbing a finger at the air.

Adrienne (as Laurie thought of her) wore silk shirts and leather jackets and a single silver earring. Laurie was sure she was a dyke, but whenever Laurie managed to work lesbian references into the classroom discussion Adrienne always answered with historical or political points that supported lesbians but said nothing about herself. Even when she sat in a coffeeshop with Laurie and some of the other students she never spoke about her life outside art history. Once, Laurie tried to follow Adrienne after class. She had noticed that Professor Beker had recently been finishing exactly on time and then hurrying away instead of sitting on the desk surrounded by students trying to get close to her. She has a new lover, Laurie decided, and imagined Adrienne striding off campus and into the arms of a small woman with a delicate face surrounded by a halo of fur. But when Laurie shadowed her professor, using the snow to cover the sound of her boots, all she saw was Adrienne getting into her ten-year-old Porsche and driving alone onto the icy streets.

One day Professor Beker displayed a slide of a cave painting of beasts surrounding a man dressed like a stag and playing a musical bow. For half an hour she built up a complex argument to show that the man, whom she called "the Sorcerer of Lascaux," derived his power from the Goddess and was therefore the work of women. The cave of Lascaux, she said, formed a giant uterus, a generator of female energy. Laurie sat squirming through this whole speech. Several times she started to put her hand up and then dropped it. She looked around the room, wondering when someone was going to say something. Finally she raised her hand.

Adrienne frowned. "Yes, Ms. Cohen?"

Laurie said, "Isn't that picture actually from the cave of Les Trois Frères?"

Adrienne stared at her, then the slide. For a long moment there was silence, and then Adrienne said, "Well. I guess we're all indebted to Ms. Cohen. She seems to have caught me in the wrong uterus." There was a ripple of nervous laughter, which stopped when Professor Beker went on to explain that the essential argument remained. Later, after the class had ended, Laurie moved to the front of the room, but Adrienne had already slipped her notes and slides back into her briefcase and was heading out the door.

Two weeks later Laurie presented a paper to the class on the image of Amazons in different cultures. Far from a male fantasy, as some scholars maintained, Amazons (Laurie argued) formed tribal remnants of "matrifocal" culture. Laurie had worked very hard on this paper. When she stood in the front of the room her hands shook, and she worried that her voice quavered. Professor Beker sat on the end of her desk, her arms folded. For several seconds after Laurie had finished and sat down, Adrienne said nothing. Everyone waited; Laurie stared at the floor. "Well," Adrienne said, "I think we are all impressed by Ms. Cohen's devotion to her cause. However, the study of women's history requires something a little more serious than lesbian erotic fantasies." She went on to describe the dangers of adolescent wish fulfillment, and finished with the need to avoid "excited amateurs with visions of Camp Fire Girl sex." During this speech Laurie sat with clenched fists, terrified she would start crying. When Professor Beker had finished, Laurie prayed no one would ask any questions. The Goddess granted her wish. She did her best to imitate calm as she left the room.

Over the next several weeks Professor Beker developed the term "Amazon" as a catchword for amateurism. Her first remarks drew nervous laughter and glances at Laurie, but after a while the joke gathered its own history, and remarks about Amazons gave the class its own special unity. Sometimes Laurie found herself laughing along with the others.

Laurie never told Jaqe what had happened. When Laurie complained about her life in graduate school, Jaqe suggested she speak to Adrienne. "Maybe I'll do that," Laurie would say, and then she would change the subject.

In the second half of the year Laurie took a course in Goddess archaeology. According to the professor, ancient temples were built in the shape of a woman's body. She showed them slides and photographs of artificial hills shaped like either a pregnant belly or a giant eyeball, or both. They examined diagrams of temples and saw how you could see them as a woman lying down, if that woman had huge breasts and hips, no waist, and a knob for a head. Laurie wrote to Jaqe, "It's like those puzzles in children's magazines. See if you can find Janie, her dog, her cat, and her bicycle in this tree. See if you can spot the Goddess in this old pile of rocks."

One evening in the library, Laurie read three articles on megalithic tombs before she realized she didn't remember the basic point of any of them. She went back to the first and prepared to start again. Instead, she got up and took the article to the Xerox machine, where she copied a photo of a statue of a sleeping pregnant woman. With great patience she drew a picture of Jaqe curled up at the woman's feet. The next day she made copies of all the photos of stone circles, ancient temples, and prehistoric monuments. She drew Jaqe into all of them—in the Goddess's belly, standing on Her head, kissing the Goddess with her legs wrapped around a stone neck, half crawling out of temple doors. Each day she sent Jaqe another picture.

"Darling wonderful Laurie," Jaqe wrote. "Thank you for the pictures. I'll put them up on the sacred shrine—the refrigerator. But aren't you going to write anything?" When Jaqe called, Laurie let her do all the talking; Jaqe leaped into Laurie's silences like a woman running into a fire to save a child.

Jaqe had an exam the same day Laurie finished her last class. "I can get a postponement and come get you," Jaqe said on the phone. "I can say I'm sick. They'll never know. And I can study on the bus."

"Forget it," Laurie insisted. "I can find my way back by myself. You just do well on your exam."

Jaqe thought Laurie's voice didn't sound as convinced as her words. "I love you," Jaqe said. "If you change your mind, if you need me, I'll come right away. I don't care what exam I miss."

"I do. I don't want you missing any."

"Do you love me?"

"More than anyone."

"More than the Goddess?"

"Lots more. She's got the whole world to worry about. All I really care about is you."

Jaqe left her Russian history exam early in order to meet Laurie's bus on time. She'd answered every question, though she knew she could have written more on the essay comparing Peter the Great and Catherine the Great—"those two great Greats" as Louise called them. It wasn't just a lack of time. She kept thinking of Laurie, how sick she'd looked the last time Jaqe had seen her, how she sounded on the phone like she was trying not to cry.

At one time a great portion of the city's drunks, prostitutes, and ambulatory schizophrenics had occupied the main bus terminal like a foreign army. In recent years, however, that army had grown so large the city had launched a counter-coup and expelled them back into the street. Instead of ordinary doors, the bus station now had a wall of glass that slid apart only when a guard in a bulletproof booth pressed a button. "For admittance," a sign read, "first show ticket to porter." A ticket booth stuck out into the sidewalk, with more bullet protection for its inhabitants. Outside the glass wall men and women lay on the pavement like trolls guarding the entrance. Some drank magic elixirs from paper bags. Others had laid out filthy blankets with plastic jewelry or old magazines to sell to tourists. Still others walked up and down, whispering or shouting to people either passing by or invisible.

The building occupied a whole block. As Jaqe hurried along the street to the entrance, she could see buses slide into their slots and she kept thinking Laurie had arrived early and what would she do when Jaqe wasn't there? She paused near a tall man in a white caftan. A stand in front of him displayed copper earrings and bracelets, small bottles of oil or perfume, and a pile of pamphlets with a bearded face smiling on the cover. "Follow the twisting path with Dr. Root," the pamphlets declared.

The man in the caftan leaned toward Jaqe. "Talismans," he said. "Potions of wisdom and protection. Made from genuine ingredients, original recipes. Amulets to protect you on your journey."

"I'm not going anywhere," Jaqe said, and slid around him, only to have a woman in a torn dress and a purple wig step in front of her.

The woman looked over sixty, but when she stuck her face close to Jaqe's, Jaqe saw it was marked with acne, like a teenager's. She reminded Jaqe of Dan Reynolds, her high school boyfriend. "Get your ticket," the woman said. "Right to the Land of the Dead." She laughed and clapped her hands. "The Land of the Dead. Express leaving now."

Jaqe stopped herself from giving the woman a shove. Probably the whole army would rise up against her. She slid around the woman, who was still laughing at her own joke. "I don't have a ticket," Jaqe started to tell the porter, but he waved her on.

Laurie's bus was late, not early. For half an hour Jaqe walked back and forth, drank tea from a machine, and checked the announcement board in case she'd misread the gate number. Finally the bus, green and white with darkened windows, rolled into the dock. The doors opened with an explosive sigh. As the passengers stepped out, Jaqe bounced up and down on the balls of her feet. Where was she? Who were all these stupid people? She must have missed the bus, maybe she was sick and trying to call Jaqe at home. "Relax," said a man in some sort of uniform. "He's coming." Jaqe made a face at him and he shrugged. And then Laurie was there. She was wearing black jeans and a white blouse with a stiff collar, and she was carrying her blue cotton blazer over her arm and her black leather travel bag in her beautiful long-fingered hand. She ducked her head as she came through the door. When she lifted it she looked around a moment before she spotted Jaqe, and then she grinned. Her free hand pointed at the side of the bus where the driver was handing out luggage.

For some reason nonpassengers were not allowed through the doors to the parking area, so Jaqe had to wait inside the building, watching Laurie, unable to touch her. Laurie looked wonderful and terrible all at once. It was still the strong face, but now it was all drawn and thin—she must have lost ten pounds. Jaqe wanted to run and get her a double milkshake. And the way she moved—there was still that same arrogant grace, but now tension had mixed in with it, the shoulders tight, the face hardened except in those moments when she smiled or winked at Jaqe. Her luggage came, a garment bag and a black nylon duffle which she hoisted onto her shoulder. It almost made Jaqe cry, the way Laurie balanced everything so carefully, just for those few steps into the terminal.

She didn't wait for Laurie to drop her bags before she hugged her. "Welcome home," she said, and now she really did start to cry, with the side of her face against Laurie's shoulder.

Laurie laughed. "This is great," she said, "but can we get out of the doorway?" Behind her, people were trying to push through. "No," Jaqe said, and hugged her harder, but then she let Laurie move to the side and set down her luggage.

The man in the uniform walked around the two of them, as if to examine an exotic animal. "It's a woman," he said in mock amazement.

Jaqe half turned her head. "You better believe it," she said, and Laurie burst out laughing.

Outside the terminal the woman in the purple wig rushed up to Jaqe. "Back from the dead already?" she said. "And with a refugee too."

"Friend of yours?" Laurie asked, but Jaqe was already hailing a cab.

In the apartment, Jaqe had set up a bouquet of pink roses in an old orange juice bottle she'd washed down and then painted with a spiraling red stripe. Around the bottle she'd placed a circle of painted eggs left over from the "Celebration of Spring" she and Louise had hosted before the beginning of exams. The women in the party had stood in a ring with the eggs in a bowl on the floor. They passed around a bundle of burning sage and sang an old Turtle song more or less translated into English. Then each woman had picked up her egg, held it in the air and asked "Grandmother Earth" to help her face her most difficult task: an exam in organic chemistry, a term paper on the theme of revenge in Greek Lit, or a conversation test in colloquial German. To end the celebration several of the women had wanted to eat the eggs, but Jaqe said they should leave them in the bowl, as "carriers of power." "Psychic batteries," someone joined in. In fact, Jaqe really had wanted to save the eggs for Laurie, for even though she claimed her egg represented her paper on images of family conflict in European folklore it really meant—all the eggs meant—

Laurie returning safe and happy from her exile at the frozen lake. After the party, when everyone had gone home, Jaqe had written Laurie a long letter, carefully light and amusing, about the party, each of the women's costumes, and how she had saved the eggs from destruction, though she didn't say why. The letter went on for five pages, and Jaqe hoped it would inspire, or shame, Laurie into a reply. Instead of words, she'd gotten back a drawing of an egg half buried in a hillside. Inside the egg was a Xeroxed photo of Jaqe, asleep on the couch in Bill and Janet's living room. When Jaqe received the picture, without even a signature at the bottom, she cried for half an hour.

Now, when Laurie came in the door and saw the roses and the eggs, her own eyes teared and her face seemed to shiver. She dropped her duffle bag and hurried into the bathroom, where she turned on the water and sat down on the edge of the tub to cry. Jaqe didn't know what to do. She wished there was some spell she could say, or magic food she could feed Laurie to bring her back. But, despite the party with the LSU women, Jaqe didn't believe in magic words, and all she'd made for dinner was a salad with different kinds of pasta and a thick blue cheese dressing. When Laurie came out of the bathroom she'd washed her face and was smiling again. "It's good to be back," she said, and Jaqe ran to hug her again. But there was something wrong with the smile, and Jaqe could feel the jerkiness in Laurie's arms, even when they weren't moving. She pulled away. "Are you tired?" she asked. "I made a salad, but you can lie down if you want." She hated sounding like a hostess, like her mother.

"How was your exam?" Laurie said.

Jaqe shrugged. "Dumb," she said. Laurie nodded, as if that was the right answer.

They decided to eat, and then to drink tea. Laurie talked about graduate school, how nothing made any sense, how it was all just competition. To Jaqe it sounded like a report from an impartial observer. She noticed that Laurie took the smallest possible amount of pasta and still didn't finish. "You know," Laurie said as she leaned back and put her hands behind her head, "I didn't even finish my papers. Can you believe that?"

"What do you mean?" Jaqe asked.

Laurie's attempt at casualness only made her look more strained. She said, "I took them home. Three of them. I'm supposed to mail them in. Two weeks to finish three papers. Think I can do it?"

"How much do you have to do on them?"
"I've got some notes."
"Have you written anything?"
"Not really."
There was a silence, and Jaqe wondered if she should get mad at Laurie, maybe shout at her, something like "I didn't leave my exam early and fight off bag ladies so you could sit there like a lump." Or maybe she should shake Laurie's shoulders, even slap her, so Laurie could say, "Thanks, I needed that." But she knew she could never do any of those things, never touch her except to stroke those long muscles, that wonderful springy skin. She wanted the perfect fit of Laurie's mouth against hers, the feel of Laurie's nipples slippery under her fingertips, Laurie's fingers sliding inside her, with her body so light, light as a bubble, that Laurie could hoist her in the air, above the city, above the clouds and into the sun.
"Why are you smiling?" Laurie asked, her voice belligerent, as if Jaqe were laughing at her for bringing her papers home. Eyes downcast, Jaqe shook her head. Against tears, she thought of how Laurie sometimes crouched down so that her small breasts came just below Jaqe's larger ones, and then she'd stand up, pushing Jaqe's breasts toward her chin.
When they'd finished dinner they made love, or pretended to. Many of the usual moves were there, but Jaqe knew that Laurie and maybe she herself were doing it because they were expected to (by whom she couldn't say). She was glad when Laurie stopped in the middle, saying she had to piss. Lying in bed, Jaqe wanted to scream or to bite something. She turned over to lie on her belly. Near the bed, where she and Laurie had piled their clothes, she saw two objects which must have fallen out of her pockets. One was a stone, and when she reached over to pick it up she recognized the rock she'd found the year before, with the tree on one side and the ferryman on the other. She laid it in her palm and looked at it. She hadn't seen it in months. The other object was a brown bottle with a label that proclaimed itself "Dr. Root's Revival Massage Oil." Where had that come from? She certainly hadn't bought it. The man in the caftan at the bus station must have slipped it into her pocket. She unscrewed the cap and sniffed. It smelled sweet, like flowers. Was it safe? Maybe Dr. Root had slipped toxins or dope inside it. She sniffed again. It sent a slight tingle along her skin, and she smiled.

Laurie came back, looking like someone determined to go through with a difficult task. For a moment anger pushed Jaqe away from her. Jaqe thought how Laurie was treating her like one of her term papers. No, she thought, Laurie was *her* project, and if she failed the exam the remedial course would get a lot tougher. "Lie down," she said, "I'm going to give you a massage."

Laurie did her best to grin lasciviously. (Jaqe thought of those movies where some kind of fake, a robot, or a pod person, or a Martian, takes over people's bodies but can't fake the emotions.) Laurie said, "I thought you were welcoming me home."

"This is part of it," Jaqe said. "Come on, do what I say."

"Yes, ma'am," Laurie said, and saluted. She lay down on her belly, with her face turned toward the wall. Jaqe rubbed some oil on her hands and started smoothing it in long strokes down Laurie's body, beginning at the shoulders and sliding all the way to the toes. Jaqe had never given a massage before. Many of the women Jaqe knew assumed all women could do massage, as part of an inborn talent for nurturing and sensuality, the way an older generation assumed a woman automatically knew how to diaper babies or make men feel superior. All Jaqe could do was try things out and hope they worked. She thought you were supposed to find the tense places and work at them until they loosened up. As far as she could tell, everything was tense. She worked at the hips for a while, then the shoulders, then the thighs.

After some time Laurie began to sigh, then moan. Jaqe thought it was a good sign, but she wasn't sure. She rubbed more oil into her hands and went back to stroking. The more oil she used, the more her hands really did seem to know where to go, now rubbing the muscles on the upper arms, now pulling on the fingers. She poured out some more oil and touched her fingertip to her own lips. The oil stung slightly but otherwise tasted sweet, like peppermint. She dotted the oil between Laurie's shoulders and in spots along her spine, smiling when Laurie jumped at the touch of Jaqe's finger to a place just below the center of her back. As Jaqe resumed her long rubs, a pair of birds began to sing in the maple tree just outside the bedroom window. The birds were speaking, Jaqe realized, speaking actual words. She could understand them just as if they were girls in the dormitory talking just outside the door. Only, when she tried to work out what they were saying, she couldn't seem to capture the words and line them up into sentences. Something about treasure, something (or somebody) hidden somewhere, on a mountain or inside a cave.

Laurie moaned again, with her body half melted into the bed. "Do that again," she said, and Jaqe discovered she was shaking Laurie's buttocks. "The amazing vibrating woman," Jaqe said, and laughed. Laurie's moan settled into a steady purr. Jaqe gave Laurie's ass a squeeze, then swooped her hands down to the feet where she rubbed each one and then wiggled and pulled on the toes. She whispered, "This little piggy went to a faraway country, ruled by an evil queen. But now she's come all the way *home.*" She said the last word loud, and ran her hands up the insides of Laurie's legs until they met. Once again, she could hear birds, now a whole forest of birds, the whole bedroom filled with birds, all of them speaking, trading messages. Laurie rolled over and pulled Jaqe down on top of her.

Later, Laurie was licking and kissing and biting Jaqe when suddenly she laughed. She laid her head on Jaqe's thigh, with her face turned upward, toward Jaqe's curious face. "You know," Laurie said, "you're the kind of masseuse that gives the profession a bad name."

Jaqe laughed. *Thank you*, she thought, not sure who or what she was addressing. Dr. Root? She looked down at Laurie's head moving between her legs like some small hairy animal. She laughed again and laid her head back on the pillow.

Jaqe dreamed she was a bird, or dressed in a bird costume, running through an empty shopping mall and knocking over racks of shoes with her outstretched wings. A single pair of red shoes lay in the middle of the floor among a pile of broken glass. She woke to the sounds of crying and disco music from the apartment next door. Boyfriend's back, she thought. Sometimes she wondered if he beat that poor little kid. She listened a moment, then decided the crying sounded more like a child who just wasn't getting enough attention. As she snuggled closer against Laurie she remembered a record player her parents had given her once. It was soft blue, with clouds and elephants painted on the sides. And she remembered her favorite record, a song about a rabbit who never learned how to hop. It wasn't just the song she liked, but the color of the record, a bright pink. The song was good too, she thought sleepily. Silly rabbit mother, forgetting to teach her bunny how to hop. *When I have a baby*, she thought, *I'll make sure to give it hop lessons all day long.* Her hand made hopping motions on Laurie's breast. She turned to lie on her back, staring at the ceiling. *I want a child,* she thought. *I want a baby.* Stupid, she thought. Stupid idea. She turned again to curl her arm around Laurie and hug her until she woke up.

Four

The Three Papers

For two weeks Laurie tried every day to work on her papers. "No problem," she'd tell Jaqe. "All I need is to find the right spot." First she tried the university library, but the term hadn't ended yet, which meant the library was full of students desperate before their last exams. Better to relax, she thought, and went to the cafeteria. Only, she always seemed to find old friends there, women who wanted to tell her about the LSU, a guy she used to go drinking with, former Frisbee partners. It felt good to go out on the lawn and just play for a while. She could strut again, catch the Frisbee behind her back with that flick of the hip which sometimes drew sighs from the younger women. In the cafeteria she would sit with her feet up and her hands behind her head. She felt like she'd gotten back something she'd forgotten; but she wasn't getting her papers done. So she left the campus and went to a women's coffee shop, and then a café.

"Sweetheart," Jaqe said. "Maybe you should just stay here."

"Too many distractions," Laurie said, and kissed Jaqe's shoulder, naked in a tank top. Besides, Laurie insisted, it was going great.

Four days before Laurie's deadline, Jaqe's parents called and insisted she come home for a visit. Jaqe didn't want to go. Laurie needed her. Laurie wouldn't eat without Jaqe cooking for her. Laurie needed Dr. Root's magic massage oil. Though Jaqe had hid Dr. Root in the back of the medicine cabinet since that first night, she imagined Laurie's back seizing up in the middle of typing her last paper. Jaqe would have to stand behind her, rubbing and pounding Laurie's beautiful muscles while the sentences poured from her elegant fingers. Laurie, however, insisted she could work better alone.

Though she didn't like to admit it, Jaqe was relieved at the thought of getting away; it also helped that she could see her parents without Laurie and it wouldn't mean a surrender. "When you come back," Laurie said, "everything will be done, and then we can celebrate." She added, "Give your mother a kiss for me."

Jaqe laughed. "On the lips?"

Laurie winked and said, "Anywhere you like."

After Jaqe left, Laurie packed her notes and walked half an hour to a bar she knew where she could order a beer and sit all afternoon under the protection of the woman working the tap. In a kind of automatic action she stood for a moment leaning with her back against the bar with her elbows up, and turned her head, first left, then right, with the breeze of a smile and a raised eyebrow. Hardly much point. Though the bar was mixed gay and straight, the dykes didn't come in much until evening. There were a couple of gay men at the end of the bar, three more men at a table, a woman playing pool in the back, and in the corner by a window, a small woman who looked old enough to be Laurie's grandmother. She was reading a newspaper, but when Laurie looked at her she raised an empty shot glass, as if in salute.

Laurie ordered a beer and sat down at a table for two. She spread out her papers and looked out the window at traffic. Four days. Three papers. She shook her head and laughed. She'd have to stay up every night just to type the damn things. She knew she couldn't do them all, of course, but she could write and ask for another extension for two of them. The important thing was to do one, just one, to prove she could do it. She looked at her notes on "Constants in the transplantation of rituals from Stone Age to present." What constants? she thought. In the Stone Age, did people sit around in the sun getting tanned? If they did, they certainly didn't worry about holes in the sky giving them cancer.

She looked at her hands. They looked good. A slight gold color, not too dark, a nice glow. She moved her fingers to watch the up-and-down ripple of the muscles fanning out from the wrists to the base of the fingers. She looked good, she knew. Cotton shirt, pale blue, with a low neck and loose cut that flowed gently over her breasts. White baggy pants with a wide black belt. Hair a little long but slicked back to accent her wide forehead. She glanced out the window at a woman in a pink sundress. Laurie thought, *Why isn't Jaqe here?* She laughed.

For the rest of the afternoon Laurie tried getting a start on her papers. She wrote a first paragraph three times and crossed it out each time. She switched to a part she felt more sure of but after a while decided the idea needed to flow from the beginning. She ordered another beer, a turkey-and-onion sandwich, then another beer. She played pool for an hour or so, thinking maybe the exercise would loosen her mind. The woman—Pat was her name—could have passed for a man, Laurie thought, except for the large breasts. Pat knew the game; her attempts to play down to Laurie's level were obvious. When she suggested they play for money Laurie laughed and said she had to work on her papers. Pat shrugged and went back to practicing. Laurie noticed, with surprise, that Pat's nails were manicured.

That night, when Jaqe called, Laurie said she was making great progress and recited a list of points she claimed she'd put into her paper on rituals. When Jaqe said it sounded exciting and she couldn't wait to see it, Laurie told her she'd met a woman that day who was either a pool shark or a stockbroker.

The next two days Laurie went back to the bar each afternoon and stayed until the bar started filling up with yuppie gays and dykes coming to celebrate their roots before dinner. Through the day she would sit and stare at her work, or try writing. She imagined writing a whole paper and then rubber-stamping "Bullshit" on each page and mailing it in. When she realized there was no time to get a rubber stamp made up she began laughing so hard she wondered if someone would come running up and slap her. The people in the bar changed, except for the old lady in the corner, who was there every day when Laurie came in.

On the last afternoon before her deadline Laurie knew she should write her letters asking for extensions. Instead, she just sat, thinking of heroic scenes from old movies.

She jumped when the hand came down on hers. Looking up, she saw that the old woman was sitting beside her. Laurie glanced down to the hand that still lay on top of hers like someone sleeping on a narrow bed. The skin had an almost translucent quality. "You look sad," the woman said. Laurie shrugged. She pulled her hand loose, but instead of going away the old woman simply nodded at Laurie's notes and crumpled sheets. "Term papers?" she asked. Laurie said nothing. The woman smiled. "You're not much of a one for conversation."

"I'm sorry," Laurie said, and felt herself blush. Goddess, she thought, the great butch Laurie Cohen turns into a femme for little old ladies. She added, "I'm not feeling very well."

A single finger tapped the pile of blank paper. "No wonder," the woman said, "with all of this to do."

"Well, since I've got so much to do," Laurie said, "maybe you could leave me alone." She pretended to study her notes.

"I could help."

"What? What are you talking about?" Laurie stared at her. Instead of folds of flesh the woman's wrinkles had become a network of tiny lines drawn across smooth skin. Laurie imagined a fortune-teller studying this face to learn the history of the world.

The woman said, "I often write papers for students in trouble. It gives me something to do."

"And I suppose you know all about subject–object grammatical implications. Or matrifocal archaeology."

"I can read your notes."

"My notes are shit."

"That's all right," the woman said. "I'm sure they'll do fine."

"Thanks for the vote of confidence. Except it doesn't matter. It's too late." The woman didn't answer. Suddenly angry, Laurie said, "I've got to get these done—done and to the goddamn post office—by tomorrow. Think you can do that?"

The clear eyes settled on Laurie's. "Yes."

In the few seconds Laurie didn't speak, it seemed to her that the whole world had gone silent, that outside in the street the cars had stopped, that here in the bar no one talked or poured beer or moved a glass. And then she said, "Oh, yeah, sure. You can just zip through all three in one night. I suppose you can guarantee an A on every one, right?"

"It's not so difficult. I'm a fast study, and an even faster typist."

Laurie made a show of setting her papers in order. "Excuse me, but I'm busy."

"What have you got to lose?" the woman said. "You cannot do it yourself. You know this."

"And what do you charge for this miracle?"

The woman waved a hand. "If you are satisfied with my work we can arrange a price."

This is crazy, Laurie thought. *Wait'll I tell Jaqe.* "Sure," she said. "Why the hell not? Where do you want to perform your wonders?"

"We will work at your house. You have a typewriter?" Laurie nodded. "And enough paper?"

"Oh, I've got loads of paper."

The woman stood up. "Good. Then we will go." She was nearly out the door by the time Laurie had packed her book bag. Outside, the woman hailed a taxi. Soon Laurie was making coffee while in the living room the woman had already begun to type.

The old woman worked all night, scanning Laurie's notes, typing, reading, typing again, always lining up the finished page face down in a precise pile beside the typewriter. For the first hour or so, Laurie attempted to ask what approach she was taking or to look over her shoulder, but the woman ignored her, and after a while Laurie went into the bedroom and tried to read or watch TV. Later she found herself sitting in a chair and watching the old woman, who sat upright, completely motionless except for her birdlike fingers.

Laurie wasn't sure if she was asleep or awake at the moment the old woman picked up the pile of papers and banged them twice on the desk. "Done," she said. "Do you wish to look them over?"

Laurie rubbed her eyes. "Wow," she said. "What time is it?" She lifted the windowshade. The sky was blue, the air warm and dry. "You really did it?" she asked. The old woman just sat there, her back to the desk now, her hands clasped in her lap. Laurie walked over and picked up the first pages. The paper concerned a radical feminist grammar, and as Laurie began to read she suddenly remembered the excitement she'd felt the first time she'd come across these ideas—the description of patriarchal language as the establishment of dominant relationships, the place of women as "others," as objects, the possibility of language, and therefore thought, that did not require objects. It was all there in precise, smooth prose: the facts, the references, the arguments, the critique of academic positions within the correct academic framework. In fact, Laurie realized, the woman had written exactly what Laurie herself would have written if she'd overcome her paralysis.

She scanned the other papers. When she set them down she arranged them in neat piles, the way the old woman had done. "This is incredible," she said. "They're brilliant." But they were more than brilliant. They were her. She said, "I can't possibly pay you what these deserve."

"Do not worry," the woman said. "There is no need to pay me now."

"But I've got to pay you. A job like this deserves something special."

"Then I shall ask you for something special. But not now. When I return, you will pay me." She rose with no sign of weariness. At the door she said, "Goodbye, Laurie Cohen. I am glad I was able to help you."

"Wait a minute," Laurie said. "I don't even know your name." But she stayed by the window as the woman swung the apartment door shut behind her.

Laurie went into the bedroom, thinking she would lie down for an hour, then take the papers to the post office. Instead, she pulled on her sandals, grabbed her keys and some money, and left the papers behind her to go downstairs to the street. What a wonderful day, she thought, looking up at the sky. The sun was already baking the stiffness from her shoulders, while the slight breeze carried away the heat. She heard a whoosh of noise and turned to see the tree that stood in front of the apartment building shake its branches at her. Laurie laughed. It looked so sparkling in the early light. She wondered if it had rained during the night, for the leaves appeared sprinkled with tiny jewels, each one a different color as it picked up some stray bit of light. If she looked long enough she could imagine objects hidden in the tree: toys, tiny houses, animals crouched on the branches. Laurie walked closer. She'd never realized how tall the tree was. The topmost branches moved gently in the wind far above the apartment building.

She jumped up and grabbed a low branch. Her legs swung in the air until she could brace her foot on a knob, which allowed her to push herself onto a branch. Soon she was surrounded by leaves and wood. She could hear birds, though she couldn't see any, could hear their chatter and the flap or hum of their wings. At one point she came across a nest of twigs and wire and pieces of paper. Something lay inside—a chick, she thought, or an egg, but when she climbed up to it she saw it was a doll, a plastic baby that some bird must have carried up in its beak. The blank eyes made Laurie laugh so hard she almost lost her footing and had to grab tight to one of the branches.

She felt so good, so free of all the things that worried her. Why did she ever stop climbing trees? If only Jaqe were here. Maybe they could build a tree house. Sitting with her eyes closed and her back to the trunk, she thought of making love with Jaqe, on a platform deep in the woods. Jaqe was different from the other women Laurie had known. Laurie remembered the wild ones, who wanted to do everything, including reaching all the way into each other's bodies. And the shy ones, who had to take everything step by step, like learning to drive. And the ones who expected her to act like a man, and the ones who got angry if she did anything that in any way resembled a man. But Jaqe—Jaqe knew just what she wanted, what she needed. Sex with her might be slow or fast, noisy or quiet, but never timid, never confused. Sometimes it was Laurie who got scared. Making love with Jaqe could bring her body to a state where her orgasms seemed to go on and on, even after she and Jaqe had finished, officially finished and washed up and gone to eat or just to the supermarket. Her body would have seemed to calm down, to settle into a low tingling, when suddenly something would happen—a look from Jaqe, or a touch of her hand—and it would start up again, waves of orgasm running through her like fever, and she would become scared, because you're not supposed to live like that; other people didn't live like that, they kept things clear and separate.

She began to climb again. She could hear the city now, buses, a truck horn, street construction. It all came from far away, like noise from a television left on in another room. She discovered different regions in the tree. In one place she wanted to jump up and down on the branch with happiness. A little farther on she became sad and wanted to howl for every humiliation she'd ever suffered. She climbed a little higher and all the pain left her, as if the wind had blown it away. She stopped now, and looked up through the leaves at the sky. It looked warm and blue and soft, like a baby's blanket.

In her old bedroom in her parents' house Jaqe lay asleep beside a stuffed tiger she'd found in a box in the basement. She'd stayed up later than she'd expected, doing something she'd promised herself never to do again—arguing with her parents about Laurie. They'd gone on about Jaqe coming home for the summer when they knew damn well she would stay with Laurie. Of course, what they really meant was leave Laurie altogether, go "back" to what they considered normal desires. She tried to point out that she had never shown any interest in men. A mistake, for her parents told her she couldn't give something up if she'd never given it a fair chance. Jaqe still might have gotten out of the whole thing if she hadn't made a further mistake—of comparing her parents with Bill and Janet Cohen. Her mother began crying all over again, and her father went on about sickness, and how parenting wasn't a popularity contest. By the time Jaqe had calmed them down, it was two in the morning.

So now she lay in bed and dreamed she was planting a tree. The tree was short and delicate, about half her height, with yellow leaves, and with its roots wrapped in a bag. The bag was full of holes, so that dirt and tiny jewels fell onto Jaqe's bare feet when she lifted the tree and set it into a hole on the top of a hill. She scooped dirt onto the roots with her fingers, and when she looked up she saw that she was standing in a circle of trees, old dried trees with twisted branches. Somewhere she heard a woman, or maybe a boy, singing. She couldn't make out the words. When she turned around the tree she'd planted had grown. It reached above her head, the branches still thin and graceful, the leaves bright with sun. She began to cry. No, it wasn't her crying, it was a child, a little girl sitting on the ground, with her back against the tree. She was wearing yellow overalls and held a bone in each hand. "What is it?" Jaqe said to her. "What's wrong?"

"My mommy doesn't love me," the little girl said. "I did something bad and my mommy took me here and left me."

"It's all right," Jaqe said. She hugged the little girl. "It's all right. I'll take you home."

Jaqe woke up suddenly, as if someone had clapped into her ear. Without waiting for her heart to settle, she rushed downstairs to the phone. She should have called last night. It had just gotten so late, she'd thought either Laurie was working late and shouldn't be disturbed or Laurie had gone to bed exhausted and shouldn't be woken up.

It took several rings before a groggy "hello" came over the line. "I love you," Jaqe said. "I'm sorry I didn't stay and help you. I'm so stupid. Do you forgive me?"

Laurie laughed. Sleepy, she sounded relaxed, more like the real Laurie than at any time since she'd gone off to graduate school. She said, "I forgive everything you've ever done, in this life and all others. How's that?" When Jaqe didn't answer right away, Laurie said, "I love you. I love you forever."

Jaqe said, "What happened with your papers? Did you get them done?"

"Yeah," Laurie said. Jaqe could hear the smile. "All done. Right on time. Elegant as hell, too."

"That's great. So you've mailed them off?"

"Uh-uh."

"What do you mean?"

"I threw them away. Tore them up and threw them down the incinerator."

"Oh my God," Jaqe said. "Why?"

"Because I don't belong there. I had the papers in my hand and I looked at them, and I thought, No, I can't do it. If I send these now I'll never get out."

"What do you mean? What are you going to do?"

"I've already done it. I sent in my letter of resignation. I'm free, darling. Free and in love. Are you proud of me?"

Slowly, Jaqe nodded. When she realized Laurie couldn't see her she said, "I love you. You're my brave honey. I'm proud of you forever."

Five
The Treasure of Thorny Woods

It took Laurie only three days to find a job, in a bookstore downtown. The man who owned it, Mark, was the brother of one of the LSU women and was happy to hire Laurie on his sister's recommendation. The shop was small and stacked with books in such a cluttered way it amazed Laurie at first that Mark could find anything at all. Mark described the store as specializing in "literature and its friends," but it really followed the vagaries of Mark's own taste and fascinations. There were books on archetypal psychology but no self-help best-sellers, books on witchcraft, including spells to be done at different times of the year, but none on manifesting miracles in your job and love life. There were books on African American religion, interspecies communication, the history of cosmology; there were books on flamenco and square dancing (but none on ballet or disco), and books on the structure of international finance (but none on personal investment strategy).

A large man who always wore jeans and a yellow T-shirt, Mark slipped through the stacks of books without knocking them over, a trick beyond Laurie and most of the customers. Writers often came into the store to sit with Mark on folding chairs and drink passion-fruit tea. They complained about publishers, gossiped about other writers, or described the structure of a new novel or the stupidity of rival anthropologists or difficulties in setting up proper controls for a study of human sexual response under stress. At first, Laurie assumed Mark knew as much as all the writers in all their subjects; he could even talk with a woman who had written several books on myth and religion but came in to discuss her earlier work on the history of knitting. Once, after a linguist had left with the solution to a problem that had blocked his work for days, Laurie blurted at Mark, "How do you know all this stuff? Where do you find time to learn it all?"

Mark sucked on a Popsicle the linguist had given him. He said, "I don't watch TV." After a while Laurie discovered that Mark knew how to listen—half like a sponge, half like a mirror. "You've just got to learn people's language" he said.

Laurie assumed that Mark had hired her to do the practical work, like taking money when he was talking or stocking the shelves from the piles on the floor. When she'd been working a couple of weeks, however, Mark asked her, "Don't you like books, Laurie?"

Laurie looked up from the stack she was straightening. "I like books a lot," she said.

"Well, tell me something to order then." Nervous, Laurie suggested the work of several Québecoise literary critics who sought to transmute passion into text. Mark scribbled the names on the back of a telephone bill. "Terrific," he said. "That's the stuff." So Laurie began studying catalogues, literary magazines, and even the academic journals she'd despised in school. She and Mark would look at everything that came in, and if she wanted to read something she could take it home, read it through, and bring it back as long as she didn't smear the pages or bend the spine. "I'm happy," she told Jaqe. "I'm actually happy."

"That's wonderful," Jaqe said. "When are you going to tell your folks?"

Laurie insisted she couldn't tell her folks about leaving school until she saw them, and she couldn't do that until she got some time off from the store, and since summer was the busy season and she'd just started . . .

One day, Jaqe went into the store and asked Mark for a copy of the I Ching. He brought out his own copy from under the counter, but when he offered her his three Chinese coins, she reached into the pocket of her baseball shirt and brought out three silver coins. About the size of quarters, they showed a turtle on one side and a pair of toads on the other. "Hey," Mark said, "where'd you get those?"

"Found them in the street," Jaqe said. "That's why I thought I better speak to the I Ching. I figure the turtle stands for yin and the toads for yang. What do you think?"

"I think the oracle wants to tell you something."

In the back of the shop Laurie was examining a box of books to see whether some white flecks meant a man had been masturbating over them. This was a hazard of the book business, Mark had told her. It didn't matter if you didn't sell pornography or even serious literature with erotic passages. People got excited about pretty much anything and would slip in the back of the store when no one was looking. Once, Mark said, he'd chased away a masturbator and when he looked at the book that had caused such impatience it turned out to be a field guide to moths and butterflies. Mark told Laurie she wouldn't have to clean such things up, but she should let him know if she found anything. Laurie was trying to examine the books without getting too close when she heard Jaqe's voice. "Jaqe!" she shouted, and ran to the front to hug her as if they hadn't seen each other in months.

Mark said, "Look at the coins Jaqe found."

Laurie held them in her hand. She ran her fingers along the smooth edges. "They look really old," she said. "Maybe they're worth something."

"I don't want to sell them," Jaqe told her. "I just got them."

A friend of Mark's had come into the shop and was looking at the coins. This man was writing a long poem he described as "the seeds of all knowledge." Evenings and weekends he wore a black caftan he claimed he'd stolen from an Iranian cleric. During the day, however, he sold ice cream sandwiches from a counter in a department store and so had to wear a white jacket and pants. Holding Jaqe's coins, he looked like a lab assistant about to try different kinds of acid on an unknown alloy. "There's no writing," he said. "Maybe they're medallions." He looked at the turtle side. "The Chinese used tortoises for divination. There's three of them. You could use them for the I Ching."

"What a wonderful idea," said Jaqe. She picked up the gray book. "And look, here's the I Ching now."

Mark said, "What do you want to ask it?"

"Should Laurie take this weekend off and visit her parents?"

"Hey, wait a minute," Laurie said.

Mark said to Jaqe, "Are you going to toss them? Maybe Laurie should do it."

Laurie said, "Maybe I should toss them back in the street."

Jaqe thought a moment. "It affects all of us, so maybe we should all do it. Two lines apiece." She turned to the poet. "I'm sorry to leave you out, but there're only six lines." He waved a hand.

Jaqe did the first two lines, then Mark. Complaining about "communal destiny," Laurie did the top lines. The hexagram was 48, "The Well." It explained how people came and went, but the well stayed the same.

"Great," Jaqe said. "It's settled."

"What's settled?" Laurie said.

"We're visiting your folks."

"It doesn't say a word about my parents."

"It talks about the source, doesn't it?"

The poet said, "Sounds clear to me."

Laurie said, "Jesus Christ, you didn't even throw any coins."

"How's this?" Mark said. "You can leave early on Saturday afternoon and come in late on Tuesday."

"All right," Laurie said. "I don't believe this. All right. We'll go see my parents."

"And you'll tell them?"

Laurie made a face. "Yeah. I'll tell them."

It always made Jaqe smile to see the Thorny Woods "bus station," the parking lot of a hardware store, with tickets sold in a coffee shop across the street. Laurie's parents were already there when the bus pulled in, Bill in loose white slacks and a blue shirt with large yellow flowers, Janet in a sleeveless orange dress with a flared miniskirt bottom. "Your mother looks great," Jaqe said as she waved through the window. "Great legs."

"Better than mine?" Laurie asked.

"Nothing's better than yours. Especially wrapped around mine."

"Just remember that."

"Will you stop it?" Jaqe said. "You've been such a pain since we left the city."

"This was your idea, remember?" Laurie stood up to yank her tote bag from the overhead rack. "Come on," she said, "or the bus'll pull out before we can get off. And wouldn't that be a shame?"

Jaqe held her hand. "Kiss me first."

Laurie said, "This is Thorny Woods. Girls don't kiss in Thorny Woods."

"I don't care," Jaqe said. "Kiss me right now or I'll scream." Laurie shrugged and then she looked around at the curious faces.

"Hey," the bus driver called, "you two getting off or what?" Laurie grinned and grabbed Jaqe in her arms. "Jesus," the bus driver said. Laurie heard a wolf whistle and slow applause as she and Laurie dashed off the bus.

Outside, Bill was laughing and shaking his head. He did a kind of shimmy while Laurie hugged her mother. "You two are really something," he said. "Better watch out or you'll start a forest fire." When he hugged her, Jaqe found herself putting her head on his shoulder. It felt so solid, so welcoming.

On the way to the car Janet put her arm through Laurie's. "I'm so glad you're here," she said. Jaqe smiled at the sound of that voice, like a pastel painting of rolling hills.

Bill fingered Jaqe's hair. "You could use a cut," he said. "Want me to do it?"

"Wow," Jaqe said. "That'd be great. You sure you have time?"

He put on a fake tough-guy voice. "For you, sweetheart," he said, "I've always got time." Jaqe laughed.

Laurie had planned to tell her parents after dinner, but on the way home to pick up Ellen and change for a restaurant, Bill said, "So how's the life of the scholar? Getting a good rest?"

"Sure," Laurie said. "I mean, I'm working hard at the store, but that's kind of like a rest." She yelped as Jaqe poked her with her elbow.

"Are you all right?" Janet asked.

"Look," Laurie said, "there's something I've got to tell you."

Janet's face tightened, and Jaqe thought how she suddenly looked like a mother. "Go on," Janet said.

"Could we stop somewhere?" Laurie asked.

"We're almost home," Bill said. They were driving along a tree-lined road that ran from the highway to the housing development.

"Honey," Janet told him, "pull over." When Bill had parked the car on the shoulder, Janet reached over and shut off the engine. She put on the blinker and then nodded to Laurie.

Laurie stared at the back of the front seat. "The thing is," she said, "I'm not a scholar anymore."

Bill said, "I don't get it."

"I've dropped out."

"Resigned," Jaqe said.

"Resigned from graduate school," Laurie said.

Bill said, "Jesus, what'd you do that for?"

Janet said, "We knew you were having some problems, dear—"

"It wasn't just problems," Laurie said. "It didn't make any sense. I don't belong there."

Her mother said, "Maybe you could take a leave of absence. Don't they have that?"

"It's too late, Mom. I've already made it official."

"Are you having trouble?" Janet asked. "You could have asked for help."

"What could you have done, change all of graduate school?"

Bill said, "Maybe you could try somewhere else."

"Dad, it's not for me. It just isn't."

Janet said, "Is it because of those papers? Couldn't you get an extension?"

"Mom," Laurie said, "I told you, I resigned. I'm no longer a student there."

Jaqe said, "And besides, she did the papers. She finished every one of them."

"I don't understand," Janet said.

Jaqe waited, but when Laurie said nothing, Jaqe said, "It was the papers that made her realize. She could do them, but they didn't mean anything to her. She knew she had to get out."

Laurie said, "I felt like if I didn't do it now, I'd never do it."

Janet said, "I just wish you had told us. Maybe we could have helped or something."

"Hey," Bill said, "she's a big kid now. She knows what she's doing." He winked at Jaqe. "Right? I'll bet Jaqe's learned that."

"I don't need any help," Laurie said. "I mean, I did the right thing."

Janet asked, "What are you going to do?"

"Well," Laurie said, "for now I'm working in the bookstore."

"That's hardly a career."

Bill said, "She probably just needs some time." Leaning over the seat as if he were about to climb into the back, he said, "If my Laurie says she did the right thing, that's good enough for me. Right?" His voice bounced off the metal and glass.

"Of course," Janet said, and her voice had gotten softer again. "We love you, darling. Whatever you do is fine with us."

Bill held out his arms. "How about a hug?" he said. For a moment Laurie sat where she was, looking at the back of the front seat. Then she leaned forward. Bill put his right arm around her. "Come on," he said to Jaqe, "you too. I want both my favorite women here." Jaqe slid forward and put her arm around Laurie's waist as Bill scooped her up. His slightly pudgy fingers squeezed her shoulders.

When Bill let go, Janet bent over to kiss Laurie on the cheek. She said, "We love you, darling."

"I love you too, Mom."

"Great," Bill said. "Now let's go home; we'll pick up Ellen and we'll go celebrate." He started up the car. "After all," he said, "you've made a big decision, right?"

"Right," Laurie said.

Jaqe thought, it was so easy. If only her own folks could act like Bill and Janet. Even a little. She sighed.

"What is it?" Laurie asked. Her voice sounded sharp.

"Nothing," Jaqe said. "I was just thinking about my parents." To her surprise, Laurie turned away and looked out the window. When Jaqe took Laurie's hand she thought at first that Laurie would pull away, but a moment later she turned around and put her free arm around Jaqe's shoulder. She pulled Jaqe to her and kissed her on the lips. For a moment, before she closed her eyes, Jaqe glanced at the front. Janet was looking out the window, but Bill, she saw, was grinning as he looked in the rearview mirror.

That night they were making love in Laurie's bedroom at the back of the house, when Jaqe decided that Laurie was making too much noise. "Shh," she whispered, and patted Laurie's shoulder.

"Don't stop," Laurie said. When Jaqe moved her hand again Laurie let out another explosive breath.

Jaqe moved away from her. "Laurie," she said, "Please."

Laurie shook herself as if coming back from a dream. "What? Why did you stop?"

Jaqe smiled. "You were making so much noise."

"Oh God," Laurie said, and let her head fall back on the pillow. "Do it again."

Jaqe said, "Can't you be more quiet?"

"Grunts of happiness," Laurie said. "Explosions of ecstasy."

"Can't your ecstasies explode a little more softly? You'll wake up your sister."

Laurie laughed. "Nothing wakes Ellen up. I once had to throw water in her face to get her up for school."

"Well, your parents then."

"They don't mind."

"I mind," Jaqe said. "I love your parents, but I don't want them knowing everything we do."

Laurie said nothing for several seconds, only lay there on her back as her breathing settled. Finally, she said, "Do you really love them?"

"Yes, of course. They've been so good to me. I wish my parents could accept you the way yours accept me."

Again silence, then, "I guess there's not too many like them."

"They're really special," Jaqe said.

"The treasure of Thorny Woods."

Jaqe laughed. "That's right. And you should appreciate them more. But that doesn't include letting them hear every bump."

"On the rocky road to orgasm?"

"Sometimes I think you're just showing off."

"If you've got it, flaunt it."

"Not to your parents."

Laurie sighed. "Maybe we should just go to sleep."

"Because you can't grunt and scream? I didn't say we had to stop. Just—just more quietly."

"I guess I just don't feel relaxed."

"Why do you have to shout to feel relaxed?"

"I just do, okay? I don't want to censor myself."

Jaqe stopped herself from some furious answer. Instead, she kissed Laurie on the mouth. "I'm sorry I upset you," she said.

"It's all right. I love you, Jaqe."

Jaqe said, "I feel so lucky having your parents. I feel almost like I lost one set and got another in return."

Laurie said, "Let's go to sleep."

The next day, after breakfast, Janet announced she was taking the girls shopping. Laurie said she didn't need anything, but Janet insisted it wasn't a question of need. "Buying your daughter clothes is a perk of motherhood," she said. When Ellen said she wanted to watch a swimming meet on television Janet told her she couldn't spend her life in front of a box. "You can watch people swim among the dresses." Ellen made a face.

Laurie grinned at Jaqe. "You want to come see the glories of our local mall? I'll buy you a present."

"An offer I can't refuse," Jaqe said.

Janet said, "How about if *I* buy you a present? You're one of my girls, too, you know."

Jaqe felt shy for some reason and lowered her eyes. Before she could thank Janet, however, she felt Bill's fingers stir her hair. "I've got an idea," Laurie's father said. "You let them go get you a present, and I'll cut your hair. What do you say?"

"I'd love to have you cut my hair." She looked at Laurie. "Do you mind?"

A strange look formed in Laurie's face and then vanished. Grinning, she said, "Suppose I get something you don't like?"

"I'll be happy with anything you get me."

"But suppose I get something for myself and you think it's ugly?"

"It'll become beautiful the moment you put it on. You could buy a hair shirt and it would turn into gold the moment it touched your skin."

"I could stay here," Laurie said, "make sure he doesn't cut it too short."

"Laurie," Janet said, "your father is capable of cutting Jaqe's hair without your help."

Again the strange look flickered over Laurie's face. Jaqe said, "Sweetheart, are you all right?"

"Yeah, of course," Laurie said. "I would just like it if you came along."

Janet said, "Oh, stop fussing. You'll get some great clothes and Jaqe'll get a great haircut."

Jaqe asked Laurie, "Is that okay? I'll come if you really want me to."

Laurie said nothing for a moment, then she shrugged. "No, it's okay. It's fine."

"Are you sure?"

"Yeah, of course."

Janet sighed loudly. "Well, I'm glad that's settled." To Laurie she said, "Now go brush your teeth or whatever you need to do." She waved a finger at Ellen. "You too. Come on, go get ready." Ellen said, "Oh, Mom," but Janet told her, "Move."

In the driveway a few minutes later, as Jaqe kissed Laurie she thought again of her own parents, how hysterical they would be if she and Laurie so much as hugged each other in front of the house. "I'm so lucky," she told Laurie.

"Make sure he doesn't do anything you don't want."

Jaqe laughed. "I'll keep a close watch," she said.

Inside, Bill held up a green smock with snaps up the front. "Here," he said, "go put this on instead of your T-shirt."

"Why can't I put it on over my T-shirt?" Jaqe asked.

"Whatever you like, but Janet's found it doesn't close completely at the top. This way, if any hairs get on your shoulders you can just go in the shower and brush them off."

"I guess so," Jaqe said. She took the smock and went into her and Laurie's bedroom. The polyester felt cool against her skin. When she folded her T-shirt and laid it in her overnight bag she spotted something gray in the corner of the case, underneath a bead necklace she'd worn the night before. When she reached down she discovered the gray stone with the tree and the ferryman. A squeamishness passed through her as she squeezed the stone in her hand. She was sure she hadn't packed it. Maybe it had been in her extra jeans. She put it in the pocket of her shorts and went back to Bill.

"We'll do it in the guest room," Bill told her. "Janet'll scream if we get any hair in the living room and I don't like the light in the den or the kitchen."

"What about the bathroom?"

"I don't like working in there. Too small. Too hot, too."

"Should I wash my hair?"

Bill smiled at her. "I'll wash it. Part of the service for my extra-special customers."

Jaqe smiled back at him. "Thank you, sir."

"First part of the service is a short massage."

"Massage?" Jaqe asked.

"A thing of mine. The cut goes better if the customer's relaxed."

Jaqe said, "Am I supposed to lie down or something?"

Bill laughed. "No, no, we just do your shoulders." He grabbed a chair from the dinette and set it in the middle of the living room. "Madam," he said, with a slight bow.

Jaqe curtsied with the smock and sat down. As Bill's hands began to knead and push her muscles she smiled, thinking of Dr. Root. Then the smile softened at the feel of her shoulders loosening, and she let her head tilt back. She must have made a noise because Bill said, "That sounds very nice."

"Do you massage all your clients?" Jaqe asked.

"Only the ones I really care about. Besides," he added, "some of them are so heavy you wouldn't want to touch anything but the hair." Jaqe didn't answer. Bill slid his hands to the ends of her shoulders and held them as he bent down and kissed Jaqe lightly on the cheek. Surprised, she turned and looked at him, but he'd already straightened up. "Now we'll go wash your hair," he said.

Jaqe said, "I can just do it myself."

"Hey, you're in the beauty parlor. A wash is part of the service." He led her into the bathroom, where he'd set out a folding chair by the sink. Bottles of salon shampoo and conditioner were lined up along the counter. When Jaqe sat down, Bill wrapped a towel around her shoulders and tucked the edge into the collar of her smock. "I had this sink put in special," he said.

Jaqe leaned back. She wished she could watch what he was doing, but all she could see was the ceiling. Behind her she heard the water running, and then she felt his hands brush her neck and the sides of her face as he lifted her hair back. "Loosen up," he said, "you've just had a massage."

Jaqe did her best to drop her shoulders and let her head rest in Bill's hands. When he finished rinsing out the conditioner he wrapped her hair in another towel, thick and fluffy, and gave her head a good rub. Jaqe sighed. "Nice, huh?" Bill said. "You should get Laurie to wash and dry your hair for you."

In the guest room Bill laid a plastic tablecloth on the floor and set the dinette chair in the middle facing the bed. The white outer curtains were closed so that filtered sunlight glowed in the room. Jaqe said, "It's such a nice day. Let's open the curtains."

"Sorry," Bill said as he gestured her to the chair. "Janet gets furious if I let in direct light. Says the furniture will fade."

"Well, can we turn the chair then? If I face the bed, I'll just get sleepy." Wrong move, she thought. He'll suggest lying down. The thought surprised and embarrassed her. All he did, she told herself, was kiss her cheek.

Bill turned the chair to the side so that Jaqe was facing the dresser with her back to the windows. "How's that?" he said.

"Fine," Jaqe said. She sat down.

Bill's hand rested against her neck as he held her hair. "You've got beautiful hair," he said. "You're the kind of client I love to work on."

"Thanks." She thought, *Why didn't I go shopping?*

"What would you like me to do to you?"

"Cut my hair."

Bill laughed. "Right. How do you want it?"

"Pretty much the same, I guess. Just, you know, more shape."

"You've already got a great shape. But I'll see what I can do."

One more line, Jaqe thought. One more, and the beauty parlor shuts down. Bill settled in to separating her hair, clipping it in bunches, snipping off split ends. Once again, Jaqe felt rotten for misjudging him. "Do you cut hair much yourself?" she asked.

"No, usually I've got too much to do running the business."

"Do you miss it?"

"Sure, sometimes. But then I get to work on someone wonderful. Like you." There was a silence again, and then Bill said, "You know we all feel really lucky that Laurie's got you."

"I'm lucky I've got her," Jaqe said.

Bill was combing locks of hair and clipping off the ends. As he worked beside her, Jaqe could see the gleam of the scissors, dotted here and there with black spots, like mold or corrosion.

Bill said, "You know, Janet and I have always supported Laurie. We figure, as long as she's happy, you know? But I'll tell you the truth, we're real happy she's found you. Some of those other girls were kind of wild, if you know what I mean. Go after anything."

"None of the women I know are like that at all," Jaqe said.

"Maybe you just like to see the best in people. Anyway, Laurie's got you now, and you *are* the best." He bent down and kissed her shoulder.

Jaqe twisted away. She said, "Let's stick to the haircut, okay?"

"Hey, come on," Bill said. "You know I think of you like my own daughter." A moment later he announced, "Done."

Jaqe turned to look in the mirror. He'd cut it a little shorter than she'd expected, but even with her hair damp she could see it had more curl, more . . . excitement. She said, "It looks great."

Bill inclined his head. "Thank you, madam. Shall I blow-dry it?"

"I think I'll just go outside and let the sun dry it." She started to get up, but Bill's hands held her shoulders.

"I'm glad you like it," he said. "If I didn't know it was impossible, I'd say it made you even more beautiful than before."

"I'm getting up now," Jaqe said. Before she could move, Bill bent down and kissed her on the lips. Or tried to, for Jaqe snapped her head away and all Bill got was her chin. As hard as she could, Jaqe shoved him away and jumped up for the door. But he was already there, grinning as if they were playing a children's game.

"Hey," he said, "doesn't the hairdresser get a tip?"

"I'll give you a tip," Jaqe said. "Keep away from me or you'll really regret it."

"You don't mean that," he said, and moved toward her.

"Like hell I don't." Jaqe tried again for the door only to have Bill grab her arm as she tried to get past him. With his free hand he took the scissors from his shirt pocket. He said, "Don't you know you should always act nice to a man with a sharp object? Or one of us could trip and get hurt."

Jaqe stood very still. "C'mon, Bill," she said, "throw that away. I'm sure we can work something out."

"Yeah?" Bill said. He hefted the scissors as if they weighed several pounds. "Is that a promise?"

"A promise," Jaqe said.

Bill looked again at the scissors, then Jaqe. He grinned. "What the hell," he said, and tossed the scissors on the floor next to the bed. Immediately, Jaqe tried to pull loose her arm. "Hey," Bill said, "we had a deal."

"Go to hell," Jaqe said.

"What's the matter with you? What are you so worked up about? Are you worried about Laurie? Is that the problem? Don't. She knows all about it." When Jaqe stopped struggling he grabbed her other arm by the wrist.

Jaqe said, "What do you mean? What are you talking about?"

Bill's grin made her sick. He said, "Laurie and I, we've got an agreement. Share and share alike."

"You're lying," Jaqe said. She realized she was shouting. "How can you say something like that about your own daughter?"

"It's true, that's how. We've always done it this way. When they start missing the real thing too much, Laurie sends them to me. Then I give them back to her all calm and happy." Suddenly he let go of one arm to pull open the snaps of her smock. He bent down to kiss her breast, his mouth open, his teeth shining in the filtered light. With her free hand Jaqe tried to shove him away. He didn't seem to notice, only pushed his hand inside the back of her shorts. She could feel his pudgy fingers push between her cheeks.

"You lying bastard!" Jaqe screamed, and jerked her knee up between his legs.

It wasn't a direct hit, or at least he didn't curl up in agony like she was hoping. But it did loosen his grip enough so that she could wriggle free. When she kicked at him again, this time with her foot, she missed even wider, getting him in the knee. But it was enough, for he stumbled and fell against the chair Jaqe had sat in for the haircut.

Seeing him on the floor, Jaqe wanted to kick him again and again, hit him with the chair, the mirror, anything she could grab until he took it all back, admitted it was all lies. But he had the scissors again, he was getting up. *Get out*, she told herself. *Run.* As she scrambled out the door something struck her leg, and she yelped in pain. But she kept going, while behind her Bill yelled, "It's true! Just ask her. You're the first one to complain. The first one. Ask her!"

Jaqe kept running when she got out of the house, hardly even slowed by the limp that had taken over her left leg. She didn't know if Bill would chase her in the car, but just in case, she took the first turn she came to and then the next. When she'd looked back a few times with no sign of him, she stopped to inspect her leg. A narrow stream of blood ran down the thigh from a cut a few inches above the knee. Though it didn't look deep, it throbbed every time she took a step. She thought of the black spots on the scissors and knew she should get the wound disinfected. But all she could think of was the danger that Bill might be following the drops of blood. She found some old tissues in her pocket and did her best to press them against the wound as she walked.

Sweat was pouring off her. It had to be in the eighties and the polyester smock didn't help any. What an idiot she was to let him talk her into taking off her T-shirt. She stopped a moment to catch her breath. A teenage boy with a black dog came toward her. Nervously, Jaqe checked the smock to make sure all the snaps were closed. She must look ridiculous, she thought, like an escapee from something. *Goddamn him*, she thought.

The boy looked her over as he bent down for a stick. For a moment he hefted it in his hand, reminding Jaqe of the way Bill had hefted the scissors. But then he threw the stick. The dog ran after it, the boy followed, and then they were gone; Jaqe was alone again. It can't be true, she thought. Of course it wasn't true. Laurie would never think of making a deal like that. Any kind of deal. It was impossible. That sonofabitch. How could he say something like that? About his own daughter. She passed a lawn with a ring of stones around a plastic statue of a boy and girl holding hands. Jaqe wished she could grab up all the rocks and run back to throw them at Bill.

It was then that she realized that she didn't know where she was. Laurie's housing development was much larger than her own, with many more streets. Jaqe caught her breath. There was no need to worry, she told herself. She couldn't go back anyway, not until she was sure Laurie had returned (damn her leg, she thought, and decided to ignore the pain). She could always knock on someone's door and ask to use the phone. Or just ask for directions. She looked around. All the houses looked the same, blank and closed. Where were all the people? Even the boy with the dog had vanished. It's all right, she told herself. She just had to wait. She kept walking. When she took away the tissues the bleeding had stopped; the cut looked dark around the edges.

What would Bill tell Laurie? Would he make up some story? She wished she could see Laurie first, tell her exactly what happened. She remembered Laurie saying "They won't mind" last night when Jaqe worried about the noise they made making love. Did Bill hear them? Why wouldn't he mind? Because he knew he was getting his turn the next day? "No!" she said loudly. "It's not true."

The street she was on curved to the left, and suddenly Jaqe found herself facing the wooded entrance to a park. She looked back. If she was lost she probably should stay inside the development. But the park looked cool. And suppose Bill decided to chase her after all. All he'd have to do was cruise up and down the streets until he spotted her. She limped toward the woods.

Six

Candles in the Sun

The path into the park was narrow and overgrown with thorns so that Jaqe had to pull aside one branch after another to make any progress. Despite her care, the thorns kept scratching at her wound, making her gasp in pain. The path was so tangled she couldn't think how anyone could use it at all.

Maybe there was another entrance. Maybe they kept this one closed as a kind of museum exhibit of what it looked like before the houses came. They called the town Thorny Woods, after all. Maybe this park was really the remains of woods going back thousands of years. When she stopped to catch her breath, she discovered the smock had torn at the right shoulder. That bastard. That lying bastard.

She felt like such a jerk—falling for all that "special client" crap. She remembered all the things she'd said to Laurie about how great Bill and Janet were. She wanted to cry. What an idiot she was. Second parents, she'd called them. She remembered how Laurie had tried to get her to go to the mall. "Make sure he doesn't do anything you don't want," Laurie had said. Jaqe felt dizzy, out of breath. Don't think about it, she told herself. Stay calm.

She looked at the mass of thorns. It looked impossible to get through. But when she looked over her shoulder the ones behind her appeared just as thick as those in front. She had no idea how she'd gotten this far. When she took a breath, her leg beat with pain. She stared ahead. They were just bushes after all. It was so quiet. She could hear a bird somewhere and—very faintly—a child crying, but aside from that she might as well have been in a woods hundreds of years ago. Okay, she told herself, this can't go on forever. The thing to do was go forward. At that moment she noticed a stick standing upright in the web of branches. Someone had made a walking stick from it, for the bark was peeled away and a string of colored beads was tied to a notch cut near the top. Carefully, Jaqe pulled the stick loose from its cage. It felt warm, almost polished, as if someone had used it for years before leaving it. Jaqe half leaned on it, half used it to push the branches away. It comforted her to have something to do, something to hold and use. It made her feel less . . . less like an orphan.

When Jaqe heard the crying, she almost thought it was herself. But the voice was a child's, somewhere ahead of her. Using the stick, she pushed through the thorns. Soon she came out into a meadow, a wide soft hill ringed all around with old trees, many of them gnarled and bent, with thornbushes in the small spaces between the trunks. What a strange park, Jaqe thought, for there were no picnic benches, no baseball fields, nothing but grass, wildflowers, and trees. The trees stood like a fence against the outside. Toward the far end of the meadow, however, just past the rise of the hill, Jaqe saw a small circle of trees, younger than the others, straighter, more graceful. In the center rose a bushy tree with a rough bark and thick scaly leaves. Without thinking, Jaqe walked toward it. There was something blue; when she came closer she realized they were berries, small bright things like jewels.

Again she heard the child crying. Even with the stick it hurt Jaqe to walk, but she moved faster, and when she reached the top of the hill she could see a girl sitting on the ground with her back against the young bushy tree. The girl wore yellow overalls, but her blond hair shone brighter than the cloth. In front of her, on a red scarf, lay a small pile of bones. They looked old, all smooth and polished, like Jaqe's stick. The girl just sat there, looking at the bones and crying.

Jaqe stood the stick against the tree and sat down in front of the child. "Are you lost?" she said. The girl shook her head. "Do you want me to take you home?" The crying got louder.

Nervously, Jaqe reached out to touch the child's shoulder. It was wet with tears. "Do you want to tell me what's wrong?" she said. As if Jaqe had touched a spring, the little girl leaned forward with her arms out for Jaqe to scoop her up. "It's all right," Jaqe said as she held the child tight against her torn smock. "It's all right. No one's going to hurt you anymore." She wasn't sure what she meant, but it seemed the right thing to say. Jaqe too began to cry. At first, she worried that the girl might get scared, but when the girl held Jaqe even more tightly, Jaqe let her whole body weep. The two of them rocked back and forth in the sun.

Slowly they came to a stop. When Jaqe gently separated herself, the girl asked her, "Would you help me?"

"Of course," Jaqe said. She started to get up, thinking the child wanted to go home. But instead the girl asked, "Can you help me bury them?"

"What?" Jaqe said, and then realized the girl meant the bones. She was already trying to dig a hole in the grass beside the bushy tree. Jaqe asked her, "Where did you get them?"

"They're my brother's," she said.

Jaqe smiled. "Does he know you've got his collection?"

The girl shook her head. "Please help me," she said. "We've got to make them safe."

"Safe from what?" Jaqe asked, but the child wasn't paying attention. The dirt seemed too hard for her, and the more frustrated she got, the more frantically she poked at the earth. "Let me do it," Jaqe said. The pain made it unbearable for her to kneel, but she stretched out her leg and began pulling with her fingertips. A moment later she began using the stick like a pike to loosen the dirt. The girl's worry must have been catching, for Jaqe worked very fast, jabbing with the stick, shoveling with her hands. She had no idea how much time had passed, but suddenly they were done, and she was sitting back, breathing hard, with the stick in her lap. Before her was a neat mound of dirt, packed down with bits of grass and torn flowers. The little girl sat quietly now, her hands in her lap. Her yellow overalls were covered with brown stains.

"It needs a stone," the child said.

"A stone?"

"Sure. They've always got to have a stone."

Jaqe looked around, but all she could see was dirt. She grinned. "You know," she said, "I think I've got a stone right here." She reached into her shorts pocket and with a flourish took out the flat rock with the tree and the boat. "Here," she said. "How's this?"

The girl held it in both hands. "Wow," she said. "It's beautiful." Jaqe felt like singing as the little girl set the rock in the center of the mound of dirt. Very carefully, the child pressed the stone into the ground and packed some dirt on top of it. "We better hide it," the girl said, "so no one'll find it."

Jaqe nodded. "That sounds like a good idea."

Looking around, Jaqe spotted a small mound of fresh leaves. They were dry and brightly colored, as if an early autumn had come for just this group of leaves. Together Jaqe and the girl grabbed armfuls and carefully placed them on the fresh dirt. "How's that?" Jaqe said.

"It's beautiful," the little girl told her. "Thank you. You're the kindest lady I ever met."

Jaqe smiled and bent down to give the child a hug. When she straightened up she glanced toward the top of the tree. The light hit the leaves in an odd way, so that it looked like she could see a face, a child's face, in the branches. The face was smiling, and Jaqe's heart opened; for a moment even her leg stopped hurting.

But then she looked at the ancient trees at the end of the meadow, and her eye fell on a dark area embedded among the thorns and branches. She shuddered, and now when she glanced down at her leg, the ugly green and black of her wound made her recoil in disgust. How had it gotten so bad so quickly? It was as if days or weeks had passed in the short time Jaqe had been in the woods.

The little girl leaned her head against Jaqe's head. Suddenly Jaqe became very tired. All that digging. When she looked down, she saw that the little girl had fallen asleep, curled on the ground with her head against Jaqe's thigh. Gently, Jaqe moved the child and lay down beside her. For just a moment she thought she saw a face, not a child's, not peaceful, in the dark trees. But then she had to close her eyes; she could no longer force them open. With the stick in her hand, she put her arm over the child and fell asleep.

She was standing in a chill room, almost bare, with just a plain wooden table and four chairs, and at the other end a stove with a large black pot. She strode to the table to arrange a life-size doll in one of the chairs. Carefully, she propped up the doll's body, with the legs under the table and the hands neatly folded in front of it. It looked so funny she could hardly keep herself from falling over laughing. A doll in a golden coat! Cheerfully, she walked over to the stove, where the doll's head lay beside the pot. It was one of those plastic heads, with a smiling mouth, rosy cheeks, and eyes that closed when the doll bent backward. Only, the smile had chipped and the eyes had rolled backward permanently so that all you saw was white with little flecks of red. She giggled. It really did look so funny. She picked up the head and did a little dance step as she moved back across the room to set the head carefully on the shoulders. She adjusted it and stepped backward. It was very important, she knew, to get it right.

She was sitting in the dirt, playing with a pair of sticks in the corner. She spoke bits of dialogue for them and allowed one to chase the other and then knock her down. But she had to do it all silently, very silently, or the mother might hear and punish her. She sneaked a glance at the mother stirring a pot of stew on the stove. The mother wore a dress with bright colors and little bits of metal on the shoulders. She herself wore a torn smock and no shoes. The mother turned, and she ducked her head, afraid the mother might have seen her staring.

But no, the mother only said, "Your silly brother has fallen asleep again. Go give him a push and wake him up." She got up from the floor and walked to the table, where her brother sat upright with his hands folded in front of him. She touched his shoulder. No answer.

The mother said, "You have to do it harder than that. You know how deeply he sleeps." The mother sounded so cheerful. She took a deep breath and pushed her brother with both hands. His head leaped off his shoulders and rolled across the table.

Jaqe woke up with a shout. *God*, she thought, *what a nightmare*. She felt the small body under her arm. She thought, *What am I going to do with her*, and then, *What am I going to do with me?* She sat up, gasping with pain, but careful not to disturb the child. As soon as Jaqe moved her arm, however, the girl began to twitch and her face twisted, as if some terrible dream had seized her. "It's all right," Jaqe said softly, and touched her shoulder. The child made a noise. Her arms shot out and grabbed at the air. "It's okay," Jaqe said, and hugged her. "It's okay." The girl woke up to stare at Jaqe without seeing her. "It's just a dream," Jaqe said.

At that moment, she looked beyond the girl to the fence of trees. Once again, she thought she saw that angry face. It was just a suggestion, really, nothing more than a gleam of eyes, a flicker of movement. And yet Jaqe had never felt such a stab of terror. She wanted to run, hide in the dirt, but she knew that would leave the girl all alone. Breathing hard, she stared at the trees. It all looked normal now. It was so hard to tell, the woods were so dense. There—she saw it again. Jaqe stood up. Leaning against the tree, she waved the stick in the air. The beads rattled against each other. "Keep away from us!" she shouted. "Get out of here."

She heard a rustling sound in the bushes. It lasted only a second, and then the silence came down again. Jaqe leaned on the stick. She felt foolish, shouting like that. If she had seen anything at all, it was probably just some harmless animal. She hoped she hadn't scared the child.

But when she looked down the girl was gone. *She's run away*, Jaqe thought. *I scared her and she ran into the woods*. She could get really lost. Or injured. There were all those thorns. "Come back," she called. "It's all right. No one'll hurt you." Why hadn't she asked the girl's name? "It's all right," she shouted again. "Come back and I'll take you home." Nothing.

She tried to run, not knowing where to go, but in only two steps, she cried out in pain and fell to the ground. As she fell, her body turned toward the meadow. And there she saw something so strange that for a moment she forgot the girl, forgot the pain in her leg, even forgot Laurie and Bill. The entire meadow was filled with burning candles. Hundreds, thousands of candles, all sizes and shapes, some thick and bright, others thin, delicate. The air above the flames shimmered and shook. And in front of them all, in the midst of grass white with melted wax, stood a single low candle, sputtering, as if about to go out.

Jaqe turned; she didn't know why, but that sputtering candle terrified her more than everything that had happened. Frantically, she scanned the trees, looking for a way through. She saw an opening, a space between the trees. She started out, leaning heavily against her stick, then stopped. What if the girl came back looking for her? She needed to leave a sign so the child would know Jaqe had gone for help. She laid the stick on the ground, pointing at the path where she now limped away from the meadow.

The trees looked different here, not so old and bent. She limped quickly, sometimes bracing herself with the branches. And then she came to the end, and stood for a moment, dizzy and sick in the bright sun of the housing development. Holding her hand above her eyes, she looked around, hoping she could recognize something or at least see someone she could ask for directions.

There was nobody, and nothing looked familiar. The houses didn't even remind her of Laurie's. Jaqe wondered if she had come out into some other development on the other side of the park. But then she looked closer at the houses and saw they really were the same—split-level, shingle siding, contrasting roofs. Only—only, they looked so old, so dilapidated, the paint peeling, gutters all rusty, shingles coming loose, bare spots on the roofs. Jaqe fought hard against panic. She tried focusing on the ground, but everywhere she looked she saw decay. The paving in the road had broken up; weeds and wildflowers overran the lawns, they looked like no one had cut them in weeks, even months.

Jaqe made a noise, half sob, half whimper. Her leg throbbed so badly it felt twice its size, and she felt nauseous from the pain. Everything looked deserted, as if somehow everyone had left, as if a war had come, killing everyone with fallout, or neutron bombs, leaving the buildings whole and killing all the people. *Stop it*, Jaqe ordered herself. She squeezed her hands into fists and took a deep breath.

She heard a rattling noise nearby. When she looked, she thought she saw someone walking around the side of a house. Jaqe limped across the street. She called out, "Excuse me? Hello? Hey!" And then she stopped on the edge of a lawn. She hadn't seen a person at all, but a doll, one of those life-size cardboard skeletons people hang up for Halloween. A gust of wind shook it, and once again the legs and arms rattled against the house like someone about to run away. *Oh God,* Jaqe thought, *Help me.*

A soft noise came along the street behind her. When she turned, Jaqe saw a small red car, a two-seater, roll to a stop before a droopy tree with no leaves and a gray trunk. The car looked as worn out as the houses, with faded paint, rust holes along the bottom, a large dent in the back fender, even a crack in the side window. The tires, bald as a dead tree, sagged on the road. Inside sat an old woman with skin so covered in delicate lines her face looked like a map of the world. The sun seemed to penetrate right through her skin to light up her bones and give the impression that her body shone with its own radiance. Despite her fragility she sat upright in the car, with her hands lightly on the steering wheel. She wore a light green dress with a piece of multicolored chiffon that fluttered out from the shoulders like a cape. Her fine white hair danced in the breeze.

The woman got out of the car. Without any plan of what she wanted to say, Jaqe walked across the road. The old woman held out her hands, and Jaqe's own hands drifted up to them. When the woman smiled, the sun shone directly on her teeth, so that Jaqe, dazzled, had to turn her face for a moment. When she looked again the white straw had darkened and softened into tumults of red hair. All the cracked lines of the face had faded; the skin shone. Beneath the thin dress, Jaqe could see the soft curves of a young body. Behind the woman, the red car, smooth and spotless, perched on whitewall tires that looked about to smile.

Jaqe tried to pull her hands away, but the woman held them fast without any pressure. "Hello, Jaqe," she said. "How lovely to see you again."

"Let go of me," Jaqe said. "I know what you are."

Mother Night laughed. "Do you?"

"What have you done to this place?" Jaqe demanded. "What did you do to the people, the houses?"

"Oh, Jaqe," Mother Night said, and shook her head. "You have it all wrong. This sort of thing happens when I *don't* do anything."

"I don't believe you," Jaqe said. "You did this. You took them all away." Mother Night didn't answer. "What do you want from us? Why can't you leave us alone?" Again no answer. "You've got no right. It's not fair." She wanted to kick her, to knock her down in the road, to throw her back against her little red car.

Mother Night said, "Look at me, Jaqe."

Jaqe turned her head away. "No! Leave me alone." Again she tried to pull away, and again Mother Night held tight to her hands. Slowly, her breath as heavy as the old car that had labored up the road, Jaqe brought around her eyes. She didn't know what she expected to see, maybe a dark shadow licked by flames or a skull-like head with a lolling tongue. But all she found was that sweet face, and those smiling eyes. Hardly knowing she was doing it, Jaqe bent down in the street to lay her head against Mother Night's belly.

Mother Night said, "That's a nasty wound, Jaqe. Let me see." She bent down to touch Jaqe's leg.

Suddenly the pain was gone; Jaqe gasped in surprise. She smiled. It felt so good, so peaceful. When she looked at her leg, the place where the wound had been shone bright and joyous. A memory came to Jaqe from years ago: a warm wave, and she and her mommy lying in the surf on the edge of the sea.

Somewhere down the street she heard a noise. Lazily she inclined her head. It sounded like a girl, she thought, about ten or eleven, calling to a friend. From somewhere else came the cough of a lawn mower. Jaqe stood to look up and down the street at clean lawns decorated with bushes and flower beds. Water from the sprinklers darkened the smooth streets and the freshly painted houses. At one end of the street a woman sunbathed in a lawn chair. At the other end, a man in sweatpants and a headband braced himself against a tree and pushed as if he would uproot the world.

"You see," Mother Night said, "it's really very simple."

Jaqe started to nod, then stopped herself. Mother Night's smile washed over her. "There's a girl," Jaqe said, and pointed vaguely toward the park.

"She's all right," Mother Night said.

"You don't understand. She ran into the woods. She's all alone. We've got to find her."

"She's fine. You helped her. You buried the bones for her, don't forget that. You don't know what will come of that."

"But we can't just leave her."

"She'll do fine. Really she will."

Jaqe grimaced. There was something—something about a dream. She said, "What happened to the girl's brother?"

Mother Night said, "That doesn't concern you."

"But—"

"It's all right, Jaqe. Trust me." Jaqe didn't answer. "Trust me," Mother Night said.

"I can't," Jaqe said. "I can't trust you. You'll take Laurie from me."

"Oh, Jaqe," Mother Night said. "Is that the problem? You should have told me. I will make you a promise. I will never take Laurie from you. Does that help?"

Jaqe clenched her fists against the relief that tried to wash over her. "How can I believe you?" she said.

Mother Night smiled again. Her shrug sent her dress rippling down her body. She said, "Why should I lie to you?"

"I don't know. I can't stand the thought of losing her."

"Then free yourself from torment. Trust my promise." Jaqe said nothing. Mother Night said, "Poor Jaqe. Maybe as the months go by and Laurie remains with you, you'll come to believe that I mean what I say."

A gust of wind blew Jaqe's hair across her face. It lifted Mother Night's hair and the cape from her dress so that they flared like flags. Jaqe closed her eyes again, only to see Bill shouting filth at her. "I've got to get back," she said.

Mother Night started toward her car. "I'll drive you."

Jaqe took a step, then stopped. "Is it safe?"

"I've never had an accident."

Jaqe couldn't help herself. She began to laugh, first nervously, then with a shout that drowned out the lawn mower. She opened the door of Mother Night's car and sank down in the leather seat.

As they drove away, something made Jaqe look back. On the edge of a lawn burned a single candle, fresh and strong, with a flame that held steady in the afternoon sun.

Seven

The Children of the Sky

Jaqe and Mother Night sat parked across the street from Laurie's house. With the doors and curtains closed to protect the air conditioning, the house looked to Jaqe like a castle with the drawbridge up. But at least the garage door stood open, revealing Mrs. Cohen's minicompact parked beside Bill's Buick. They were all there, the whole gang.

Jaqe looked at Mother Night. "I guess you can't come with me."

"I'm sorry," Mother Night said. "I've got an appointment."

Jaqe shuddered, remembering a story she'd read once. "Okay," she said. "It would probably just make me nervous." she got out of the car.

Mother Night held out a hand. "Good luck, Jaqe," she said.

Jaqe hesitated a moment, then jumped her hand out to shake Mother Night's. "Thanks," she said. At the door, before she rang the bell, she looked back. As the red sports car turned the corner, a thin hand waved out the window. And then Jaqe was alone. She took a breath and jabbed the bell.

Bill answered the door. "Hey, Jaqe," he said. He called out, "Here she is. No need to worry." Jaqe resisted the urge to shove him as she marched into the living room. Bill said, "Glad you're back. I told Laurie you'd just gone for a walk, but you know how nervous she gets."

Laurie said, "Hi, sweetie. We got you a present." Janet added, "Laurie was so nervous it wouldn't fit. I promised her we'd bring it right back if it didn't."

Jaqe stood in the middle of the room, looking from one to the other. In the back of the house she heard a TV laugh track; Ellen must be watching a sitcom. Jaqe thought, *They look so goddamn normal.* And, *It's not true. It can't be true.*

"Jaqe," Laurie said. "What's wrong?" When she came closer she saw the torn smock, the dirt stains on Jaqe's face and hands, the scratches up and down her legs and arms. "Oh my God," she said. "What happened to you?" She tried to take Jaqe's hands, but Jaqe pulled them away. Laurie said, "What's wrong? Why aren't you saying anything?"

Bill said, "Did you fall or something? She must have fallen."

Janet fingered the torn smock. "Why are you wearing this?"

Jaqe jerked her shoulder away. She didn't want any of them touching her, not even . . . She said, "I didn't have time to change. I had to leave in a hurry."

Jaqe thought Laurie glanced at her father, but she wasn't sure. Laurie looked about to cry as she asked, "Honey, what's wrong? Please tell me."

"What's wrong," Jaqe said, "is that your father has a very peculiar idea of a haircut."

"Huh?" Bill said. "What's she talking about?" He looked at his wife. "Can you figure out what she's talking about?" Laurie was staring at the floor, her fists clenched.

"Jaqe," Janet said, "you're not being very clear."

"No? Then how's this? Your husband tried to rape me. Is that clear enough?"

"What?" Bill shouted, and Janet's golden purr leaped a register as she said, "How can you say that? That's disgusting." Laurie stared down at the floor.

"What's disgusting?" Ellen said. She stood in the archway of the hall leading to the back bedrooms.

"Get out of here," Janet ordered. "Go to your room."

"Let her stay," Jaqe said. "She's got to learn about her father sometime."

Janet said, "Don't you tell me what to do with my child. She doesn't need to hear your sick fantasies." To Ellen she said, "Go to your room. Don't make me tell you again."

Coolly, Ellen looked from her father to Jaqe, and then to Laurie. She glanced once more at her father, smiled briefly and shrugged, and then shuffled back to her television.

"Jesus," Bill said. "I don't know what she's talking about. All I did was cut her hair."

"And rip open my clothes. And cut me with the scissors—"

"That's a lie," Bill said. "You did that yourself."

"And stick his hand inside my pants—"

Janet stamped her foot. "Stop it. Stop making up filth about my husband." She shook her head, "Oh Jaqe, poor Jaqe, you must be so confused. We took you in. We treated you like our own daughter."

Laurie slammed her fists against the paneled wall. A Degas print bounced off its hook and onto the floor. "Shut up," Laurie ordered her mother. "You know goddamn well she's telling the truth."

"Laurie!" Janet said. "This is your father."

Laurie paid no attention. She took two steps toward her father and hit the heels of her hands against his shoulders. "Goddamn you," she said crying. "Goddamn you. You couldn't keep your fucking hands to yourself."

Jaqe wanted to run. She wanted to put on her own shirt and run outside before she threw up. Bill was saying, "I didn't touch her. I didn't go near her," and Laurie was shouting something about too many lies, and Janet was going on about how Jaqe needed help, living in a sick fantasy world, and now Laurie was telling her mother, "You know who the sick one is. You know," and Jaqe knew she had to get out.

"Laurie," Jaqe said, "take me away from here," but Laurie was shouting something at her father, or maybe her mother. "Please," Jaqe said.

Jaqe didn't know if Laurie actually heard her or just saw the tears in her face. She broke off whatever accusation she was launching and reached over to Jaqe, only to stand there with her hands half rising, then rubbing against her jeans, unable to reach all the way to touch her lover. Jaqe said, "Get me out of here."

Laurie said, "I'm sorry."

"Please," Jaqe said.

"Did he—how far did he—"

"I'm okay," Jaqe told her. Her own voice sounded funny to her. "Just take me away from here."

Janet said, "Jaqe, you look sick. Why don't you just lie down?" Her hand slithered up toward Jaqe's shoulder.

Laurie slapped it away. "Keep your hands off her," she said, and finally, as if the movement had released her, took Jaqe in her arms. "It's okay, sweetheart," she said. "I've got you. It's okay. We'll go upstairs, and I'll pack your stuff, and I'll call a taxi."

Boxes, plastic bags, and clothes with tags on them lay on top of the bed. Laurie swept them onto the floor and started throwing things into their canvas bags. Her hands shook, and twice she dropped things. Jaqe meanwhile pulled off the smock and threw it against the wall. When she'd pulled on a T-shirt she sat down in a pink wing chair that had stood in the corner of Laurie's room almost from the day Laurie was born. Jaqe stared at the floor and only looked up when Laurie had just about finished packing. "Laurie," she said. Laurie stood still but didn't look at her. "How did you know I was telling the truth and your father was lying?"

There was a pause, then Laurie shrugged. "Of course you were telling the truth," she said. "I love you. You'd never make up a story like that."

"But you told your mother that she knew it was true. What did you mean?"

"Well—I don't know—just that she should know you'd never lie."

Jaqe said nothing.

Laurie called for the taxi from the old princess phone her parents had installed for her back in junior high school. While they were waiting, Janet knocked on the door. "Laurie," she said, "I want to talk to you."

"Go away," Laurie said.

Janet rattled the locked door handle. "I'm your mother," she said. "I demand you let me in."

Laurie shouted, "Get away from us!"

Jaqe and Laurie said nothing until they heard the sound of the taxi honking for them. Then Laurie went over to Jaqe and squatted down in front of the chair. "You okay?" she said. Jaqe nodded. Laurie said, "I'm sorry, Jaqe. I'm really sorry."

"Let's just go," Jaqe said.

They rushed through the house. In the living room, Bill was gone but Janet was waiting, ready to grab Laurie as they made for the door. "You can't do this," Janet said. Laurie shook her away and yanked open the door. Janet said, "She's sick, Laurie. Can't you see that?" But Laurie was already rushing for the cab, while Janet stood in the doorway.

The cab driver was a young woman with red spiky hair. She lounged back in the seat, seemingly paying no attention to her passengers. Laurie climbed in, but Jaqe only stood there. The driver wore a black tank top and black cutoff jeans. Next to her on the front seat lay a leather jacket. All Jaqe could see was the satin lining, but she knew that if she turned it over she'd find a gold labyrinth and words in flowing script.

Laurie said, "C'mon, Jaqe." Jaqe stood in front of the open car door. *She promised*, Jaqe told herself. *She gave me a promise.* When she heard Janet's footsteps behind her, she jumped in and slammed the door. Laurie said, "The bus station. Let's go." The driver made a cocking motion with her fingers and the car rolled away.

When they got to the bus station/hardware store, Jaqe suggested that Laurie run into the coffee shop for tickets and a schedule while she paid the driver. Thrilled to be doing something, Laurie half sprinted across the road. The driver ran her fingers through her hair as she examined herself in the rearview mirror. "That's five dollars," she said. Jaqe took five dollars and fifty cents from her purse and dropped it in the woman's hand, careful not to touch the skin. "Thanks," the woman said.

Jaqe opened the door, then turned back. "Can I ask you something?" she said.

The woman shrugged. "Sure. Go ahead."

"Can I trust her?"

"Trust her?"

"You know who I'm talking about. Does she mean what she says?"

The driver grinned. "Kid, Mother always means exactly what she says."

Jaqe didn't know if this reassured her or not, but she couldn't think of anything else to say, so she got out of the car. She saw Laurie coming back across the street and was about to meet her when she turned once more. The driver was looking up at her, still grinning. Jaqe said, "Tell her thank you for me, okay?"

The driver nodded. "Sure thing." She whistled softly as she put the car in gear and drove away.

"Good news," Laurie said as she strode up to Jaqe. "There's a bus in an hour. We can have something to eat in the coffee shop."

Jaqe stared at her. Laurie stood there like her old self, weight on one foot, hands in pockets. *Doesn't she care?* Jaqe thought. *What the hell was all the screaming about?* She said, "I don't want to wait. That's just where your folks will look if they come after us."

Laurie's eyes fixed on the ground. "I guess so," she said. She straightened up. "Let's take a walk."

They headed down Church Street to the fountain, a Victorian display of stone flowers and winged nymphs. A few children splashed in the water at the bottom of the statue while their mothers sat on benches ringing the fountain. Laurie said, "Why can't grown-ups do that? What do you think people would say if you and I ran in the water, shrieking and flapping our hands?"

"Laurie—" Jaqe said. She stared at the edge of the sidewalk, squinting against the splash of sun coming off the water.

Laurie kept walking, even speeding up as if she wanted to get away. Finally she stopped, shook her head, and turned and came back. She said, "Let's talk about it later, okay?"

"No," Jaqe said. "It's not okay at all. I don't understand how you can, I don't know, act like we're on a picnic or something."

"I'm not acting like we're on a picnic. I just . . . I just can't talk here.

"What's wrong with here?"

"It's where I grew up. Why can't we wait till we get home?"

"That's hours, Laurie. I can't sit on the bus, looking over the scenery and talking about the weather. Your father almost raped me." She thought of the cut on her leg, the pain, how it had swollen and turned green, and she thought of the candle sputtering out in the meadow.

"Shh," Laurie said, and actually put up her hands with the fingers spread. When she saw what she was doing, she dropped her hands. "I'm sorry," she said.

Jaqe said, "I'm not going to shut up. I don't care if everybody here has known you since you were a baby jumping up and down in that fountain. We can't just forget about this."

"I'm not planning to forget about it. I promise we'll talk about it later."

"It'll just get harder. It's not just the rape. I trusted them. I trusted them like my own parents. I trusted you."

Laurie said, "What's that supposed to mean?"

"How could you let him—" Jaqe stopped, dizzy and out of breath. She had a strange sensation that Laurie was rushing away from her. When Laurie touched her shoulder, Jaqe made a frightened noise.

Laurie said, "It's all right, honey."

Jaqe shook her head. "Let me alone."

"You don't look good. You've got to get out of the sun." Laurie took Jaqe's bag and led her to a bench under a tree a few yards from the fountain. Some kids were sitting there, eating ice cream from a small family grocery across the street. Laurie told them, "My friend's sick. Can we sit down?" One of the kids grimaced and the other rolled her eyes, but they moved. "We must be getting old," Laurie said to Jaqe. "They think we're grown-ups."

Jaqe bent forward, her eyes focused on a small ring of pebbles lying in the grass. They looked very far away, like a prehistoric ruin seen from up in the sky. She took a deep breath, then another. The dizziness was passing.

"Are you okay?" Laurie asked.

Jaqe sat up. "You've got to stop pretending," she said.

"I don't know what you mean."

"You knew, Laurie. That's why you wanted me to come shopping with you."

"I just wanted your company."

"Don't lie to me. You were scared. You knew what he'd do if you left me alone with him." Laurie didn't answer. "God," Jaqe said. "Why didn't you tell me?"

"What was I supposed do, tell you you better come along or my dad might attack you? How could I say something like that?"

"So you did know."

"I didn't know," Laurie whispered.

"You just said—"

"I was scared."

"Why were you scared? What were you scared of?"

"I'm sorry, honey. Really I am. I'm so sorry."

Jaqe couldn't look at her. She said, "How did you know?"

"I didn't. Not really. That's why I didn't say anything. I was just scared—"

"Why were you scared?" Laurie didn't answer. "Did he tell you?" Jaqe asked.

"Tell me?"

"Did he say, 'Laurie, you go off with your mother, I want to have some fun with Jaqe'?"

"No! Jesus, Jaqe, do you think I'd let him say something like that?"

"He told me you knew. That you approved."

"Goddamn him," Laurie said. "I'll kill him. I'll kill him."

"He said the two of you had an agreement. 'Share and share alike' he called it."

"That's insane. You didn't believe him, did you?"

"He said I was the first one to complain."

"That fucking bastard," Laurie said. She jumped up as if she'd run back to the housing development.

"Sit down," Jaqe said. Laurie was marching back and forth. "Please sit down, honey. I need you to talk to me." Not looking at Jaqe, Laurie came back to the bench. Jaqe said, "Why would he say such a thing?"

"Because he's crazy. Because he deserves to lie in a pit with women throwing rocks at him."

"He didn't get the idea from something, maybe something you said?"

"No!"

"Then how could you know what he was going to do?"

"I don't know. How many times do I have to tell you?"

"But you were scared. That's not normal, Laurie. People don't worry about their fathers raping their girlfriends as soon as they leave the house." Laurie said nothing. "Please," Jaqe said. "Please, honey. I've got to know."

"You promise you won't leave me?"

Jaqe hugged her. She said, "I'll never leave you."

"And you won't hate me?"

"I promise I'll never hate you." Silently she added, *And I always mean what I say.*

Jaqe let go of Laurie, except for Laurie's hand, which she held in both of hers. Laurie lifted her head and stared across the street, as if she wanted to read the specials listed in the grocery window. She said, "He did it before."

"What? What do you mean?"

"He attacked—he raped one of my friends."

"Oh my God," Jaqe said. "When?"

"Three years ago. I was with a girl named Margaret. She was one of the ones who started the LSU. There was me and Margaret and Sharon and Judy." She stopped for a moment, and Jaqe wondered if she was going to have to keep pushing her. But then Laurie said, "Margaret was really pretty." She smiled briefly and added, "Not as pretty as you, but you know what I mean. Petite. Cute. The kind of woman no one would ever take for a dyke. Sometimes on marches, like Gay Pride, reporters would come up to her and say, 'Are you a lesbian?' Like they wanted to add, 'How could someone as pretty as you be a lesbian?' I used to get so pissed off." She sighed. "Anyway, Margaret and my father got along really great."

"Like me."

Laurie laughed, a sound like a bark. "Yeah. We'd go home on weekends, or my folks would come to the city and take us to dinner. And they'd bring Margaret little presents sometimes. I remember once on Valentine's Day, they sent this silly ornate card, a big velvet heart, with a special message for a daughter-in-law. And wherever it said son, they'd crossed it out and written daughter."

"Sounds sick."

"Yeah, well, everyone at the DCC thought it was really great. They were all having trouble with their parents, and my folks just seemed different. Special."

Jaqe nodded. She remembered everyone telling her stories of how special Laurie's parents were. Everyone including Laurie.

"Anyway," Laurie said, "we came home one weekend. To get away from the dorm. I was living in the dorm then." She stopped, took a deep breath. "My mother wanted to show me something at the temple. Some damn project she was working on in the sisterhood. We took Ellen—no, that's not right—Ellen had gone to a friend's house."

"And Margaret stayed home with your father?" Jaqe could see the wetness glistening in Laurie's eyes.

Laurie said, "He offered to cut her hair."

Jaqe said nothing. Nauseated, she became scared the dizziness would come back. She held on tight to Laurie's hand.

Laurie said, "I came home and he was watching television. Can you believe it? The fucking sonofabitch was watching some goddamn hockey game. Can you believe it?"

"Where was Margaret?" Jaqe said.

"In the bedroom. My room. She was all wrapped up in a couple of blankets. I mean, she'd put her clothes back on, and then she'd put the blankets all around her. She wouldn't talk to me, Jaqe. It took me, I don't know, five minutes or something, to get her to tell me what had happened."

"What did you do?"

"I ran and screamed at him. I think I even threatened to kill him. Shit. I wish I had."

"And he denied it."

"Yeah. Said he had no idea what I was talking about."

Just like today, Jaqe thought. She said, "And your mother?"

"Backed him up. Said Margaret must be crazy. Fucking bitch."

Just like today, Jaqe thought. And, *Laurie, how could you let him do it again? To me?* She said, "You could have called the police."

"You know how hard that is with lesbians."

"If there was . . . if there was penetration, you could have proved it."

"C'mon, Jaqe. They would have just said she went out and screwed some local guy and then accused my father to cover it up."

"You could have tried." And they could try now, she knew. Skip the bus, walk into the Thorny Woods police station. But it would just be her word against Bill's. This time—thank the Goddess—there hadn't been any penetration. "What did you do?" she said.

"Margaret went back to school. She had a car and she wanted to be alone. So I took the bus. When I got back to the dorm I went to find her. She didn't want to see me. She didn't want to speak to me. She didn't blame me, she said, but she just couldn't be with me." She looked at Jaqe. "You won't leave me, will you?"

Jaqe shook her head. "I told you," she said, "I'll never leave you." Laurie looked like she would start crying again, but instead she just sat there, bent over with her hands clasped. Jaqe flinched at the harshness of her own voice as she said, "What about the others?"

"There weren't any others," Laurie said. "Margaret was the only one. I swear it."

"That's not what I mean. I mean the others at school. What did they say?"

"Oh," Laurie said. "Yeah." She sighed. "They didn't know. Margaret made me promise not to tell anyone. Everybody figured she just dropped out of school."

"Did you want to tell them?"

"Of course . . . No, that's a lie. I'm sorry, Jaqe. I was so ashamed."

"So you let everyone think Bill and Janet were the great lesbian parents."

"I didn't—it just—they kept putting on their act. And everyone loved it. Everyone kept saying how great my parents were."

"Did you believe it?"

"I guess sometimes. It just seemed so much easier sometimes. To believe what everyone else believed. And . . . and it never happened again."

"Until now."

Laurie said, "I wanted to tell you. Please believe me, Jaqe. Please."

Jaqe remembered all the stories. Bill defending Laurie, Janet going to a dyke bar. But she also remembered the time Laurie had screamed at her to throw away the graduation-day photo of Bill with his arm around Jaqe's shoulder. And the way Laurie had fought against visiting her parents. She said, "I believe you." She put her arms around Laurie and hugged her. For a long time they held each other, twisting sideways on the bench. And then Jaqe pushed her away. She said, "We better get back to the bus."

Neither of them said very much on the way back to the city. For a while, Laurie held Jaqe's hand, but she let it go when Jaqe just looked out the window. There wasn't much to see, just concrete and low hills with trees, and every now and then a gas station or a small shopping center when the bus left the highway to make a stop on the edge of some small town. As the hours passed Jaqe found it harder to breathe, harder to swallow. She couldn't seem to get comfortable, constantly shifting in her seat, until Laurie asked if she wanted to lie down. "Don't be stupid," she said, and when Laurie offered her lap or her shoulder for Jaqe's head, Jaqe told her to leave her alone.

Jaqe tried to make herself relax. She tried deep breathing but gave it up when she noticed the little girl in the next seat staring at her and then whispering something to her mother. She tried reading—Mark had given her a book of animal stories—but the bus made her nauseous, so she shoved the book back in her bag. She tried going to the chemical toilet next to the backseat; the smell drove her away. Stuck in her seat again, she tried not to look at Laurie and her sickly expression, like some homeless beast hoping someone will take her in off the street. Jaqe told herself that wasn't fair, Laurie just wanted to take care of her, to make it up to her.

She shifted in her seat to look at the passengers around her. They struck her as distasteful, even frightening. A few seats back, a man slept on the seat, his arms and legs tucked into his body as he lay on a pile of crumpled newspapers. Jaqe imagined him dead, dead for weeks on that seat and no one noticing. When he started to snore, she found herself wanting to shove his paper in his mouth. Across the aisle, the little girl was staring at her again, as if planning some nasty trick the moment Jaqe would pass near her. Jaqe imagined the girl sitting in front of her house and someone coming up in a car to grab the child and throw her into the backseat. Jaqe shook her head, pushing away the image. When she looked again, the girl held some cloth doll and was twisting its arms around its body. The girl's mother had the kind of perm that looked like every hair had gone into place according to a master blueprint stuck to the mirror of the beauty parlor. Jaqe wondered if Bill had constructed it; she imagined his pudgy fingers touching the woman's face, stroking her neck.

Jaqe shivered. She thought of the girl in the woods, the way the child had hugged her when they'd buried the bones, and the way she'd run away when Jaqe tried to protect her. Jaqe didn't know if she could have done something. Mother Night said the girl was okay. The image of the candles came to her, the meadow filled with fire. And the candle on the lawn, burning bright.

Jaqe heard a noise outside. She turned to the window and saw three women on motorcycles passing the bus. The setting sun lit up their red hair, their black leather. They went by too fast for Jaqe to read the gold letters stitched across the back of their jackets. *Leave me alone,* she thought. *Please leave me alone.*

The driver took the bus off the highway and into the parking lot of a convenience store where he announced, "Ten minutes, folks, we've got about ten minutes," and hurried off the bus.

Laurie stood up. "Are you getting off?" she asked Jaqe. Jaqe didn't answer. Laurie said, "Can I get you something?" When Jaqe said nothing, Laurie told her, "I'm going to go get a soda." She hesitated, then bent down to kiss Jaqe, whose mouth seemed to move away all by itself. Jaqe whispered, "I'm sorry, I didn't mean that," but Laurie was already striding down the aisle, moving in a jerky parody of her normal walk.

I've got to do something, Jaqe thought. She got up and left the bus. In the parking lot the humid air stank of spilled gasoline. It clung to her so that when she tried to wipe the sweat from her forehead it felt like she was smearing grease into her skin. Maybe she should have gone to the police. Maybe she should have lugged Laurie to the police station and forced her to tell her story. Maybe she should have sent Laurie ahead and gone to the police alone. But she didn't want to get rid of Laurie. She just wanted. . . .

Jaqe walked into the store, where the smell changed to pizza and hot dogs from a small keep-hot-all-day display next to the cash register. The bus driver stood there, biting on a pizza slice and dripping tomato sauce onto his gray uniform. His face gleamed with excitement, his teeth looked long and sharp, as if they only chewed the soft food as a disguise, as if they could bite through anything. Jaqe felt strange looking at him, as if someone had twisted things around inside her head. When she turned away, the fluorescent light in the aisles made everything look overly bright and hard, like a lurid painting of the consumer society. Jaqe walked up and down, looking for Laurie. When she didn't find her, she became scared, though she couldn't think of why; she knew Laurie must have gone outside or something. But the fear still rose in her, and the fact that she couldn't attach it to anything only made it worse.

She knew she'd better get outside, but when she turned around the woman and the little girl from the bus were standing in the aisle. The girl reached up for a bag of candy, and her mother slapped her hand away. The mother said, "You keep whining and you'll get something all right," and she jerked her hand up above the girl's face. Jaqe moved to the next aisle. The driver stood there, leafing through a gun magazine and eating a hot dog.

In the last aisle a door opened in the wall and Laurie came out, rubbing her hands on her shorts. Jaqe ran and threw her arms around her, as if she had to hold her down or Laurie would float up to the ceiling. "Hi," Laurie said, and looked around nervously as she hugged Jaqe.

"Get me out of here," Jaqe said. In the parking lot she breathed in the gasoline air.

"Are you all right?" Laurie asked. When Jaqe said nothing, Laurie held her hand and led her back to the bus.

At the door to the bus, Jaqe stood and watched Laurie ascend the steps. The fear had settled down in her, like a dark pool hidden somewhere in her body. She hurried inside when she saw the driver coming up behind her.

Jaqe asked Laurie for the window seat again, and when they rolled onto the highway she stared outside, looking for motorcycles. Most of the way to the city Laurie read her book while Jaqe sat turned away from her. Sometimes Laurie put the book down and looked to her lover as if she wanted to kneel down in the narrow space between the seats and beg Jaqe for forgiveness. Twice she tried putting an arm around Jaqe. Jaqe only looked out the window.

Later, while digging in her bag for a half roll of peppermint Life Savers, Jaqe came across the three I Ching coins she had found in the street. Medallions, Mark's friend had called them. She held them up to examine them in the weak reading light. She'd never noticed the markings on the backs of the turtles. They looked like the continents, as if the turtle wore the Earth itself as a shell. She turned the coins over to look at the pairs of toads, the way they stared so intently at each other. She thought of the toad dance, the first time she'd seen

Laurie, the way they'd danced together. She thought of Mother Night.

Jaqe found a notebook in her bag and set it on her lap. With both hands she made a shell around the coins to bounce them around each other. She worried for a moment that Laurie might get angry, but then she made up her mind not to think about it. When she dropped them on the book all three came up toads. Nine. Yang. She opened the book and drew a line with an X in the middle. Five more times Jaqe tossed the coins, and five times they came out the same. Jaqe stopped writing after the third line. She'd planned to look it up when she got home, but there was no need. Six yang lines meant action. And because they were nines they would change into yin. Peace. Action brings peace. What? she wondered. What the hell should she do? She looked out the window. No motorcycles.

At the bus station Laurie sat while the other passengers hurried off. Jaqe looked at her. Laurie was bent forward with her head down and her elbows on her knees. "Can we get off?" Jaqe asked. "I'd like to go home."

"Sorry," Laurie said, and jumped up, almost banging her head against the rack.

The station blared at Jaqe with all the noise of loudspeakers, crowds, video games, and fast-food stalls. At the same time a buzz sounded in Jaqe's ears, getting louder and higher pitched as she moved toward the exit. Outside, Jaqe looked around for Dr. Root, or the woman in the purple wig who had tried to sell her a ticket, but they were both gone. Maybe the cops had chased them away. She stepped into the street and the buzzing jumped another level. It drowned out the cars, the buses, the sirens, the people shouting at each other up and down the block. Laurie asked, "Should we take a cab?" but Jaqe wasn't listening. She stared across the street at a teenage boy and girl who sat together in front of a closed jewelry store, their backs against the metal grate, their knees drawn up tight as if they hoped they could make themselves small so the police wouldn't notice them. A couple of nylon backpacks lay between them. The boy held tight to a rolled-up piece of foam about an inch thick. Scattered crumbs lay about their feet, like the end of a trail from a home where they could never return.

The girl's shoulders looked squeezed together, her whole body compressed as she bent forward to get something from her backpack.

A half-empty bag of junk food, Jaqe saw. The way they bent forward, with the car lights flickering over their faces, they looked to Jaqe like birds, like children of the sky whom some enchantment had imprisoned in the bodies of human beings.

Something tugged at Jaqe's arm; she jerked it away. Beside her, Laurie sighed. "Come on," she said. "Let's go." When Jaqe didn't answer or move, Laurie said, "What do you want, anyway?"

Jaqe turned her head now. "Justice," she said. "I want justice."

Eight

Greenthumb and Redshoes

Jaqe met Mother Night in a cemetery. Mark had suggested it to her. "If you need to find a violinist," he pointed out, "you go to a concert hall. If you're looking for a professor you try the universities."

She'd gone to Mark one evening after the store had closed, after

Laurie had gone home expecting Jaqe would be there waiting for her. Mark was sitting by the counter, alone, with a review magazine and a red pen to mark the mistakes he always discovered in the reviews. "I need to find someone," Jaqe said, and then, after a deep breath, she told him about Mother Night.

For a while Mark sat back in his desk chair, rubbing his cheek with a fingertip, as if nothing was more important than checking his beard stubble. Jaqe thought for sure he would tell her she needed serious counseling, or else detoxing in a spiritual recovery program. But all he said finally was, "Why do you want her? It sounds to me like you'd want to keep away from her."

"I can't tell you that," Jaqe said. "I just need her help for something."

"You want to put out a contract on someone?"

"No!"

"Just asking," Mark said mildly. He added, "Is Laurie okay? She hasn't looked right lately."

"Laurie's fine."

"She moves like someone's jerking her muscles."

"I said she's okay!"

Mark nodded. "Yeah, she says that too. So I guess if you both say it, it must be true."

"Look," Jaqe said. "I'm doing this for Laurie as much as for me. No, that's not true. I'm doing it for myself. I just have to pray it will help her. Or at least not hurt her."

Mark shrugged. "Not much you can do except hope. Praying is good. Praying is always good. So. You want to find this Mother Night. Too bad you can't kill a dragon."

"What?"

"Recommended by all the authorities. You kill a dragon, taste the blood, and you understand the language of the birds. And then the birds tell you where to find Mother Night."

"Why would the birds know?"

Mark laughed. "Good point. The authorities never seem to consider that question. Of course, dragons were really fluid earth energy, and killing them meant pinning the energy down in one place so people could plant crops and build cities. What would a modern dragon be? Maybe a nuclear power plant." He stopped as Jaqe headed for the door. "Hey," he said, "come back."

"I'm serious about this," Jaqe said. "It may sound weird to you, or dumb, but I don't care."

"I know," Mark told her. "I'm sorry. Please sit down again. I'll make some tea." He went into his storeroom office at the back of the shop. A couple of minutes later he returned with a tray containing two brown mugs and a white book. There were no words on the cover, only a drawing of a toad sitting on the back of a turtle. "What you need," Mark said, "is to go to the Land of the Dead."

Two nights later, Jaqe stood in a small cemetery by a small country road. "You don't want one of those big city places," Mark had told her. "For one thing, they've got cops around in case of vandals or weirdos. For another, they've crowded things up so much Mother Night would never notice you." He added, "Or hear you. The dead make a lot of noise. I found this out once when I spent a few nights in a cemetery. Some of them get lost and upset, and some like to sing—for some reason, the dead all sing off-key, I don't know why—and some just like to complain." So he had loaned her his car and given her directions to a "nice rustic little place" where most of the graves went back two centuries and the residents had given up making trouble.

The cemetery sat behind the only church in a tiny village near the state border. The church itself didn't look very old, with its single white steeple and plain cross. The cemetery, however, must have gone back to colonial times, for many of the gravestones had sunk so far into the ground it was impossible to read who was buried there. The cemetery was smaller than the church, and much smaller than the lawn in front or the parking lot alongside. As far as Jaqe could tell, anyone who died in the neighborhood these days took up residence somewhere else, probably someplace more modern, with room for elaborate stone tributes.

At first Jaqe parked in the church lot, but then she thought how a cop might spot the car and come looking for her. So she drove back to the village green and left the car in front of an antique shop, under the protection of an overhanging oak. When she walked back she noticed an odd rock across the road from the church at the edge of a wood. A huge boulder about five feet high and six or seven feet long, it perched on five small rocks, like footstools. From a certain angle Jaqe could see a profiled face in the boulder, a round indentation for an eye, a jutting block for a nose and a crack in the rock for a prim mouth. The stone swept back from the "forehead" so that the whole thing looked like the elongated head of a snake, or maybe a turtle. When Jaqe looked underneath, among the footstools, she noticed something white, and when she bent down she saw they were bones, small and polished, like the remains of a doll. Somewhere behind her, Jaqe heard a noise and she hurried across the road and behind the church.

For over two hours Jaqe sat at the edge of the graveyard, with her back to one of the larger stones, a memorial to a certain Jack Hunt, who had died more than a hundred years ago. It was chilly in the cemetery, and Jaqe had to pull her knees up against her chest to keep from shivering. This is nuts, she thought. Mark and his stupid ideas. The next thing, she thought, he would tell her to sacrifice a chicken. She laughed. Maybe she should cut her finger and scatter some blood over the tombstones.

Jaqe had been sitting there for two hours and seventeen minutes—she had just checked her watch—when she heard footsteps. Like some small dog she scurried behind the tombstone, trying to compress her body and still look out at the graveyard. An old man came from the parking lot into the cemetery. Over his shoulder he carried a bag, which he set down with a thump. Next to it he placed a plastic bag, like the kind used in supermarkets. He sat for a moment, head bowed, looking very tired. With a sigh, he emptied the bag. A bunch of clothes fell out, along with some dirt, a few rocks, and some string. Working efficiently, the man molded the dirt into the rough form of a body. He placed the stones for eyes and a nose, and used the string to form a mouth. He looked critically at this sculpture a moment, then made a few small changes, lengthening a dirt leg, rolling a stone a little higher up the head. He then took the clothes and laid them out along the body. When he finished he reached into the shopping bag for what looked like a bottle of beer. With the experienced skill of a waiter, he took an old-fashioned bottle opener (a church key, Jaqe realized) from his pocket and flipped off the cap. Shaking the bottle, he poured the liquid all over the clothes and the effigy.

For several seconds, nothing happened, while the man tapped his foot and Jaqe held her breath. Then the clothes began to flutter, as if a wind had risen. At that moment, a speck of dust flew into Jaqe's eyes. She squeezed them shut, and when she opened them again the clothes were occupied. A young man with long matted hair was sitting up, rubbing his eyes, stretching. He grinned up at the old man, who looked down at him with disgust. The young man said, "I guess I did it again, huh?"

The other gave him a hand and pulled him to his feet. "One of these days," he said, "I'm just not going to bother."

"Yeah, sure," the young man said, and laughed.

The older man made a face. "You stink."

"Well, what do you expect?" said the other, and the two of them walked off toward the parking lot. Only after they'd gone did Jaqe notice that the sculptured pile of dirt had vanished.

She was about to get up when she heard someone else coming. A woman came around the church, young, about Jaqe's age, with straight blond hair. She wore a long loose dress that fluttered softly against her body. An animal loped alongside her—a dog, Jaqe thought, but then she saw it was a fox. The woman said, "Is this the place?"

"Yes," the fox said. "Now you must do what you promised." It spoke in a high sharp voice, with some kind of accent that Jaqe found hard to follow.

"I can't do that," the woman said. "You've done so much for me."

"And you must do this for me," the fox insisted. The woman began to cry. "Have I ever asked you for anything?" The woman shook her head. "And have I ever told you to do anything that turned out badly?" Again she shook her head. "Then do what I tell you."

The woman reached into her handbag and took out a gun. Before Jaqe could do anything, the woman shot the fox. Jaqe gasped, but the woman didn't seem to hear her. When the fox had stopped twitching, the woman, weeping now, bent down and took out a small axe from her bag. In five quick chops she cut off the fox's head and then its feet. Blood spattered her face and her lovely dress. Sickened, Jaqe looked away. A cry of surprise made her turn back again. The mutilated corpse of the fox had vanished. In its place, a young man sat kneeling on the ground. He started to get up, fell on all fours again, then finally made it to his feet. The woman stood before him, staring at his handsome face, his silk T-shirt, his black linen trousers. In a soft tenor voice, with only a trace of the fox's accent, he said, "The man who tried to kill you and fell over the cliff was my older brother. He changed me when a fortune-teller told him I would take over the family business." He held out his hands and the woman took them. Together they walked out from the graveyard.

Almost the moment the two vanished around the corner of the church, Jaqe heard footsteps from the other side. This time a middle-aged woman came into view. She was crying as she carried the body of a girl about ten years old. She laid the body down on the grass, in the same place where the man had shaped the dirt and the woman had shot the fox. This woman, too, carried a bag, a child's knapsack shaped like a teddy bear. The woman reached inside and took out a quart-sized metal can. When she opened it Jaqe smelled gasoline. The woman poured the whole bottle over the dead child.

Instead of lighting a match, however, she sat back on the grass and spoke to the corpse. "Who are you?" she said.

The mouth didn't move, but a whisper came from the body. "I am the child of Mother Night."

"Where do you come from?"

"I come from the dark in the back of the sky."

"And where are you going?"

"Away from there and back to here. Far away and forever home."

In one movement, the woman lit a match and threw it on the dead child. "No!" Jaqe screamed, but she was too late. The gasoline flared up, a flash of light that blinded Jaqe as she jumped to her feet. When Jaqe could see again, the little girl was standing next to the woman, who bent down and hugged her. The smell of gasoline had vanished, replaced by a faint sweetness, like some delicate perfume made for a child's birthday. The girl picked up the knapsack and the two started to walk away.

"Hey!" Jaqe called to them. "Just a moment. I want to talk to you." They stopped to turn and look at her for a moment, but then kept on walking. A hand on Jaqe's shoulder stopped her from following them. She turned, and there stood three of Mother Night's helpers. They all wore their leather outfits. Heavy makeup masked their faces: violet eyeshadow and dark blue mascara, red lipstick and slashes of red across the cheekbones like scars. The moonlight shone in their red hair. Behind them, by the corner of the churchyard, stood their motorcycles. The one who'd grabbed Jaqe's shoulder said, "Mother wants to see you."

"I'm right here," Jaqe said.

The woman grinned. "Yeah, well, Mother's across the road. Over by the turtle." The big stone, Jaqe thought. So it was a turtle and not a snake. The three women turned and walked toward their motorcycles. Her hands on the handlebars, one of them turned to look at Jaqe. "Hey, kid," she said.

"Don't call me that," Jaqe said. "I'm as old as you are." The three laughed, and Jaqe blushed.

"Fine," the woman said. "All I want to know is, are we going to have some fun?"

"I didn't come here for you to have fun," Jaqe said. Before they could say anything else she turned and headed out of the cemetery. As she rounded the church corner she heard the roar of motorcycles.

Mother Night was standing with her back to Jaqe, with one hand on the stone, and her head tilted up, as if to talk to the petrified face. Jaqe thought how it always surprised her to see how short Mother Night was. Mother, as the redhead had called her, wore a striped tunic, belted at the waist with a braided rope belt. The tunic flared out over a long skirt whose flowing rivers of color sparkled in the dim light. On her head she wore a hard skullcap, set with feathers, clustered jewels, and strips of lace. When she turned around, she was wearing a necklace of charms, ribbons, and, in between, a series of small polished bones. Jaqe glanced under the rock. The bones that had lain there had vanished. Mother Night smiled at her. "Hello, Jaqe," she said.

"Hello," Jaqe said. "Thank you for coming." Mother Night nodded. Jaqe said, "That was quite a show you put on." Mother Night smiled, a delighted grin, like a child. Jaqe said, "Did you set it all up just for me?"

"You went to such trouble to find me, it seemed only fair to give you something a little special. But it wasn't *just* for you, you know. The work needed to get done."

"I didn't know you did that kind of work."

Mother Night fluttered a hand. "Oh, I do many things." For a while they just stood there, Mother Night lounging against the boulder, Jaqe with her shoulders up and her fists clenched. With a quick smile, Mother Night said, "What do you want, Jaqe?"

Again silence, this time for nearly half a minute. Just as Mother Night turned away again, Jaqe said, "I want justice."

Mother Night turned to stand directly before Jaqe. A gust of wind blew a strip of lace from her hat across her eyes. She didn't move it. She said, "Are you sure?"

"Someone did something to me. And to Laurie. I want him punished."

Mother Night nodded. "I understand," she said. A moment later she added, "Do you?"

"I don't know. But I don't think it really matters. I know I want justice."

Softly, Mother Night clapped her hands. "Fine," she said. "We will see what we can do."

In the road, just behind Jaqe and to the side, the five women appeared, all of them this time, and without their motorcycles. "Well, what do you know," one of the women said. "It looks like we're going to have some fun after all."

Bill Cohen carefully rolled up the sleeves of his blue shirt to just above the elbow. He looked at himself in the bedroom mirror, turning first to the left and then to the right. He pouted a moment, then pulled his belt a notch tighter over his jeans. In the bed, Janet groaned and stretched out her arms. Something about the gesture enraged Bill, but he shrugged the feeling away and went back to the mirror. Leaning closer, he rubbed his prickly beard shadow. Bill always shaved in the evening; smooth for Janet, rough for the women in the beauty parlor. When he glanced back at the bed, Janet was sitting up, with Bill's two pillows behind her own. Like a fucking queen, he thought.

The word reminded him that he had to get rid of Malcom, the British faggot who'd been working for him in the Main Street branch. Gays were one thing, Bill thought; you couldn't escape it in this business, but Malcom had started camping it up just too damn much. Bill himself didn't care, but the customers were starting to make faces. Maybe that sort of thing went okay in the city, but not in a place like Thorny Woods.

Janet said, "I'll be at the club this afternoon. I'm meeting the girls to talk about our casino trip."

"Do whatever you like," Bill said. He checked his pockets for his wallet and keycase.

"Honey," Janet said. His back to her, Bill made a face. "We've got to talk," his wife told him. "About Laurie."

"What's to talk about?"

"Maybe we should call her. Go see her in the city or something."

"What for, so she and that nutty girlfriend of hers can make up more lies about me?"

"I don't care about that."

"Thanks a lot. Well, I do care."

"I'm sorry," Janet said. "I didn't mean that the way it sounded. I just meant, can't we all forget about it?"

"Fine with me. You know I don't hold grudges."

"Well, maybe we should call them."

"She'll call us when she wants to. Probably when she needs money." For some reason, an odd memory came into his mind—a time when Laurie was a kid and wanted to go fishing of all things, so Bill had gotten them a couple of cheap poles and they'd spent a couple of hours sitting in a boat on Silver Lake. She was some kid, Laurie. For a moment, he really wished she'd just get over her nuttiness.

Janet said, "But what if she doesn't?"

"Look," Bill said. "I've got no time now. I'm opening on Park Street today. Mrs. Nelson has a nine o'clock."

Janet giggled. "Isn't she the one you hate?"

Bill laughed. "I never hate my clients. She may be ugly as sin, but she pays well."

As Bill left the bedroom Janet called after him, "Will you think about calling Laurie?"

"You bet," Bill said, without looking back. "Promise."

In the driveway, he noticed something odd across the street in front of the Holloway house. A motorcycle stood there, a long black thing, glistening, as if someone had sprayed it with water. In front of it, leaning against the gas tank, stood some kid in a red leather jacket. Bill thought it was a boy at first until he noticed the outline of breasts behind the crossed arms. He found it a little hard to see her face—the sun shone directly in his eyes—but he thought she looked kind of pretty, despite the punky red hair. He grinned as he opened his car door. Maybe Jim Holloway had decided to try out some rough trade. He glanced back once more. He wouldn't mind trying some himself. Just as Bill turned on the car engine the woman kick-started her motorcycle, a roar that made Bill jump in surprise. By the time he'd pulled out of the driveway, the motorcycle had vanished around the corner.

At House of Hair, Helen, the assistant, was waiting outside the door when Bill pulled up. He parked the car, then gave her a cheery good morning as he unlocked the door. Helen was okay, Bill thought. Worked hard, didn't just hang around too much. He reminded himself to make sure Meg or Gail was teaching her. While Helen made coffee and arranged things in the shop, Bill looked over the books for the different branches. Over the next fifteen minutes the rest of the staff came in, gossiping, complaining, all the time-wasters he had to tolerate for the sake of morale.

They were all sitting around the counter, laughing at someone's inane joke, when suddenly the noise died down. Bill turned around to see everyone looking at a tall redhaired woman standing in the entrance. She stood over six feet, with wide shoulders and gentle curves flowing down her body. She was certainly the type to draw attention, but Bill stared at her with extra fascination, for she looked so much like the biker she might have been the girl's older sister—her sophisticated older sister, for this one wore a dark red linen suit and alligator shoes—or was it snake? They were hardly the kind of clothes you saw very often in Thorny Woods, at least not in House of Hair. Along with a small shoulder bag to match the shoes, she carried a gleaming black briefcase, eelskin probably, with a catch that looked to be solid gold. The catch was shaped in some design or other, concentric circles with lines running through them.

She smiled at Helen, whose mouth hung open slightly, as if she'd never seen anything quite like her. In a soft deep voice, the woman said, "I'd like my hair done. Washed, cut, and styled." Her hair was short, but not too short that Bill couldn't think of various possibilities. At the moment, it was partly pushed back and partly straight up in a style that must have required sculpting foam and hair spray.

"Do you have an appointment?" Helen asked.

The woman smiled, "No, I'm sorry."

Helen said, "Well, let me see who's free." She ran her finger down the schedule.

"Excuse me," the woman said. She turned slightly and pointed a long finger at Bill. "I want him."

"I'm sorry," Helen said. "Mr. Cohen is booked this morning."

"That's all right," Bill said quickly. "I can squeeze her in after Mrs. Nelson."

Helen said, "But you've got Mrs. Steiner then."

"I said it's all right." He turned to the woman. "I hope you don't mind waiting a little."

The woman smiled again. "Not at all," she said. "I brought some work to do. Why don't you see your two appointments first? I wouldn't want you distracted."

Confused somehow, Bill said, "Well, if you're sure you wouldn't mind."

Just as the woman sat down in one of the black tubular chairs Bill had recently installed, the first clients came in. Meg and Mark took them, helping them into smocks, sitting them down and easing their hair into the wash basins. Mrs. Nelson was late, as usual. Bill was wondering if he could take the redhead when someone who looked like yet another of her sisters came into the shop. This one was short, with large hips and a round face. She was dressed in a wholly different style, but one which stood out in Thorny Woods as much as the other woman's red suit and outrageous leathers: She wore a dress that looked like something from an old movie about the South Pacific—low cut, pale yellow, with huge flowers in every color from fuchsia to turquoise. Her red hair hung in loose curls in no particular style.

"I'd like a cut," she said. "And I want the boss to do it."

"That's not possible," Helen said.

Bill grimaced at Helen's rudeness. He moved forward. "Good morning," he said, "I'm Bill Cohen," and for some reason he bowed slightly.

The woman in the flowered dress said, "Do that again."

Confused, Bill bent over. He heard giggles as he straightened up. "I'm rather busy," he said, "but if you don't mind waiting . . ."

"That's fine," the woman said.

"It may be up to an hour."

"No problem." She sat down next to the other and picked up a hairdo magazine.

Bill looked around the shop. Didn't anyone else notice the resemblance?

Flower Dress held out her hand to the other. "I'm Amy," she said.

"My name is Lillian," Red Suit said. When they smiled the link became even stronger, almost like twins despite their different shapes.

Wait a minute, Bill thought, wait a minute. Dress—Amy—was wearing a pendant on a gold chain, and Bill was pretty damn sure it was the same design as the catch on the other one's briefcase. He tried to see, but the Suit—Lillian—had set the briefcase on the floor with the catch hidden against the leg of the chair. He was wondering if he should go ask to see it, when Mrs. Nelson came in.

Taking her jacket, it was all Bill could do to keep the disgust out of his face. Besides her natural ugliness, the woman had no taste, none at all. That flouncy dress she wore—he glanced back at the two redheads. What a difference, he thought. It almost embarrassed him for them to see Mrs. Nelson in his shop. While Helen sat Mrs. Nelson down and began washing her hair, Bill wished he could give her to Meg, or even just shove her out the door, and go to work on Lillian. But Mrs. Nelson came regularly, and often for expensive work, and who knew if Lillian would even come back at all. He glanced at Lillian again, quickly, so people wouldn't notice. He decided he would wash her hair himself, give her a special head and neck massage.

Bill was just seating Mrs. Nelson in the chair by the window when yet another stranger came in. She looked nothing like the others. For one thing, she had blond hair (looked recently cut, Bill thought), and besides she lacked the flair, the style, despite a pair of oversize sunglasses that hid half her face. And yet she wore a dark red leather jacket a hell of a lot like the one the biker had worn in front of Jim Holloway's house. When she spoke it came out low, as if she didn't want anyone to hear. "I'd like a perm," she said. She added, "I don't have an appointment."

"I'm sorry," Helen said, and glanced over her shoulder. "There's no one available."

"That's all right," the woman said. "I'll wait." Before Helen could say anything else, Leather Jacket sat down at the other end of the row of chairs from Amy and Lillian.

"Bill," Mrs. Nelson said in that awful pout, "do you think I should change my hair?"

I think you should chop it off and eat it for lunch, Bill thought. He hated it when she pouted. Ugly women should never act coquettishly. The law should forbid it. He suggested a style that would "lighten" the face, and then he asked if she wanted, if she dared, to go blonde.

"I don't know," she said. "I'm not sure I'm ready for that."

Neither is the world, Bill thought, *but what the hell*. He started work, parting the hair into clumps which he held in place with plastic clips.

Usually Bill chatted with Mrs. Nelson, even worked slowly to give himself time to build up that intimacy that kept people like her steady over the years. Today, however, he worked efficiently, hardly speaking even to answer her questions, for he kept looking past her to the three women in the waiting area. Which perhaps is why he didn't see what was happening to Mrs. Nelson's hair.

"My hair!" she screamed. "What are you doing to my hair?" She slapped his hands away.

Bill stared down. All over Mrs. Nelson's head, swatches of hair had turned bright green. And where there had been curls and moistness, the green hair stuck out straight and strawlike. Bill took hold of a green clump. The whole thing came out in his hand. As Mrs. Nelson screamed again, Bill looked around the room. Everyone stared at him. His mouth open, he turned and tugged on two more clumps. They came loose; the bald spots shone in the fluorescent light. Mrs. Nelson shoved Bill, who fell against the counter, knocking over a blow dryer. "Get away from me!" she screamed. "Get away, get away."

"Mrs. Nelson," he pleaded. "Marian. Please sit down." Mrs. Nelson was yanking at the smock, trying to pull it off without unsnapping it behind her neck. "I don't understand what happened," Bill pleaded. "Please sit down."

The smock came loose and Mrs. Nelson grabbed her jacket and bag. As she ran to the door, bits of hair fell from her head to litter the floor with scraps of green. Bill glanced again around the room—the staff and regular clients looked embarrassed, Amy and Lillian were smiling, and the third woman stared at the floor—and then he ran after Mrs. Nelson. Or started to, for when he opened the door to look for her, he saw instead someone else. Across the street, leaning against her motorcycle, stood the biker in the red leather. Bill wasn't sure, but he thought she nodded at him. He went back inside.

In the steel chairs Amy and Lillian had gone back to their reading, while Leather Jacket—the other Leather Jacket—still studied the floor. Throw them out, Bill told himself. Get rid of them. Instead, he went back to his station to shake his head at the clumps of green hair. Meg came over to whisper, "Jesus, Bill, what did you put on that woman's hair?"

"Nothing," Bill said. "C'mon, Meg, I didn't even finish cutting it."

"Well, something—"

"The shampoo! Or the conditioner. Helen must have used some

garbage on her. Sweep that mess up, okay? Get it out of sight." He strode over to the counter, where Helen was pretending to study the appointment book. "Come in the back," he ordered her. In the staff room Bill said, "Now what the hell did you do to Mrs. Nelson's hair?"

"I just washed it, Mr. Cohen. Honestly."

"Don't give me that crap. You must have grabbed the wrong bottle."

"No, really. I'll show you." She rushed past him to the sink out front, where she grabbed a couple of plastic vials from the garbage. "Here," she said. "See?"

Bill wanted to slap them out of her hands, to shove her lying face against the wall. But everyone was watching him, he could feel them. "All right," he said, "but you ever do something like that again—" He let his voice drop, unable to think of an adequate threat.

Right then, Mrs. Steiner came in. Bill glanced at her, then pointed a finger at Helen. "You keep away from her, you hear me?" he whispered. "I'll wash her hair myself."

Helen whispered back, "I swear to you, Mr. Cohen—" But Bill had already turned to smile at Gabi Steiner.

He was sitting her down at the sink when he heard the roar of motorcycles. It started loud and got stronger, as if a whole pack of them was about to drive right through the plate-glass window. Though Bill wanted to scream at them to shut up, no one else seemed to notice. Mrs. Steiner purred softly as Bill rubbed the shampoo into her scalp. He moved her to a seat and started to work.

This time Bill saw it first and then the other hairdressers and customers saw it. Mrs. Steiner had taken off her glasses and closed her eyes, and only when all the gasps alerted her did she snatch her glasses from the counter to stare at herself in the mirror. Half her hair had turned green. Huge tufts of it lay on her shoulders and lap. "What have you done to me?" she shouted.

"I'm terribly sorry," Bill said. "It must be the shampoo. A bad shampoo. Please sit down. Please. We'll fix it."

"Don't touch me," Gabi Steiner said. When she jumped back, more hair fell to the floor. "How could you do this?" she said. "Are you insane? Don't you know my husband's a lawyer?"

"We'll fix it," Bill said. "Please."

"Don't you come near me." Mrs. Steiner snatched her purse, quickly, as if Bill would try to grab her if she came too close reaching for it. She pulled the smock over her head like a shawl, then ran out the door.

Bill stood in the middle of the shop and looked around the room. Everyone was staring at him, the workers, the customers—Amy and Lillian sat back with their arms folded, smiling at him. The third woman leaned forward with her fists on her knees. She didn't smile like the others, but he could feel her eyes right through the dark glasses. "What the hell's going on?" he said. "What'd I do? I didn't do anything." He picked up a pair of scissors from a table. When he looked at them in his hand, the blades had turned all green and moldy. Bill yelped and dropped the scissors. The pin must have rotted away, for the two halves fell apart when the scissors struck the floor. "I'm going home," Bill said to no one. "I'll come back later."

When he stepped outside, however, he made a noise and moved back against the building. Across the street, three women, almost identical, leaned against black motorcycles. In perfect unity, they raised their hands in front of their shoulders and began a slow, rhythmic clapping. "Oh Jesus," Bill said. "What the hell's going on?" He looked over his shoulder, as if he could hide in the shop. Inside, however, the three women had gotten up from their seats and were walking slowly toward the door. Lillian raised her hands like birds and brought them together in a single clap.

He ran for his car. It took him several seconds to get his key into the lock and turn it. When he jerked on the handle the door swung open, but the handle itself turned green, like something that had lain for years on the damp floor of a forest. Bill got into the seat; gingerly he pulled the door shut. The inner handle stayed the same, but the outer one fell off onto the street.

Bill glanced over his shoulder before he started the car. The women were looking in his direction, but they hadn't moved. Bill turned on the engine and sighed when it worked, when the key didn't turn green and fall out of the ignition. All the way home, he checked the rearview mirror every few seconds, but no one was following him. During the ten-minute ride he drove through two red lights and almost lost control on three curves.

He didn't bother to park in the driveway, just left the car on the lawn and ran inside. He made sure the bottom lock was on, but when he tried to close the dead bolt on top the knob turned green and came off in his hand. "Goddamn it!" Bill shouted, and threw the useless thing against the wall.

He looked around nervously. "Janet?" he called. "Ellen?" No answer came, and Bill whistled his relief. He closed the living room drapes, then opened them a crack to let in some light. For a few seconds, he just walked around the living room. Got to relax, he told himself. Whatever they did to him, he was safe now. Get a beer, he thought. Watch TV. He went into the kitchen, wondering if Janet had found time in her busy schedule to buy some beer before she went to her goddamn club. He grabbed hold of the refrigerator door handle. It came off in his hand, a green antique that smelled of rot.

He was having trouble breathing now. He went into the bedroom and lay down on the bed. "Help me," he moaned. A wave of excitement passed through Bill's body and he realized he had an erection. *What a time*, he thought, but then he laughed. If that didn't calm him down, nothing would. He jumped up for a couple of the magazines he'd hidden on the shelf behind the boxes of tax forms and old receipts. Back on the bed he pulled off his shoes and threw them, basketball-like, into a chair across the room. He was already feeling better. He undid his pants and shimmied them down around his ankles. He pulled down his underwear and lay back on the bed. "Here we go," he said out loud. Delicately—he didn't want to rush—he wrapped his hand around the base of his penis.

It turned green.

Bill screamed. He screamed, and pulled up his underwear and then his pants, and kept on screaming. Until, in the midst of his shrieks, he heard laughter. And applause. He turned around, and all six of them stood there, the bikers, Amy, Lillian, and Sunglasses, three on either side of the door. All but Sunglasses were clapping slowly in unison. "Why are you hurting me?" Bill said. "I never did anything to you."

"Like hell you didn't," Sunglasses said. She threw the glasses on the floor.

"Jaqe!" Bill shouted. "Oh God, Jaqe, thank God it's you." He crawled across the bed toward her. "Tell them to stop. Tell them to make it all better." The women laughed.

Jaqe said, "Haven't you figured it out? I'm not going to make them stop. I told them to do this. They're following my idea."

"Then tell them to stop." Jaqe shook her head. "Why?" Bill pleaded. "I never did anything to you."

Jaqe shouted, "You tried to rape me. You almost killed me with those scissors. You lied about Laurie."

"I didn't mean any harm. I just wanted to have some fun."

Jaqe spit on him. It wasn't much, just a dribble, and Jaqe looked even more surprised than Bill, but the laughter of the women rose like a sudden wave rearing over his head. And then Jaqe began to laugh too, and clap, and stamp her foot. Bill ducked his head, covered his face, and ran out of the bedroom.

In the living room he found the front door open and leaped from the house. Bill wasted only a few seconds trying to get the car door open. When the key fell off the ring onto the grass he took off, first along the street and then on people's lawns when the pebbles on the pavement hurt his bare feet.

He ran jerkily, out of breath almost immediately. His left side hurt, but he kept going. Every few seconds he looked over his shoulder. When he didn't see them he felt along his crotch. *Still there*, he thought to himself. *Oh God, God, it's still there.*

At the end of the housing development Bill came to the back entrance of a shopping mall under construction. He glanced back once more and then dashed into the huge building. Inside, he bent over with his arms on his knees and tried to catch his breath. But then he heard the sound of motorcycles and he began to limp along the mall avenue.

The construction team must have had the day off, for the whole place was empty. Apparently they'd almost finished it; quite a few of the stores had names and even merchandise. Bill had thought of opening a branch here, and had even come along on a local merchants' get-acquainted tour. Now he tried to remember the layout, and where he could find a place to hide. Where the hell was everybody? Where were the guards? Where were the men? Bill saw a row of telephones and ran to them. He didn't have any coins, but maybe you didn't need any to get the police. He grabbed the first phone. Dead. The second. Dead. And then he heard rhythmic clapping.

As Bill ran down a side corridor his feet began to sting. He looked at the floor and saw it was strewn with broken pieces of colored glass. Already his feet were bleeding. He almost turned back, but at that moment the women came around the corner. They moved slowly, the five redheads perfectly in step, Jaqe slightly to the side. Bill looked all around. In front of an empty store window lay a pile of red shoes, as if someone had set it out for a demonstration display and then knocked it over. Bill stepped on his toes through the glass until he could sit down on the pile and find a pair big enough to fit him. He had just pulled them on and jumped up when the women reached him.

In each direction he thought of running, one of the women was standing in front of him. The clapping speeded up. Bill began to hop from one foot to the other; why was he hopping? He realized that his feet hurt worse than before—and not just from the glass, for when he looked down the red shoes glowed with heat and wisps of smoke leaked out from the sides, smoke from his feet. His feet were burning. He tried to kick off the shoes, to pull them off, but they wouldn't come loose. And all the time he kept on dancing, faster and faster, to the beat of hands and the sea roll of laughter. "Please," he begged. "For God's sake." He could smell himself burning.

The faces reveled in the heat, their mouths open, their eyes wide, Jaqe just like the rest of them, worse, her face all twisted as she whooped her laughter and stamped on the floor. The red leather jackets glowed in the heat, but Jaqe's face glowed brighter than any of them. "Help!" Bill shouted. "Somebody help me!" Jumping up, he tried to see over their heads, find a guard, a worker, anybody. He only saw a woman, another woman, this one motionless in a long dress. "Get a guard," Bill shouted to her. "Call the police. Hurry." He screamed in pain, for the hurt had spread upward from his feet and the whole bottom half of his body was sizzling. The woman didn't move.

But Jaqe did. She stopped clapping and looked around at all the women and then at Bill, whose body jerked in agony, still in perfect time to the sweep of hands. For a moment, it seemed to her that the women, not Bill, were on fire, that fire blazed out from their unburning bodies to fill the whole mall with furious light. When she looked down at herself, flames flickered around her own hands. "No," she said softly, "no, this wasn't what I planned."

She bent over and started to throw up but then stopped, as if she realized that that wouldn't serve any purpose. She began to shove the women and pull at their hands. They ignored her. Jaqe took off the jacket and threw it at Lillian, who leaned back slightly and let it fly past her. "Let him go," Jaqe demanded. "This wasn't the idea." The women laughed louder. One of them contorted her face and stamped her feet in imitation of Jaqe two minutes earlier.

Jaqe turned to the woman outside the circle. "Make them stop. Right now. Make them stop! Do you hear me?"

The woman waved a finger. Slowly, reluctantly, the five lowered their hands. Though they looked angrily back at the woman and at Jaqe, none of them spoke. In the center of the circle Bill fell to the floor and pulled the shoes off his charred feet. The air smelled of cooked meat. He hid his face in his hands and cried.

Jaqe said to Lillian, "This wasn't what we planned."

Lillian folded her arms. "You were certainly enjoying yourself."

There was silence for a moment, then Jaqe said, "That's why it had to stop." She added sarcastically, "I'm sorry to spoil your fun."

Lillian shrugged. "No problem. We've used this trick before."

"Yes," Jaqe said, "I'm sure you have."

"Want a ride back to the city?"

"No, thank you. I'll take the bus."

"We're a lot faster," Lillian said.

"I don't doubt it. I'll still take the bus." Behind her, Jaqe could hear Bill Cohen wailing and beating the floor, in terror and pain. She shook her head and turned to walk away. If she saw the woman in the long dress she gave no sign, but only strode off across the bright colors of the broken glass.

Nine

The Butterfly Tree

Laurie sat on the floor, her back against the front of the gray couch. Alongside her stood a half-empty bottle of beer. Laurie picked it up and set it down without drinking or even looking at it. On the television an aging tennis star tried to keep up with her teenage opponent. Laurie didn't care much about tennis. She watched because the aging star was a woman-loving woman. And because it gave her something to do while she waited for Jaqe. I've got to go away for a couple of days, Jaqe had told her. Where? Sorry, can't tell you. Well, what for, for Goddess's sake? Uh-uh. Secret. "Goddamn it," Laurie said, and took a swallow of beer. She made a face. Flat. Laurie laughed. If she wanted to be a tough beer-drinking bull dagger she'd have to learn to finish off a bottle in less than two hours.

On the TV the teenager scored a dazzling passing shot and the crowd screamed with excitement. Laurie thought, Bastards, they just want to see an old dyke go down in flames. The worst thing, the goddamn worst thing, was that Jaqe had told Mark. Where did he come in? He was Laurie's *boss.* "Jaqe knows what she's doing," Mark had told her when Laurie had said she was worried.

"How do you know?" Laurie had asked. Mark had gone back to reading a small-press catalogue. Laurie had pulled it out of his hand. "You know where Jaqe is, don't you?" Mark had shrugged. "You know what she's doing, don't you?"

"Not in detail," Mark had said.

"Not in detail? What the hell is that supposed to mean? Why would she tell you and not me?" Laurie had had to clench her fists to keep from crying.

Mark would only say, "She needed my help." And then he'd refused to talk about it.

The television cheered, and Laurie realized she'd missed some crucial play. She snarled at the close-up of the former champion nervously chewing her bottom lip.

A knock came at the door. Just what she needed, neighbors. Maybe boyfriend had come back and wanted to borrow a cup of dope. Maybe she could not answer, pretend she'd gone out and left the TV on to discourage daytime burglars. Another knock. Laurie growled and got to her feet. When she opened the door Jaqe stood there.

"What's wrong?" Laurie asked. "Why didn't you use your key?" Jaqe looked like a frightened child. Her hair went in all directions, her clothes were stained, as if she'd fallen, and her face was streaked, with smears of makeup under the eyes and along the cheeks.

"I can't come in," Jaqe said.

"What do you mean?" Laurie reached out to her but Jaqe jumped back.

"No!" she said. "I don't want you to touch me."

"I don't understand," Laurie said. "What is it? Oh God, is it my father? Did he find you and attack you or something?"

Jaqe shook her head. "No. No, I—" She stopped, closed her eyes a moment, then took a breath. "*I* found *him.*"

"What do you mean? What are you talking about?"

"I—I did something. I wanted—I thought it was—I wanted justice."

"Oh my God," Laurie said. "What did you do?"

"No. I can't tell you. Not yet."

"Is he—did you—is he alive?"

"Yes."

Laurie sighed. "What did you do, then?"

"Not yet. I need you to help me."

"Help you how? Do you have some plan or something?"

"I don't mean about that," Jaqe said. "About him. That's—that's finished."

"Then what do you need?"

"I need you—what I did—I thought it was right—it was right, but it's cut me off. From the world. I need your help, Laurie. I need you to bring me back."

"Back where?"

"To the world of humans. To you."

Laurie closed her eyes, raised a hand to her lowered face. There was silence for what seemed a long time, and then Laurie dropped her hand. She nodded, softly, then held out her arms.

Jaqe shook her head, crying. "I'm sorry," she said. "I can't. I want to accept it, what you're giving me. I'm just—I'm just too far away."

Laurie said, "What do you want me to do? Tell me what I should do."

"I don't know. I want you to think of something. A purification. Something to bring me back."

"You mean like some kind of Goddess ritual?"

"No! I'm sorry. I'm sorry, it just—it has to be something to do with the world, with humans. With you."

Laurie made a noise. "Wait in the hall," she said.

Jaqe leaned against the wall, head down, one hand covering her face. When Laurie came into the hall a few minutes later, Jaqe shrunk away.

"It's okay," Laurie said. "I won't hurt you."

Jaqe shook her head. "It's not that. It's just—I don't feel fit to touch."

"Was it that bad? What you did?"

"No, no, that's not it. I—I've got to come back to the world, Laurie, or else I'll just pull you away from it."

"That's what we're going to do," Laurie said. "Bring you back." She carried a large plastic shopping bag. "Come with me," she said, and turned toward the stairs.

"Where are we going?" Jaqe asked her.

"The bottom," Laurie said. She led Jaqe down to the basement, where she took out two scarves from her bag. She held them up, one black silk, the other a polyester tourist scarf with garish pictures of the city's landmarks. "Remember this?" Laurie asked, raising the polyester, and Jaqe smiled slightly. They'd bought it as a joke during a day when they'd played at being country tourists in the big city.

Laurie said, "Okay. This one—" She held up the black. "This one represents the place you are now. I'm going to toss it to you and I want you to cover your eyes with it." To Jaqe's frightened look she said, "You have to accept where you are now before I can lead you back." Jaqe shook her head. "And you have to accept that I will help you and not hurt you." They stood there motionless for a moment, then Jaqe nodded.

Laurie held up the other scarf. "This one will be our link. The line that allows me to reach down and bring you to the light. Okay?" Jaqe nodded again. Laurie took a breath, then threw Jaqe the black silk. Jaqe held it in her hands a moment, then tied it over her eyes.

To herself, Laurie whispered, *Thank you.* Out loud she said, "Good. I'll wave the other one near your hands, and when you feel it, grab hold of it. Okay?"

"Okay," Jaqe said.

"Get ready," Laurie told her. She laid one end of the scarf in Jaqe's left hand. Jaqe took hold with both hands. "Now we've got a connection," Laurie said. "Don't let go. Do you understand?"

In a little-girl voice Jaqe said, "I won't."

"I'm going to lead you out of here," Laurie said. "So you know what we're doing. I'm going to take you up in the elevator. To the top floor."

When they reached the top, Laurie pulled Jaqe to the stairs that led to the roof. "We're out of the darkness," Laurie said when they came outside. "Can you feel the sun?" Jaqe nodded. "Okay. I've brought you here, so now I'm going to let go of the link and set up the next stage. But you won't get lost, because you're already here. Is that all right?" Jaqe didn't answer. "Say if it's all right."

"It's all right," Jaqe said. When Laurie let go of the scarf, Jaqe bunched it up in her hands and held on tight.

A couple of minute later, Laurie said, "Now take off the darkness and throw it away." Jaqe didn't move. "Come on," Laurie said gently. "Just get rid of it." Jaqe pulled the blindfold off her head and threw it out of sight, behind the stairwell. She squinted at the bright sun. In front of her, Laurie stood in a wide circle made of torn-up pieces of junk mail. Around Laurie, and all about the roof, gold and black and green and blue butterflies darted in the air. Laurie came to the edge of the circle and said, "Pass me the end of the link." Jaqe held out the tourist scarf for Laurie to take hold.

Slowly, Laurie pulled Jaqe toward her into the circle. They stood facing each other, not touching except through the scarf. "Good," Laurie said. "I'm going to let go again. I've got just a few more things to do." While Jaqe watched, Laurie moved about the circle, setting down objects from her bag. "This is to establish the four human directions," Laurie said. "Uptown," she announced, and put down a bill from the electric company, with a piece of brick to hold it in place. She walked to the other side of the circle, said, "Downtown," and laid down a newspaper turned to the financial page. "East side," a glass she'd taken home from a women's bar. "West side," a leftover croissant.

"There," Laurie said as she straightened up. "This is the human world. Now you have to let go of the other one." Laurie reached into the plastic bag again and took out a large pad of paper and some felt-tip pens. She laid them down at Jaqe's feet. "I want you to draw this other place," she said. "And what you did there. Can you do that?"

"Don't watch," Jaqe said. Laurie turned and stood with her back to Jaqe. Jaqe squatted down and took up the pens. She held them for a while, with the pad in her lap, and then she began to draw. She drew a huddled figure—Bill—with his hands over his head, as if someone were beating him. She drew flames around his body, and then she drew the six women around him, with flames around their hands and faces. She labeled one of them "Jaqe" and drew the face all twisted, the teeth as fangs. She stopped, breathing heavily as she looked at the picture. She bent over again, and using a red pen she drew Mother

Night in a long dress, standing on top of a rock shaped like a turtle. She colored Mother Night's face black, but then she drew a golden light around her head and body. Jaqe held the drawing in both hands as she got to her feet. "Okay," she said.

Laurie turned to see Jaqe standing with the drawing held face down against her chest, as if she feared Laurie would try to snatch it away from her. "Tear it up," Laurie said. Jaqe shook her head. "Come on, Jaqe," Laurie told her. "Come back to me. Please."

"Do you love me?" Jaqe asked.

"I love you," Laurie said.

Jaqe tore the paper in half. "Forever?" she asked.

"Forever after," Laurie said.

Jaqe tore the paper in quarters. "Do you forgive me?" she asked.

"For all the actions and for all time."

Jaqe said, "No matter what I did?"

"No matter what you did?"

Once more Jaqe tore the paper, and then again. Crying, she said, "I love you, Laurie."

Laurie said, "And do you forgive me?"

Jaqe said nothing as she looked from Laurie to the pieces of paper lying in her open hands. "I love you," she said.

"Do you forgive me? I can't bring you back if you can't forgive me."

"I forgive you," Jaqe whispered. Then louder, "I forgive you." She tossed the pieces of paper at the sky. A gust of wind took them and they swirled about, then vanished into the sun. Jaqe came into Laurie's arms. As they kissed each other they closed their eyes, so that neither one of them saw the thousands of butterflies that came over the edge of the roof. In a single form they flew, the shape of a tree, a huge blue and green and black and gold tree whose branches stretched high above the women's heads. In the middle of the branches lay the sun, the face of a child in a circle of light.

That night, Laurie woke up to find Jaqe by the bedroom window, looking out at the street. "Honey?" she called. "Are you okay? What are you doing?"

Jaqe turned around. "I want a baby," she said. "I want a child."

Part Two

The Child in the Stone

One

The Baby in the Tree

Laurie did not know what to make of Jaqe's desire for a child. At first she made nothing of it, as if Jaqe had said something odd in an emotional moment. Laurie certainly had enough to occupy her, with her father in the hospital and her mother's insistences—in vain—that Laurie go visit him. However, in the middle of all the conflicts, Jaqe said it again—"I want a child"—and Laurie began to suspect that her lover was serious.

"Please," Laurie said to her. "Can't we just finish things with the previous generation before we start working on the next one?"

Eventually Laurie's mother gave up, and Laurie began to think her life might settle down for a while. But as the months passed, Jaqe became moody, sometimes refusing to eat, sometimes staring at the floor while Laurie would tell her stories from the shop, like the one about the customer who had come in requesting "rude photos" of the British royal family.

One evening they went to a housewarming party for Louise's new apartment. Laurie had not seen Louise or the others for weeks. She dressed very carefully, in a red silk blazer and black jeans, and she carefully slicked back her hair and even used Jaqe's lipstick to accent her cheekbones. When she saw that Jaqe did not intend to change from the T-shirt and worn-at-the-knees jeans she'd had on all day, Laurie demanded she put on something "dynamic." Jaqe said she didn't care. "Well, I do," Laurie said. "I don't want all those baby butches to think we've degenerated into old marrieds."

Jaqe shrugged. "It's just not important."

"Well, what is? You've been moping so much it's like you don't care about anything."

"I told you," Jaqe said. "I want a child."

"Oh great," Laurie said. "That's terrific. I'll tell you what. You put on your backless strapless topless so I can get all worked up, and then after the party I'll stick my genuine autographed Radclyffe Hall dildo up you, and start a bun in the oven. How's that?"

When Jaqe looked about to cry, Laurie said, "I'm sorry, honey. I don't mean to act like an idiot. I just do it so easily. Do you forgive me?"

"I mean it," Jaqe told her. "I want a baby."

"I really am sorry." When Jaqe said nothing, Laurie said, "I promise we'll talk about it later. Okay?" She grabbed a white blouse and pants from Jaqe's closet and tossed them on the bed. "Why don't you wear these?" she said. "It's getting late."

But when they got home Jaqe didn't bring it up again, and Laurie announced that she needed to get right to sleep so she could help Mark in the morning, before the store opened.

Over the next weeks, Jaqe went back to school and Laurie involved herself first in work and then in a campaign to include education about women-loving women in the public schools. Jaqe became steadily more listless. She lost weight and her face became pale, with a sag around the mouth. She dropped most of her courses a few weeks into the semester. One night, in bed, Laurie looked at Jaqe and saw her staring over the pages of a book on feminist theories of architecture. Laurie realized that Jaqe had not turned a page in half an hour. "Good book?" she asked. When Jaqe didn't answer, Laurie saw a picture in her mind—herself slapping Jaqe, or shaking her by the shoulders. To her own great surprise, Laurie began to cry.

Jaqe looked as if someone had called her from a great distance. For a moment, she squinted at Laurie, then put her arms around her. "It's okay, sweetie," she said. "It's all right. Everything's going to be all right."

Laurie pulled away. "No, it's not all right," she said. "You keep vanishing. I don't know where the hell you go, but you go someplace." She started to cry again. "I'm scared you'll leave me."

Jaqe looked down. "I'm sorry," she said. She raised her eyes back to Laurie. "I don't mean to . . . to vanish. You know I love you. It's just—I told you, I want a baby."

"Jesus," Laurie said. "How can you have a baby? What about college? And money? Babies cost a lot of money."

"I don't care," Jaqe said. "We can find a way. Other people do it. People have babies all over the world without a lot of money. And I don't care about college at all."

"Well how do you think we can *make* a baby? Haven't you forgotten a pretty important ingredient in the recipe?"

Jaqe smiled gloriously at her. "You'll figure it out. You can do anything."

Laurie laughed. "Thanks. I may be butch, but I'm not that butch."

"Alice got pregnant."

"Oh great," Laurie said. "I don't want you picking up strange dicks in chess clubs." Alice, an ex-girlfriend of one of the LSU women, had seduced an acquaintance to get pregnant. To check him for intelligent genes, she'd challenged him to a chess match.

"She didn't join a club," Jaqe said. "She met him in a café."

"Alice was alone," Laurie insisted. "She could do any crazy thing she wanted. You've got a partner."

"Maybe Mark—"

"No!"

Jaqe grinned. "I just meant that maybe he'd have an idea."

"Can't we keep this at home?" Laurie said. "I'm sure you and Mark have a wonderful relationship, but he's still my boss. He doesn't have to know all our problems."

"A baby's not a problem. A baby's a sacred gift from the Goddess of Life."

"Great," Laurie said. "Maybe she'll mail us a gift certificate. But let's keep this Goddess promotional program to ourselves for now, okay?"

And yet, two days later, Laurie asked Mark if he would like to have a beer with her after work. Sitting in the same bar where she'd once tried to write her papers, Laurie told him of Jaqe's "obsession," and asked him if he could help her figure out what to do about it.

Too large for the narrow wooden chair, Mark still managed to look at home as he sat with his hands folded on the scarred tabletop. An empty cappuccino cup sat on either side of him. Mark had been talking cheerfully about the "category error" of using computer models for dream interpretation, but had stopped the moment Laurie had begun to speak. Now he shrugged slightly, and said, "If she wants a child, why don't you give her one?"

Laurie lifted her hands in a gesture of despair. "Not you too," she said. "Am I the only person who ever took sex education in school?"

"They didn't talk dirty when I went to school."

"Well, let me explain it. Men and women may look exactly the same to you and Jaqe, but there's a crucial difference where you can't see it. The man's got this collapsible tube—you've probably noticed it when you've gone to pee—"

"You worry too much about technicalities. If you can't make the baby, you can act as the agent."

"Great," Laurie said. "Do I get ten percent? Anyway, it still comes down to that one requirement. The technicality."

Mark said, "There are more ways to make a baby than you realize." The waitress came to ask if Mark wanted more coffee, or Laurie more beer. Laurie shook her head, but Mark said, "Do you have a child?"

"I certainly do," she said. "A two-year-old little maniac. Would you like to have him? He gets along great with everybody. As long as you do whatever he says and don't expect to sleep."

"There," Mark said to Laurie. "See how simple it is?"

Laurie made a face. "I don't think she means it."

The waitress said, "Try me."

Mark asked her, "How did you get pregnant? Did you use the orthodox method?"

Startled, the woman shrank back, but Mark only smiled blandly at her. "Actually," the waitress said, "not really. My husband . . . we used artificial insemination." She shook her head. "Why did I say that? I've never told anyone before. We promised each other we wouldn't tell."

Mark took her hand, for just a moment. "It's all right," he told her. "You haven't done anything wrong. This woman needed help, and now you've helped her."

When the waitress had hurried away, Mark said, "There. That's one method."

"Clinics don't take lesbians."

"You're too full of objections. How do you know who clinics take or don't take? Anyway, you don't need a clinic for artificial insemination. All you need is a donor and a turkey baster. If you read more, you would know that."

Laurie said, "If you're offering—"

Mark waved a hand. "No, no, don't worry. I don't do that kind of work. Of course, I could act as arranger. So you and Jaqe won't have to know who the donor is."

"I don't know," Laurie said. "I don't like it." She waited for Mark to tell her she just didn't want children.

Instead, he said, "And if AI doesn't work—did you ever notice how the same term is used for artificial insemination and artificial intelligence?—if AI doesn't work, you could try dreams."

"Dreams?"

"I read a book recently where a woman gets pregnant from a dream. Kind of an odd dream, something to do with eating jeweled hot dogs at a Persian baseball game."

"Mark," Laurie said, "that was a book. This is life we're talking about now."

"How do you know everything that happens in life?"

"I know how to make a baby."

"People have always known how to make babies. Only, they sometimes know different things. Some people know that babies come from walking alone under a full moon. Maybe at some future time people will think it astonishing that we thought babies came only from sexual intercourse. They'll say things like 'Didn't they notice how many women had intercourse and didn't get pregnant? Didn't they ever study the dreams of pregnant women?' "

Laurie got up. "I've got to go," she said.

Mark waved to her, as if she were already traveling down the street. He said, "Give my love to Jaqe." Laurie nodded.

Outside the door she looked back through the window. Mark sat back with his hands behind his head as he talked to the waitress, who looked confused but nodded her head.

Winter was coming, and Jaqe kept getting sick. Colds, flu, backaches. Sometimes she would wake up more tired than when she went to sleep. When Laurie asked her to go for blood tests, Jaqe didn't answer, just shrugged. She wasn't eating right, Laurie knew. Laurie made elaborate dishes from a vegetarian cookbook; Jaqe just ate a few bites and left the table. The same went for steak or ice cream or home-delivered pizza or Chinese food.

Sometimes Jaqe woke up in the morning with her eyes wet, as if the tears couldn't wait and had started in her sleep.

Laurie said to Mark, "It's like someone's cast a spell on her. And she won't get help. When I tell her to see a shrink or something, she says she knows what's wrong."

"Maybe she does." Mark said this without looking at her. He had just bought a computer and was playing a game in which a digital hero had to climb a tower and rescue a princess while packs of digital witches on broomsticks tried to knock him to the ground. He said to Laurie, "Maybe you should just give her what she wants."

"Come on," Laurie said. "Even if the medical miracle of donor insemination provided a baby, what would we do with it?"

"What does anyone do with a baby? Shit!" he said, and slammed his fist on the counter. A teenage girl jumped, and turned around from the stack of books she was scanning. Mark said to her, "The witches won again. There's just too damn many of them."

"Wow," the girl said. "That's the best news I've heard all week."

Mark put his face closer to the screen, as if he could look past the tower to some wider scene. "You're right," he said. "It all depends on how you look at it, doesn't it?"

Winter was coming, and Jaqe kept getting sick. She went out without a coat, walking sometimes for hours in just a sweatshirt and jeans. One morning, Laurie followed her. First she made sure Jaqe dressed properly. As Jaqe was leaving, Laurie gave her an apple and a small knife to peel off the pesticide and wax. Half a minute after Jaqe had left, Laurie suddenly grabbed her pea jacket, pulled on her cowboy boots, and ran down the stairs. Despite her worries, it excited her to play detective, and she found herself smirking as she occasionally hid in doorways. Mark's going to love this, she thought. She remembered the day she'd followed Adrienne Beker, but she pushed the thought away as she bent down to fake tying a shoelace while Jaqe waited at a walk sign.

Laurie followed Jaqe all the way to the park in the middle of the city. Jaqe seemed to pick up the moment she entered the park. Her shoulders straightened and she no longer looked at the ground. Without buildings or crowds to use for cover, Laurie worried that Jaqe might spot her, but Jaqe never turned around or looked to the side. Jaqe clearly knew where she was going, for she moved swiftly along the path and then across the grass, past the rocks and the pond and the people admiring the colors of the leaves. Finally she stopped before a large tree with gnarled branches that stuck straight out to the sides, like a candelabra. At the bottom the roots half stuck out of the ground, forming a tangled ball.

Jaqe stood before the tree for over a minute, with her head tilted slightly backward. Finally she began to walk around the tree, with her eyes on the ground, as if searching for something. Laurie did her best to hide behind a cluster of young maples, but she needn't have bothered. By a small group of rocks Jaqe found a short stick, about a foot long, lying on the ground. It looked like a fallen branch, except that someone had peeled off the bark. Jaqe kneeled down with one knee on the grass. In sharp, practiced movements she used the stick to scratch some sort of picture in the dirt in front of the tree. Then she got up, laid the stick against the ball of roots, and stood there looking at what she had done.

With a sigh, she took out the apple and knife Laurie had given her. She began to peel it, but she must have cut herself, for Laurie saw her hand jerk away. And then Jaqe squeezed her finger, with great concentration it seemed, until blood started to flow. Like someone watering a plant, she sprinkled the blood on her drawing. Laurie could see Jaqe's lips moving, but she couldn't hear the words.

When Jaqe headed back the way she'd come, Laurie decided not to follow her. Instead she waited until Jaqe was safely out of sight, then went up to the markings Jaqe had made on the ground. Jaqe had drawn a copy of the tree, Laurie saw. There was the straight trunk, the branches like layers of arms. Only, Jaqe had made a couple of changes. Instead of the twisted roots, she'd drawn a pattern, a maze, at the bottom. And at the top she'd carefully scratched the figure of an egg, set between a circular sun and a crescent moon.

That night, Laurie dreamed of women in trouble. There were women whose husbands beat them, old women evicted from tenement apartment buildings, women whose lovers had deserted them after a fight in the middle of the night, women with incurable diseases and no health insurance, women thrown out by their families. In the dream, Laurie stood in the parking lot of an all-night convenience store. She wore a yellow raincoat and a baseball cap with a feather stuck in the side. One by one, the women slipped into the store. Laurie saw a professor of hers from graduate school, and then a young woman who looked nothing like her sister Ellen, yet was Ellen. The dream-Laurie whispered, "I'm sorry. I know it's wrong, but I've got to think about Jaqe now."

Inside the store, a young woman in a mechanic's outfit stood behind the cash register. She wore her red hair slicked back, and her hands were stained with grease as she took people's money. She never spoke openly to the customers, but when one of the desperate women came up to her, the mechanic would tell her softly, "Mother Night can help you. Go to the water and find Mother Night."

Laurie stood at the back of the beach, at the edge of the sand dunes. In front of her, close to the water, stood a shack with streaked walls, a sloping tarred roof, and windows too dirty to see inside, except where the glass had broken to reveal the gray darkness of a room impervious to the sun. Laurie stood there all day, while women came one by one to pass through the broken door.

Laurie heard a child cry, a strange whooping noise that went on and off like a siren. When she looked around, however, she only saw an old tire lying in the sand, and inside it a pile of colored rocks. Laurie looked back at the edge of the world, where the sun was sinking helplessly into the water. She rushed into the shack.

Mother Night sat behind an old desk of scarred wood. She wore a denim jacket and jeans, and she sat with her legs up on the desk so that Laurie could see the scratches and cuts on the bottom of her basketball shoes.

"Please help me," Laurie said. "Jaqe wants a baby and I don't know what to do." For a long time Mother Night didn't move, and the dream-Laurie wondered if Mother Night was dead. But then she swung her legs down and said, "Come on," and led Laurie outside, where the sun slapped her eyes.

When she could see again, Laurie discovered they were standing on grass. Mother Night wore a long green dress with wings of white silk fluttering on the shoulders. Behind her, the sea rolled up to the edge of the grass. Laurie wished the old woman would put her arms around her. Instead, Mother Night pointed at the ground.

A group of stones lay piled on the bare dirt. Oval shaped and about eight inches long, they were painted gold or red, and when Laurie bent down she saw faces drawn on the flat surfaces: elliptical eyes, long thin triangles for noses. There were no mouths. Laurie lifted up a red stone with spokes of yellow light painted around the edges. Somewhere she heard a baby cry, and then a motorcycle. When she looked up at Mother Night, the sun behind the old woman made it hard to look at her.

Mother Night said, "This face is the child. If you plant it in Jaqe, it will grow from the Earth to the Sky."

Two days later, on her day off, Laurie went out of town to the beach. On the subway she kept telling herself she should go to the city beach, where at least she knew the trains were running. When she got off the subway, would she find a bus this late in the year? But when she got to the end of the train line there it was, a battered old city bus with no one on board but a man with an aluminum camera case, another man asleep across a couple of seats, and the driver, a young woman with short red hair. The bus started up as soon as Laurie sat down.

Laurie hadn't been to the beach in autumn in years. She walked past the parking lot, with its scattered cars bright in the sun, past the closed toilets and snack bar, and along the slightly damp sand until she stood near the edge of the water. She sighed. What the hell had she come here for? She looked around. There were more people than she'd expected—mostly fishermen with long poles anchored in the ground, but also a few runners, a couple of photographers, and a girl about ten, who was trying to control her kite in the strong wind. Laurie didn't see anyone who looked anything at all like Mother Night.

Laurie could hardly remember what the old woman looked like. She'd only seen her once, at that dance a couple of years ago. And all Laurie's attention that night had gone to Jaqe. She said out loud to the air, "What a dumbass thing to do."

Heading back to the parking lot, Laurie heard someone say "Shit!" When she turned she saw the girl with the kite, only now the kite lay on the ground, tangled in string. Laurie walked over and started to untangle the wooden cross with its painted diamond of paper.

"This is some picture," Laurie said to the girl. The yellow kite showed a bare-breasted dancing woman, with a black spiral painted over her face.

"My mom made it," the girl said. "She's an artist." For several minutes she and Laurie worked together to raise the woman into the sky. When Laurie said goodbye the girl said, "Thanks, lady. You're really great." She reached into her jacket pocket, then held out her closed fist. "Here," she said. "Do you want this?"

When the girl opened her hand, Laurie saw a small stone, dark gray, with short lines covering both sides. "Umm, thanks," Laurie said to the girl, who immediately took off down the beach with her kite flapping behind her. Laurie looked at the stone again. If you looked at the lines a certain way, you could see pictures. A bent column of white above a line of white looked like a ferryman standing up in a boat. He even held a pole, a diagonal line running from one corner of the stone to the other. On the other side, a whole web of fine lines ran from either side of a thick vertical column. At the bottom of the column, a mass of lines tangled around each other, like the string from the kite.

No. No, Laurie thought, not the kite, *the tree.* The lines in the stone made the same picture Jaqe had drawn in the park—the trunk, the stepladder branches, the ball of roots on the bottom. "Hey!" Laurie called to the girl, but the child was too far down the beach. She looked at the stone again, holding it close to her face, searching for the egg Jaqe had drawn in the top branches. There was something there. But not an egg. Too much sticking out. Like—like arms, and legs! "It's a baby," Laurie said out loud. She held the stone tightly in her fist, which she shook slightly in front of her. "It's a goddamn baby!"

When Laurie got home, she found Jaqe curled up on the couch with a blanket around her despite the late-afternoon sun heating up the apartment. Jaqe was watching TV, a talk show featuring nuns who had discovered their mother superior was a serial murderer. The host smirked as he explained that he and the audience took this "tragedy" very seriously, and only joked to relieve the tension.

"Hi," Laurie said. "It's me." Jaqe didn't answer. Laurie said, "I brought you something from the beach." Jaqe turned her head.

Laurie hesitated. She wondered if Jaqe would see the resemblance, if she should explain it to her. Instead, she just held it out.

The effect made her jump back in surprise.

"Where did you get this?" Jaqe cried out as she grabbed the rock from Laurie's hand.

"I told you," Laurie said. "At the beach."

"Who gave it to you? Was anyone there?"

For some reason, Laurie shook her head. "Just some fishermen. And photographers. And a girl with a kite."

"A girl? How old was she? Was she wearing yellow overalls?"

"No. She was about ten, I guess. Maybe a little older."

"You didn't see a younger girl? Around seven?"

"No," Laurie said. "There was no one like that at all." Tell her, she ordered herself. Tell her the kid gave it to you. But then Jaqe would know she'd lied at first, and Laurie couldn't stand the thought of Jaqe thinking of her as a liar.

Jaqe said, "And . . . the woman who introduced us. At the dance? Was she there? Today, I mean. Did you see her?"

Laurie shook her head. "No," she said. "I haven't seen her since that one time."

But Jaqe had stopped listening. Instead, she was squinting at the stone, at the tree side, the top of the tree. "Something's different," she said. "There's something . . . It's hatched!" She hugged Laurie. "It worked, it worked." She separated, only to kiss Laurie. "It's going to be okay," she said a moment later. "You did it. You did it. It's going to be okay."

Two

The Baby in the Jar

The next day Laurie told Mark to warm up the turkey baster and look around for a healthy donor. “He’s got to be smart,” Laurie said. “Well, I don’t mean genius. You know, not stupid.”

"I understand," Mark said.

"And healthy. I mean, no hereditary diseases." Mark nodded. "And, uh, not too homely, okay?"

"Got it," Mark said. He held up three fingers. "No dummies, no sickies, no uglies."

Laurie stared at the floor. "Oh," she said, as if she'd just remembered something. "I told Jaqe it was my idea. I hope you don't mind."

Mark reached out a hand to tilt Laurie's chin until she was looking at him. "It's fine," he told her. He smiled. "It's all going to be fine." When Laurie started to cry, Mark took her in his arms and hugged her almost half a minute before the two of them went back to work.

It took Mark over a month to find someone. During this period Jaqe began to eat and sleep properly, even to get back to studying for a couple of her suspended courses. Every night, when Laurie came home from work, Jaqe greeted her with a bright hello, a hug and a kiss, and then the question "Any news?"

"Sorry," Laurie would murmur, and rush off to wash her hands, as if she'd come home from working in a garage or a foundry.

"Haven't you got someone?" Laurie asked Mark. "She's driving me crazy." When Mark told her it took time and delicate negotiations, Laurie said, "All he's got to do is jerk off in a warm jar."

Jaqe stopped walking to the park without a coat, she'd even gone back to cleaning the house and cooking, a great relief to Laurie, who always did her best to do her share but never felt she had much "aptitude for the finer points," as a girlfriend of hers had once said. One day she came home to find Jaqe hanging cards on the two large plants framing the living room window. The dieffenbachia had grown almost to the ceiling since the time Laurie had given them to Jaqe for their one-month anniversary. "Our private forest," Jaqe had called them. She'd trimmed them, Laurie saw, and now she was carefully tying on the cards with colored thread. The cards all showed babies surrounded by lace and fluffy clouds and chorus lines of dancing storks. Jaqe said, "I just thought I'd create a good atmosphere. And we can use them later for birth announcements."

"Can't you find *someone?*" Laurie asked Mark. "I can't take it anymore."

"Actually," Mark told her, "I've got a prospect."

"Great," Laurie said, without much enthusiasm. "When can he report for work?"

"I'm still negotiating," Mark said.

That evening, Laurie told Jaqe she had some catch-up work to do at the store and went to a women's bar she used to visit before she knew Jaqe. For a couple of hours, she tried to work up some enthusiasm for dancing, or at least finding someone to talk to. But the music only hurt her ears, and the women all looked too young or too flashy or too cold.

When Laurie got home, Louise was there laughing with Jaqe at some joke. Jaqe jumped up and gave Laurie a kiss. "Yecch," she said. "Were you drinking beer?"

"Yeah," Laurie said, afraid she would blush. "I stopped at Pete's on the way home."

"Here's one for Pete," Jaqe said, and kissed Laurie again.

"Hi," Laurie said to Louise.

Louise grinned at her. "Hi, boss."

Laurie looked at their excited faces and knew something was going on. She waited while Jaqe glanced at Louise, who giggled. Finally Jaqe said, "Louise has been helping me calculate the best time."

"The best time?" Laurie repeated. She felt slightly queasy.

"You know, for donation."

Louise added, "And we're also planning how to set it up. We figure Jaqe will want to lie in the bedroom, which leaves this room for the mystery man."

Laurie wanted to scream at Jaqe, to shout at Louise, to run away. Instead, she stroked Jaqe's face, which shone as Jaqe said, laughing, "I thought maybe we should get a pile of old *Playboy*s and *Penthouse*s. You know, to give him inspiration. But Louise said we wanted a more spiritual atmosphere. So we could use pictures of the Great Mother instead."

Louise giggled. "You can include it in the contract."

"There's no contract," Laurie said. "We won't even know who it is."

Louise ignored her. "Hey," she said. "I just thought of something. When a man's wife has a baby he gives out cigars, right? It's pretty obvious what the cigar stands for. But what can a dyke give out? Maybe turkey sandwiches. The breast meat, of course." She and Jaqe laughed so loud, Laurie wished she was back in the bar.

Later, Laurie said to Jaqe, "Why the hell did you have to tell Louise?"

Jaqe shrugged. "Why not? She's my friend. Anyway, she really does know a lot about cycles. She works in that clinic."

"I don't care where she works. She's a gossip. She'll think it's so great she'll just have to tell everybody. We'll be lucky if she doesn't write an article about it."

"It is great," Jaqe said. "Why should we keep it a secret?"

"Because it's our baby. You and me."

"I know that," Jaqe said. "That's why it doesn't matter." Laurie tried to turn away, but Jaqe grabbed her and hugged her until Laurie put her arms around her.

For the donor, Mark chose finally the poet who sold ice cream sandwiches during the day and wrote about the "seeds of all knowledge" in the evenings. Unlike the other men Mark had approached—who all feared Mark would let the child know its father's name so that ten or twenty years later some stranger would knock on the door with a bill for child support—the poet, whose name was Aaron, found the idea enticing. "Aaron will raise his rod," he told Mark, "and let the multitudes pour forth." He put only one condition to Mark—that the anonymous mother give him two weeks to prepare himself and his "microscopic ambassadors."

Louise would have been delighted. Aaron did not use any Goddess pinups, but he did meditate every evening in a circle of upright "stones" he'd fashioned out of papier-mâché. Every morning, before going to his department-store booth, he stood on his head for five minutes—"to awaken the seeds and fill them with light" he wrote in his journal. "I have always," he told Mark, "taken my responsibilities seriously."

As Louise prepared Jaqe, and Mark prepared the "mystery guest" (as Louise called the donor), Laurie began to concentrate more and more on "living a normal life." Now she started to go out for walks, not, she told herself, in a stupor like Jaqe, but just to get away from the laboratory atmosphere of her apartment. Sometimes at night, when Jaqe would wiggle up against her, with her head against Laurie's breast, Laurie would think of pushing her away, even as she put her arm around Jaqe and held her in a warm hug. One night she discovered she wanted to hit Jaqe, to slap her or even punch her, and she got out of bed to stand in the kitchen until she could calm down.

It surprised Laurie when she learned that Jaqe assumed Laurie would administer the planting. Commander Turkey Baster, Jaqe called her.

Laurie said, "I thought you'd get Louise to do that." Instantly she felt like a jerk, though she wasn't sure why.

Jaqe said, "She's just helping me figure out what to do."

"So now you want me to play the father?"

"I'm sorry," Jaqe said. "Don't you want to?"

Laurie shrugged. "Sure. Of course." She remembered her dream, Mother Night telling her to plant the seed in Jaqe.

Jaqe did her best to look lewd. She said, "You've put lots of other things inside me. What's wrong with a turkey baster?"

Laurie said, "It's just what's in it." She added, "I'm sorry, honey. I didn't mean that."

"Try not to think about it," Jaqe said. "Pretend—I don't know—pretend it's turkey juice."

Laurie found herself grinning. "Maybe you'll lay an egg instead of giving birth."

"That's right," Jaqe said. "And when it hatches we'll find a baby girl with golden wings and a beak in place of a nose."

"And everyone will call her Turkey Nose. But then when the dragon imprisons the princess, Turkey Nose will use her beak to pick the lock."

"And her wings to carry the princess over the dragon's fiery breath."

Laurie said, "And we'll all live happily ever after."

According to Jaqe and Louise's reckoning, Jaqe's ovulation that month would coincide with the full moon. When she heard this, Laurie thought of telling Jaqe to skip the turkey baster and just go for a walk, naked, on the rooftop. She told Mark the idea, but he suggested Jaqe might not go for it.

It amazed Laurie how simple the technique was. The donor would "ejaculate" (as Mark insisted on saying) into a warm sterile jar. Then he, Mark, would draw the contents into the baster and pass it to Laurie, who would squirt it into "the waiting chamber" (Louise's term), trying to get it as close to the cervix as possible. "I guess it doesn't sound too bad," Laurie said to Mark.

"Not bad at all," Mark assured her. "It's a wonder folks don't do it this way all the time."

A few days before the time, Jaqe told Laurie to ask Mark to ask the donor if he could do it a second time the day after. "For insurance," she said. Over Laurie's protests, Jaqe pointed out that even married couples who did it the old-fashioned way sometimes missed the target.

Laurie said, "Let's try it once, okay? If it doesn't work, we can do it more times next month."

Laurie wanted them to do it at Mark's house. She wanted to say, "So we won't have to smell it after he's gone," but instead she suggested that they wouldn't want him to know how to find the apartment.

Jaqe refused. "I want to do this in my own home," she said.

Laurie told her, "Suppose he suddenly decides to investigate who lives here. Or just watches the place for pregnant women."

"I don't care," Jaqe said. "Mark can blindfold him." Nor would she accept Laurie's idea that they wait in a diner until Mark telephoned them to say the baster was ready. "I don't want to take a chance," Jaqe said. "We'll wait in the bedroom and Mark can hand it to you through the door."

Great, Laurie thought. A prisoner in my own bedroom while some jerk jerks off in my living room.

On the morning of the full moon, Jaqe found it hard to decide what to wear. Should she choose something sexy, like the short red dress she'd bought once to shock everyone at the LSU? Or something maternal? (The closest she could find was a checked blue-and-white jumper over a white blouse with a lace collar.) Finally she put on jeans and a T-shirt Louise had given her, with a picture of the moon and a profile of a naked woman bending a bow to shoot an arrow at the stars. To Jaqe's surprise, Laurie wore a gold silk shirt and tight black jeans; she had even polished her black cowboy boots.

Aaron had no trouble at all deciding what to wear. When Mark came to pick him up, Aaron carefully framed himself in the doorway. He wore his black Iranian caftan, with a silver phallus on a chain around his neck. A black leather bag hung from his shoulder. He had waxed his beard and mustache until they gleamed in the winter sun. As they drove to the home of the mother, Aaron explained to Mark that he would need to chant for at least ten minutes "to awaken my seed for its mission of potency." Mark advised against it, pointing out that Aaron didn't want the women to hear his voice.

When they arrived, Mark went to knock on the bedroom door to make sure the women knew the other team was there. Aaron meanwhile walked about the room, investigating the walls and the furniture and nodding his head. Mark saw, with relief, that Laurie and Jaqe had remembered to put away any photos, as well as letters or envelopes displaying their names. He smiled when he saw that someone, Jaqe probably, had set out a bowl of homemade popcorn.

Aaron sat down on the couch. From his bag, he took out a photo stand with a picture of a smiling man with a long curved mustache. His guru, he explained, and set it on the coffee table. In the kitchen, Mark found an empty peanut butter jar kept warm in a pot of water over low heat. Jaqe—Mark assumed it was Jaqe—had crossed out "peanut butter" on the label and written in "sperm." Next to it, on a white linen napkin, lay a new turkey baster.

In the other room Jaqe sat on the bed, fully dressed, with her legs stuck out before her. Laurie stood frowning by the window, wishing she was somewhere else, wishing she'd never agreed to the whole thing. She thought, I hate this, I should have just sent her off to the chess club. Do it the old-fashioned way and get it done. What am I supposed to do if I have to go to the bathroom? *He* can go to the bathroom all he likes. She thought how men used the same instrument for urination as for—the other thing—and the thought made her sick.

"Honey?" Jaqe whispered. "Come sit by me?"

Laurie winced, then did her best to clear her face before she turned around. "We're not supposed to talk," she whispered back. "*He* might hear us."

"Please," Jaqe said. Laurie sighed, and walked to sit on the edge of the bed. "Sit next to me," Jaqe told her when Laurie sat with her back against the wall. Jaqe took Laurie's hand in both of hers and laid her head on Laurie's shoulder. "Thank you so much," she said. "I love you so much."

Laurie surprised herself by wanting to cry. "I love you too," she said.

"I'm sorry we have to do this," Jaqe whispered.

"It's okay."

"I know you hate it. *I* hate it. There's just no other way."

"It's okay," Laurie repeated. "It was my idea, wasn't it?"

"Put your arms around me." Laurie hugged her, then kissed her, first on the soft round cheek she loved so much, then on the mouth.

They heard a small bang in the living room, and then a mumbling.

Jaqe giggled. She whispered, "Maybe he's having trouble getting it up."

Laurie said, "We forgot the *Playboys*. I guess that was our job."

"As the hostesses," Jaqe said.

Now Laurie was giggling too. "We put out popcorn," she said. "Isn't that enough?" The two of them laughed into their hands like sisters staying up after Mom and Dad had ordered them to go to sleep. Again Laurie kissed Jaqe, but then another bang, like a door slamming, set them off again. Laurie whispered, "Maybe he's gone into the bathroom. Isn't that where they're supposed to do it?" She made a pumping motion with her hand, and both of them had to bury their faces in the pillow to keep the laughter from escaping the room.

Suddenly Jaqe grabbed Laurie's hand and pulled it under her T-shirt. When she felt that wonderful shape spreading out past the palm of her hand, the delicate hardness of the nipple against her fingertips, Laurie discovered herself shocked with joy, as if she'd never expected to feel this again. She lifted the T-shirt to kiss Jaqe's belly, then the skin just under and around the breasts, and finally the nipples, moving first one, then the other, with the tip of her tongue. As Laurie was getting undressed, she heard a faint sound, like a sigh or a moan, from the other room. She ignored it and got into bed to press herself against Jaqe, who wrapped her arms and one leg around her lover.

They froze in position at the sound of a knock on the bedroom door. "We're going," Mark called. A moment later, they heard the front door shut. "Just like a man," Laurie said, still whispering. "Always coming and going." They swallowed their laughter in a kiss, during which they lay sideways and rocked back and forth.

Abruptly, Jaqe pushed away from Laurie. "Go get it," she said softly.

Laurie made a kind of purring noise. "In a moment," she said. She tried to draw Jaqe close again.

Jaqe held up her hand as a barrier. "No," she said, "not now."

"It'll stay safe," Laurie insisted. "It's good for an hour."

"Please," Jaqe said. "I want to feel like it comes from you."

"What?"

"Hurry," Jaqe urged her, and Laurie scrambled off the bed and into the living room, where the syringe still lay on its napkin, but now filled with thick yellow-white liquid. Laurie had to stop herself from gagging as she picked it up. She was grateful that Mark had done the work of drawing it into the syringe, but she wished they didn't make turkey basters transparent.

When Laurie came back in the bedroom, Jaqe lay on her back with her legs apart and her knees up, and a pair of pillows under her ass. For a moment Laurie imagined Louise instructing Jaqe how to position herself, and her stomach spasmed with jealousy. But then she saw Jaqe's shy and frightened smile, and it struck her that Jaqe, like herself, was one of those rare lesbians who had never gone through a try at heterosexuality, who had never slept with a man. She sat down on the side of the bed and held Jaqe's hand briefly, while Jaqe turned her head so as not to lose sight of her. Laurie noticed that Jaqe's other hand gripped the stone Laurie had gotten from the girl at the beach.

"Ready?" Laurie said. Jaqe nodded, and Laurie took a breath. She didn't know why this seemed so difficult. It wasn't any more complicated than putting her fingers in Jaqe, was it? She bent down and touched the lips, sighing when Jaqe opened so easily.

Jaqe said, "Get it in as far as possible."

"Right." Silently, to the baster, Laurie said, *Okay, gang, do your stuff.*

Later, when Jaqe had fallen asleep, Laurie slid carefully out of bed, dressed, and went for a walk. Away from home, she felt able to breathe, really breathe, for the first time in hours. She walked to a nearby bridge that connected two of the city's boroughs across a filthy river. It was an old bridge, without lift or grace, painted a dreary gray. Because it was old, however, it still had a footpath, and Laurie could go out halfway and stand leaning over the railing to look at the water. She stood with her elbows on the rail, the top half of her body extended slightly over the water, not thinking, just watching. Down below she saw some small green shapes and thought they moved. *Turtles?* she wondered, but didn't think it was possible. From somewhere—she couldn't tell which side of the river—she heard a sudden growl of motorcycles.

A breeze swept across her face. She looked up suddenly, as if she'd see a girl fly past, with golden wings and a turkey beak instead of a nose. She saw only a seagull and, far above, a plane. When she lowered her eyes, she spotted a man walking toward her from the other side of the river. She turned and headed for home.

That night, Jaqe laughed in her sleep, a sound so amazing it woke

Laurie, who thought, as if it never had occurred to her before, how much she loved Jaqe, loved her all over again. Jaqe's eyes opened. She smiled when she saw Laurie. She said, "I dreamed you put a child inside me. She was all the way up in a tree—" She turned to look out the window. "That one, I guess. And you got her down and opened my belly and laid her right inside me. Then you closed me up and sprinkled some water on me. From a watering can." She laughed. Then she opened her mouth for Laurie to kiss her.

Five weeks later, when she was sure she'd missed her period, Jaqe went for a test. "You did it!" she told Laurie when her lover came home from work. Laurie only looked at her. "You did it," Jaqe repeated. "It worked. We're going to have a baby."

Three

The Child in the Water

A month went by, and the first major snow came and covered the city for two whole days. Below Jaqe and Laurie's window a dog leaped up and down in the snow, carried away with delight at the chance to run, free of cars and leashes. Two months passed, and the cold wind from the river drove the homeless out of their cardboard boxes and into the eternal light and noise of the shelters.

It was during the second month of Jaqe's pregnancy that Laurie asked her if she planned to tell her parents. "I don't know," Jaqe said. "I get scared just thinking about it."

"The thing is," Laurie said, "if you don't do it soon, they'll know as soon as they see you." Jaqe nodded. "Unless you want to tell them on the phone."

"No," Jaqe said. "No, I guess I don't want to do that."

"Then maybe we should go there pretty soon." Later, Laurie thought how she never would have expected herself to push Jaqe to visit her parents. Maybe, she thought, this baby thing wasn't so bad after all.

But when Jaqe finally did decide to tell her parents, she told Laurie she wanted to go alone. "Maybe it'll go a little easier," she said, "if I just see them by myself."

"Maybe it will," Laurie said.

"It's just this one time."

"Sure."

"I'm sorry, honey," Jaqe said. "I just want to—you know what they're like. And I haven't seen them in so long."

"It's okay," Laurie said. "Seeing your folks is not exactly my favorite treat."

Jaqe's parents picked her up at the train station on a cold day with the sky white with expectant snow. Jaqe had not seen them in a long time, she realized, not since before the trouble with Laurie's parents. On the train she'd wavered between telling herself they made it impossible and wondering if she could have done more to get them over their prejudice, or just accept them the way they were. When she saw them coming toward her on the platform she realized how much she feared they would have gotten sick, or aged terribly, in the few months she'd been away from them.

Her mother put her head on Jaqe's shoulder and hugged her so long Jaqe looked around to see if people were staring at them. Her father stood by, smiling as if for a photograph. *They know*, Jaqe thought. They could see it somehow. But then another thought came to her, and she felt a little queasy. *They think I've broken up with Laurie*. Gently she pushed her mother away, only to have her father give her a shorter, if more crushing, hug. "Come on," she said lightly. "Let's go. It's cold here."

"Welcome home, baby," her father said. He grabbed her overnight bag out of her hand.

Jaqe said, "Laurie sends her love."

Her father winced, but her mother managed to say, "I hope she's all right?"

"Of course," Jaqe said. "She just had to work. She's taking inventory in the bookstore."

Her mother made pot roast. "Your favorite," she told Jaqe. Jaqe didn't remember ever having a favorite dish—before she'd discovered her name everything had tasted alike to her—but she thanked her mother, who ran up and hugged her again before setting out the rolls and applesauce. Throughout dinner, Jaqe's parents talked constantly, sometimes both at once, her mother about neighborhood gossip, her father about local politics, crime rates in various places, and a Japanese company's plans to build an auto factory on the other side of the county. A couple of times they would ask Jaqe a question about school or Louise or the weather in the city. Her one-sentence answers satisfied them, and they jumped back into their monologues. Jaqe kept ordering herself to tell them, to break into their speeches with an announcement. When her mother offered her coffee and she asked for tea she thought of saying, "Coffee's bad for fetal development, you know," but she couldn't make herself do it.

After dinner, Mrs. Lang waved a hand at the table and told Jaqe they would leave the dishes. She said, "I always hope I'll come back in the kitchen and find some elf has done them for me." She tried to look meaningfully at her husband, but he'd already headed for the den to turn on the television.

On the screen a woman was telling jokes about rewinding her biological clock. A moment later she gave way to a desert scene and a husky voice announcing a "new generation" of automobile. Talking loud over the television, Jaqe told her parents she wanted to tell them something. They looked at each other, and then at her. "Could you turn the TV off?" Jaqe said. In the sudden silence she heard herself sigh. "Do you remember," she said, "when you told me you looked forward to having a grandchild?" Neither of them spoke. "I've decided to have a baby," Jaqe said.

"What?" her father said. "Oh, come on."

"Jacqueline—" her mother began, but stopped when her daughter said, "Jaqe."

"This is ridiculous," her father said. "You're joking, right?"

Mrs. Lang said, "You're not even married, honey. Don't you think that you should wait until you're married?" Her face lit up. "You haven't gotten married, have you?"

Jaqe thought of how if she was Louise she would say, "I married Laurie two years ago." Instead, she told her parents, "I don't need a husband to have a child."

"How are you going to support a child?" her father asked.

Her mother said, "Sweetheart, don't you think maybe this one time—just this once—you've gone a little too far? Don't you think that's a possibility?"

Mr. Lang said, "Can't you just finish school? You can decide stuff like that later."

"You don't understand," Jaqe said. "I've already decided. I'm pregnant."

"Jesus Christ," her father said.

"Dear," his wife said. "Please."

"She's pregnant and you're worried about my language?"

Jaqe's mother said to her, "Are you sure? You haven't made a mistake?"

"Of course I'm sure."

"How do you know?"

Jaqe thought of a cousin who'd once said, "A woman knows the moment it happens. She can feel the new life quicken inside her." Jaqe said, "The traditional method. I missed a period."

"There are many reasons you might—"

"Mom, I went to the doctor. The tests are positive."

"Excuse me," her father said, "but I was under the impression Laurie's a woman. She hasn't changed it to Laurence, has she?"

Mrs. Lang said, "Please, dear, don't make it worse."

"How can I?" he told her. "I'm just trying to figure this out." To Jaqe he said, "You mind telling us the father of our future grandchild?"

"There is no father," Jaqe said.

Mr. Lang rolled his eyes. "Now we're really in fantasyland. Let me tell you something, young lady, there are some things a man is still good for."

Jaqe said, "I did it by artificial insemination."

There was silence for a moment, then her mother said, "I didn't know they took . . ."

"Lesbians," Jaqe finished for her. "The word is lesbians." She thought how soon she'd start marching, carrying placards. She thought of a T-shirt: "Don't ask for a father. I did it with a turkey baster."

Her mother said, "How far—how many months?"

"Two months."

Mrs. Lang sighed. "Then it's not too late."

"Too late?"

"For an abortion. Usually I don't believe in them—"

"I'm not having an abortion," Jaqe said. She saw her mother cringe, and she realized she was shouting. She pushed her voice back down as she said, "I want this baby. I planned this baby. Artificial insemination does not happen by accident." It occurred to her that her parents might not believe her. They might assume she made up the AI story to save Laurie's honor, or even to deceive Laurie after she'd gone with some man and gotten caught.

Mrs. Lang said, "Please don't get angry. We're just worried for you. You read the papers."

"The papers? What have the papers got to do with it?"

"Well, all of the trouble with single-parent families."

"I am *not* a single parent."

Her mother started to cry, and her father slapped the arm of his chair. "Don't shout at your mother!" he shouted. Jaqe got up and began walking toward the doorway. "What are you doing?" her father said. He sounded more surprised than angry.

"Nothing," Jaqe said. "I'm going upstairs. I want to lie down."

Her mother ran after her. "Are you all right? Should we call the doctor?"

Jaqe laughed and shook her head. "I'm fine, Mom. I'm just tired."

"I guess you need your rest," Mrs. Lang said. She stood in the doorway of the den and watched Jaqe walk down the short hallway to the stairs.

Upstairs, Jaqe lay down for just a few seconds before she got up to find the photo album of herself as a child. She looked at the baby pictures, all of them, but none of that old urgency rose in her. Suddenly she became scared she'd made a terrible mistake. Could she change her mind, do what her mother said and get an abortion? She thought of all the trouble she'd made for Laurie, then realized Laurie would probably rejoice if Jaqe got rid of the baby. It's not fair, she thought. Doing everything alone. It's not right.

Don't panic, she told herself, *just don't panic*. Quietly, Jaqe put on her sneakers and her coat and slipped downstairs and out the front door. She took a couple of deep breaths before she hurried across the lawn and up the street, nervous her mother would spot her and come running with a few extra scarves or a hat. The road was slippery, with patches of ice that had melted in the day and then refrozen in the evening chill. Hugging herself against the wind, Jaqe walked to the place where she remembered seeing the women dancing that night. It was very hard to tell—so many months had passed. She bent down to the ground. Frowning, she traced her finger on what looked like very faint lines, the remnants of a drawing of a tree. With a pebble she scraped away some packed snow to reveal what looked like remains of a labyrinth. She reached in her jeans pocket for the stone Laurie had found on the beach. It looked the same—except for that clear picture of a child in the top branches.

The sound of a car behind her made Jaqe stand up and move to the side. A police car passed her, and she thought of the way the women had looked so startled when the patrol car disturbed their dance. She turned over the stone; she'd never really studied the other side, the one with the ferryman poling his boat along a river of white quartz. Funny, she thought, when you looked at it close, it all dissolved into meaningless lines, but when you just glanced at it, it was so clear.

Voices down the street made Jaqe look up to see a small group of people leaving a house and heading for their cars. In the dim light they all looked to Jaqe like skeletons. Skeletons in coats and boots, skulls in hats and earmuffs, laughing and chattering, bone hands opening car doors, skeleton arms sticking out of sleeves as they waved goodbye. Jaqe squeezed shut her eyes. When she looked again, skin and meat safely covered the bones. *God*, she thought, *I've got to get some rest*. And then, *Please. You promised to leave us alone. You promised.*

Three months passed, and Jaqe went into the park once more to stand under the tree. She wore a warm coat now, and a scarf Laurie had specially bought for her one night from a street vendor under a full moon. She walked around the tree until she found a single brown leaf, sodden with snow, lying right at the base of the trunk. Jaqe studied it, even taking off her gloves to trace the lines with her finger. She couldn't really see anything, and yet she found herself crying, with her shoulders quivering and her chest making soft hiccuping noises.

She felt a tap on her shoulder, and when she turned around a woman in a red coat and hat and a blue scarf smiled and held out a hand to her. Jaqe jumped back until she realized she didn't know the woman, who was simply smiling and holding out a small package of tissues. Jaqe smiled back, took a tissue, and blew her nose. When she realized she had crumpled the leaf, she dropped it and walked home.

Four months passed and the last snow came, replaced two days later by warm air like a soft blanket draped over a waking child. Patches of green replaced brown in the park. In the city's largest church, women dressed as gargoyles ran up and down the aisles shouting "Murderer!" at the priest. They threw fake blood on the organ and the altar and the statues of the saints.

Jaqe's mother called. She and Jaqe's father wanted to apologize, she said, for speaking "in the heat of the moment." She waited, as if Jaqe would say, "I'm sorry too, Mommy," but Jaqe said nothing.

Five months passed and young men dressed as medieval fools broke into a corporate meeting to invite the executives to a dance of life, a procession against disease. Jaqe went to her parents' for the weekend. She returned with a package of baby clothes from a cousin whose husband had gotten a vasectomy after their second child. When she got back she found a note from Laurie, who'd gone several hours earlier to play softball in the park.

Six months passed and the tree in the park grew berries, shiny red balls picked by birds and groups of foragers under the guidance of men in hiking boots, long pants, and shirts with long sleeves. In a bar one afternoon, Laurie complained to Louise about the breathing classes she had to go to with Jaqe. "It's not the exercises," she said. "It's the class itself. I mean, it's full of all those straights. Newlywed types. And yuppies. I don't know which is worse. The newlyweds are all smiles and glows, and the yuppies are all serious. Do everything right. Just like making the right career moves. And they're all straight. And married. None of them are even just living together. Can you believe it?"

"How do you know?" Louise asked.

"Because when the class started, the teacher called them all Mr. and Mrs. and nobody corrected them."

"Maybe some of them are lying."

Laurie shrugged. "Who the hell cares? We're still the only dykes in the whole class."

"Do you get any—"

"No, no one bothers us. Everyone pretends not to notice. No stares or smirks, everyone's happy to talk to us. They just have a little trouble figuring out what to *say*. I mean, the women don't know what to say because I'm not the one that's pregnant. And the men don't know because I didn't *make* her pregnant. And you know they're just wondering who the hell *did*."

Louise said, "You should come back to the DCC."

Laurie shrugged. "How can I? I'm not a student. I'm an old married woman."

"You don't need to be a student. We miss you."

"Half of you don't even know me."

"They've heard about you."

"Oh, great. The living legend." Laurie tried to sound disgusted, but Louise saw the way Laurie brushed back her hair with her hands, extending the long tapered fingers like combs.

Laurie leaned forward. "You know the worst? You want to know the worst?" Louise nodded. "The men are all so fucking caring. So sweet. And concerned. And dedicated. Shit, it's like they're all trying to be women. And you know something? They're doing a better job of it than I am. And I *am* a woman."

"I know," Louise said. "I noticed."

Laurie sighed. Not for the first time, not even the tenth, she thought of kissing Louise. She thought exactly how she would do it. She'd touch her hand and then maybe her leg, just above the knee, not long. Then maybe a stroke of her shoulder, the hand sliding down like slow water. They'd be smiling at each other by then, and by the time the kiss started it would come without any nerves. Exciting, oh yes, with all the thrill of that first time you kiss a woman. But no nerves. Inevitable. She looked at Louise and started to smile. And instead broke out laughing.

For a moment, Louise squinted at Laurie, then she too started to laugh. Laurie looked at her and shook her head, and Louise laughed again. "Come on, you old married woman," she said. "Let's go see Jaqe." They got up. "Maybe we can bring her some booties."

Seven months passed. Malcolm, a man in Jaqe and Laurie's building, began to talk to people who couldn't hear him. He'd read an article, he told Laurie, about how you could help people in comas by telling them the news, saying you loved them, telling them how everyone missed them. If it helps with comas, he thought, why not with other situations? He talked to news announcers on television, encouraging them to report good news. When he read a novel he talked to the characters, telling them they could make better lives for themselves. In a rainstorm one night, Laurie saw him standing in the street. The next day he told her how he'd stood there over an hour, just repeating "It's all right. It's okay. No one's going to hurt you. Calm down. It's okay."

"I know it sounds kind of weird," he told Jaqe, "but don't you and Laurie talk to the baby?"

"The baby's alive," Jaqe said.

"Well, sure, but it can't hear your voice. It probably wouldn't even understand English. Anyway, the rain is alive too."

One day he came running into their apartment, waving a book. "Look," he said, "look at this." The book was the *Tibetan Book of the Dead* and it explained how the Tibetans sit with their dead bodies and talk to the soul for forty-nine days.

Jaqe pulled Laurie into the bedroom. "Get him out of here," she whispered.

"Come on," Laurie said. "He doesn't mean anything. He's just excited."

"I don't care. Get rid of him."

Over the next weeks Malcolm took to slipping into funeral parlors late at night. He would claim to be a relative who couldn't sleep and wanted to sit with the body. All night he would whisper encouragement, assurances of a safe journey, of joy and adventures, interspersed with news, gossip, weather reports. Then he would slip out before morning and the arrival of the family.

When he got caught one day and the police allowed him a phone call, he called Laurie. Only, Laurie had left for work, and it was Jaqe who answered the phone. She refused to talk with him, said if he put the police on she'd claim she'd never heard of him. When he shouted at her, "Then just tell Laurie. Please!" Jaqe hung up.

Eight months passed. The berries on the tree grew plump and dark, almost heavy enough to drop off by themselves. Jaqe's blood pressure floated upward. She stopped eating salt and lay on the couch all day, watching the same cable news features over and over. Safety featured very strongly in these reports. A man had invented a personal shield, lightweight and easy to carry yet made of the same material and strength as police bulletproof vests. Various people interviewed said it sounded like a valuable adjunct to urban living, only they wondered if they could get it in front of them in time to stop the bullet.

Other news items stressed personal expression. A man wanted to draw pictures on the roofs of Jaqe's city. Looked at alone, each roof would contain meaningless lines and squiggles. But if you went up in an airplane—or better yet, a space station—the buildings would vanish and you would see spiders and trapezoids and crouched cats and ornamental circles on the wings of birds with human feet. "Messages for the ancestors," the man called the drawings and Jaqe imagined her great grandparents, and their parents, moving into abandoned space stations. The idea upset her, and she changed the channel.

A woman came to the door, and Jaqe had to get up. The woman wore shorts and a tank top, and carried a clipboard. She came, she said, to do a building census—how many units, how many apartments and how many storefronts or offices, how many occupied and unoccupied. She asked Jaqe, "Do you know if anyone has ever been born in this apartment?"

"Not yet," Jaqe said, and smiled as she looked down at her belly.

"Oh, wow," the woman said. "You must think I'm really dumb. Well, that's great. I mean, the baby."

"Thanks," Jaqe said.

"And do you know if anyone's ever died here?"

"No," Jaqe said. "And no one's going to."

"Hey," the woman said, "I didn't mean anything." She held her clipboard up as if it were a personal shield. "They just tell us what to ask. That's all."

"I've got to lie down," Jaqe said. She slammed the door.

At first she thought that the pain was in her side and that it came from slamming the door too hard. Only when she sat down on the edge of the bed and the pain jerked her backwards did she realize that the "thing," as Laurie called it, was happening. And then the pain vanished, and Jaqe just sat there, not sure what to do, wondering if it was real, if she should do anything. She realized she didn't want to call Laurie, she didn't want to hear Mark say that Laurie had gone out and he didn't know where. Or worse, she'd tell Laurie and Laurie would say she couldn't leave, she had to stock inventory or something.

It was warm that day, and even with the windows open, Jaqe was sweating. She gasped again, thinking it was the pain until she realized it was something else, the sound of a motorcycle. She went to close the window. With her hand on the wooden sash she looked down to see a child, a girl about seven in a ragged dress, playing hopscotch. All by herself, and with great concentration, the girl moved among the chalked squares, back and forth, as if her fate, or the fate of her family, depended on it. Jaqe began to cry, a deep longing that pushed its way through her body. And then the pain kicked her again and she knew she had to call Laurie.

Listening to Laurie almost made Jaqe start crying again. Laurie spoke in a wild rush, telling Jaqe to call the doctor, saying how much she loved her, how maybe they should meet at the hospital, and saying "Right, right" when Jaqe reminded her it would take hours before anything really serious happened. At least, she thought to herself, that's what the book said.

Mark sent Laurie home in a taxi. Laurie thought of the last time her parents had visited her, how they'd taken her and Jaqe to a French restaurant and given them cab fare home, which Laurie had wanted to spend at a disco and take the subway home, but Jaqe wouldn't let her. Sitting alone in the cab, Laurie missed her mother, even her father. She knew it was the fantasy she missed, the let's-pretend parents. "Even so," she whispered, "it was such a *good* fantasy." Now she was about to become a mother herself—or a father—or something. She couldn't believe it. What the hell was she going to do?

Labor lasted two days. Much, much too long, Laurie thought. She and Jaqe followed all the exercises, the breathing, the massage—nothing shook loose the *thing*. Laurie found she couldn't think of it as a baby, just as an object hurting Jaqe and making her scream. Even though the midwife kept rubbing Jaqe down and soothing her belly, and telling her she was fine, everything was okay, Laurie kept expecting some doctor to pull her aside and tell her Jaqe was lost, they could save the damn baby, but Jaqe was lost.

After two days, Laurie and the doctors decided to persuade Jaqe to agree to a cesarean. Jaqe might have agreed right away if the doctor who'd talked to her hadn't had red hair, and hadn't stood next to Laurie. "Leave her alone," Jaqe kept saying, and both Laurie and the doctor had assumed Jaqe meant the baby, and together they tried to reassure Jaqe that no one would harm the child. Jaqe just became more and more frantic. And then the doctor touched Laurie's arm, and Jaqe shouted, through her own jolt of pain, "Let go of her! She promised. I need her."

Laurie felt herself blush. "It's okay," she told the doctor. "She doesn't know—I mean, she usually—she's not jealous usually." She thought, *Shit, I can't stand this, I just can't stand it.*

The doctor smiled at Laurie, who blushed again. "It's all right," she said. "Women in labor are officially absolved from all responsibility for anything they say or do. Didn't anyone tell you that? We'll send in someone else."

After the operation, with Jaqe still unconscious, and the baby sleeping in the nursery, Laurie sat outside the coffee shop in the hospital lobby, with her head down and her elbows on her knees, and told Louise she felt ashamed. "I just feel, I don't know, I guess I feel unworthy. Does that sound crazy?"

Louise said, "Jaqe's a lot to be worthy of. But even Jaqe can say something dumb. Especially when she's screaming in pain."

"Yeah, I know, I know," Laurie said. "The thing is—" Her back curved lower, as if she wanted to hide between her own legs. "The thing is, she was right."

"What?"

"I mean, I didn't *do* anything. I don't even know the woman. But I thought about it."

"Well, so what?" Louise said.

"Shit, there's Jaqe shrieking in pain, out of her mind almost, and I'm sizing up some hot number."

"Come on, you don't even know if she was gay."

Laurie shrugged. "She was," she said, and Louise laughed. "Anyway, that's not the point. I was thinking about her, and not about Jaqe."

"Oh sure," Louise said, "you've got to think about Jaqe every moment. Goddess help you if you fantasize about someone else."

"When she's in pain like that, shouldn't I be thinking about her?"

"Weren't you? Haven't you made yourself sick thinking about Jaqe?"

"I guess so," Laurie said. "Sometimes it seems like all I really think about is me."

"It's called being human. Women are human. Men are allowed to think of themselves all the time, but not women. We're supposed to put everyone else first."

Laurie said, "Spare me, okay? You know, the whole time Jaqe was there, groaning and grabbing hold of me, I just kept wishing I was somewhere else. I kept feeling like everyone was staring at me—because I wasn't a man. I kept wishing I could run away. Or wave a magic wand."

"Women don't use magic wands. We use cauldrons."

Laurie smiled. "Yeah. Poor Jaqe. She sure could have used a magic cauldron. Or something. And those goddamn breathing exercises. They didn't do shit."

"You're just scared," Louise said. "And that's okay."

"Is it? What are Jaqe and I going to do with a child?"

"What anybody else does. Raise her. Go goo-goo. Bounce her on your knee. Dress her in ruffles and wheel her proudly through the neighborhood."

"Thank God at least it's a girl."

"Goddess," Louise said, and they both laughed again.

"Give me a hug," Louise said. Laurie looked around. "Don't worry about it," Louise told her. "No one's going to care if you and I hug each other. And I give you permission to fantasize about me. All you want. Because I'm sure going to fantasize about you." Laurie laughed again, and reached out for Louise. With her arms around Laurie, Louise whispered, "Congratulations, Mom."

Laurie grinned. "Don't call me that," she said. "Just don't call me that."

Near Laurie and Louise, a group of men in black suits and black felt hats sat around an older man with a gray-white beard that reached halfway down his chest. The older man wore a top hat, as if at a wedding. When he stood up, one of the younger men bent forward and kissed the older man's hand.

While Laurie looked at the men with a fascinated disgust, Louise went over to them. Though the young men formed a loose wall between Louise and their leader, Louise managed to peer through them. "My friend's just become a mother," she said, "and she's kind of nervous. Do you think you could bless her?"

"Louise!" Laurie cried, and ran to yank her away. The men said nothing, just stared curiously after them.

In the recovery room, the light hurt Jaqe's eyes. She saw a woman in a rag dress, holding open her arms, smiling. Jaqe wanted to run to her, but she couldn't move. She'd eaten, or drunk, something, and now she couldn't even find her legs. The woman's hair looked on fire, her arms gigantic. "No!" Jaqe screamed, and heard her own voice in a whisper. "I won't go."

"Honey?" came a voice. "Sweetie? It's me."

"Laurie?" Jaqe said. She managed to reach up a hand. Laurie grabbed it before it fell. "Hi," Jaqe said, feeling dumb. She wondered if Laurie was crying. The lights and the noise made it hard to see. Laurie bent over and kissed her fingertips—not at all the way she'd done it that first time, but still it reminded her, and she smiled.

"How are you feeling?" Laurie asked.

"Okay, I guess. Where's the baby? I want her."

"She's fine," Laurie said. "She's in the nursery."

"She's okay? They haven't found anything wrong, have they?"

"She's perfect. She weighs six pounds and seven ounces. She has squiggly little hands and toes, and right now she's fast asleep, dreaming of her mommy."

Jaqe tried to laugh—Laurie talking like that!—but it hurt, and she made herself stop.

With an effort, Jaqe moved herself a little to the side. "Come in bed," she ordered, patting the sheets.

Laurie said, "Come on, honey, I can't—"

"Oh, be quiet," Jaqe said. "No one's going to mind. If you don't come hug me, I'll shout and open my stitches."

Laurie sat on the bed with one leg up and the other on the floor, like someone in an old movie before they relaxed the code. She put her arms around Jaqe, who rolled her upper body against Laurie's breasts—almost, Laurie thought, like a baby hungry for milk.

Four

The Child in the Street

They named the baby Kathryn. Kathryn Alice Lang. Kate, Jaqe insisted, not Kathy, not Katy, just Kate. They'd chosen the name before the birth, of course, just as Jaqe had insisted they get Mark's lawyer to write them a paper appointing Laurie the child's guardian "if anything, you know," as Jaqe put it.

Otherwise, Jaqe had said, her parents would try to grab the baby for themselves. At the time, they both knew that Laurie would give the baby to Mr. and Mrs. Lang the first chance she got. Just as they knew that Laurie hardly cared what they were going to call the child. Now, however, as she and Louise stood looking through the nursery window, Laurie found herself saying, "She really looks like a Kate, doesn't she?" She blushed at Louise's loud laugh. "No, I mean it," she said.

"I'm sure you do," Louise told her.

"I mean, look at her hands. Like she can't wait to grab hold of something. That's kind of a Kate thing, isn't it? And look at that red hair."

"I just love her hair," Louise said. "It's so gorgeous."

"Do you see any other kids with red hair? Red hair and Kate. Perfect combination."

Jaqe didn't think so. The first time she saw her daughter after the C-section, when she was fully conscious, before she even touched her, she said to Laurie, "How did she get red hair?" as if someone had played a trick on her.

"Well," Laurie said, "your hair's blond, so she clearly didn't get it from you. And I'm a brunette. So that leaves only one candidate."

"Why didn't you tell Mark I didn't want anyone with red hair?" Jaqe was crying now. Laurie remembered the stuff in the pregnancy books about postpartum depression, and she began to wonder, frantically, if they could give Jaqe hormones or something. *Goddess*, she thought, *spare us this one. Please?*

The nurse smiled. "Why don't you hold her?" she said. Before Jaqe could say anything, the nurse placed the baby in her arms.

Later, Laurie reported to Louise, "It was like a magic trick. Like the baby had some kind of magic wand or something."

"I keep telling you . . ." Louise said.

Laurie laughed. "I know, I know. The wands are for boys. Girls have cauldrons and boxes."

The first time Jaqe held Kate—nervously, and then more firmly when she discovered her daughter's strength and solidness—that first time Jaqe probably would have been happy just to hold and touch her, or maybe delicately kiss her forehead. Kate, however, had other ideas, reaching for her mother's breast with a sureness that said, "Finally. No more imitations."

Jaqe looked up at the nurse. "What do I do?"

"Don't worry," the woman said. "Your daughter will take care of it." At first, Jaqe cried out, more in surprise than pain, at how hard Kate was sucking on her. But then, as Kate settled in to taking care of it, Jaqe found her free hand stroking the baby's head, even following the tight red swirls with her fingertips. She sighed, and let her body sink deeper into the bed.

Jaqe's parents noticed the baby's red hair as well, though the curls seemed to strike them more than the color. "What a head of hair," Mr. Lang said. "Sure isn't like Jaqe's."

"Dear . . ." his wife cautioned him, as if they'd rehearsed platitudes in the car. She then added, "It really is curly, isn't it?"

Later, standing in the hall with Laurie, Mr. Lang said, "Tell me something, Laurie, just between you and me—" (Man to man, Laurie thought.) "What kind—what sort of a person are we talking about here?"

"Who?" Laurie said.

"You know who I mean. You know, the father. What kind of genes are we talking about here?"

"Oh, him," Laurie said. Don't play, she warned herself. It struck her suddenly how much she *needed* these people. "Actually," she said, "I don't know."

"What do you—you don't know?"

"That was the deal. Jaqe and I don't know his name; he doesn't know ours."

"But how did you—we thought—"

"My boss arranged it."

"Some company you work for. That's a hell of a fringe benefit."

Laurie made herself laugh. "I guess so. I never thought of it like that. But Mark's more than a boss. He's like a best friend." Or a brother, she thought. Or a father?

"And you trust him?"

"Absolutely."

"He wouldn't pick any—anyone unsuitable?" Laurie shook her head. So did Mr. Lang. "I guess I just don't understand this." Laurie thought, *No one asked you to.* "And what if the baby wants to know who her father is? You and Jaqe can't even tell her. Do you think that's right?"

Laurie's hand clumped into a fist, but she kept her voice calm. "We talked about that," she said. "With AI in the clinics—artificial insemination—they keep the names on file, the donors. Except they don't release it until the child is eighteen and can ask for herself. So that's what we're doing. Mark put the name and everything in a safe deposit box, in a kind of trust for Kathryn. Until she's eighteen. If she wants it. That seemed fair."

"Fair," Mr. Lang repeated. "Jesus. Look," he said, "I'm sorry. If I've said the wrong thing. It's just—I'm just not used to it. All this stuff. We didn't do things like this—" He stopped.

"In your day?" Laurie said. Mr. Lang's face tightened. And then he saw Laurie's grin, and he started to snicker. And then the two of them were laughing, while inside Jaqe's room someone made a burbling noise and the baby cried, for just a moment.

Jaqe and Kate stayed in the hospital five days. They might have left sooner, but Jaqe's blood pressure leaped upward after the surgery, and even though it went down again, her doctor wanted to monitor her for a while. Laurie visited them on her lunch hours and every evening, telling herself she couldn't wait to get them home again so she wouldn't have to run around. And yet, she knew it gave her a kind of peace to know exactly what she needed to do. In the hospital, it made her nervous every time she had to learn something new with Kate—to burp her or give her a bottle if Jaqe needed to sleep, to change her diaper, even just to hold her for the first time. She kept feeling like she should know what to do, and that everyone—the nurses, Jaqe's mother, even Jaqe—would laugh at her clumsiness or talk about her when she went home.

At the same time it amazed her how wonderful it was just to hold the baby, to spread her hands across that tiny compact body, to feel the weight against her chest and shoulder. One evening, she was holding Kate and sitting in the chair alongside Jaqe's bed when the baby began to cry, and a moment later began groping for Laurie's breast. Laurie rushed Kate over to Jaqe, who was laughing and wincing from the surgery at the same time. "It's okay," Jaqe told Laurie, and then motioned her closer to whisper, "I know how she feels. I miss sucking them myself. In fact," she said, "why don't you—" She began to unbutton Laurie's shirt.

Laurie jumped back. "You can't do that," she said.

"Why not? The curtains are up. No one will see."

"Not so loud," Laurie whispered. "Suppose the nurse comes in?"

"Then we'll stop," Jaqe said, and laughed again.

"But you're feeding the baby."

Jaqe laughed louder, then groaned and reached with her free hand to hold her belly. She said, "I love it when you act puritan."

On the day Jaqe and the baby came home from the hospital, Louise volunteered to clean the apartment. When they came inside they found that Louise and some of the other women had set out baskets of fruit and strung the walls with ribbons and banners of welcome and congratulations. A vase of flowers and a giant bowl of fruit sat on either end of the table, with a giant stuffed lion between them. The lion, golden with a black mane, sat back on its haunches, with its front paws held forward. A note around its neck said, "Hi! I'm Nora (short for Leonora). Louise sent me to welcome you home and stand guard over Kate and her two sweet mommies." While Laurie held Kate, Jaqe hugged the lion and kissed its nose. "Thanks, Nora," she said. "Happy to have you in the family."

"Why don't you get in bed?" Laurie said. "I don't want you getting sick."

"That's okay," Jaqe told her. "Nora will protect me."

"Great," Laurie said. She thought, *A crummy job, a tiny apartment, and a baby. But at least I've got a stuffed lion.* She looked at the toy. She thought, *I sure as hell wish you could protect us. Maybe you'll come alive at night while we sleep, and clean the house, and feed Kate, and go out and hunt food for us.* But Kate started to cry as soon as Laurie put her down in the crib Jaqe's parents had bought for them, and Laurie knew she better fix the problem, whatever it was, before Jaqe insisted on taking care of it instead of resting. Laurie realized how hungry she was, and how she had no time to eat, no time for anything.

Over the next three months, the people around Jaqe and Laurie gave different reasons for Kate's almost constant crying. Colicky, some said. Diaper rash, others claimed. A test of wills, the pediatrician suggested, which only caused Jaqe to insist they find another doctor. "I'm not having my daughter described as a tyrant," she said. Louise thought that maybe Kate had brought some great truth into the world, some mystery of the womb or even earlier, and now could not understand why nobody would listen to her. Others considered the crying existential or maybe political—outrage against the powerlessness of babies. Mark described the problem as "temperament."

"That's a big help," Laurie told him. "So now you're telling me she's going to be like this no matter what we do, and *in fact—*" Her voice rose, and she feared she would become hysterical, a possibility that filled her with shame as well as fear. "We better *not* do anything, because any attempt to shut her up will just be stifling her natural *personality.*"

The fact is, Laurie did not really care why Kate cried so much, often refusing to sleep for more than twenty minutes at a time. She just wanted it to stop. She needed to sleep, she told herself. She would sell her soul, if she had one, just for one uninterrupted night. "Hell," she told Mark, "is made up entirely of young mothers. They've got to pretend it's a bad deal when God or the tourists come around, but otherwise they just sleep the whole time, or else they sit around and discuss current events, and sip mint juleps."

And yet it wasn't just the exhaustion, or the destruction of her time with Jaqe, that drove the panic through Laurie's body. Instead, it was terror that she just couldn't *do* it. That this endless series of tests would expose her inadequacy. She thought of single mothers, of fathers, especially fathers, who managed to keep it all rolling forward, and she thought if they could do it—if men, whose bodies weren't even tuned for babies, could do it—what the hell was wrong with her?

She remembered stories she'd read as a kid where the evil king or stepmother (was she a stepmother? she wondered. An assistant mother? A vice mother?) challenges the princess with impossible tasks. Find a sliver of gold in a huge pile of straw. Bring all the water from the bottom of the mountain up to the top. The tasks all had to be done at night, in a single night. With a fury that amazed her, Laurie thought how the goddamn princesses had it easy, for, win or lose, the test finished by morning. And the animals they'd befriended earlier in the story would do the work. Groundhogs or something found the gold. Flocks of pelicans carried up the water. So that's the problem, Laurie thought. She forgot to do good deeds for animals. Now there was nobody to help her.

Maybe if Jaqe hadn't come home still weak from the surgery, she would have done more those first few weeks and Laurie could have relaxed. Or maybe Jaqe did do her share, more than her share, for as well as nursing, Jaqe got up more when the baby cried, and changed her more. Or maybe she didn't. Laurie discovered she couldn't tell, she just could not measure it all. Nor did it really matter, for even when it was Jaqe who got up, Laurie still lay awake, listening first to

Kate's crying and then to the silence, waiting for the crying to start up again as soon as Jaqe would turn away, like someone listening to a drip from the ceiling and finding the silence more unbearable than the sound of water striking the pail.

One night, during a break with Kate asleep, Laurie put on the all-news TV station. To her disgust, they had finished the current headlines and gone on to feature a special on "children having children." Laurie surprised herself by watching it. Along with the statistics and the poignant stories, and the middle-aged men speaking darkly of welfare's burden on the middle class, there were stories of mothers beating their babies and fathers running away from home. Laurie wondered which category she might fall under.

Later that night she went to a bar, the first time since Kate and Jaqe had come home that Laurie had gone anywhere except to work and the supermarket. She knew she shouldn't do it; Jaqe hadn't fully recovered, even after three months, and in fact had been feeling flushed lately, so that Laurie was afraid Jaqe might be coming down with something. But Kate was sleeping—over an hour so far—and it was Laurie's day off, which meant that Jaqe had gotten some real rest and probably could handle it if the baby woke up. Laurie wrote Jaqe a note, saying she was going out for a short while, the baby was fine, and she loved Jaqe, whom she called "sweet cushion" (after her habit of sleeping with her head against the side of Jaqe's breast).

When Laurie went inside to lay the note on the pillow, Jaqe looked so sweet, with her lips puckered out slightly as if offering a kiss, that Laurie almost took off her clothes and got in bed beside her. But the idea of staying home panicked her. It seemed like a challenge, or a last chance. Whether she wanted to go or not, if she stayed home now she was lost. And besides, she told herself, Jaqe needed to sleep.

In the bar, Laurie drank so much vodka and cranberry juice that she had to throw up in the ladies' room. It was like some self-fulfilling prophecy, she thought, not even sure what she meant. She hated being sick, and she hated even more the extra burden of fear that now came with it. What if she got really sick, and couldn't take care of them, couldn't work? She didn't even have medical insurance. Jaqe's parents paid for insurance for Jaqe and the baby, putting them on their family plan as if Laurie didn't exist, and there was nothing Laurie could do about it. But she herself had no coverage at all.

When she thought she probably didn't have to throw up anymore,

Laurie flushed the toilet and wiped the bowl with a wad of toilet paper. On the way out she passed a woman about eighteen years old, dressed in a tight leather miniskirt and leaning toward the mirror over the sink to put on dark red lipstick. Laurie wasn't sure, but she thought the woman stopped to smirk as Laurie passed her.

Outside, a little girl about seven or eight years old, with red hair, was playing hopscotch on a pattern drawn in pink chalk on the sidewalk. The girl wore yellow jeans with rolled-up cuffs and a blue T-shirt covered with gold stars and crescent moons. A bright green barrette in the shape of a frog held back her hair, whose redness made Laurie wonder if this was what Kate would look like in a few years. She frowned. Kate was prettier, she thought. This girl was okay, but Kate . . . She looked down at the ground, as if someone passing might catch her thoughts and laugh at her.

She lifted her head again to watch the girl play. Instead of numbers, the girl had drawn crude pictures in each of the boxes. Some were recognizable, like a crude tree or a stick figure of a bird. Others appeared like abstract circles or squares crossed by squiggly lines. Maybe, Laurie thought, they represented characters the girl considered perfectly obvious.

The child played the game a little differently than Laurie remembered. She would toss something—a piece of bone it looked like—then hop after it, mouthing some jingle or formula, to the square where it fell and bend down to pick it up while still standing on one foot. Without turning around, she would make her way back again, hopping backwards through the squares to the bare sidewalk.

Laurie looked at her watch. Ridiculous, she thought. A kid her age shouldn't be out so late. Where was her mother? God, she thought, a parent three months, and she was judging other people's failures. Besides, the child looked perfectly safe and happy. Except, Laurie thought, she appeared frustrated with her performance. She seemed to do something wrong each time she picked up the bone, some offense against her private rules which brought out a sigh or a roll of the eyes, before she would retreat out of the pattern. Laurie wondered if the goal of the game might be to go all the way through the pattern and out the other side, and some mistake or other always forced the girl to back out instead of continuing.

Maybe, Laurie thought, she should wait until the girl finished, and then see if she needed help getting home. Somehow, the thought of seeing the child leap triumphantly out the far end of the pattern caused a twitch in Laurie's fragile stomach. Anyway, she told herself, she couldn't hang around. Her own family needed her. *Her* family. For once, the thought pleased her, and she walked a little more lightly, despite the queasiness.

The closer she got to home, the more worried she became. Suppose something had happened when she was out drunk? Suppose the baby had started screaming and Jaqe had leaped up too fast and hurt herself?

When she got home Jaqe was sitting on the couch, asleep, with Kate resting against her breast. Kate must have woken up, rousing Jaqe from bed, and then when Kate quieted down again, Jaqe had fallen asleep where she was sitting. They looked so . . . so *honest,* Laurie thought. Not at all like the images of mother and child you saw on TV, where the woman always appeared perfectly made up and looking like she slept fourteen hours a day, with soft music playing. Jaqe's face looked slightly mottled, and her lips pushed out like Kate's did when she was getting ready to attach herself to Jaqe's breast.

Funny, Laurie thought, how you think of yourself as a child until you get one of your own. Like being wrenched inside out, a mirror image of who you used to be. Except somehow you start looking like a child. She imagined Jaqe's face looking like that when she was, oh, six months old. The thought made her want to wrap her arms around both of them and squeeze them as tight as she could—except that Kate would just start screaming.

Besides, Laurie knew she stank. Shame rushed through her. She hurried to the bathroom to strip off her clothes and wash her face and brush her teeth.

Back in the living room, Laurie kneeled by the side of the couch, watching Jaqe's face quiver as she breathed. Jaqe had on the bathrobe Laurie had given her to wear in the hospital. The once-gleaming white robe was now pink, from the time Laurie had washed it in the same load with Jaqe's red jeans. Stains spotted it as well, though whether from the baby throwing up or just from Jaqe trying to eat while holding her daughter, Laurie couldn't tell. Jaqe hadn't knotted the robe very tightly, so that Laurie just had to spread the flaps slightly to expose Jaqe's belly and much of her breasts.

Laurie moved around to the front of the couch, where she squatted with her legs slightly apart. The posture spread her vaginal lips enough that she could smell her own arousal. She had to press her mouth closed to keep from laughing. As softly as she could, Laurie ran a finger from below Jaqe's throat and down her chest to her belly, just above her scar. Laurie closed her eyes. Pregnancy had made Jaqe's soft skin smoother than ever, and the—release—of the baby had not changed that. Laurie tried to think of a metaphor for Jaqe's skin, but nothing was adequate, certainly not butter or silk.

She moved the tip of her finger back and forth between the inner line of Jaqe's breasts, pressing them to feel the springiness against her fingertips. She wondered how much she could do without waking Jaqe up, and how little it would take—just touching the sides of her breasts? licking them? licking the aureole around the nipple? the nipple itself?—to move her own body to orgasm. Maybe she could slide open the bottom of the robe and move her face or at least her lips along Jaqe's thighs to just below the crotch, without actually waking her.

But it was Kate who woke up. She opened her eyes and instead of crying or moving her hands she only turned her head slightly to stare at Laurie, as if she were studying her. Laurie tried to stare back until Kate's unflinching steadiness turned her away.

Now Jaqe woke up too, with a sputtering noise and a squeezing of her eyes before she opened them fully. She jerked her head to the side, as if to make sure Kate was there. Only when she confirmed that her child was all right did she move her gaze to discover Laurie squatting naked in front of her. "Wow," she said, "I hope you didn't go out like that."

Laurie was so relieved that Jaqe wasn't angry with her that she nearly fell backward onto the thin rug. She said, "I was just . . . umm . . . my clothes were dirty."

Jaqe nodded. "So you got rid of them. A wise policy."

Jaqe didn't seem to notice that Kate was staring at Laurie. Jaqe herself was staring, though with a lot more expression than her daughter, and Laurie felt like someone had put her on display. She was about to give up and get dressed, when Jaqe reached out and said, "Give me your hand."

Jaqe pressed Laurie's hand against her own mouth, sucking with her open lips while she licked the hollow of Laurie's palm. Laurie cried out with her eyes closed. She would have fallen over if Jaqe had not been holding her.

Jaqe moved Laurie's hand down to her breast, rolling the palm around the nipple. "Oh God," Laurie whispered. Without taking her hand away, Laurie waddled forward so she could bend over and kiss the side of Jaqe's belly, careful to avoid the scar. She moved away when Jaqe moaned.

Jaqe said, "I like that. Why did you stop?"

Laurie said, "I thought maybe I was getting too close. You know, to your surgery."

Jaqe pulled her back. She said, "That sound you heard was pleasure. The same goes for any unexpected movements. I promise to let you know if you're hurting me."

Laurie felt flickers of movement through her body, the distant beginnings of orgasm. Instead of kissing Jaqe's side, however, she glanced the other way, where Kate was still watching her, empty of any expression except maybe curiosity. Laurie said, "Maybe we should put the baby away."

Jaqe glanced at her daughter. "Do we have to?" she said. "She's quiet right here."

"Well, what if we're . . . in the middle of it, and she wakes up?"

"The middle of it?" Jaqe repeated. "What do you think she'll do? Report us?" She laughed at Laurie's shocked expression. "Sweetie," she said, reaching out to stroke Laurie's brush haircut, "don't be so squeamish. Do you really think Kate would understand anything that's going on? And even if she did, it's only love, isn't it? You're not a Freudian, are you? You don't think Kate secretly desires me, and wants to do away with you?"

Laurie looked again at the baby, averting her eyes quickly from that steady gaze. "No, of course not," she said. "But suppose we're . . ."

"Making love? Screwing? Licking and sucking?"

"Making love," Laurie said. "And suppose she does get uncomfortable. Or suppose you wanted to change position."

"Or thrash around," Jaqe said.

"Or thrash around." Laurie stood up. "Why don't I put her to bed, and then we can do whatever we want." She thought to herself, *Until she starts screaming.*

Jaqe sighed, but she was smiling as well. She held the baby up to Laurie. "Here," she said. "Maybe you should give her her pacifier. Then she can have something to suck on, too."

In the bedroom, Laurie laid the baby in the crib the Langs had given them. It seemed too warm to tuck her in, so she just made sure

Kate could reach her stuffed toad and turtle. (Kate had never shown any fondness for Nora the lion, so instead of living in the privileged zoo of the crib, Nora remained in the world, standing guard over the room from the top of a chest of drawers.) Laurie checked to make sure that Kate's feet could reach the mobile of musical spheres hanging from the ceiling. Finally she gave her the rainbow-colored pacifier Louise had given them, Kate's favorite. Throughout this process, Kate didn't make a sound, leading Laurie to bend over and examine her as well as check for fever.

Instead of rushing back to Jaqe, Laurie went to piss, then washed her hands and face, telling herself she wanted to get everything taken care of for their first chance in so long. All the same, she thought, why couldn't they just have gone right on and *done* it when they were both so hot? Guiltily, she reminded herself that she was the one who'd wanted to get rid—to put the baby to bed. But it was Jaqe who'd wanted the baby in the first place. Without Kate they wouldn't have to worry about someone else, a third party, when they wanted to do something that was supposed to involve just the two of them.

Laurie closed her eyes to picture Jaqe. She wanted to remember her before she saw her, remember the way her skin had looked when she was asleep, the feel of Jaqe's nipple against her palm. She smiled as her skin tingled and a pulsing began between her legs. She nodded her head and swayed slightly to her own rhythm. She laughed, trying not to make noise. She was ready.

But when she came in the room, Jaqe said to her, "Did you make sure she was on her side?"

Shit, Laurie thought. They were supposed to keep the baby from lying on her stomach because of SIDS, Sudden Infant Death Syndrome. Medical researchers had found that fifty percent (or something, Laurie couldn't remember the actual number) of SIDS babies had been lying on their stomach when their mothers found them. So even though they had no idea what this meant, if anything at all, Jaqe insisted they keep Kate on her side or her back if they were going to be out of the room and she was likely to fall asleep. The problem was, Kate liked being on her belly. As soon as they turned away she would flip herself over, sometimes doing it again and again, and laughing, like it was a game. They could prop her up, using pillows and stuffed animals to hold her, but even if the baby didn't manage to shove them away, Laurie wondered if the props themselves might be more dangerous than the remote chance of the mysterious SIDS. And besides, maybe Kate would sleep longer if they let her find her own position.

"She's fine," Laurie said. "She's wide awake."

"But she's so quiet. If I can't hear her, I'll just worry all the time." Laurie sighed loudly and headed back to the bedroom, where she propped Kate against the side of the crib with a rolled blanket. She had to smile at Kate's burbly look, her roundness and pliancy. Stroking her bottom, Laurie imagined herself turning into a giant bird and lifting the baby high above the smoke and anger of the city to carry her to some far land where no one ever cried or got sick, or needed to run away into sleep ever again. Maybe that was how stories got started, she thought. Out of longing and fear.

When Laurie returned again to the living room, Jaqe asked, "Is everything okay?"

"She's fine," Laurie said. "Sucking on her rainbow stick and staring out the window."

Jaqe smiled and held out her arms. "Then come here," she said. "Right now." Instead of kneeling on the floor again, Laurie sat down alongside Jaqe. Taller, she had to slide back a little to put her head on Jaqe's shoulder while Jaqe hugged her.

"Kiss," Jaqe said, and Laurie sat up to hold Jaqe's face in her hands while she kissed her. Jaqe moved a hand down Laurie's spine until she found the spot where a sharp press jolted Laurie's body so that her skin nearly bruised Jaqe as she arched away.

Laurie reached forward to hug Jaqe very tightly before she opened her mouth wide on Jaqe's neck, moving her whole head in a circular motion while sliding her tongue across the skin. Jaqe cried out and scratched her fingernails along Laurie's back.

It seemed to Laurie as if she was speeding up—moving from Jaqe's neck to her side, and then under her breasts, and then to her nipples—much faster than she really wanted. It's because of the baby, she told herself. Kate could start crying at any moment and they'd have to stop with their bodies surging. But she knew it wasn't just Jaqe's daughter. It was as if they had to follow a magical performance, and any mistake would ruin everything.

Jaqe wasn't worried at all. When Laurie slowed slightly, circling around the middle of Jaqe's breasts with her tongue, Jaqe just settled deeper into the couch, smiling happily and making soft noises, more like her daughter than ever, like an enlarged photo. Then, when Laurie speeded up again, licking Jaqe's right nipple and moving the left with her finger, Jaqe began to push against her, turning sideways so she could lift a leg to go around Laurie's waist.

Laurie thought how sucking Jaqe's nipple was something else lost because of the baby. She used to love pulling really hard so that the nipple would slide through her slightly open teeth. But now milk would squirt out, and even if Laurie had not minded the extreme sweetness, the flow of liquid confused her.

So she moved her mouth to Jaqe's thighs, kissing first one then the other, until she moved her whole face against Jaqe's vulva, holding the thighs open and apart with her hands. Jaqe let out a yell, muffled to avoid alarming the baby, but still a yell, of joy, or triumph, or maybe just power.

Laurie felt her own rush of power when another swallowed cry and a flexing of Jaqe's thighs signaled her orgasm. They had done it, Laurie thought. *She* had done it: outlasted, outwitted, outsmarted their three-month-old daughter.

But the push inside her own body seemed to evaporate, and when Jaqe finally told her, "No, stop," Laurie just sat back and sighed, holding back when Jaqe tried to pull her close, until she realized that Jaqe might ask what was wrong, a question she didn't want to have to answer. It was just timing, she told herself as Jaqe kissed her with a wide wet kiss that slid over half her face. They could get away with one of them, but there was no way the baby would let both of them go through to orgasm. As Jaqe continued to kiss her, Laurie found herself listening for the baby as if for the sounds of a rescuer.

And then something happened. Jaqe had her arms around Laurie and was kissing her cheek, her ear, tickling Laurie a little like the way you might tickle a child, when suddenly Laurie remembered something she often forgot, even before Kate, which was how it felt to let Jaqe take over, to give up directing what Jaqe should do to her, and what she would do to Jaqe, and instead just slide fully into Jaqe's hands and mouth and belly and legs. The very thought stroked her with excitement, and when Jaqe ran her fingernails from Laurie's thighs all the way up Laurie's back, she felt that movement that begins at the toes and swirls upward, pausing at the groin to gain strength before it reaches up through the breasts, ready to burst, before it flows out the face and the top of the head.

For a second, Laurie wanted to tell Jaqe to lick her nipples or just to offer them, arching her chest toward Jaqe's mouth, but then she remembered again. Do nothing. Nothing. Become a leaf, or just a breath, lifted in the wind of orgasm.

Jaqe pushed her thigh up between Laurie's legs, not harshly but with enough force for Laurie to cry out. And yes, the sound brought the baby's yell—of competition, or curiosity, or just coincidence. For once, however, Jaqe did not jump up, but in fact whispered to Laurie, "It's okay. We can just let her cry, it's all right." For Laurie it didn't matter; she was beyond worry other than the fear that Jaqe might stop, and she didn't have to fear that at all, for now Jaqe slid two fingers deep into Laurie's vagina, far enough that the heel of her hand covered Laurie's clitoris. Laurie didn't know if she was crying or just breathing raggedly. Instead of moving them in and out, Jaqe wiggled her fingers and vibrated her hand. Laurie cried out again as her back and legs arched and her fingernails dug into Jaqe's sides. (An image flashed in Laurie's mind, the taut bow of the Moon Goddess, who shoots her silver arrows of healing deep into women's bodies.)

It was the kind of orgasm that is always new, always something you've never experienced before, even when you know you have, and in fact even when you remember that exact feeling of newness. And Jaqe let her ride it, with Jaqe's fingers now pushing deeper and harder in time with the undirected movement of Laurie's hips (or was it the other way around?), while Kate called out to them, her gulping cries in perfect time with Laurie's thrusts.

Laurie could tell the exact moment the rhythm broke. It wasn't Kate but Jaqe who broke it. "I'd better go see how she is," Jaqe whispered, and slid her body away from Laurie, who until that moment had thought she could go on for hours. As if a spell had broken, Kate's magical song reverted suddenly to the shrieks that had knifed through Laurie's head for three months. Or maybe the spell hadn't just collapsed. Maybe Jaqe had snapped it deliberately. Watching Jaqe close her bathrobe, like a grease-stained shield of modesty, Laurie wondered if Jaqe had sensed the flow between Laurie and Kate, and blocked it, wanting to keep her place as the pivot between them.

The thought depressed her, and she wished she could gulp it back, like someone literally swallowing her words. But the more she assured herself that Jaqe would never do such a thing, the more ashamed she felt for thinking it. She was just tired, she knew. Worn down by a constant wind of screaming.

The cries stopped, and Laurie assumed Jaqe was feeding, the only time when Kate stayed constantly quiet. Laurie got up, feeling almost as sick now as when she'd come home. She remembered how it used to be after sex. The quiet lying softly in the bed, the little sounds she and Jaqe used to make to each other (baby noises, she realized now), the occasional prodding or kissing along each other's bodies, maybe plans for the day if it was morning or rolling into sleep if it was night.

Shaking her head, Laurie got up and walked into the bedroom. Jaqe sat in the worn pink chair the two of them had once dragged up from the street, and, yes, Kate was at her breast, claiming the property rights of the hungry. As soon as Laurie sat down on the arm of the chair, Kate moved her eyes slightly, to Laurie's face. Laurie looked at Jaqe, who smiled at her.

Laurie bent down to kiss Jaqe's cheek. She frowned. "Do you feel hot?" she asked.

Jaqe laughed. "I would have thought that was obvious."

"No, really, I mean it." She touched Jaqe's forehead. "Are you all right?"

"It's just the flames of love pumping through my veins." Laurie rolled her eyes. "Really, honey," Jaqe said, "I'm just wonderful." She tilted up her head and pursed her lips for Laurie to bend down and kiss her. "Absolutely wonderful."

Five

The Baby on the Bridge

Laurie discovered she could hear Kate crying even after she'd stopped. She discovered this in the shower one day, where she'd gone in hopes the sound would drown out the baby. But Kate's shrieking sliced through the torrent of water. Laurie thought of turning the hot water high enough to scald herself so she would have an excuse to scream even louder than Kate. Only when dizziness forced her to turn off the water did she discover that the baby had stopped crying, probably had stopped minutes ago.

Laurie stood there, dripping, with her arms out slightly as if to let the water run off, and she thought, *I'm going to hear this forever.* Some switch in her head had been thrown, and now, at parties, in the bookstore, on the subway, she would hear that high pulse of rage, or pain, or just power, throbbing and throbbing in her head.

If only she could do something. Drying herself off, she imagined someone kidnapping Jaqe and the baby, shutting them away in a dungeon deep in the mountain, so that Laurie would have to ride out and rescue them (after a decent night's sleep). But she couldn't do anything about the crying. Once, she'd even tried to offer the baby her breast. Jaqe was trying to sleep, and Laurie had held Kate while she clumsily undid her shirt. But after a minute or two of trying it out, Kate knew when someone was cheating her. She removed her mouth to yell for the real fountain of peace. With disgust stoked by exhaustion, Jaqe had gotten out of bed and pushed Laurie aside to grab hold of the baby.

It was worse for Jaqe; she too had tried to escape into the shower, only to find that the sound of her child not only penetrated the wall of water but also prodded her breasts to squirt milk. Laurie had heard a thump in the shower. She'd been rocking Kate in her arms, trying to quiet her so Jaqe could get washed, and maybe eat breakfast at the table, when she heard the noise. For a second she looked from the baby to the bathroom door, confused, before she set Kate down and ran to help Jaqe. She found her leaning back against the wall, her eyes squeezed shut and her hands against her forehead as streams of white arced across the shower stall to drown in the fall of clear water.

The only thing that worked at all, Jaqe found, was never putting the baby down. If Jaqe carried her everywhere—and it had to be Jaqe, Kate could tell the difference instantly if it was Laurie, or Mrs. Lang, whether from the feel of the arm, or the weight, or the pressure, or maybe, as Jaqe believed, the smell of the milk "brewing" in Jaqe's breasts—if Jaqe carried her everywhere, then Kate just might stay quiet for more than a few minutes. And Jaqe had to *hold* her. Kate wouldn't accept riding in a sling, even the kind that nestled her against Jaqe's breasts. She demanded Jaqe's arm around her. Jaqe took to doing everything with her right hand, joking that her left arm soon would look like Popeye's. She became skilled at things like making coffee, combing her hair, even washing her face and getting dressed with just one hand. If necessary, she could slide Kate from one side to the other to put on a blouse or a dress.

Only, as she told Louise, she could do everything, but never quite right. Her hair always looked messy, probably, she said, because she never dared take the time to condition it properly. She had to limit her meals to the things easiest to prepare, usually ready-to-eat foods, and even this became difficult, or actually dangerous. Once, she cut herself opening a sardine can, and when she had to put Kate down to wash and bandage the cut, the baby's screaming drove her to do it all quickly, as quickly as possible, so that she didn't really clean the cut and sterilize it the way she would have done in what she called her "previous life."

Keeping clean was the hardest. She told Louise that she smelled all the time and only waved her (free) hand when Louise insisted it wasn't true. She wore the clothes that were easiest to put on and take off, and since neither she nor Laurie seemed to have enough time to go down to the washing machines in the basement, most of her clothes were stained. It would have been pointless to try to keep them clean, anyway. Preparing and eating food quickly, while holding the baby, made sure her clothes received a portion of whatever she ate. "I'm like a walking museum of food," she told Louise.

Worst of all—and this she could not make herself tell Louise—she could not keep her body clean. It wasn't just the infrequent showers or the dirty clothes. She couldn't even wipe herself properly when she went to the toilet. If she laid Kate down in her crib, the crying would cut through Jaqe until she just wanted to finish what she was doing and get back to Kate and make it stop. And if she held the baby while sitting on the toilet, the awkwardness as well as concern for the baby's cleanliness made her rush to get it all done. It was such a simple thing, she knew, something you mastered before you even went to school. Somehow she just couldn't do it. And she couldn't talk about it, not with Louise, and certainly not with Laurie.

Jaqe was scared for Laurie. She knew how hard Laurie was trying, always staying cheerful, positive, promising relief and solutions that never came. She wished she *could* talk to Laurie, not for herself, but for Laurie. It seemed so unfair, Jaqe thought. Laurie didn't want a child, and now, having a child who cried without rest and a lover who could never do anything, Laurie never complained, never got angry, just kept trying and trying to make it right.

Laurie, in turn, couldn't talk to Jaqe. She was convinced that Jaqe suffered so much more than she did. How could she dare to say anything? And Laurie knew that she at least could get away to the quiet of work. Getting away didn't help, however, for Jaqe's greater pain exaggerated Laurie's own inadequacy. And getting away just made it harder to go home. For the first weeks, when it became clear that Kate would not stop shrieking, Laurie thought constantly of the stories of women who beat their babies. She would check herself, examine her urges, look at her hands whenever she had to pick Kate up, as if they might change into fists without her knowing. But instead of a desire to beat or hurt her baby, Laurie just wanted to leap down the stairs and out to the street, where she could suck deep on the polluted air. Only—she remembered—it was men, fathers, who did that, abandon their families. She couldn't even do things like a proper woman, she thought. She wasn't the baby's mother or its father. She was nothing. And there was no one she could talk to, no one. Louise would just lecture her about women-loving women claiming their rights as full parental partners. Mark would stay calm and say something sensible, if a little strange. No one could understand. No one could help.

When Jaqe got sick, neither she nor Laurie realized it at first. Jaqe was so tired and confused all the time anyway—what difference could it make? True, Laurie could feel the heat radiating from Jaqe's body, but Jaqe had always been warmer than Laurie, she'd always heated the bed in winter, so that if Laurie ever shivered in the middle of the night she only needed to slide closer to Jaqe's body, put her arms over Jaqe's shoulders, her leg over Jaqe's hip, and warmth would flood her cold thin body. So it took a while for them to understand that something was wrong beyond the confused and joyful agony of trying to satisfy a yelling child.

Even when Jaqe started throwing up she could tell herself it was just stress, and the need to eat in such a fast and sloppy way. Or that it simply was the flu she'd had a few weeks earlier, swinging back for a return visit. And if her hand burned with pain where she'd cut it awhile back, well, that too was nothing special. It was her own fault, she knew; she never should have done anything so foolish as to try and yank open a sardine can with just one hand.

She had, in fact, worried about the cut at first, especially when it sent a line of puffy red blisters up her wrist. For several days she'd just kept washing it with alcohol and making sure to keep it covered, from fear that Laurie would see it. Laurie had far too much to worry about already. Finally, she'd just set Kate down in her crib, and with the steady rhythm of Kate's shrieking pushing her to hurry (she thought, dreamlike, of the days when she could take her time with simple tasks, do them right, and even pause afterwards to admire what she'd done), she sterilized a large needle as best she could in fire and alcohol, and then pierced her way along the line of pustules until all the green and red and yellow liquid poured down her hand into the sink. Afterward, she'd washed and then lightly dressed the wound with a row of Band-Aids, once more covering the whole mess with a long-sleeve T-shirt so that Laurie wouldn't get alarmed, wouldn't think Jaqe had tried to hurt herself in a moment of panic. And then she'd rushed back to Kate, offering the reward (or bribe) of her breast to her daughter's impatience. In a day or two, the skin had healed enough that Jaqe could do without the Band-Aids and concealment, just using a little makeup for the areas that remained discolored.

Only when diarrhea joined the occasional vomiting did Jaqe admit she was in trouble and maybe needed to see a doctor. Even then she didn't want the doctor for herself, but only because the illness made her afraid to feed Kate, even to hold her. They returned to keeping Kate much of the time in her crib, or set up on the couch or the chair in a wooden cradle Mark had given them. Laurie bottle-fed Kate, a practice which enraged Kate.

Jaqe lay in bed, feeling out of balance, the alignment of her body all wrong without her baby against her side or her breast. At least twice a day, Jaqe would get out of bed and walk heavily into the kitchen or living room, loosely clutching her bathrobe, to stand hesitantly before Laurie and Kate. "Why don't I take over?" she'd say.

"Honey," Laurie always answered, "go back to bed, okay? Let me take care of it. Okay?" Jaqe would stand there a moment, half raising her arms to reach out for Kate, who was demanding the real thing, and then another stab of pain, or maybe dizziness, would strike her, and she would rush to the toilet or simply back to bed.

Somehow Laurie persuaded the doctor to come. He confirmed that Jaqe did indeed have a high fever, as well as other symptoms. He pronounced that she had a severe case of a flu that was going around.

(Jaqe imagined it visiting people's houses, knocking politely, and then leaping down their throats when they gullibly opened the door.) Jaqe did not tell him about the cut, or the infection. Laurie was standing alongside her, and Jaqe didn't want to admit she'd concealed something. Besides, she told herself, the flu was an infection, so any treatment the doctor gave her would apply as well to whatever traces were left on her arm.

And in fact, the doctor did give her a course of antibiotics, along with orders to stay in bed, keep warm to the point of sweating, drink as much as possible, and rest, rest, rest. He might have stayed a little longer and examined a little more closely if not for the screaming child pulsing in his head and throughout his body.

Jaqe hated using her parents' insurance to pay the doctor. She hated it not for herself, but for Laurie, who left the room to heat up a bottle for the baby, as if to avoid watching an obscene act between Jaqe and the doctor. Jaqe wanted to rush up to Laurie and tell her it was okay, it didn't mean that Laurie didn't love her or didn't take perfect care of her, it was just money, and anyway it was the fault of the political system, a patriarchal structure gimmicked against women's independence from their fathers. But she was just too tired, too weak. She could hardly talk at all, and besides, she never *could* do that stuff very well, even after years of listening to Louise.

Laurie had to send Louise for prescriptions, since she didn't want to leave Jaqe with the baby. Louise offered to watch Kate so Laurie could go for the antibiotics and food supplies, but Laurie insisted she needed to stay. Kate wouldn't like it if her mother was sick and some stranger was there. Louise wanted to say, "Well, what'll she do, cry?" but poor Laurie looked so close to tears herself that Louise didn't dare. So instead she saluted, and said, "Okay, boss," a phrase that seemed to bring Laurie closer to tears than ever.

Mark, too, offered his help, mostly by telling Laurie to take as much time as she needed. Laurie didn't want time, she wanted to work, she longed just to stand in the chaos of books, stand and breathe amid the noiseless whispers of print, the aromas of words.

Mark came for a visit the evening after the doctor. It was not the first time he'd come there since Kate's birth, but the conjunction of Mark's visit and Jaqe lying in bed reminded Laurie of Kate's conception. If Laurie expected to feel resentment, or regret, she surprised herself with a wave of gratitude for Kate's presence in her life, so vivid it almost knocked her onto the rug. She rushed over and picked up Kate and held the body tight against hers, wishing she could satisfy her the way Jaqe did.

In the past, Mark had made sure to talk with Jaqe, bringing her news of the outside world, as if Jaqe lived in some isolated settlement far from civilization. But now, with Jaqe too miserable for visitors, Mark spent his time with Kate. Laurie expected Mark to talk to the baby, to discuss some intellectual concept with her, maybe the feminist linguistics he'd learned about from Laurie. Instead, Mark held Kate firmly in front of him—and stared at her. At first, Kate did nothing, just looked back at him. After a moment, however, she began to squeeze together her face muscles in preparation for crying. Laurie rushed forward, not sure if she was rescuing the baby or her boss, but Mark only motioned her away with a shake of his head. He said, "Why don't you go see if Jaqe needs tea or anything."

At the archway leading out of the living room, Laurie looked back. Kate's face seemed to quiver, as if trying, and failing, to hold on to the launch of a cry. In the bedroom, Jaqe moaned, whether at sight of Laurie or just on principle, Laurie couldn't tell. "Um, sweetie?" she said. "You want some tea?"

Jaqe squinted at her, like Kate trying to figure out Mark. "God," Jaqe said, "Goddess. I'd love some tea. Blackberry."

From the kitchen, Laurie could glimpse Mark, still holding on to Kate, who had given up any plans of an outburst, and now was reaching out to poke Mark's face, so much fleshier than that of either of her two mothers. As Laurie was passing through the living room with the tea, Mark leaned forward and whispered something to Kate. The baby smiled widely and then shook slightly, laughing uproariously without any sound.

Laurie said, "What did you say to her?"

"I told her a joke," Mark said.

"A joke?" Laurie repeated. She remembered all the funny sounds she'd made for Kate, the gulping motions with her mouth, the rolling of her eyes, none of which ever stopped the river of noise for more than a few seconds. "You mind telling me that joke?" Laurie said. "Maybe I could repeat it to her when you're not here."

Mark shook his head. "Oh, I wish I could," he said. "But now she already knows the punch line. Besides, you had to have been there."

"Shit," Laurie said, moving toward the bedroom. "I wish I was there now." She found Jaqe asleep. Laurie set the mug and saucer down on the chipped mahogany night table Jaqe and a woman named Janine had found on the street one night. As gently as she could, Laurie stroked Jaqe's hair, all greasy from days without washing.

She returned to the living room to see Mark laying a sleeping Kate down in her cradle. He said, "I better get back to the store."

"I've got a better idea," Laurie said. "I'll take care of the store, you stay here with Kate. You can try out your whole nightclub act on her."

Mark pushed his lips in and out, as if pondering the suggestion. "No," he said. "No, I think she needs her mother."

Laurie had to force herself to keep her voice down. She said, "I'm not her mother, Jaqe is."

Mark said, "Give Jaqe my love. Tell her I hope she gets over this as soon as possible."

"Why don't you stay for dinner?" Laurie said. "We could order a pizza."

"I'm sorry," Mark told her. "I have to go."

She listened to his footsteps, feeling her breath tighten as the sounds grew softer. Even after she knew he was gone, she couldn't stop staring at the door, as if any moment he would change his mind and come back to help her. Or she imagined yanking open the door, running after him. The baby was sleeping, she told herself. What harm would it do? They could go to Wally's, the bar around the corner from the store, where she and Mark used to go sometimes after work, and Mark would ask her to point out women she found attractive, and tell him why.

She started to cry, silently so she wouldn't wake Jaqe or Kate. Stop it, she told herself. Jaqe mustn't see her looking so weak, or helpless. And by telling herself to stop, she did. She was no longer crying. But it seemed to Laurie that the tears didn't really stop, they only stayed inside. Her whole body was filling with tears, her lungs, her heart, her kidneys drenched in sorrow and fear. She didn't understand. It was just a colicky baby. Just a lack of sleep. I'm no good, she thought. I just can't do it. Why couldn't Mark have stayed? She needed someone to help her. He wouldn't have had to do anything. Didn't he understand that? She just needed help.

Jaqe, meanwhile, was dreaming. It was a simple dream, one she'd had several times since getting sick. She was sitting in a rowboat with her family. She knew they were her family even though she didn't recognize any of them. There were three of them, two adults and a child. Maybe they were her parents and Kate, though that didn't make any sense, since where was Laurie? In the dream, she wanted to ask who they were, but she didn't dare. She couldn't even see their faces, because they all sat hunched over in front of her with their heads partly covered by loose coats or jackets pulled up high over their necks. No one was rowing. Instead, someone was standing up behind her, pushing the boat through the water with a long black pole. Jaqe wanted to turn and look at him (she knew it was a man, maybe by his strength in moving the boat so sharply through the water), but she didn't dare, frightened she might disturb the boat.

They were crossing a river, or at least moving toward an island. Jaqe thought there were people on the island, for she thought she saw movement among the trees, but she couldn't see anyone. The boat moved so quietly, not a sound from the water or the people. On one side, the left, the surface never stirred. On the right, however, every push sent out ripples, even small waves, though always without a sound.

Evening was filling the air around them, and everything was turning gray, giving up whatever color had tried to cling to it. The island, with its thick trees, was darker than the open water, where bits of light still rested on the mirror surface of the river. On the island, she could see people's eyes moving between the trees, like dull lightning bugs.

Without warning, the boat struck the shore. Jaqe sat up, surprised. The people ahead of her all shuffled off and vanished in the trees. Jaqe stood up in the boat, struggling for balance. She had to get off, she knew, she had to step into the water and then onto the gray island. Why couldn't she just go back? The boat had to go back the other way, didn't it? Why couldn't she just wait and travel back with it?

Someone stepped out from the trees. It was dark, and Jaqe couldn't tell if it was a woman or a man; all she could see was someone tall and skinny. The figure reached up to the side of its face. It seemed to tug at something. Without thinking, Jaqe reached up a finger to the skin just below her ear. She began to scratch . . .

She woke up wet. Her whole body was damp. Her cotton nightgown clung to her, soaked. She hoped it wasn't ruined; her parents had given it to her when she first left for college. Even the sheets were wet, especially, she realized, right around her hips. An awful thought struck her. Shivering slightly, she got herself out of bed and pulled down the top sheet. While the sheet as a whole felt clammy, an actual wet spot, about eight inches across, stained the sheet about halfway down the bed. She bent down, sniffed it, then pulled back with her face wrinkled in disgust.

She'd wet the bed, she realized. She'd actually wet the bed. She turned her head to check the door, as if Laurie would come in and catch her. For the first time since she woke up, she realized that Kate was crying. Of course, she thought. The noise had become part of her world. She squinted, concentrating on the sound. It was okay, she thought. Not pain, or terror, or even overwhelming hunger. Jaqe could wait a few minutes before she had to show herself to Laurie.

She took off the nightgown and grabbed her bathrobe from the chair across from the bed. She smiled as she put it on. Laurie had managed to wash it for her, not getting out all the stains, but at least giving it a nice feel against her damp body. The strange thing, she thought as she hurriedly stripped the bed, was that she actually felt much better. She was still weak; in fact, she wasn't sure how long she could stand up without something to hold on to. But she felt rested, soaked with sleep as well as sweat and urine.

Urine, she thought, shaking her head. She pulled off the mattress pad and touched the mattress. As far as she could tell, it hadn't soaked through. Goddess, she thought, how could she do that? Were they going to have to get a rubber sheet, like the one in Kate's crib? Maybe Laurie could diaper her while she was diapering Kate. She giggled, then pressed her lips together, even though Laurie could hardly hear her over the baby's crying.

When she'd taken off the pillowcases and piled everything on the floor, she sat down in the pink chair with her head forward, and her hands gripping the chair arms. Maybe she really was better, she thought, as she shook her head. Maybe she'd poured out all the sickness. In every way possible. A wonder, she thought, that she hadn't drooled all down her chin. She got herself up, took a deep breath, and headed for the living room.

The baby lay in her cradle on the couch, with her face compressed in the effort of crying. Jaqe thought she was right; Kate looked . . . normal. Laurie stood nearby, except that she wasn't looking at Kate, she had turned herself to the door. "Honey?" Jaqe said. When Laurie didn't turn around Jaqe called louder, "Laurie? Sweetheart?"

Laurie spun around as if jolted. She was smiling, with a pained look that meant she didn't feel like smiling at all. "Jaqe," she said. "Why aren't you in bed?"

"I'm feeling a lot better," Jaqe said, hoping Laurie couldn't see her dizziness. "I think I've sweated it all out."

"Really?" Laurie said. "Wow, that's great. Are you sure?"

Jaqe stared at Laurie's rigid smile. What was wrong with her? She sounded like she had a bad scriptwriter. "I think so," Jaqe said. "I must have. Everything's so wet. I had to strip the bed. I even stripped the mattress pad. Do you think maybe you could wash it all for me? I'm really sorry to ask."

"No," Laurie said loudly. "No, of course I'll wash it." She looked from Jaqe to the baby. "I was just going to—I mean, I'm sorry about that. The crying, I mean."

Jaqe moved closer to Laurie. She had to fight a pull toward the baby so strong that she felt she must be walking lopsided. But for once, she was more worried about Laurie. The absurd thought occurred to her that Kate could take care of herself, but Laurie needed help.

"Give me a hug," Jaqe said. Laurie squeezed her, though not as long as Jaqe would have liked. "Honey," Jaqe said, "I've got an idea. Why don't you go out for a while? You haven't gotten any fresh air for days."

Laurie shook her head. "I'd better do the sheets," she said.

"When you come back," Jaqe said.

"The baby needs—"

"It's okay, honey. Really." Jaqe stroked Laurie's face. The skin felt hard. She wished she could lay Laurie down on the bed, stretch her out and rub her down with Dr. Root. *Oh God*, she thought, *I love her so much.*

"Are you sure?" Laurie asked. Jaqe nodded.

"I'll just go for a little while," Laurie said. She moved off toward the bathroom. "I've got to pee first." Jaqe heard the door close. She took a deep breath, then went and picked up her daughter.

In the bathroom, Laurie squeezed her fists as hard as she could, trying to keep in a panic that threatened to knock her over. What if she went out and couldn't make herself come back? She realized suddenly that Kate had stopped crying. Maybe Jaqe was feeding her. The silence unbalanced her, like a strong wind that abruptly dies away, leaving you braced against something no longer there.

She took a deep breath. It's just for a little while, she told herself. Jaqe would do fine without her. Jaqe always did fine.

Laurie went into the bedroom for her keys and wallet. About to leave, she grabbed her old leather jacket from the closet. She hardly wore it anymore. Jaqe didn't like it for some reason. She folded it so that the lining showed and not the leather, then draped it over her arm.

In the living room Kate was sucking on her mother's breast, oblivious to whatever pain or enthusiasm had led her to cry just minutes before. Laurie wondered if she should stay. Kate was quiet, Jaqe was feeling better, maybe she should touch Jaqe and kiss her, rub her down with hot water and soap, and dress her in fresh clothes. She must have taken a step toward Jaqe, because Jaqe said, "No, you go out. I'm fine. Really. You need some air."

Laurie nodded. "I'll just go for a few minutes.

"Take your time," Jaqe insisted. "We'll be here." Alone, Jaqe leaned back heavily against the couch. She felt so dizzy, she wasn't sure how long she could sit up. It had taken all her energy to persuade Laurie to go out. At least, she thought, the fever had broken. That was all that mattered.

In the street, Laurie thought she heard the sound of motorcycles, blocks away. She felt a little foolish in her tough biker jacket without a bike.

She went to a bar a few blocks away, an old-fashioned neighborhood place where she could sit in a wooden booth in the back and drink beer, and the men would leave her alone. She told herself that the beer was a magic potion, a gift from the Goddess to take away her fear.

Only, it didn't work. Like someone who's taken the wrong potion, she found her panic rising with every glass. Finally, she just dug out her money (she tried to calculate how much beer she'd drunk by the size of the bill, but gave up) and left.

Outside, she shivered slightly. It was still light, but a fog had rolled in from the river, making everything vague and damp. Leaning against a car, she knew she should get back. Make dinner for Jaqe. Shit, she thought, she hadn't even washed the damn sheets or made the bed. But instead of hurrying home, Laurie walked to the bridge crossing the narrow filthy river between the two boroughs of the city.

The bridge both looked and felt old, maybe because of its clunky yet ornate style, or the fact that the city had let it get all grimy, with rust spots showing underneath the flaking gray paint. Compared to the glamorous suspension bridges in other parts of the city, this simple post bridge, with its two lanes of traffic and its anachronistic footpaths, looked like a neglected stepsister.

Laurie walked out to the middle, where she stood holding on to the railing and looking out at the city. The fog had covered the dense glut of buildings on either side. Silence settled onto the bridge. Silence and dimness. Laurie wished she'd worn something warmer than a tank top under her jacket. The day had been so hot before. She hugged herself. She could always zip up the jacket, but she'd never really liked that look. Leather jackets should hang open. Otherwise, what was the point?

Somewhere in the blankness Laurie heard laughter. It sounded like a child. She thought of her family, of the times they used to go places together, laughing and having a good time. *I need help*, she thought. *I need someone I can count on. Not just for me, for Kate, for Kate.* She just wasn't enough. Jaqe's parents weren't enough. They tried hard, she knew that, but even if they could get over their own . . . their own anger, what could they do about everyone else's?

Laurie had never admitted to herself how much the world frightened her. Despite all the demonstrations she'd organized with the LSU, all the speeches she'd made, all the women she'd seduced with her posture of power, she believed in women's weakness—no, women's vulnerability—with a deep conviction that Louise, and even Jaqe, would have found alien as well as frightening. Women didn't really exist, Laurie thought. In a world invented by men, women moved like shadows, illuminated in direct light only as paintings, or maybe just illustrations.

Holding on to the railing, Laurie tried to shake these thoughts out of her body. It's just alcohol, she thought. Alcohol and sleeplessness. Everything looks weird when you don't sleep. She knew that.

But the thought wouldn't leave. Two women raising a child. A girl child. If only Laurie could get some protection for her. A godparent. Didn't people used to have godparents to watch over them? Not just a ceremonial title, but someone who really cared.

That's it, she thought, giddy. Kate needed a godparent. Mark came to mind, but Laurie shook her head. Too weak. Mark was too much like a woman, unattached to the world, happy to be a shadow, a thought rather than a substance.

Laurie squeezed shut her eyes, rubbed her hands against her face. Just go home, she told herself. Go home and wash clothes. But when she opened her eyes she stared through the fog at the buildings on the far side of the river. The way you could see some and not others, the way the mist formed around them, the way a pair of lit-up buildings glared at her—somehow, it all formed a face. The face of an old bearded man. A grandfather looking at the generations of his children.

Laurie thought of all her friends in support groups, the way they talked of their Higher Powers, and when you pressed them they meant God. A grandfather God who always took care of you. She remembered, as a child, when her father used to take her to Hebrew school, how she'd hold his hand as she walked, and she remembered the pictures in the books, God sitting on his throne in a white dress with his beard brighter than the sky. She shook her head and laughed. What better godparent than God?

And then, to her amazement, she said out loud, "You *bastard!* You goddamn sonofabitch. Are you really there? Can you hear me? You made this world and then you gave it all to *men.* Fuck you." She discovered herself crying, and angrily rubbed her face with the sleeve of her jacket.

Don't look at it, she ordered herself. Look away and the hallucination will vanish. She did her best to stare past the city entirely, to the hills beyond the buildings. Despite the fog she could make out their shapes, dark and round and moist.

The hills looked like a woman, she thought. No, *felt* like a woman. Living forever, silent in the Earth. Laurie thought back to her graduate school classes. The Goddess, she thought, so old that nobody even knew her name anymore, only the names men had given her after she'd retreated into the rocks.

Goddessparent. Wasn't the Goddess supposed to love you and take care of you? Nourish you like a cow, a queen bee, with her milk and honey. "No," Laurie whispered. "You never do anything. All these centuries of pain and rape, you've never done anything to stop them. You just don't care. How can I trust you?"

Shit, Laurie thought, *there's nobody that can help us. Nobody.*

The sound of an engine made her look toward the end of the bridge in the direction of home. Instead of a car, she just saw a woman walking toward her. The woman wore a patchwork dress with dangling sleeves and a flat black hat with a long red ribbon tied around it so that the ends floated in the breeze past the stiff brim.

Laurie was about to turn away when the woman said, "Good evening, Laurie. How are you today?"

"Mother Night?" Laurie said. She thought back to the dance where she'd first met Jaqe. She remembered the old woman by the punch bowl who seemed to know both of them. "Mother Night," she repeated.

The woman nodded. "I'm happy to see you again, Laurie," she said. "And congratulations. On becoming a mother."

Laurie shook her head. "I'm not a mother," she said. "Jaqe had the baby, not me."

Mother Night shook her head. "You love Kate, and you worry about her. And you know you cannot leave her or separate from her, no matter how much you might desire it. Aren't those the qualities of a mother?"

Laurie began to cry. "She doesn't need a second mother. She needs a godmother."

"Yes, I know," Mother Night said. "Tell me, Laurie. Would you like *me* to become her godmother? I promise to watch out for her. And I'm very well connected."

Laurie remembered her dream. The dark woman at the beach, sitting with her feet up on a scarred wooden desk. And earlier in the dream, the woman in the convenience store who'd told her, "Mother Night can help you. Go to the water and find Mother Night." She stared now at the woman in front of her. Mother Night wasn't laughing or anything. She looked like she meant it, like she really cared. Laurie thought how even if Mother Night promised to be Kate's godmother and then forgot about it, what could she lose? She took a breath.

Before Laurie could speak, a bird, a brown-and-white pigeon, settled onto Mother Night's shoulder. The old woman turned to smile at it, then stroked it with a finger.

The bird died. It didn't fall over, it just . . . crumbled. The plumpness shriveled, the feathers withered into gray sticks, the eyes dried into dust and blew away. Mother Night took the corpse from her shoulder and set it gently on the railing.

Laurie found herself gasping for breath, for speech. She said,

"You're . . . you're . . . De . . ." She couldn't make herself say the word.

"Of course," Mother Night said. "Didn't you know? Who better is there to protect your child? Who could better shield her from pain and loss? Do it, Laurie. Make me her godmother, and I will show her how to live."

Laurie's head hardly moved. Someone passing by would never have known she was nodding. But she was. Though no sound came out, the lips and tongue formed the word "Yes."

Mother Night smiled joyously. "Thank you," she said. "It's been a long time since I had someone I could care for. You have made a wise choice." She turned now and walked back off the bridge, her step graceful and confident. Laurie only stood there and watched her. She felt strange and relieved all at the same time. Her body had become so light that a flexing of her toes would have floated her up to the top of the bridge.

At the end of the bridge, Mother Night turned to look back once more at Laurie. Only, now her face had changed, had become grayer and frailer. She looked like someone Laurie knew. Like—

Oh God, Laurie thought. She looked like the old woman. The woman from the bar. The one who'd written Laurie's graduate papers. Three papers in one night. All of them perfect. The one who wouldn't name her price. Another time, she'd said, they'd talk about it another time. Something special, she'd said. And now? "It's been a long time since I had someone I could care for."

"No!" Laurie screamed. "Come back here. You can't have her! I didn't mean it!" But Mother Night was gone, vanished into the fog.

"Kate!" Laurie screamed. "Oh my God, Kate!" She began to run.

Jaqe's head jerked as she woke up. She was sitting on the couch, with Kate asleep at her breast. Excess milk had dribbled down her and the baby, streaking them with white. Jaqe grunted at the pain in her neck, but when she lifted her head the pain moved like an electric shock down the rest of her body. She groaned. She'd thought she was better, but now she felt so weak again. Everything was shivering, and she had the terrible thought that if she gave in to it, the shaking would turn easily into convulsions. She could feel a wetness around her thighs. Frightened she'd lost all control of her bladder, she looked down.

It took her a moment to recognize the redness as blood. Why was she bleeding? She was still nursing, she wasn't supposed to get her period until after Kate was weaned. Gently as she could, Jaqe laid the baby in her cradle. Mercifully, Kate didn't wake up. Holding on to chairs and tables, Jaqe made her way to the bathroom. She stopped at the door. A candle was burning on the top of the toilet tank. A plain stubby candle on a plate covered with wax. Only the smallest amount was left of it. Already the wick had started to sputter.

Jaqe backed away, shaking her head and moaning. The kitchen, she thought. Didn't they keep candles in the kitchen? Under the sink or something? She could replace it before it went out.

Jaqe banged her shoulder against the door as she lurched from the bathroom. She paid no attention to the pain, only rushed to the kitchen. But as she rounded the corner into the ill-equipped kitchen, with its ancient refrigerator and cracked linoleum floor, she stopped short. Mother Night sat in a chair alongside the red Formica table. She was drinking a glass of milk. "Hello, Jaqe," she said. "I'm happy to see you again."

Jaqe began to cry. "It's not fair," she said. "You promised."

Mother Night shook her head. "No," she said. "I promised you I would never take Laurie away from you. I never said anything about taking you."

"I won't go," Jaqe said; then realizing how absurd that was, she said, "I—I've got protection."

Mother Night set down the glass and leaned forward. "Really?" she said. "How exciting. Bring it out. Let me see."

Jaqe left the kitchen and went into the living room, where she stood, swaying. She could just run, she thought. Dash down the stairs and try to find Laurie. Oh God, she missed Laurie so much. But she couldn't leave, she knew that. She couldn't just run off and leave her daughter. Protection. Protection. What could she use . . .

She ran for the laminated jewelry box where she kept the stone with the labyrinth and the baby. Mother Night would have to respect that, wouldn't she? But Jaqe couldn't find the stone, not anywhere. Nor could she find the bottle of Dr. Root's massage oil. When she went through her night table, however, she came across one of the drawings Laurie had sent her from graduate school, a xeroxed photo of a prehistoric temple, with Jaqe drawn in, asleep at the altar.

She returned to the kitchen and held it up at arm's length, like a shield. "Here," she said. "This is my protection."

Mother Night looked solemnly at the paper. "What are your demands?" she said.

"I won't go with you. That's all. Kate needs me. And Laurie needs me. I'm not going."

Mother Night shook her head. "I'm sorry, Jaqe. I can't do that. Name something else."

"Is this because of Laurie's father? Because of what I did to him?"

"This has nothing to do with Laurie's father. It only has to do with you."

"Then why? It's so unfair. He gets to live and I don't. That's wrong."

"I know," Mother Night said. "What I do is not about fairness. But think of this. He lives because you chose to release him. You gave him life. Not for his sake, but for your own. And for Laurie, so that you would be worthy of her. You cannot choose what will happen to you, but when you faced the choice for someone else, you chose life."

"Then let me go. Let me stay with my family." She added, "The candle. Give me a new candle. Another chance."

For the first time since Jaqe had known her, Mother Night became angry. "Don't you think I've already done that?" she said. "Do you remember when Laurie's father cut you? And you went into the woods? Those woods were not a safe place, Jaqe. They would have swallowed you forever if I had not reached out for you. I gave you an extension then. So you could bear a child. I cannot do any more than that." Jaqe said nothing, only stood there, still holding the picture. Relaxed again, Mother Night said, "Make another demand."

There was silence for a moment, and then Jaqe said, "Kate. I want you to take care of her. Watch over her. Make sure no one gets to her and hurts her. Can you do that?"

Mother Night nodded. "Yes, Jaqe. I give you my promise. I will watch over Kate as if she were my own child."

Jaqe began to cry. "And Laurie," she said. "Will you take care of Laurie?"

"I will do what I can."

As Jaqe looked at Mother Night the old woman seemed almost to dissolve. She was still sitting there, still smiling, but she had grown slightly transparent. An odd thought came to Jaqe—that she had known Mother Night for a very long time, that once there was no one but the two of them, the Mother and the Daughter, inseparable. But Jaqe had changed that. She had gone away and met Laurie. Instead of just a daughter, she had become Jaqe. She said, "If I go with you—if I return—I won't stop loving Laurie. I hope you know that."

Mother Night nodded. "Absolutely. That is just the way it should be." She stood up and held out her hands.

Jaqe was about to take them when she heard, somewhere behind her, Kate crying. "Oh," she said, "the baby. I better go see if she's okay."

Mother Night said, "I'm sorry, Jaqe. Laurie will see to her. And remember, she's under my protection now."

"Oh. That's right," Jaqe said. "I forgot." She laid her hands on Mother Night's palms. The small fingers circled around hers. Jaqe closed her eyes.

Laurie became sick on the way home. Goddamn alcohol, she thought. She wanted to stop and throw up, right there in the street like some homeless person. But she couldn't stop; there was no time. She had to get home before Mother Night got there. She was out of shape, she knew, and weak from lack of sleep and too much beer, but couldn't she at least outrun an old lady?

She reached the apartment building finally, and nearly screamed at how difficult it was to get the key in the lock and open the downstairs door. Finally, she got through it and ran up the stairs to her own front door, which took even longer. "Jaqe!" she shouted when she got inside. "Jaqe? The baby. Is she okay?"

It took her a moment to realize that Kate was crying, screaming in fact, as loudly as any time in the months since her birth. "Oh God," Laurie said, "Oh, Goddess. She's *okay.* She's all right." She picked Kate up and held her a moment, just to make sure she didn't feel hot or anything, then put her back down.

How was she going to explain all her shouting to Jaqe? It didn't matter, she realized. She'd think of something. Better not to tell Jaqe what had happened. She'd probably just imagined it anyway. She found Jaqe in the kitchen slumped over the table. Laurie pulled up a chair to sit across from her. Should she wake her? Anyone who could sleep through a noise like that deserved her rest. *Goddess,* she thought, *I love you. I love you so damn much.* She stroked Jaqe's face.

There was something wrong. Laurie could feel it instantly. She knew Jaqe's skin. Asleep or awake, sick or healthy, it made no difference. Laurie knew how Jaqe felt. There was no give, no energy, no . . . Laurie shook her shoulder. "Honey?" she said. "Sweetheart?" She lifted Jaqe's head. The eyes swung open, empty.

"Jaqe!" Laurie shouted. She continued to shout, though she had no idea what she was saying. Then, *911*, she thought, *call 911*. But all she did was shake Jaqe's shoulder. And scream. Only when she heard the sound of the baby piercing through her own voice did she stop. She put her face right up against Jaqe's, trying to convince herself she could find some sign, some tiny fantasy of breath. Nothing. She put her hand on Jaqe's breast, a place she knew better than any spot on her own body. Nothing. Put her on the floor, she thought. Pound on her chest. Breathe into her mouth. But she knew there was no point. Jaqe had been dead for too long. Jaqe had been dead since that moment on the bridge, when Mother Night had turned and looked back at Laurie with the face of the old woman.

Laurie was hugging Jaqe when she saw the Xeroxed photo with the drawing she'd made. She picked it up off the floor and carried it with her to the baby. Laurie picked up Kate and held her in one arm. "Look," she said, dangling the drawing in front of Kate's face with her free hand. "Look, this is your mommy. Isn't she beautiful? Oh God, isn't she beautiful?"

Kate stopped crying. She reached out and took hold of the drawing. From that moment on, Kate would never cry without purpose again. She would yell for Laurie only when she needed food or changing or serious attention. Otherwise, she would play, or sleep, or watch the world—in peace and gentle silence. Laurie, of course, knew nothing of this. She knew only that her daughter was laughing, and the sight of this miracle opened her heart with joy even as pain rocked her back and forth, and tears filled her mouth, meeting the great sobs that were rising up from her throat.

Part Three

The Girl Who Played with Death

One

Fly with the Crows

Kate could never understand why Laurie wanted nothing to do with Kate's wonderful godmother. Even when Kate was very young, before she could even talk very much, Kate knew there was something wrong between the two. Once, when Kate was just three, Laurie was in the kitchen making dinner, leaving Kate to play with a set of dolls in funny costumes Uncle Mark had given her, when a sweet smell broke Kate's concentration. She looked up happily, for even though she'd never smelled it before, she knew right away what it must mean. And sure enough, there stood the Lady With the Hats. (Kate thought of her that way until the age of three, when the Lady—who seemed to wear a different funny hat each time Kate saw her—explained what a godmother was.) She wore a long dress with lots of folds and what looked like real green plants growing all over it. And her hat—it was all big and floppy, like the dress, but where the dress had plants the hat had people! Or at least what looked like faces hidden in the creases. And just the tiniest whisper of voices, hundreds of them, it seemed. The Lady set the hat down on the floor, and Kate crawled up to it.

On her hands and knees, like a puppy, she put her face up close, trying to see all the people hidden in the hat, trying to hear the funny sounds they were making. She began to laugh loudly; it was all so much fun. Though the Lady put a finger against her lips, Kate paid no attention. Soon she heard Laurie-Mommy call from the kitchen. "Kate, sweetie? You okay?" Kate made a noise, by which she meant, "Come in, hurry. This is wonderful." To her surprise, the Lady looked sadly at her, then picked up the hat from the floor and set it back on her long red hair.

"Honey?" Laurie said from the doorway. "What is it?" Kate turned to look at her. Thrilled that Laurie could now meet the wonderful Lady, Kate laughed again. But when she turned back, the Lady had gone.

Soon after she learned what a godmother was, Kate discovered she better not talk about her. She discovered this on a day when she'd gone on a trip in Godmother's cute red car. Godmother had taken her away from day care, as she sometimes did (Kate didn't know what she told the day care ladies, but it always worked), and had driven her to a huge park or zoo where you could see the bones on all the animals. Later, when Kate tried to describe the zoo, Laurie said, "That sounds like quite a place. Did you go there all by yourself? Or did someone take you?"

"Of course I didn't," Kate said. "It was Godmommy."

Laurie laughed. "God took you on a trip? That must have been very exciting. Did you fly in his beard?"

Kate rolled her eyes. "Not *God*, Laurie. My *Godmommy* took me. In her red car."

The effect amazed her. Laurie bent down and grabbed Kate by the shoulders, really hard. And then she *shouted*. Laurie *never* shouted. "I want you to keep away from her! Do you hear me? I don't want you going anywhere near her. I don't want you even talking to her." Kate stared at her. She didn't cry or try to get loose; she just stared. Laurie pulled her hands away from Kate's shoulders as suddenly as she'd grabbed them. "Sweetie, *I'm sorry*," she said. "I'm sorry." She put her arms around Kate and held her close.

Kate liked that. Usually Laurie had so much to do she never had much time for touching. So now Kate felt like a present, with Laurie the gift wrapping. Finally, Laurie let her go, only now she held her shoulders again, except not so hard, and said to her, "Kate, I want you to promise me something. It's very, very important. Do you understand?" Kate didn't answer. Laurie said, "I don't want you ever going anywhere with her again. And if she comes to see you, I want you to run and tell me. Do you understand what I'm saying?"

Kate nodded. "Promise me," Laurie said. Kate still said nothing. "Sweetie," Laurie insisted, "you've got to promise me this. I can't tell you how important it is." When Kate asked why, Laurie said, "I can't tell you that. You just have to promise. *Please*."

"Okay," Kate said, and Laurie, who was suddenly crying (crying! Laurie never cried, just like Kate herself), hugged her again. Of course, Kate had crossed her big toe over the second one, which meant the promise didn't count, a rule she'd learned from Alvin, a boy in day care.

So Kate learned early to keep her godmother and Laurie in separate places in her life. She couldn't even use Godmother as a threat. Once, when Laurie wouldn't get her an ice cream (Laurie claimed she'd already eaten two chocolate chip cookies, an argument that made no sense of any kind to Kate), Kate had said to her, "I'll bet my godmother would let me have ice cream."

But instead of forcing Laurie to prove her generosity, the challenge only got Kate a yank on the arm from Laurie, who had started to shake. "Don't you ever say that," Laurie told her. Then she bent down to hold her daughter. "Shit," she said. "I'm sorry, honey."

"You hurt me," Kate said, more surprised than upset. "I have to draw with this hand." She held the hand up, as if testifying at a trial.

"I know," Laurie said, "I'm really sorry." She started crying. (Crying again! Even just talking about Godmother made Laurie cry.) Suddenly Kate was crying too, though she wasn't sure why.

When Kate started school she also started seeing more of her godmother. Mostly this meant sneaking away at lunchtime. Her godmother would pick her up, standing at the school gate just like one of the grandparents who took kids home for a hot meal. She didn't come every day, of course. She had things to do. Each day at lunch, Kate would run to the playground. If she didn't see Godmother, she would sigh and go back to eat her sandwich with the other children. But then the next day Godmother might be there, ready to take Kate on some adventure that, no matter how long it lasted, always ended just in time to bring Kate back for class.

Sometimes Kate even saw Godmother talking with the other women, laughing at some joke together, though the conversation always stopped as soon as Kate came running up for a hug. Godmother was always so much easier about stuff like that than Laurie. When Laurie came to pick her up she always just stood there, with her hands in her pockets, not speaking to anyone while she waited for Kate to show up so they could leave. Laurie would walk away so fast that Kate would have to run a little to keep up with her, at least for a block or so, and then, once they'd gotten away from the other parents, Laurie would go back to normal, talking cheerfully to Kate and remembering to hold her hand.

Kate worried a little that Laurie might find out about Godmother visiting her at school. Maybe one of the grandparents might tell, not knowing that Kate wanted to keep it a secret. "I just love Kate's godmother," one of them would say, "she tells such good jokes," and then Laurie would start shouting and flapping her arms, like she did when she got really upset. But when Kate told Godmother about this, Godmother just put an arm around her and said, "Don't you worry, darling Kate. Laurie won't know until the time comes for her to know, and then she will know everything. So you see, we're not really lying. We're just waiting to tell her."

"I guess," Kate said. They were standing in the top story of a funny old house in some neighborhood with nothing but single homes, and grass around them, like at her grandparents' house. But this house looked like the kind of house Marianne, a girl at school, called spooky, a word Kate could never understand. When Kate asked her godmother if indeed it was spooky, Godmother laughed and said the house was "a fine old Victorian," whatever that meant, and just needed a little work. They were standing in a bare room that smelled a little, like no one had cleaned it in a long time, standing before a window all closed with funny wooden doors Godmother called shutters (at first Kate thought she'd said "shudders" and laughed, since the wood stayed absolutely still). Kate was still thinking about Laurie when Godmother took hold of the shutters and said to her, "Get ready now, darling Kate. This is what we came to see." She took a large step back and as she did so she pushed open the shutters.

At first, all Kate could see was darkness. This made no sense at all, since they had come here in the middle of the day. She knew vaguely that time sometimes did funny things when she went with her godmother, but still . . . She turned to look at Godmother. "Is it a picture?" she asked.

Godmother put her hands on her hips, as if angry, but Kate knew she was playing. She grinned as Godmother said, "A picture? Now what are you talking about?"

"It's so dark," Kate said.

"Don't let the darkness lure you," she said. "Look at the light." And Godmother pointed straight out the window.

Though Kate wondered what "lure" meant, she looked dutifully past Godmother's arm to the distant center, where she now saw a throbbing ball of light. At first it just looked like a dot, but the more she stared at it, the more it filled her eyes. "What is it?" she said finally.

Godmother bent down beside her. "It's a dying star," she whispered. "See how it spins and pulses? Stars get very excited when they die."

Kate smiled. "Stars can't die."

"Of course they can," Godmother said. "They don't believe it, I admit. That's partly why they get so disturbed. But everything dies."

"Everything?"

"Well, almost everything. I'm sorry we couldn't get any closer, Kate," she said, "but the closer it comes to death, the hotter it burns. A foolish resentment, but what can you do except respect its feelings?"

"What happens when it really does die?"

"Ah, that's partly why I wanted you to see it. Something quite special happens when a star dies. First it blows up. A little bit like a balloon if you blow in it for too long. Can you picture that, Kate?" Kate stared harder out the window, then she nodded. "Good," her godmother said. "However, it's after the explosion that the truly interesting part begins. The bits from the star go floating through space for a long time. Sometimes nothing happens to them. But sometimes—" She paused, to make sure that Kate would give her full attention.

"Sometimes they join with bits from other dead stars, and together they all form a new star, healthy, young, and all full of energy. And *sometimes*, bits of the dead stars will come together as hard balls of rock circling and spinning around the new star. These are the planets. And over time, on some of these planets, really tiny bits of rock and dirt will change and become *alive*. And once life starts somewhere, well, there's really nothing that can stop it."

Kate turned to her and grinned. "Cool," she said.

Godmother nodded. "Exactly. So you see, Kate, you and Laurie and Mark and Louise and all your friends are all made out of dead stars."

Kate stood there, thinking for a moment. Then she turned and looked back at the star. "Is it going to explode now?" she asked. "Can we see it make people?"

Godmother smiled and stroked Kate's hair. "No, I'm sorry," she said. "It takes much, much too long for us to stand here and wait for it. You do have to return to school, you know."

"Can't you write me a note?"

Godmother laughed. "I suppose I could. But I don't think that's such a good idea." She took Kate's hand and they headed for the stairs.

By the door of the empty room, Kate turned back to look once more at the dying star. She said, "When it makes people, will it make another one of me?"

"No, Kate darling. You are the only one of you who has ever existed."

"Oh."

Kate was silent all the way down the stairs. When they got into the car, however, Kate said, "Do you know Uncle Mark and Aunt Louise?"

Godmother shrugged and waved her hand. "Oh, I know everybody," she said.

In the car on the way back to school that day, Kate thought about the grown-ups in her life, and what they thought or knew about her godmother. She wished she could ask her mother. Her real mother, that is. She loved Laurie-Mommy very much, but she just couldn't talk to her. If her Jaqe-Mommy hadn't died, Kate bet, she could have told Kate all about Godmother. And they could all do things together. She wished Jaqe-Mommy could have come and looked at the star with them. Jaqe-Mommy would have liked Godmother and wouldn't have told Kate not to talk about her.

Kate knew this because of the time she had asked Godmother about her name. She'd been almost five at the time, and it suddenly struck her that she'd always just called her Godmother, and didn't even know her name. That night she pretended to fall asleep until Laurie had left the bedroom and closed the door. Then Kate had scrunched her face up and squeezed her hands and whispered, "I want my godmother to come." When she opened her eyes, there stood Godmother, wearing the patchwork dress Kate loved so much.

"What's your name?" Kate asked her after she'd hugged her and kissed her, and Godmother was sitting on the edge of the bed.

"Well, that's not so easy to answer. I have a great many names."

"You mean like middle names? My middle name is Alice."

"Yes, darling," Godmother said. "I know." She stroked Kate's cheek. "But that's not really what I meant. You see, I move around a great deal. And when I go to so many places, it's just much easier for people in each place to call me something in their own language."

"But what's your real name?"

Godmother put her face closer to Kate's, as if she was telling her a special secret. "Call me Mother Night," she whispered.

"Mother Night?" Kate repeated, keeping her voice equally low. "That's not a name. That's—" She couldn't think of the word she wanted. "It's like a book."

"Ah," said Godmother. "You mean a title." She nodded her head slightly. "But you know," she said, "it's not really a title. My name, that is. Older women used to be called Mother all the time. And Night is a perfectly good name, don't you think?" Before Kate could answer, Godmother added, "And most of all, dear, it's the name your mother calls me."

"Laurie?" Kate said.

Godmother smiled. "Jaqe."

Kate's mouth fell open. "You knew my Mommy Jaqe?"

"I know her very well," Mother Night said. "She asked me to look after you, because she misses you so much."

Kate smiled happily. After a moment, the smile faded, as she thought about what Godmother had said. She asked, "Can dead people miss people?"

"Of course," Mother Night said. "Living people miss dead people, isn't that true? You miss Jaqe, don't you?"

"I don't know," Kate said.

Godmother laughed a little. "No, I suppose you wouldn't. Not really miss her, that is. You were very young at the time."

"Can I go see her?" Kate asked.

"I'm afraid not."

"*Yes.* I want to see her."

Godmother touched Kate's shoulder, but Kate jerked away. Godmother said, "It's just not possible."

"It is!" Kate shouted. She jumped out of bed. "If she misses me so much, why won't you let me see her?" With Laurie, Kate knew, she could sometimes get what she wanted just by saying it enough. But now Godmother took Kate's shoulders in her hands, holding her in a grip that didn't hurt but wouldn't let her squirm away. Not that she didn't try. She thrashed about saying, "It is! It is! I want to see her!" while Godmother said nothing at all until finally Kate just stopped, breathing very fast and very loudly.

They stood there for a while, Kate shaking, Godmother on one knee to look Kate in the face. "I will make you a promise," Godmother said finally. "As soon as it becomes possible, I will take you to see her. All right?"

"I guess," Kate said.

"Good." Godmother stood up and took Kate's hand. "Now you need to go back to bed." She picked Kate up and set her down on the mattress, next to Nora, Kate's stuffed lion. "Goodnight," Godmother said, and kissed her cheek. As Kate closed her eyes, she wondered when she would get to meet Jaqe. And then she wondered why Laurie hadn't come running in when Kate had shouted at Mother Night. And then she stopped wondering about anything much at all as she fell asleep.

If it frustrated Kate that she couldn't see her Jaqe-Mommy, it bothered her much more that she couldn't tell people about her godmother. After all, Laurie just didn't like Godmother for some reason.

That was too bad, but there really was nothing she could do about it. But if other people didn't know Kate's godmother, they could hardly dislike her, could they? So it was so unfair that Kate couldn't talk about her.

Actually, it wasn't that Godmother forbid her. Mother Night didn't seem worried about it at all (except that she didn't want to upset Laurie). The problem was, people just didn't believe Kate. In school she found this out early, when she tried to tell a girl named Sylvia about a trip she had taken with Godmother in a balloon. The balloon was bright red with white stripes, and they had flown so high all the houses looked smaller than the houses on the train set Sylvia's brother acted so creepy about. (That was why she'd told Sylvia instead of anyone else, because it was such a good joke on Sylvia's brother.) They'd flown so high that Kate had gotten to wear Cara's red leather jacket. (Cara was one of Godmother's friends. There were five of them and they were the coolest women in the world; they rode real motorcycles, and sometimes Godmother would let one of them take Kate for a ride.) Up there, they found themselves among a whole bunch of crows, big black things flapping and flapping just to keep their place while they all cawed and cawed. Godmother said they were having a conference, which was like a big meeting, to try and decide something they'd been arguing about for a very long time. Godmother had explained it to her, but Kate didn't really pay attention. She just liked listening to the sound of them all cawing at each other. Finally, Godmother said that Kate needed to get back to school. Cara played around with the balloon for a bit, and then they floated down to Earth.

When afternoon recess came, Kate pulled Sylvia over behind the jungle gym and told her everything. But instead of getting excited, or laughing at how the birds sounded, Sylvia just looked at Kate like she was really weird. Finally, Sylvia said, "That's *stupid.* That's a stupid story, and *you're* stupid."

"It's not," Kate said, and soon, before she even realized it, she and Sylvia were pushing and pulling at each other. Kate won, kind of, because Sylvia ended up running away, though she stopped a few feet back and shouted, "I don't care! It's still stupid."

That afternoon, when Laurie offered to take Kate over to see her friend Jeannette, Kate said no, she just wanted to stay home. She tried to sound cheerful, but she must have messed it up, because Laurie kept saying, "Sweetheart? Pumpkin? Is something wrong?" and poor Kate had to keep saying no, she was okay, until finally Laurie just let her watch TV, though every now and then she'd look at her with her worried-mommy face.

The next morning, everything seemed all right again. Kate woke up Laurie by sneaking up to her on the sofa bed and tickling her feet, which gave both of them a chance to tickle and hug each other before they had to get dressed and eat breakfast. It was always easiest for Laurie to hug Kate first thing in the morning, before she had any time to think about it. School went fine, but then right before the bell rang, Mrs. MacCracken gave Kate a note and told her to give it to her mother. "I'll expect an answer back," she said, "so make sure you give it to her."

Kate didn't exactly give Laurie the note, but she did allow Laurie to find it when she emptied Kate's frog-shaped lunchbox. Kate was playing with a toy fire truck, pretending that the two little figures on top were a handsome prince and a beautiful princess, when Laurie called her in to the kitchen. Kate stared at the floor as Laurie said, "This is a note from Mrs. MacCracken. She says you're making up stories. Is that true?" (To herself, Laurie thought, *What a ridiculous question*, but she managed to keep from smiling.) Kate said nothing. "Well?" Laurie said. "I want to know."

It was so unfair! Kate thought. All she'd done was tell the truth, but now she was going to have to lie and pretend that she'd lied. When she hadn't. Otherwise, Laurie would find out she'd lied about not seeing Godmother anymore.

Laurie was standing with her arms folded and all her weight on one leg. "I'm still waiting," she said. "Did you make up stories?"

"I guess," Kate said.

"You guess?"

"I just told Sylvia. That's all. And it's her fault, anyway, because she said I was stupid."

"Well, she shouldn't say that. That's not a nice word. But what did you tell her?"

"That I—that we went up in a big balloon and we could see all the houses."

Laurie bent down next to her. She stroked Kate's shoulder for a moment, but then she pulled back her arm. She said, "I guess that doesn't really sound so bad. Is that what you'd like to do, sweetheart? Go up in a balloon?"

"Yeah," Kate said. "It's real cool. You can see birds flying up close." Maybe if Laurie liked the idea, the next time Mother Night came to take Kate in a balloon, they could bring Laurie along. She imagined them flying over Sylvia's house and dropping things on her until she'd look up and they all could make faces and wave.

Laurie said, "Well, maybe sometime for a special day we can find someplace that gives balloon rides."

Kate tried to sound enthusiastic as she said okay.

Laurie switched now to her teacher-mommy voice. "But you have to remember, sweetie, it's okay to tell people stories, but you have to admit you made them up. Otherwise, they won't like it."

Kate managed to stop herself from screaming, *I* didn't *make it up.*

Laurie went on, "Telling stories is good, but only if we do it for fun. If we do it to impress people and it didn't really happen, that's not so good. Do you understand?"

"I guess," Kate said.

Laurie stood up. She said, "Good. Then I'll write Mrs. MacCracken a note saying we talked about it and it won't happen again."

"Okay," Kate said, and then she went back to her prince and princess, sending them to put out a fire in the royal palace.

But Kate hadn't really finished with the question. The next time she saw her godmother, before Mother Night could even say if she planned anything special for them, Kate said, "Can we go fly in the balloon again? And can we take Sylvia?" But Godmother said no. Even when Kate pleaded and begged, and offered to pay her a quarter, Godmother refused. "But I want to show her I'm not lying," Kate said.

"Of course," Godmother said. "Few things draw us more powerfully than vindication. But I'm afraid, Kate, it simply will not work. Even if you could convince Sylvia, so that she completely supported you, the others would turn against you both. I'm afraid, Kate, there are some battles no one can win."

"I don't care. I don't care about any others. I just want to show Sylvia."

Godmother shook her head. "No. And I will tell you why. We could take Sylvia with us everywhere, show her everything, and she still would not believe. She would refuse to see. She would think we were tricking her. Kate, darling, people believe what they have learned to believe. Never anything more, and never anything less. If you show them something different, they just will not hear it or see it. I'm sorry, dear, but that is simply the way people are."

"But I'm not like that," Kate said.

Godmother smiled happily. "That's because I've been visiting you since you were a baby."

After her fight with Sylvia, Kate decided she really didn't like most kids very much. It was so much more fun to do things with Godmother and the Motorcycle Girls. The girls didn't come along all the time, so it felt very special when they did. Their names were Gloria, Lillian, Amy, Cara, and Ester. Sometimes only one or two came along, maybe to drive Godmother's big blue car while Godmother played with Kate in the backseat. At other times all of them showed up, and they'd go roaring down the road, Godmother in her car with Kate next to her, the MGs all alongside or behind. They drove very fast, it seemed, at least a lot faster than Grandpa Lang in his station wagon. And no one ever got in their way, and they never had to stop for a light. It was so much fun that Kate never got bored, or hungry, or even needed to go to the bathroom.

Best of all was when Godmother let Kate ride with one of the MGs. Usually it was Cara, who talked in a tough voice and looked a little like a boy, with her short hair and small breasts and hips, and her hard hands, as if she worked outside in winter and never wore any gloves. But she also was very gentle with Kate, helping her climb over things if they were out walking in some rocky field, or giving Kate her jacket to wear if they went someplace cold.

Kate loved wearing Cara's jacket. Even though it reached all the way down past her behind, and her hands disappeared inside the sleeves, and it weighed so much her shoulders hurt the next day, she always got excited wearing it, and pretending to walk tough, like Cara. They all said she looked like one of them, with her red hair. She could have been their kid sister. She wished Godmother would give her her own jacket, but Godmother only promised to do so "later," whenever that was. She could imagine how cool it would look, the dark red leather with the ridges on the shoulders, the gold silk lining, and the words "Mother Night" stitched on the back, above that funny picture of the circles with lines in them. "Mother Night" were the first words that Kate ever learned to write. Even before Godmother told her that was her name, Kate learned the words by tracing her finger endlessly over the letters on Cara's jacket while she sat on the back of her motorcycle.

Though Cara was Kate's favorite, she also loved Lillian and Amy. Lillian was extremely tall and very beautiful, with hair that was almost as short as Cara's, but somehow didn't look at all like a boy. The same with her voice, which sounded even deeper than Cara's. Amy looked more like a girl than the others. She had long curly hair, and big soft breasts, and a bottom that rolled when she walked. At home Kate sometimes tried walking first like Cara and then Amy (though never Lillian, who moved in some kind of way that Kate loved to look at but could never figure out). Amy wore more makeup than the others. Sometimes she even wore a dress, usually with lots of color and pictures of flowers. Kate didn't see Gloria or Ester as often. Godmother said they had to do errands for her, and Kate imagined them riding their motorcycles into the supermarket to pick up a chocolate cake or a bottle of milk. But they were still Motorcycle Girls, and so Kate loved them.

And if the Motorcycle Girls weren't enough friends, Kate could play with the dead people. Kate was almost six before she realized that not everybody could play or talk with dead people. Godmother had taken her to see them so often she just thought everybody knew them. She only began to understand when Louise came over one day all unhappy and crying, and when Laurie was making tea for her, Louise said something about her aunt dying and how bad Louise felt that she never got to tell her something. "Well, why don't you go tell her?" Kate said. "Then you can make her happy."

Laurie said, "That's very sweet, honey."

Kate said, "Well, why doesn't she then?"

Louise bent down to hold Kate's shoulders. She was crying. "Little Kate," she said, "that's really kind of you. And I wish, I really wish I could do that. But we can't really talk to dead people, you know. That's what makes it so sad when people die." Kate said nothing.

The next time she saw her godmother, Kate asked her, "Can't most people talk to dead people?"

"I'm afraid not, darling Kate," Godmother said. "It's something I do and the girls do. And you do it because you come with us. Do you understand that?"

Kate nodded. "I think so." Then she added, "But why don't they?"

"People used to," Godmother said. "But a long time ago people got scared. And so they stopped doing it, and they didn't teach their children, and soon everyone forgot. And now, they can't even hear or see the dead when the dead are standing in front of them."

The funny thing was, the dead sometimes did just that—stand in front of people waving their arms or making funny noises. This didn't happen all that often. Most dead people kept to themselves, either alone or in groups. But sometimes one dead, or a group of them, would go all crazy and run around in traffic jams, banging on car windows and waving their arms, or else dance all around people walking in the street. Kate just thought it so funny that dead people could go right up to someone's face and stick their tongues out or jump up and down, and the living person would go right on talking to friends about where to go for dinner, or how you couldn't take children to the movies anymore because of the violence.

Actually, the "raucous dead," as Godmother called them, didn't act up very often. Most of the dead people Kate saw didn't bother living people much. Sometimes they just stood and looked at things. She would see them standing at a bus stop reading the sign over and over. Or else she'd see one examining a door, or staring down into a garbage pail. Others were more cheerful. They played music on big radios and danced up and down the street, waving their arms and strutting. When they danced, Kate loved to watch them. She would ask her godmother to stop the car and let her out to dance with them. Sometimes Godmother refused, saying they were going someplace special (like the day with the dying star), but other times they all got out and danced. Kate would wave her arms and stamp, the MGs would clap their hands, and even Mother Night once or twice twirled about, holding out the ends of her dress like a bright banner of many colors.

According to Cara, the dead really liked radios. They hated television and computers, and telephones just confused them for some reason. But they would listen to the radio all day long. And they'd broadcast too. The dead ran their own radio stations, playing funny music from a long time ago, and special messages from one group of dead people to another. Ester said once that living people could tune in to dead radio but were "too stupid" to understand what they were hearing and always switched it off again. Shocked at what Ester had said, Kate told her, "That's a bad word." Laurie-Mommy had told her never to call people that.

Laughing, Mother Night told Ester to apologize and to ask Kate to forgive her.

"But it's true," Ester said. "They *are* stupid."

Godmother shook her head. "If Laurie has told her not to use that word, then we will not use it either."

Ester shrugged. "Sorry, kid," she said. When Kate told her, "You're forgiven," Ester bent down to kiss Kate on the cheek.

It was easy to recognize the dead. Some of them actually looked like the pictures—all bones, which clacked a little as they walked. These were the oldest, Amy told her. With the really, really oldest some of their bones were broken or had holes or brown spots. But even the newest dead, who still kept their regular bodies, looked different. Their skin hung loosely, like hand-me-downs that didn't fit right. And when they spoke, their voices often came out funny, all slurred, or else the opposite, high and squeaky.

The real funny thing was, the dead could appear and sound normal if they really wanted to. Lillian called it "wearing flesh." When the dead did look normal, living people could see them and talk with them. Kate wondered why they didn't just do this all the time. "Why should they?" Cara said. As dead people they could do whatever they wanted, so why should they go to all the trouble of disguising themselves?

The dead liked parties. They would find some house where the owner had gone away and put up decorations—strings of dead flowers, flags full of holes, small piles of creatures who'd been dead so long they'd become stone ("settled down" as someone put it), and banners with dead jokes and slogans, like their favorite, "Better dead than red." Then they'd play their radios and laugh and dance, sometimes for days. Kate wondered why no one ever complained. The strange thing was, Lillian told her, living people just didn't hear it. They were just kept awake all night, turning about and making faces and wondering why they couldn't sleep.

Once, when Kate was nine, Laurie took her to a party. She didn't want to go, really. The grown-ups would just complain about things, or tell dumb jokes, or even dumber stories about their kids, and as for the kids themselves, well, Kate still didn't really like other children all that much. But Laurie said it would be good for her, and Louise promised to take Kate to the museum (Kate loved to look at the old paintings) if Kate went along and didn't make too much of a fuss.

The party turned out to be mostly adults, but there were several other kids, and some of the parents had brought balloons and games to keep the kids busy. Kate pretended to play with them (she didn't want Laurie to accuse her of "brooding," Laurie's favorite word), but what really interested her was a tall skinny man in a white suit. Kate didn't know what it was about this man, whose name was Matthew. He didn't look that different from anyone else. He had long hands, which he waved about a little as he talked. He was very handsome, Kate thought. It looked like other people thought so, too, because people kept laughing at his jokes. He danced with both men and women, and when the dance ended he sometimes let the fingers of one hand slide across the person's cheeks. The gesture made Kate shiver.

Toward the end of the party Matthew stepped out of the living room and walked down the hall. To her own surprise, Kate followed him. This was silly, she scolded herself; he was just going to the bathroom. But no, he walked past it to a little room at the end of the hall. He stepped inside and closed the door. Only, the door didn't really shut all the way. Kate hesitated, then went up and peeked through the crack.

Matthew sighed, and stretched himself. The room seemed to be an office, but it was hard to tell, for Matthew hadn't turned on any lights. He just stood there for a moment—and then he took off all his clothes. Now Kate thought for sure she should leave, but she couldn't make herself do it. She wondered if he was going to do something awful as he took off his jacket and pants, and carefully folded them on a table, followed by his shirt and even his underwear. But instead of touching himself, or something else gross, Matthew kept taking things off. He stripped something from his arms and legs, and then his chest and back. Kate stared at it, not sure what she was seeing. And then she realized. It was his skin. He was taking off his skin, and with it everything else, so that he became just an old skeleton. When he had stripped everything and there was nothing left but bones, Matthew sat down on a straight-backed wooden chair. He sat with his legs together and his hands on his knees.

Kate stepped into the room. "You're a dead," she whispered, after she'd closed the door. "Wow. You're a dead."

Slowly the skull pivoted around to face her. He must have been a very old dead, because there were large gaps in the bone. For a long time, Matthew didn't make a sound. And then, from somewhere, came a slow deep voice. "Yes," it said. "Of course. But let's just keep that our little secret. Will you do that for me?"

Kate clasped her hands in front of her. She smiled, happy for the first time since she'd arrived at the party. "Okay," she said. "I really like secrets."

Two

The Streetmarket of the Dead

As Kate got older she became more and more impatient with most of the people she knew and the things they expected her to do. Holidays, for instance. Laurie made such a fuss about Christmas, taking her to Grandpa and Grandma Lang's house, putting stuff on trees, going places, even telling her dumb stories and singing songs. And of course, the presents. They all expected her to get so excited about the same things year after year. Dolls, books with little morals about tolerance, a kid's camera, paint boxes and telescopes. She did like some of the clothes, especially when Laurie let her get the things she really wanted instead of the frilly dresses and things Laurie expected her to want (as if Laurie would ever wear stuff like that). Still, the only really cool presents she got came from Mother Night.

Like the half skull of a little girl who'd died when she was the same age as Kate on the day Godmother gave her the present. The girl had died so long ago that fossils of dead flowers were imprinted on the bone. And yet, when Kate held the mouth up against her ear she could hear the faint high-pitched squeal of a little girl, and beyond that the growl of some animal. And if she looked directly into what was left of the eye socket, she could see bright colors. Kate loved the skull—"Janie," she called it for no reason—and kept it next to her pillow when she slept, imagining that Janie was sleeping alongside her and they could hug and kiss each other the whole night long.

But she couldn't tell anyone, not the kids at school, not Laurie. In fact, when Laurie asked her about it she had to lie, as she lied about so many things, telling Laurie she'd found it in the park. Laurie had looked at her awhile, and Kate tried to keep her face blank as she waited for her mother to say, "That's ridiculous. Where did you really get it?" Finally, as she had done so many times before, Laurie backed down. "It's very nice," she said, "but you better be careful. It looks fragile." Then she turned to the stove, sighing as she checked the potatoes.

Once, Kate tried talking to Louise about holidays. Louise, at least, gave Kate presents that were different, that Louise herself cared about. Like the time she gave Kate a bow with real arrows, and a green tunic, and sandals that tied all the way up Kate's legs, so that Kate could become a "goddess of the hunt."

It was a Sunday afternoon in January, and they were sitting in a women's coffee shop, drinking hot chocolate. Kate was ten. She wore a long blue sweater with a white cotton lace collar over pink tights and short shiny black boots with white fake fur. Her red hair, shoulder length, was held back by a gold barrette.

"What's up, kid?" Louise said to her.

"Nothing," Kate said, and sucked loudly on her straw.

"Beep," Louise said. "Wrong answer. You have your weight-of-the-world look."

Kate made a face. "I don't understand Christmas," she said grandly.

"Hmm, let's see. We could talk about the great mystery of God becoming man, or maybe the Virgin Mary's history as the great Mother Goddess, or maybe the consumer economy and its dependence on one month of the year. But somehow I'll bet that's not what you meant."

"I just don't understand Laurie," Kate said.

"Ah. So it's *Laurie* and Christmas. I should have guessed."

"I just don't understand why she has to make it such a big deal. It's not like she believes it or anything. She's even Jewish. And I don't care. So why do we have to do all that stuff?"

"What about the presents?" Louise asked. "Don't you care about them?"

Kate shrugged, a delicate lift of the shoulders. Watching her, Louise remembered how she used to practice elegant movements like that in the mirror, right about when she was Kate's age. Somehow she suspected that Kate didn't need to practice. Kate said, "I guess. Some of them. I like the ones you give me." She had stopped drinking her hot chocolate and was looking out the window. Louise scanned the street, but if Kate was staring at anything in particular, Louise couldn't see it.

Louise said, "I suppose it's because of Jaqe."

Kate turned around. "My mother Jaqe?"

"Uh-huh." Louise found herself pleased to have gotten Kate's attention back.

"Did Jaqe use to do all these Christmas things?"

"No. That's not what I meant." Louise took a breath. "Let me try to explain this. Laurie . . . Laurie worries all the time that she's not good enough. That Jaqe would have done everything so much better than her. So she tries to do all the things she believes Jaqe would have done. Do you understand?"

Kate squinted, concentrating. "But you said that Jaqe didn't care about Christmas."

"Well, I don't know. I don't think she did. But it doesn't matter what Jaqe actually would have done. All that matters is what Laurie thinks Jaqe would have done. And not even that really. I mean, it's like—it's like Laurie has some kind of ideal stuck in her head. The perfect mother. I don't know where it comes from. It certainly doesn't come from anything *she* would have liked as a child. Wherever it comes from, Laurie really believes in this perfect mother. And it's everything Laurie isn't. So she just fights and fights against herself all the time. And on top of that she's convinced herself that Jaqe would have done all those perfect things. So she feels doubly guilty."

"But that's silly," Kate said.

"So it is," Louise told her. "Love is usually silly. And Laurie not only loves Jaqe. She loves you. She loves you very, very much."

Kate shrugged. "I know," she said. She glanced out the window again, and again Louise looked and saw nothing more unusual than a few people looking in the jewelry store across the street, or going in and out of the deli a couple of doors down. She turned back to look at Kate. What a beautiful child, she thought. No wonder Laurie would do anything, give up her whole life for her. It wasn't just Jaqe, or doing the right thing.

Not the first time, Louise wondered how much Kate knew about the custody battle after Jaqe's death. Did she remember anything of the weeks she'd spent living with her grandparents when that damn judge granted their petition for temporary custody? Or the afternoon Mark and Laurie had driven out to the Langs' and Laurie had pleaded with them to let Kate stay with her until the judge had decided. Louise shook her head, thinking of the hours and hours she had spent with Laurie and that Gay Alliance lawyer, looking things up, practicing testimony—only to have the judge die the night before the trial. They were all set to start over when the Langs' lawyer called and announced that his clients had called off their case. Two years later Laurie adopted Kate as her legal daughter. Louise had always wondered if Jaqe's parents had simply come to their senses and realized how much work it would have been to raise another child when someone else was willing (she'd almost thought "dying") to do the job for them.

So strange, Louise thought. All of heaven and hell can battle over a child, and the kid will bounce along without the faintest idea that anything unusual has happened.

Her eyes snapped back in focus when Kate asked her, "Did Jaqe love Laurie?"

"Oh yes."

"Was Jaqe a perfect mother?"

"Of course not. No one is." Kate looked about to say something, but didn't. Louise said, "Or maybe Laurie is really the perfect mother. Maybe she just doesn't know it."

Kate seemed to think about that for a while. "I don't think so," she said.

Louise smiled. "No, I guess not. I just thought I would try out the idea."

Louise jumped at the sound of someone knocking on the window. She hadn't even noticed anyone across the street. Kate must have known, however, because she was waving and smiling and rapping back on the window. Louise looked curiously at the child on the other side of the glass. At first glance, she thought it was a girl, but that was only because of the loose dress and open red coat. If not for the clothes, however, the short blonde hair and, well, just the shape of the excited face suggested a boy. Louise scowled to herself. She of all people should . . . should be beyond such simple rules. She said to Kate, "Is that a friend of yours?"

"Yes, of course," Kate said. "It's D—It's Jimmy."

"Is Jimmy in your class?"

"Umm . . . sure."

Louise wanted to ask if Jimmy wore dresses in class, but she decided it might be rude. Instead, she said, "You think he'd like to come in and have some hot chocolate?"

Kate giggled for some reason but she still jumped up. "I'll go tell him," she said. She looked at Jimmy and pointed to the door. He nodded and the two of them ran to meet at the entrance.

As soon as Jimmy came inside, Kate whispered something to him and they both began to giggle with their hands over their mouths. Louise noticed a number of the women looking up from their conversations or their magazines or their coffees to stare at the two children. A skinny child a couple of inches taller than Kate (who herself was tall for her age), Jimmy was wearing a yellow dress with red polka dots. Red tights covered his legs, but his thin coat and suede shoes with flower patterns cut out along the sides looked more appropriate for April or May than January. He didn't look cold, though. Warm-blooded, Louise thought.

"This is Louise," Kate said. "She's my mom's best friend. They're not lovers, though. I think they should get married, but my mom says she's not interested."

Louise willed herself not to blush, determined she wouldn't let Kate's deliberate cuteness embarrass her. Jimmy dipped in a minute curtsy. "Nice to meet you," he said.

"Come sit next to me," Kate said as she slid into the wooden booth. Quickly Jimmy followed her. They sat very close, their shoulders touching. They seemed to be holding hands under the table.

"Would you like some hot chocolate?" Louise asked.

Kate began to giggle again, but Jimmy just said, "No, thank you. I've already eaten."

There was silence for a moment, and then Louise said, "Where do you live, Jimmy?"

Kate really was in a mood, because she started snickering. Louise wasn't sure, but she thought Jimmy kicked her under the table before he answered. "On Harrison Street," he said. Now Louise wanted to ask if his parents knew he came downtown all by himself (and dressed like that). She wondered why it was so hard to talk to children without prying. Or without making moralistic judgments she never would have approved of from anyone else. "What do your parents do?" she asked, thinking how she didn't really care, but it was the best she could come up with.

"I don't really have parents," Jimmy said.

"Oh," Louise said. "I'm sorry." Did they die? Or disown him? Or maybe he was disowning them.

Kate said, "Jimmy's an orphan. He . . . he lives with his grandmother."

"I really am sorry," Louise said.

Jimmy said, "That's okay. I don't really mind anymore. It did happen a long time ago, after all."

Louise asked, "You were very young?" Jimmy nodded. Just like Kate, Louise thought to herself. Funny she never thought of Kate as an orphan, but in a way she was. Except that Laurie loved her more than most natural parents.

Louise glanced around. More and more of the women were staring at Jimmy, some with clear hostility. She said, "Um, kids, maybe we should move on."

Kate shrugged. "Sure."

Outside, they all stood a moment in the chill sunlight. "Well," Louise said, "what would you like to do? Shall we go somewhere?"

Kate said, "Can we go to your house and play dress-up?" Louise stopped herself from rolling her eyes. Kate went on, "If we go to my house, Laurie doesn't have any fun clothes, or any makeup. You've got really cool stuff."

"Thanks," Louise said. Then she smiled. "Laurie used to have good dress-up stuff. Do you remember?"

Kate grinned back at her. "Sure. But then she gave it all to you." They laughed. Kate turned to Jimmy. "When I started school," she said, lifting her voice at the end in that way girls did when talking to each other, "my mom used to think she had to dress properly, like a lady. It was real funny."

Louise broke in, "That's not entirely fair. She just didn't have much clothes sense. At least not for those kinds of clothes."

Kate went on, "And she wouldn't wear any makeup, or even girls' shoes. She was drawing a line, she said. Finally, Louise and Mark made her stop."

"We didn't *make* her. We just convinced her she'd make a much better impression dressed as herself."

Kate continued, "So she gave all that stuff to Louise."

Jimmy said politely, "Do you still have it?"

Louise laughed. "Actually, I gave it to a commune of drag queens."

Looking up innocently, Kate said, "So can we go to your house and play dress-up?"

Louise laughed again. "I guess I don't have much choice, do I?"

Back in her tiny apartment, Louise set them loose in her bedroom, telling them they could try on anything but her underwear as long as they didn't tear anything. She also offered to help them if they wanted to play with her makeup, but Jimmy said, "Thank you, Louise. But we can do it ourselves."

For the next two hours Louise worked on articles for the medical journal she edited, trying to ignore the whispers and giggles coming from her bedroom. Only occasionally did she sneak a glance through the bedroom door. The bed was piled high with dresses, blouses, skirts, even her leather jacket and blazers. Shoes lay strewn about the floor. Kate and Jimmy seemed determined to try everything. One time Louise would find Kate dressed in a long gold crepe-de-chine dress, with several necklaces, while Jimmy had on her red leather miniskirt and sparkly high heels. The next time she peeked Jimmy would be wearing a fussy old grandma dress she'd forgotten she owned, and

Kate would look like a miniature career woman in a tweed suit. Or they would both be wearing lace nightgowns, sitting before the mirror fussing with each other's hair or putting on yet another layer of lipstick. When she came upon them kissing, sitting a little away from each other and leaning forward from the waist to touch lips, Louise decided she better stop looking. *I'm getting old*, she thought. *I don't even want to* try *to figure this out.*

After two hours, Louise gave them a ten-minute warning, and when the time was up, took a deep breath, then marched in like a summer camp athletic director to announce cleanup time. Kate was holding Jimmy's chin in her hand and was brushing mascara onto his eyelashes. She began to protest but stopped when Jimmy got up and began to pick up skirts and dresses off the floor. "That's okay," Louise said. "I'll put the clothes away, Jimmy. Thanks. You two get dressed and then we'll see if we can discover your original faces somewhere under all that grease."

Kate squealed and grimaced as Louise wiped her face with makeup remover and then scrubbed her with soap and water. "Will you please sit still?" Louise said. "I do not want your mother to start asking me questions." By contrast, Jimmy sat nearly motionless, his hands in his lap as he delicately offered his face to Louise's washcloth. She marveled at the touch and feel of his skin, pure even for a child, and very clear, almost translucent. When she finished she found herself staring at him for a moment until she realized he was watching her. "Thank you," he said as she stepped back.

Out in the street, Jimmy announced he would go with them to Kate's house before heading home. He and Kate held hands as they walked. Louise found herself looking nervously at people passing them, but no one seemed to pay any attention.

To Louise, Kate said, "How come you don't want Laurie to know we were playing dress-up?"

"Oh," Louise said, "you know your mom. She's just a little stiff sometimes." Just as in the café earlier, Kate looked at Jimmy and began to giggle at some private joke. Louise paid no attention. Poked by guilt, she said, "That's not really fair. Laurie . . . Laurie worries a lot. That something might happen to you."

Kate laughed. "What's going to happen to me from playing dress-up?"

"Well, she worries that people—the government—might consider her a bad parent, a bad influence."

Kate laughed even louder. "Because we played dress-up?"

Louise shook her head. "Never mind," she said.

Of course, it wasn't Jimmy's parents who'd died, but Jimmy himself. "I'm a reverse orphan," he told Kate. Dead Jimmy, as Kate called him (to distinguish him from Black-haired Jimmy, a boy in her class), was Kate's best friend. Jimmy was ten, always ten, though he'd died long enough ago that his parents had grown old enough to retire and spend a good part of their days looking at pictures of their lost son. They would talk of memories, but their memories were selective, for they forgot their distaste for him, his precociousness, his contempt for their anger and commands, his perverted insistence on sleeping in his mother's old nightgowns.

Kate met Jimmy when she was seven, at a party she'd gone to with Mother Night. In the middle of all the dancing and loud laughter she'd seen a quiet figure in a green dirndl, sitting on the floor and drawing. She'd sat down and looked at the paper. It was covered with squiggly lines, except for the center, which displayed a snarling devil face, bright red with long yellow teeth. "What are you drawing?" she asked.

"Mazes," the child answered. "You want to try it?"

"Okay."

The child gave her the pencil and pointed at a break in the lines at the upper left corner. "You have to go in here and go to the center and circle all around the Monster Man without falling into his den, and then you have to go out again without crossing the way you came in."

"Wow," Kate said. "That's really cool. Did you really make it yourself?"

"Uh-huh."

Kate set to work. Several times she thought she was making great progress only to hit a dead end. After a few minutes she said, "Are you a boy?"

"Sure," the boy said.

Kate nodded. "I like your dress," she said. "It's real pretty."

"Thank you. I like your overalls."

"You do?" Kate looked down at the denim and flannel overalls Laurie had dressed her in that morning. Usually she liked these clothes. Now they looked dull. She tried to remember what pretty dresses she had at home. She looked up. "I'm Kate," she said.

"I know. You're her goddaughter." Kate's eyes opened wide. Was she famous? Did all the dead people know her? The boy said, "I'm Jimmy."

Kate put out her hand. To her great surprise, Jimmy leaned forward and kissed her cheek. From then on they were friends, despite the fact that Kate never finished the maze, never even reached the center.

Usually they met under the protective benevolence of Mother Night, who could stretch a few minutes at lunchtime into what seemed like hours. Sometimes Mother Night would take them somewhere, a party or a play, but at other times she would sit in a coffee shop, writing with a funny old pen in a shiny black notebook while the children wandered around town in search of adventure.

The first time Mother Night sent them off on their own, Kate hesitated. "Is it safe?" she asked.

Jimmy rolled his eyes. "Of course it's safe. She doesn't have to be with you to protect you."

Kate feared she would cry. "But I'm not even allowed to cross the street," she said. She added, "Without a grown-up."

Godmother set down her book. She placed her hands on Kate's shoulders. "My darling Kate," she said. "I promise you. Wherever you go, my love and safety will go with you. No one will harm you, no stranger will touch you. Do you understand?"

Kate whispered, "Yes."

Even so, when she stepped from the darkened coffee shop into the sunny afternoon, she stood nervously just outside the door. "Come on," Jimmy said, and pulled on her hand. Suddenly Kate heard the growl of a motorcycle. She turned around to see, at the end of the block, Cara sitting on her parked motorcycle, body forward as she leaned on her handlebars. One hand moved in a half wave, half salute. Kate ran after Jimmy.

Unlike most dead people Kate knew, Jimmy wore flesh almost all the time. It made it more fun, he said, if living people could see him. He got most of his clothes by stealing them from department stores, where he would fill his arms with dresses, then go to the boys' fitting room to try them on. In the midst of all the confusion, and the outrage from mothers, no one ever seemed to notice that he left with something extra, or maybe wearing something different than when he entered. Kate sometimes came along on these expeditions, but Jimmy never let her steal anything, or even stand too close. "I don't want you getting caught," he told her. "It doesn't matter if they catch me. They can't *kill* me or anything."

They were sitting on the end of a pier that day, a place where grown-ups came to exercise and to "make eyes at each other," as Jimmy put it. It was summer and Kate was eating ice cream, something Laurie usually would not allow. Jimmy had bought it for her, with money he'd begged from a couple of middle-aged women, telling them that his family was so poor he had to wear his sister's hand-me-downs. Confused, the women had looked from Jimmy to Kate, who'd nodded vigorously and said, "It's true, it's all true." Not sure what to do, the women had given the children a couple of dollars and hurried away.

Eating her ice cream, Kate said, "But they could put you in prison. Or a *home.*" She shuddered.

Jimmy shrugged. "So what? I'd just leave. I'd go unseen on them. Pop!"

Every now and then Jimmy would go unseen on the street, sometimes right in the middle of a conversation. Usually he did this as a joke on Kate, who would go right on talking, so absorbed she wouldn't notice the sudden gauntness, the glimpse of bone through the skin, all the signs that meant only she could see him. The first time this happened, she wondered for several minutes why people kept staring at her, or whispering to each other, until one woman leaned over and said to her, "Are you talking to your imaginary friend, dear? Does it have a name?"

When Kate was eleven years old, her friendship with Dead Jimmy ended because of a streetmarket.

There were always streetmarkets in the city where Kate and Laurie lived, most of them illegal. People sometimes would set up carts, or simply lay down blankets on the sidewalk. They sold old clothes and new books, cheap copies of expensive wristwatches, wallets made from eels and snakes, earmuffs and sunglasses, healing oils and incense, earrings and magic charms, silk scarves and auto parts, fortunes and protection against evil. Most of what they sold they'd stolen, and of course they paid no taxes, so that the police sometimes closed them down, at least for a little while. But people liked the markets, at least the ones that sold new (if stolen) items from clean carts. People complained more about the ones selling filthy clothes and broken junk on the sidewalk. But since these people could scoop everything up in their blankets and move on, there wasn't much the police could do.

The market that sprang up the spring of Kate's eleventh year, however, was different. For one thing it sold only old stuff—torn clothes, broken glass, high school yearbooks from twenty or thirty years ago, bent rings, jewelry with missing stones—things that no one really wanted. The sellers made up for this lack of appeal by extremely aggressive selling. They would grab people or shout in their faces. When people tried to turn away they would jump in front of them or else follow them, ridiculing the way they walked. Several people complained of cuts or bruises, even a broken arm. To make all of this much worse, the market did not operate in the seedy downtown area, but right on the main shopping avenue of one of the city's wealthiest districts. The local shops complained of losing tens of thousands of dollars a day, as people either avoided the area altogether or couldn't get through the street sellers to enter the stores.

For weeks the hellmarket, as the newspapers called it, dominated the local news. People told their stories or showed their bruises on television, newspapers demanded action, late-night comedians told jokes. The police promised to clear them out, while implying that their helplessness wasn't really their fault. In fact, no one seemed to understand just why the police couldn't do anything. Store owners would call them as soon as the market began, then wait anxiously by their windows, listening for the sirens. And yet whenever the police arrived, the market was gone. The police cordoned off whole streets, letting nobody in or out. Somehow they only ever caught innocent shoppers who berated the police with still more tales of abuse. A few times they managed to confiscate oily sheets full of rusty tools or old torn photos. As soon as they left, however, the hellmarket returned, with even greater heaps of ancient trash.

No one seemed to know where they came from. They looked to be all colors. Their ages ranged from as young as six or seven (one woman on the news told of a little girl who bit her ankle when she refused to buy a broken yo-yo), to people who looked almost too old to walk, let alone run from the police. Victims reported various languages, suggesting immigrants. Others heard only English. While many of the sellers looked as ragged as their merchandise, others appeared well fed and were dressed in clothes that could have come from suburban department stores except that they all looked helplessly out of fashion. Even the "rich" sellers, however, attacked their customers as ferociously as their shabbiest brothers and sisters.

Kate found out about the market from the television. Laurie always put the news on while making dinner for her and Kate. Laurie didn't care about the news actually; she just believed she should expose her daughter to current events. One night Kate heard shouts from the television, and when she went to look she saw groups of people shoving one another and screaming. The camera jerked around a lot, as if people were pulling the cameraman back and forth.

Glancing in from the kitchen, Laurie didn't like the way Kate sat so close to the television, staring with such concentration at the screen. She turned down the spaghetti sauce and walked over to the TV. "Honey," she said, reaching for the controls, "why don't you put on something else? This is all just noise."

"No," Kate said, with such vehemence that Laurie jerked back her hand. "I want to see."

Laurie crossed her arms and stood watching her daughter. She'd never seen Kate so intense before. Suddenly Kate said, "I have to go there."

Laurie shook her head. "Forget it. People are getting hurt there. It's a madhouse."

"I don't care."

"Obviously. But I care. It's my job. Don't even think about going there." Laurie braced herself as she reached out and turned off the TV.

Kate must have seen enough because she didn't object. Instead, she just said, "Mom, you don't understand. I've *got* to go there."

"Kate, this is ridiculous. You're not going anywhere near there."

"But I can help."

"Help?" Laurie laughed, a short sharp sound. "I don't think so, sweetheart." Kate looked down. Gingerly, Laurie touched her cheek. "I'm sorry," she said, "I didn't mean that. I think—I think it's nice that you want to do something. But you know I can't let you do that."

"It's okay," Kate said. She shifted her gaze to the empty air.

Laurie stroked her shoulder. "Why don't you help me make the salad?"

Kate knew that her godmother would take her downtown if she asked. For once, however, Kate wanted to do this on her own, at least until she knew for sure. That night, she put a couple of subway tokens in her knapsack along with her allowance and some money from the secret bag she kept under her bed. She also tucked in a special handkerchief, delicate and pink, with lace trim and an embroidered flower. Jimmy had given it to her. To show how much he loved her, he'd said. In the morning she got up early and dressed herself in ragged jeans, sneakers, and an old sweatshirt before Laurie could come in and suggest more respectable clothes. "We're going on a field trip," Kate told her mother when Laurie objected. "To the park."

Through the morning, Kate did her best to ignore the stares and snickers from the fashionable girls in her class. During recess she went and sat by herself in the corner of the playground and drew pictures of motorcycles and labyrinths in the back of her composition book. She didn't even look up when Alice and Martine, two girls who always wore dresses, strolled past her, whispering "Lezzie" just loud enough for Kate to hear.

Finally, lunchtime came. The moment the bell rang Kate rushed from class and ran for the subway. The ride downtown took twenty minutes. The whole way, Kate bounced excitedly in her seat. Going somewhere on her own, really, without even Mother Night. But as she got closer to the streetmarket area, and could hear the noises of people shouting, her confidence began to dwindle. What if someone hit her? What if the police arrested her? She couldn't just go unseen. What if it took longer than she thought and she couldn't get back to school on time? And what if Laurie found out? Silently she repeated to herself Louise's phone number and the phone number of the bookstore, placing them fresh in her mind just in case. The bookstore would be best, if she could speak to Mark, but suppose her Mom answered? She wondered if she could disguise her voice.

The market, when she came to it, appeared both quieter and more chaotic than it looked on television. The sellers covered most of the sidewalk space in front of the stores for three whole blocks, but most of them just stood by their sheets full of junk or else sat on the ground. At the same time, there were pockets of wildness, shop owners screaming at the sellers to go away, market people grabbing some poor woman who'd tried to step past someone to go into a drugstore for a prescription. Kate saw a woman crying and pleading with the market people to leave her pen store alone, to go find some other neighborhood to destroy. Her husband had had a stroke, she said, he didn't even leave the house anymore, if this kept up it would kill him, couldn't they see that, why couldn't they just go away? The marketers, a man who looked old enough to be the store owner's father and a girl who looked about Kate's age, only laughed and offered to sell the woman an ancient pen stained with leaked ink and grime. The store owner stood crying for a moment, then ran inside her shop and slammed the door.

Kate stood at the head of the street, breathing deeply until a woman came up to her and warned her she better leave, things were quiet now, but they could blow up at any moment. Kate told her it was okay, she just had to go meet her mommy in the toy store at the end of the block. The woman looked doubtfully down the street, then offered to walk with her. "No, thank you," Kate said, and walked quickly away, slowing down only when she was sure the woman wasn't following her.

The market went on and on, piles and piles of old watches, fifty-year-old calendars, broken thermometers. Here and there people shouted, or shoved each other, but Kate didn't look. That wasn't what she'd come to see. She had just reached the end of the street and was hoping she could get back to school in time if she ran all the way to the subway, when someone grabbed her arm. As she screamed, she heard high-pitched laughter. She looked to the side and saw a child about seven years old, holding her arm with both hands in a grip so strong Kate was sure it would leave marks on her skin. The boy (or maybe it was a girl, she wasn't sure) wore a T-shirt with a picture of some cartoon character Kate had never seen before, too-short jeans, and torn sneakers with a big hole in the toe. "Let go of me," Kate said, and tried to pull loose her arm. The child paid no attention.

"Want to buy my dolls?" it said. A small pile of toys lay at its feet, including a beat-up teddy bear and a baby doll with one eye missing.

"Can I take a look?" Kate said.

"Sure," the child said, and let go one hand to reach down.

Kate managed to jerk her arm away, only to back into someone else.

"That wasn't a very nice trick," a man's voice said, and the child added, "That wasn't nice at all. You said you'd buy my dolls."

"I did not," Kate said, then realized that wouldn't get her anywhere and turned around. A man and a woman were standing there, alike enough in their faces to be brother and sister. Or maybe, Kate realized, parent and child. They both looked about Mark's age, or maybe a little older. They were among the better dressed ones. At least their clothes weren't all torn. The man wore a white short-sleeve shirt, gray pants, and white shoes; the woman wore the kind of dress Grandma Lang wore, knee length and very plain, with a short yellow cardigan draped over her shoulders. The two of them smiled at her. Kate shuddered.

"Come to find some treasures?" the woman said. "We've got a lot of treasures. You could furnish your whole house with the wonderful things we have here."

Kate stared up at them. "You're dead, aren't you?" she said. "You're all dead."

Their smiles widened. "What a smart little girl," the woman said, and clapped her hands once.

"And this stuff you're selling," Kate said. "It's all the stuff from your lives, isn't it? From when you were alive."

"Yes, exactly," the woman said. "That's what makes it so special."

Kate said loudly, "Nobody wants your old junk. Why can't you just go away and leave people alone?"

The woman put her hands over her mouth. To the man she said, "Cheeky little witch, isn't she?"

The man squatted down and took hold of Kate's shoulders. Putting his smiling face very close to hers he said, "You think you're fucking clever, don't you? Figuring us out. Well, we fucking know who you are, too. You're Mother Night's pet meat."

Kate turned her head to look up and down the street. A few marketers were watching her, but none of the living. The man laughed again. In the middle of her fear Kate noticed that no breath came out of his mouth, and she thought about the time she and Dead Jimmy had played kissing, and she realized now how she'd never felt his breath, even when they'd touched their tongues. Dead people don't breathe, she thought, even as she had trouble getting air into her own lungs. The man was saying, "What are you looking for? The motorcycle bitches? They're not here. Probably off at some battlefield scarfing up dead murderers. Or maybe you're looking for your meat police. You can forget those bed wetters."

Kate's voice cracked a little as she said, "Why do you want to bother these people? They haven't done anything to you."

"They're meat," he said. "Like you. They don't know anything. They can't even remember their own fucking families."

The woman bent forward slightly. "Why should the nons own the world?" she said. "We have as much right to the streets as they do. More, in my opinion. Aren't there vastly more dead people than non-dead? We just want our rights."

Kate was trying hard not to cry as she said, "What are you going to do to me?"

The man shoved her backward so hard that she fell down in the street. The sound of Kate crying out made the child who'd grabbed her shriek with excitement. The man said, "What do you think? That we're going to eat you? We don't eat, remember? Especially not meat. More fucking non stupidity."

Kate got up and scurried back out of reach. "You're the ones who're stupid," she shouted at them. "Think you're so great just because you're dead. Well, you can—you can . . . Fuck you!" She turned and ran for the end of the street. Behind her she could hear the dead laughing and applauding. She thought they were throwing things, too, but she didn't dare to stop and look.

Kate kept running for almost two blocks beyond the end of the market. Finally, she stopped and leaned against a wall. "Shit," she whispered to herself. She realized she was crying and took Jimmy's pink handkerchief from her knapsack to wipe her eyes and blow her nose. She hated getting it dirty. She'd only taken it for luck.

Head down, Kate began walking toward the subway. She was almost there when she realized it was too late, there was no way she could get back in time. She stopped, out of breath despite the fact that she hadn't even been walking very fast. It was so unfair, she thought. She just wanted to help. Why did they have to be so nasty? She wasn't just some stupid non-dead person. Just because Mother Night was her godmother didn't mean she was anybody's pet. She came all by herself, didn't she? And now she was late, and you weren't allowed to come back late from lunch, you weren't even supposed to leave the school grounds by yourself. She couldn't go back now. Maybe Mrs. Benducci wouldn't notice she was gone. Yeah, right. Even if Mrs. Benducci didn't realize, that creep Billy Dorfman would be sure to tell her. She could just imagine *Dork*man waving his hand and pointing to her empty desk. Suddenly she thought of Laurie. The school would tell Laurie! She would get that pained look on her face and say something like "Sweetheart, you know you're not supposed to skip school. What were you doing?" And what could Kate tell her? It was so unfair. "Meat" they called her. And "non." The dead were supposed to be her friends.

A policeman came walking toward her. He's going to know, she thought. He'll say "Little girl, why aren't you in school?" and before she could even answer he'd arrest her and put her in a cell. And call her mother.

Trying not to look suspicious, Kate dashed across the street and around the corner. She better keep moving, she thought, look like she was going somewhere. She should have just stayed out the whole day. Then she could have forged a note from her mom the next day saying she was sick. Or that someone had died. That's what Karen Schumer did. Karen skipped school almost every week. She was so dumb anyway it didn't make a difference. If they called *her* stupid meat it would make some sense.

Kate was walking around for nearly half an hour when she heard the sirens.

At first she thought she must have doubled back and the police were coming for the marketers. But when she swallowed her panic and looked at the street signs, she realized she'd traveled fifteen blocks downtown. Along with a handful of others, Kate followed the sound.

She saw the crowd and the smoke and the flashing red lights before anything else. Squeezing and ducking between all the grown-ups Kate made her way to the front, where she still saw the police cars and the ambulances and the small fire truck before the people or the accident itself. Slowly, through all the noise and smoke, and people rushing about and shouting, she made out the two cars, one half crumpled into the side of a subway entrance, the other lying on its side in a lake of glass. And the freshly dead people, two of them already safely in body bags, but two others still lying in the road, one with its head smashed beyond any semblance of a skull, the other nearly torn in half, with guts and blood and shit all mingled together. And the woman, unhurt except for all the cuts dyeing her face and clothes a bright red, screaming the name "Brian!" over and over and flailing her arms at the police whenever they tried to come close and calm her down.

Despite the police pushing the crowd back, no one paid much attention to Kate. She just stood there at the edge of the street and stared. She stared at the non-dead shrieking woman and the paramedics who finally got a needle into her. She stared at the police and the paras scooping the remaining two bodies into the heavy sacks, almost like old cake and melted ice cream being dumped into a black garbage bag at the end of a birthday party. She stared at the police car and the ambulances, and all the people working so hard to clean everything up. She just stared—until one of the paramedics suddenly looked up and saw her and blurted out, "*Kate?* What are you doing here?"

"Ester," Kate whispered.

No one seemed to pay any attention as Ester said to her, "Does Mother know you're here?" Kate shook her head. "Damn," Ester said. "She's really going to be pissed." She got up from kneeling by the body and marched over to take Kate's hand. "Come on," she said. "I better get you out of here."

They found Mother Night by a department store a few blocks away. She was talking to a man selling ice cream from a little booth alongside the main entrance. People were waiting for ice cream but the man, who had long hair tied back in a ponytail, paid no attention to them, only listened to Mother Night and nodded his head. When Mother Night spotted Kate and Ester coming she inclined her head toward them and raised her eyebrows. She left the ice cream man, who called after her, and walked to meet Kate. "Good afternoon, Kate," she said. She was wearing a long violet dress with an embroidered neckline, and a straw hat with a wide brim. "We didn't expect to see you today."

Ester dropped Kate's hand and told her to wait as she and Mother Night stepped a few feet away to talk. Kate paid no attention to them. She was looking at her hand, wet with blood Ester had carried from one of the dead people. She wiped her hand on her jeans but it still looked red. Maybe it was stained forever. Something else she wouldn't be able to explain to Laurie.

Mother Night walked back to Kate. Stroking her hair, she said, "Now. Why are you wandering the streets instead of sitting at your nice wooden desk?"

"Those people—" Kate said. Her own voice sounded funny to her.

"Yes?"

"By that accident. What—what was Ester doing to them?"

Mother Night glanced at Ester, who said nothing. Mother Night said, "Helping them, of course. Helping them adjust."

"And that woman? The non-dead one? Can you help her?"

Ester said, "Survivor. She was making a lot of noise."

To Kate, Mother Night said, "We do what we can, Kate. But we cannot help everyone."

"Then what good are you? If all you do is help dead people." She stopped herself and took a breath. "I'm sorry," she said. "It's just—it's just not fair. That's all I wanted to do. I wanted to help." She realized she was crying when Mother Night gave her a large white handkerchief, but she didn't wipe her eyes or blow her nose. Instead, she said, "And then they called me names. And I don't know what to do. I can't even go back. And I can't tell Laurie. It's just not fair."

Mother Night bent down to hold Kate against her. She looked up. "Ester," she said, "will you please get my car?" Ester saluted and walked away. Slowly, Kate managed to tell her story. When she finished she said, "I'm not just your pet meat, am I?"

"Of course not. You're my precious goddaughter." Kate nodded, as if they'd settled the issue. "And 'meat' is just not a term we use. Those people at that market sound very rude."

"Are you going to do something about them?" Kate asked.

"Perhaps. But first we must bring you safely back to school." The moment Kate sat down in the backseat of her godmother's limousine, she felt a wave of safety float away the dirt and blood. When she closed her eyes she still could see the bodies poured out onto the street, and the screaming woman, but now they played out their scenes far, far away.

At school, Mother Night walked firmly into class and straight to Mrs. Benducci at the blackboard. "Good afternoon," she said warmly. "I am Mrs. Knight, Kate's godmother." She held out her hand and waited while Mrs. Benducci wiped the chalk dust from her hand. "I'm very sorry to have kept Kate out past her lunch hour. The poor thing kept warning me and pointing at the clock, but I'm afraid I just hushed her." She leaned forward slightly and lowered her voice. "I really just wanted to show her off to my friends." With a push she sent Kate to her desk. "You didn't have a test, did you? I'd be horrified if Kate missed a test because of me."

"No. No, of course not," Mrs. Benducci said.

"Oh good," Mother Night said. She looked around. "What a lovely classroom." As she left she brushed the top of Kate's head with her fingertips.

Two days later Kate stepped onto the playground at lunch hour and saw her godmother waving to her. For once she hesitated rather than ran to the gate. She was sure all the kids in her class must be staring at her as she finally took Mother Night's hand and left the school grounds. They got into the red sports car, and as they turned the avenue the Motorcycle Girls, all five of them, came roaring up alongside them.

The market was in full session when they drove onto the street. All up and down the road the noise stopped. The sellers stood, the shop owners and their few customers looked at each other, wondering if the mayor had arrived. There was no traffic, Kate saw. She wondered if the police had cordoned off the market.

The MGs all stood very still while Mother Night slowly turned and looked around. "Well?" Mother Night said finally. "Who is going to speak?"

The man who'd pushed Kate into the road strolled forward. "Why the fuck not?" he said.

Mother Night snapped her fingers. "One," she said. "You will not talk that way in front of my goddaughter. Her mother would not approve."

"What do I care about someone's mother?"

"And *I* do not approve. I am an old-fashioned woman."

"What do you want here?" the man said. Other dead were beginning to cluster around them. "Your little non whistles and you come running? Is that what's going on here?"

"Everyone is a non," Mother Night said. "She is non-dead. You are non-living. That makes you the same, brother and sister."

The woman who'd been with him the other day stepped forward. She still wore the plain dress. "But that's just not true," she said. "We have nothing in common with them. Nothing at all. They are all so—" She fluttered a hand. "Narrow."

Kate thought of the accident, the woman screaming for Brian. She wondered if Brian was there, lined up with all the other non-living.

Mother Night said, "Then you will not mind leaving their street."

The dead began to shout. There was some kind of high-pitched whistling noise in their collective voice that Kate had never noticed before. The man said, "You can't be serious."

Mother Night smiled. The sunlight caught her teeth so that they became very bright. She said, "Oh, but I am always serious."

From the gathering crowd someone who looked like a teenage girl came forward. She wore a puffy pink sweater, grease stained, over tight stretch jeans torn at one ankle. She said, "How can you do this? How can you take their side? You're not one of them."

"Nor am I one of you. I do not belong to any side."

An elderly man in a gray suit stuck out his arm to point a rusty fork at Kate. "Except her. Except your little toy. She just chatters her teeth and you rise up in righteous anger. At us! Your lovers."

Mother Night inclined her head toward him. "I'm sorry, Geoffrey. For you alone I would wish to indulge you all. But I cannot. Your market violates the country of innocence. You will have to withdraw."

The first man said, "And what if we don't?" Lillian laughed, and he stepped back.

The woman in the plain dress wiped tears from below her eyes with the tips of her fingers. "We only wanted to pass on the things that were precious to us."

Mother Night touched her own fingers to the woman's cheek. "I know, Sharon," she said. "I know. But they don't want them. Don't you see that?"

"Well, what can we do then?"

Lillian said, "Why don't you start a mail-order house? Maybe you just need to reach a wider market."

Amy raised a finger. "But remember—no telephone soliciting."

Mother Night clapped her hands. "You will all pack up your merchandise and leave this street. And you will not return, not here or anywhere." Slowly, stooped over, the dead began to go back to their places and wrap up their sheets. All up and down the street Kate could see joy and fear rush through the living.

In the silence, Kate heard Mother Night sigh. Suddenly she remembered her godmother kissing her, and the feather of Mother Night's breath on her cheek. *She's alive*, Kate thought. *She's not dead.*

A shout broke into her thoughts. "I hate you!" it said. "You pretended to be my friend, but you're not. You're a liar." Kate turned to see Dead Jimmy standing there in a short blue dress and shiny yellow shoes. He had balled his hands so tightly into fists that lines stood out along the knuckles. If he'd been alive, Kate thought, his long nails would be cutting into his palms, maybe even dripping blood onto that soft blue.

"I'm sorry," Kate said. "I didn't mean to hurt anyone."

"You're a liar," Jimmy said again. "You're just like all the rest of them. You pretended to be dead."

"I did not!"

"But you're just another one of *them.*"

"That's not fair," Kate said. "They were hurting people. And they pushed me."

Jimmy put his hands on his hips. "Oh, they *pushed* you," he said.

"Jimmy, we can still be friends," Kate said. But she knew it wasn't true. Not because of the market. Jimmy would get over that. There was something else. Jimmy was shorter than her. How did that happen? Jimmy was *always* taller than her. Always. No, she thought. What Jimmy was always was always *ten.* And Kate—Kate was nothing always. Nothing, as long as she stayed alive.

"I hate you," Jimmy said. "You're not a friend. You're the enemy." Suddenly, he bent down and grabbed a small stone from the street. He threw it at her, hitting her in the shoulder. And then he turned and ran away.

Cara took a step, but Mother Night stopped her. To Kate, her godmother said, "I'm sorry, Kate darling. Are you all right?" She touched Kate's shoulder, and then her cheek.

"I'm okay," Kate said. She looked up and down the street. Jimmy was gone, along with the rest of them. Nothing remained of the market but a pair of pink plastic sunglasses with one earpiece missing and a book lying face down in the street. The cover of the book showed a tiny woman with wings waving a magic wand at a garden. "I'm okay," Kate said again. Kate could hear people—non-dead—laughing and calling to each other.

Mother Night nodded. "Then we had better get you back to school."

Before leaving, Kate bent down and picked up the stone Jimmy had thrown at her. She looked at it for a moment—it was gray with all sorts of white lines—then put it in her pocket.

As she sat down silently in her godmother's car Kate thought to herself, *I'm never going to die. I don't ever want to die and get stuck, like Jimmy. I'll just tell Mother Night. I don't ever want to die.*

The car and the motorcycles moved through the streets.

Three

The Courageous Knight

Before they said goodbye that day, Mother Night gave Kate a tiny silver whistle on a gold chain. "Keep this with you always," she instructed her. "Hide it in your purse or your pocket or wear it around your neck. If you find yourself in trouble just blow on it gently, and wherever I am I will come to you."

Kate blew on it, first softly then harder. A soft trilling note floated into the air. "Will you be able to hear that?" Kate asked.

"Of course. Didn't I say I would?"

Kate nodded. She thought again of the accident, and how she would need to keep the whistle close anytime she rode in a car or even the bus. Would it work backward? If she died before she could use the whistle, or if she became paralyzed and then bled to death, could her godmother bring her back? Or would she say, Why didn't you call me? Kate wondered if she should tell Mother Night right then to make sure that Kate never died. But when she looked up and saw her godmother and the MGs watching her, she just said, "Thank you," and put the whistle deep into her jeans pocket.

From that day on, Kate turned away from the dead. If she was out with Laurie and Louise and she saw dead people carrying on in the street she no longer winked at them or gave a secret wave with her fingers, but instead turned away and began speaking about school or current events or gossip from the children she knew. When Mother Night offered to take her to parties she refused, only shrugging when Mother Night asked why. Soon she found she noticed the dead less and less, and one day she was coming home from shopping for sneakers with Laurie when she realized they'd gone to the busiest part of town and she hadn't seen a single non-living person. She smiled brightly and whistled a little as she cut up celery and radishes for a salad. And yet, to her annoyance, she found that what she really wanted to do was cry.

She decided to pay more attention to Laurie. After all, wasn't Laurie the center of her non-dead life? Kate began asking about customers at the store, or the latest hot books. She considered this the best approach to her mother. She'd once heard Louise say that Laurie "should just go ahead and marry the store, the great love of her middle age." In fact, Laurie was a partner now. Mark had taken her into ownership with him when the store moved around the corner to a larger space.

Kate had realized how much this meant to her mother when Laurie had celebrated by taking out a bank loan and buying all new furniture for her and Kate. About the only thing she'd kept was a single vinyl-covered kitchen chair which she placed in a corner of the kitchen. Sometimes Kate would walk into the kitchen to find her mother sitting in the chair and staring into space, only to have Laurie jump up as soon as she noticed her daughter. Several times Kate wondered if she should ask about the chair—did it mean anything? And why did Laurie keep it? But that nervous look on Laurie's face whenever Kate caught her sitting in it told Kate to drop it. Safer, she thought, to keep to the store, and books.

At the housewarming for the new store, Kate went over to the section of women-loving women books set up by her mother. Laurie was very proud of this section. A couple of times Mark had said that that section alone had brought in enough new customers to allow them to expand. If she could just choose the right book, Kate thought, if she could just demonstrate her interest in the right subjects, she could show her mother how much she loved her.

Briefly—very briefly—she looked at a book called *What Do Lesbians Do?* Filled with drawings and even diagrams of women touching and licking each other, it instructed would-be women-loving women who couldn't figure things out for themselves. Kate would have liked to study it but didn't dare. This definitely was not the right book, she thought. As she put it back, she thought to herself how none of the drawings looked anything like Laurie or Louise or any of their friends.

For a while she looked at a novel about a couple of women from two hundred years ago who'd gone off into the wilderness to build their own house and start a farm. But she couldn't see her mother ever digging up potatoes or anything, so she put that one back as well. Finally she decided on a book called *Street-Action Womyn*, a manual of wild things any "womon" could do to "disrupt the patriarchy," such as making a rubber stamp saying "Lesbian Tender" and stamping it on dollar bills before leaving them as tips in restaurants. The cover showed two women about eighteen years old, stripped to the waist, with their faces and breasts painted blue and red and gold. And they were eating fire! Each one was pushing a flaming torch into her mouth. Kate thought how she didn't know living people could do such cool things.

But when Kate brought the book to her mother, saying in her best casual style, "Oh, by the way, Mom, could I get this book?" Laurie didn't give Kate a hug, or even smile at her. Instead, Laurie just held the book a little away from her and squinted at it a moment before she said, "No . . . no, I don't think so. Maybe when you're a little older."

Kate was about to protest that she already knew more about "Lesbian stuff" than any book could possibly tell her, when she noticed Louise looking at her and rolling her eyes as she shook her head. "Okay, Mom," Kate said. It didn't matter, after all. There were other ways to get close to her mother.

Maybe she needed more of a school-and-family approach. She started watching for amusing events at school, writing them down in her composition book so she could share them with her mother. She asked Laurie to help her with her homework, even to suggest topics for compositions or science projects. She would sit next to Laurie on the couch and lean against her so that Laurie would have to put her arm around her while they watched family comedies on television.

On the weekends, instead of putting off her mother's suggestions for outings, she began to request things. At first, she tried to think of what Laurie would like, but all she came up with was bowling and miniature golf. And then one Friday, when Laurie asked what Kate would like to do on Sunday, it struck Kate that she could choose something she really liked. Nervously, she told Laurie about an exhibition of contemporary still lifes she'd read about in the newspaper. "I'd love to go see that," her mother said.

They looked at paintings all afternoon. From picture to picture Kate pointed to things she liked and didn't like. She talked about the colors, and the difference between the weird stuff and the pretty stuff, and how sometimes the weird stuff, like a picture of medical instruments lying in a basket of fruit, was cooler than the pretty stuff. She kept talking even when they left and went for a fruit fizz at a health-food restaurant. "You should try painting," Laurie said. "You've got that set I gave you."

Kate shrugged. "That's okay," she said. "I just like to look."

Kate began to ask Laurie about her life. She tried asking about Grandpa and Grandma Cohen, whom Kate had never met, but that didn't work at all. Laurie just changed the subject, or got up and started cleaning the apartment. So Kate asked about Jaqe. She made sure to call Laurie "Mom," just in case Laurie might worry that Kate would stop loving her if she knew more about her "real" mother. She needn't have worried. Once Laurie started, she talked every day about

Jaqe. She told Kate of the things Jaqe liked to eat or wear, about places they visited, about trips they took.

"You must have loved her a whole lot," Kate said. Laurie nodded and told Kate about the dance where she and Jaqe had met. She told her how Jaqe had won the prize for most beautiful woman and then called Laurie to dance with her. Kate imagined her two mothers, the dead and the living, swirling about the floor. "That's so romantic," she said.

After the subject of Jaqe, Kate tried to ask about Laurie's other girlfriends. Laurie claimed she hardly remembered them. Anyway, she insisted, they didn't matter. Only Jaqe mattered. Kate looked at her mother a little suspiciously. She was pretty sure that Laurie had gone out on dates recently. Even if her mother would only say she was "going out for the evening," there was something about the way she dressed, and especially the looks Louise gave Laurie, that made it clear Laurie was at least experimenting. Kate certainly didn't mind. It was eleven years, after all, and Kate had never even known Jaqe. But if Laurie didn't want to talk about it, that too was fine.

They moved on to Laurie's political career. "Tell me about the DCC," Kate said.

"What?"

"You know, the Dyke Central Committee."

"Jesus, where did you hear about that? Oh, right, Louise. I'll kill her."

"It's okay," Kate said. "I won't tell anyone. I'm real good at keeping secrets."

"I just worry about you."

"Don't worry," Kate said. "No one's going to take me away from you. I promise."

Laurie sighed. "I guess after eleven years I should start to relax." She began to talk about her activist days, the marches and demonstrations, the stunts, the Valentines sent to female teachers. "It was really all just a game," she said. "And I guess sometimes not a very nice one."

"I think it was great," Kate said. "I wish I could go back in time to see you."

Laurie grinned. "Maybe I could dig out some pictures."

"Wow," Kate said. "Could you? Please?"

It took a few minutes but Laurie found an old album. There she was, shouting or raising her fist or waving a sign. There was even a picture of Laurie in a tuxedo dancing with a beautiful longhaired girl in an evening gown. "Oh my God," Kate said, and grabbed the book from her mother. "I love this. You look so cool. Who are you dancing with?"

In a flat voice, Laurie said, "Just a friend of mine," and Kate knew the conversation had ended.

Kate's campaign hit its roughest moment on a Sunday afternoon in a wooded park overlooking the river. She and Laurie had gone there for a picnic, complete with a wicker picnic basket. They'd chosen that spot because Laurie had told Kate she used to go to the park sometimes in college, before she'd met Jaqe. She'd go there when she felt unhappy, she said, and sit by the river to think sad thoughts. "Can we go?" Kate said instantly.

Laurie laughed. "Sure."

The day before the picnic, Kate decided she wanted to give her mother a present. She wished she could go sneak downtown to the department stores, but there was no time so she decided to give Laurie something of her own. She began looking through the drawer where she kept her treasures.

When she first saw the rock she couldn't think what it was doing there, with her charm bracelet loosely wrapped around it. Then she remembered. Jimmy had thrown it at her. The day Mother Night broke up the market. She looked at it closely.

It was really kind of cool. If you looked at the lines in a certain way, they formed pictures. On one side it looked a little like a tree, on the other a boat with someone standing up and poling it along a river. Kate wrapped it in blue tissue paper and wrote out a little card. "To the World's Greatest Mom."

The park was all hills and woods, the most natural in the city. They followed a trail to the very top, where the trees gave way to a small lawn leading to a cliff, with the water nearly two hundred feet below them. Even though there was a railing, Laurie made Kate promise not to go anywhere near the edge.

Laurie spread out a green blanket she'd bought in a Goodwill shop. The week before, Mark had got in a book on picnics, and while Laurie couldn't afford champagne or thousand-year-old eggs, and didn't believe Kate should eat marmalade or chocolate truffles, she did bring scones and imported mineral water. She'd even made cucumber sandwiches. Kate seemed to love it all, marveling when Laurie pulled out a thermos and served hot peppermint tea in real china cups. They sat on the blanket and wiped their mouths with cloth napkins and pressed their lips together to keep from laughing.

Now that the time had come for the present, Kate wondered if she should wait until she could get to a store after all. If she didn't have enough money, Mark or Louise could lend her some. Her face must have shown something, because Laurie squinted at her and said, "Sweetheart, are you okay?"

Kate plucked the stone from her pocket and handed it to Laurie. "Here," she said quickly. "This is for you."

Laurie grinned, and grinned wider when she saw the card. Hurriedly Kate said, "It's not much, really. It's just something I found."

"It's wonderful," Laurie said, holding the rock up to the sun. "What great markings."

Kate scurried over. Seeing that Laurie was looking at the boat side, she said, "See? This one's like a boat. With someone pushing it. With a pole." Laurie nodded. "Look at the other side," Kate said. When Laurie had turned it over, Kate said, "And this one's like a tree."

Kate was so excited that she didn't even notice the change in Laurie's face. A moment later, however, she could hear the difference in her mother's voice. "Where did you get this?" Laurie demanded. "Where the goddamn hell did you get this?"

Kate backed away. "I found it."

"You're lying. Goddamn it, don't *lie* to me. Who gave this to you?"

Kate was breathing hard. "Nobody," she insisted. "I found it in the street."

"Did *she*—did—who gave this to you?"

"Nobody!" Kate shouted.

"*Shit,*" Laurie said, and jumped up. She strode to the edge of the cliff and threw the stone as far as she could out over the river. When Laurie turned she looked all scared, and Kate didn't know if she should run. Instead, she just watched as Laurie squeezed shut her eyes, then opened them wide. Laurie started to say something, but nothing came out that Kate could hear. Finally Laurie took a deep breath, raising her shoulders and dropping them. "Honey," she said. She stopped, took another breath. "You really found that?"

"Yes," Kate said. "I told you I did, didn't I?"

Laurie nodded. "In the street, you said. What street? Where was it?"

"I don't know, just a street."

There was silence, with Laurie looking at the ground. When she looked up, she seemed about to cry. "I'm sorry I . . . threw away your present."

"I chose it special for you. I wrapped it and everything."

Laurie came over and put her arms around her. "I'm really sorry. It just—it reminded me of something."

Kate squirmed loose. "That doesn't mean you can just throw it in the water."

Laurie sighed. "I know. I'm very, very sorry."

Kate knew she should let her mother go. What she'd come for after all was closeness. But she couldn't resist saying, "You scared me. I just wanted to give you a present."

"I know," Laurie said again. She looked forlorn, like a beaten child.

Kate got up and went over to stroke her mother's hair. "It's okay," she said. "You're still the world's greatest mom."

"Even if I shout at you and throw your presents away?"

Kate gave an elaborate shrug. "Sure," she said.

Kate could not decide if her campaign with her mother had worked or failed. Sitting alone in her room, she considered the situation and decided not to pursue it. Instead, she would move on to the wider non-dead world. Children, she thought. It was time to make friends.

Kate was never very good at friendship, at least not with living kids (and she wondered now if even the dead kids only pretended to like her because she was Mother Night's pet). Some kids wouldn't even talk to her, and a few times girls whispered and giggled as she passed them. Kate didn't mind very much. She had better things to do. On the rare occasions when somebody invited her to a party she often just sat and read a book or played with a toy until some adult came and pushed her to join a game. She always did her best to win, and usually did, just so she could ignore their surprised congratulations and go back to her corner.

There were always one or two kids who thought of Kate as their friend. They were the weirdos, the kids no one else wanted. Kate knew they chose her as an easy target, someone even more of an outcast than themselves. Again she didn't mind. It gave her someone to talk to during recess and lunch on the days her godmother didn't come for her.

Kate's unpopularity bothered Laurie much more than it bothered Kate. She pushed Kate to go to parties, to invite kids over to play, to join clubs and teams. She would ask Kate if she wanted new clothes, whatever was fashionable, and when Kate rolled her eyes Laurie got mad and said it was okay to be popular, you didn't have to look different.

Now Kate began to do all the things her mother had told her to do. She went up and spoke to girls at recess, she volunteered for things, she offered to help dumb (but popular) kids with their homework, she even bought plastic jewelry in vending machines and offered them to girls she'd marked on a list kept secretly in her composition book. To her amazement, nothing seemed to work. Some kids accepted her gifts of toys or answers, but no one invited her to do things, or told her secrets, or called her to join their groups in the playground. If anything, kids made faces or walked away when she approached them. Sometimes she just wanted to scream at them, "You all think you're so great. You're just stupid. You don't know anything at all."

Trying to sound theoretical, she asked both Louise and Mark what makes someone popular. All Louise would say was, "Be yourself. If you fake it, people will know." And Mark just gave her a Mark answer. "Emptiness," he told her. "The more empty you are, the more people will try to fill you up." Great, Kate thought. Thanks a lot.

Kate thought things would change when she became friends with Alicia Curran. Alicia was in the same grade as Kate, but in a different class. Kate knew her slightly, and not just from gym or art class. Alicia was popular; you couldn't help but know her. She was pretty, with wavy light brown hair that always looked freshly brushed. No matter what Alicia was doing, or what she was wearing, she gave the impression of sitting in a gold lace dress before an ornate mirror a hundred years ago. Like Kate, Alicia was smart. Unlike Kate, who refused to pander to tne teachers by answering their questions, Alicia shot her arm straight up and often gave more details than the question demanded. For most girls, such eagerness would have left them shunned. For Alicia it somehow attracted followers. During recess she always stood at the center of a group of six or seven girls who served her with gossip or rumors—the "acolytes," Kate called them, after she found the word in a book. According to a girl in Kate's class, Alicia once told someone who wanted to be her friend, "I'm sure you must be very nice, but I'm afraid I just don't have time for any new friends."

The day Kate talked to Alicia, however, Alicia was sitting all alone on a noisy school bus. The bus was taking the entire fifth grade on a field trip to a glass tower downtown, once the tallest building in the world. There they would take the elevator all the way to the roof, where Mr. Burke, the science teacher, would explain the forest of meteorological devices that helped the smiling man on television predict the weather.

Kate hated having to go on a bus, especially a bus full of kids distracting the driver by their shouting and laughing. At any moment, the bus driver might turn around to holler at them and not see a truck or a lamppost. Sitting on the aisle as far from the boy next to her as she could, Kate fingered Mother Night's silver whistle. She'd never tried it out, she realized. Maybe she should blow it, just to see if it worked.

Trying to distract herself, Kate looked around. Alicia Curran, she saw, sat alone a few rows back. Where were the acolytes? Alicia must have banished them. She sat with her hands on her knees, eyes cast down on the back of the seat in front of her. Her lips moved. Kate stared. Was she whispering something? Then she realized: Alicia was praying.

Kate walked over and stood next to her. "What do you want?" Alicia said.

"Are you scared?" Kate said. She spoke very softly so the shouting kids behind them wouldn't hear.

"Don't be dumb," Alicia said.

"It's okay," Kate said. "I get really scared on buses. I hate them."

Alicia looked up at her for what seemed a very long time. "Do you want to sit down?" she said. She moved over to the window. "I'm not really scared. I just don't like buses. Anything can happen."

"I know," Kate said. "Cars too."

"My father drives the car. He's very good. With a bus driver you just never know."

"Uh-huh. He could be drunk. Or taking drugs." Alicia didn't answer. "I saw an accident once," Kate said. "It was absolutely gruesome.

Since then, if I have to go in a car or a bus, I just pray nothing will happen." That wasn't exactly true, she thought, touching her whistle.

Alicia said, "You're Kathryn Cohen, aren't you?"

"Kate. And you're Alicia Curran." She smiled. "It's almost the same name."

"Cohen's a Jewish name. Are you Jewish?"

"I guess. We don't light candles or anything."

Alicia leaned toward her. "Would you like to know a secret? I wish *I* was Jewish." She added, "Then I wouldn't have to go to church."

On the roof of the tower, Kate discovered that bus accidents were not the only thing that frightened Alicia. Even though the weather machines stood far away from the edge, and in fact a high fence kept people from even approaching the drop, Alicia stayed as close as possible to the door leading back to the gift shop and elevators. Though she wanted to hear Mr. Burke explain what the machines did, Kate stayed with Alicia.

Alicia said, "Don't you think it's very windy here? It could just pick you up and carry you away." She looked quickly at Kate, to see if she was laughing. Alicia went on, "I wish we could just look at it from the ground. The tower. Didn't it look beautiful?"

"Like a tower for a beautiful princess," Kate said.

"That's right." Alicia sounded surprised. She leaned closer and said, "Maybe these machines are really dragons, and a spell from a wicked witch prevents us from seeing them."

Kate pointed to a metal pyramid with a kind of windmill on top. "Maybe that's where they're keeping the princess."

"Yes. And we just think that's the wind moaning, but it's really the princess. She's calling 'Help me! Help me!' "

Kate giggled. "Do you think Mr. Burke is the courageous knight who's going to rescue her?"

Alicia shook her head. "No," she said. "I think you are."

With Alicia as her friend, Kate expected the other girls to accept her too. And they might have, except that Alicia kept them separate. When she wanted to talk to Kate she would ignore the others. "You're my most special friend," Alicia would say to her. "My knight." But if Kate tried to join her when the acolytes were clustering, Alicia hardly spoke to her. At least it made Laurie happy when Kate brought Alicia home or when Kate went to Alicia's house, a large apartment several blocks away, with high ceilings decorated with wreaths of plaster flowers.

Kate began to notice more things that frightened Alicia. Food, for instance. Alicia never ate cafeteria food but always brought her lunch. "The food they serve here is simply poison," she said. "And besides, you never know what they do to it in the kitchen. They could drip cigarette ashes in it." She lowered her voice. "Or even pee in it." People sometimes got fatal diseases from cafeteria food, she said. Alicia also wouldn't go near anyone who coughed, or looked at all hot or sweaty. She avoided going to the girls' room if at all possible, and if she had to go she seemed to take a long time washing her hands. Once, at Alicia's apartment, Kate had to use the bathroom. Afterward, Alicia went in. The door was closed, but Kate suspected that Alicia was wiping down the seat, and even the sink, with disinfectant.

For some reason she didn't really understand, Kate didn't want to ask her mom, or even her godmother, about Alicia's fears. She felt embarrassed, as if she should shield Alicia from humiliation.

Kate and Alicia remained friends, of a kind, throughout the summer. They would talk for an hour or more on the phone, or go for walks during which Alicia would tell Kate about all the boyfriends she was going to have. They looked through fashion magazines and studied the mannequins in store windows. Kate didn't care about fashion much, but it excited Alicia so Kate was happy to do it. Once or twice Kate persuaded Alicia to go to a museum or gallery. Alicia acted so bored, however, that Kate stopped suggesting it.

Alicia gave Kate a square of yellow silk and told her to treasure it always. At home, Kate didn't know what to do with it, so she folded it up and put it in her jewelry box.

And yet, despite all this, there were times when Kate would call Alicia only to hear that she was "busy" and couldn't talk. A couple of times Kate heard giggles in the background. The acolytes, she thought, and knew that Alicia was giving time to her other life.

When school started again, Kate and Alicia were in the same class, with Alicia assigned to the desk right behind Kate's. Alicia would whisper to her and pass her notes on special pink paper she hid in her desk. "Let's run away," one note said. "We can go live in a palace and tell our slaves to take all our tests for us." But sometimes, when Kate leaned back to whisper something, Alicia wouldn't answer, and if Kate tried to pass Alicia a note, Alicia pretended not to see it.

One day, Alicia's parents invited Kate to dinner. While Mrs. Curran cooked, Mr. Curran watched television, causing Alicia to roll her eyes and whisper to Kate, "I must apologize for my father. He's usually much more civilized."

"That's okay," Kate said. "My mom and I watch the news every night while we make dinner." She stepped closer to the TV, ignoring Alicia's folded arms. "What are you watching?" she asked.

Mr. Curran looked surprised at her interest. "A travelogue," he said. "They're touring the old castles of Germany and France. Kind of a comparison thing. It's sort of interesting, actually. Some of them are all restored and modernized, and others are kind of crumbling."

Kate thought he sounded nervous. "That's really cool," she said. The picture showed spikes pointing down from the ceiling in a stone room. The TV voice explained that the spikes were to catch witches flying into the room to steal babies. Kate said, "I'd like to go see places like that someday."

Mr. Curran said, "I'll bet you will, Kate. How about you, Alicia? Do you want to go visit castles in Europe?"

Instead of answering, Alicia took Kate's hand and pulled her away from the TV. "Come on," she said. Kate heard Mr. Curran sigh as she followed Alicia. In Alicia's bedroom, she said to Kate, "I'm never going to Europe. It's just too dangerous."

"You don't have to go by plane," Kate said. "You could take a boat."

"I don't care," Alicia said. "There's still terrorists."

"You're so scared to get hurt all the time," Kate said. "You can't do anything if you're just going to worry about getting hurt all the time."

Alicia put her hands on her skinny hips. "I am not," she said.

"Yes you are. You won't even go outside if it rains, just in case there's lightning."

To Kate's amazement Alicia looked about to cry. She half whispered, "It's not getting hurt I'm scared of."

"Well then, what is it?"

"Dying. I'm scared of dying."

Something jumped in Kate. Did Alicia know? Did she see the dead? Did she understand? "Me too," Kate said.

Alicia started pulling on the ends of her perfect hair. "It's just . . . I'm so scared of what happens." Kate nodded. "It's . . . I don't want to go to hell."

"What?" Kate said.

"My mother said I would go to heaven, but I know she's lying." Her voice dropped to a tearful whisper. "I was baptized too late. After I'd already sinned. I can't really remember because I was so young, but I can feel it."

"That's ridiculous," Kate said. Alicia jumped back as if Kate had shouted at her. "There's no such thing as hell. Or heaven."

"What do you know? You're nothing but a Jew."

"Please," Kate said. "Please just trust me. I know what happens when people die. I can't explain why, but I really know. I really do."

"You don't know anything. You're just a Jew. The Jews *made* hell."

"That's nutty," Kate said. Seeing Alicia's face, she decided to try something else. "I'm never going to die," she announced.

Alicia rolled her eyes. "Everybody dies. God kills everybody." Kate shook her head. Suddenly Alicia was shouting at her. "Get out! Get out of my house. You're a liar and a Jew."

As Kate backed out of the room, she heard Mr. Curran call out, "Alicia? Alicia, are you okay? What's happening?" He was emerging from the living room as Kate ran past him to the door. "Kate?" he said, then, "No, please, Kate, don't go. It'll be okay." He ran after her to the door. "I'll talk to her. Kate, come back, please." But she was already halfway down the stairs.

For two weeks Alicia refused to talk to Kate. She turned her back when Kate came up to her at lunchtime, she didn't answer when Kate whispered to her in class, she ignored the notes Kate held out behind her. When Kate called she only got Alicia's parents, who sounded embarrassed when they told her, "Alicia can't come to the phone right now." After several of these calls, Mr. Curran finally said, "Look, Kate, you seem like a really nice girl, and personally I think my daughter is making a big mistake here. But the thing is, she doesn't want to speak to you. I'm sorry. Believe me." He sounded very sad.

And then one day Alicia didn't come to class. All that afternoon Kate wondered if she should call or go see her. If Alicia was sick maybe she'd like a visit. Kate thought of bringing her a magazine. Maybe she could wear the yellow square of silk. It would cheer Alicia up. Finally, however, she just told herself that she better stay home and do her homework.

Alicia didn't show up the next day as well. Kate wondered if she should speak to the acolytes. She almost went up to two of them after school. But she couldn't stand the thought that Alicia might have spoken to them and not her. What if they'd visited Alicia? And what if she'd said, "Don't tell Kate Cohen (the Jew) anything about me?"

The following day the teacher made an announcement. "I have some sad news," she said. "As you all must know, Alicia Curran has been absent the past few days." Kate held her breath. Maybe one of the terrible accidents Alicia feared so much had finally happened. Could you *make* an accident happen just by being frightened of it? The teacher said, "She will be gone for another few days, I'm afraid. Her father had a heart attack two days ago. I'm sorry to have to tell you that he has passed away." She held up a large card with a picture of flowers on the front—a condolence card, she called it—and passed it around for everyone to sign.

Kate forced herself to keep her head down, her face grim, so that no one could see her excitement. Now Alicia would have to listen to her. No one else knew about death like she did.

At home she kept the same downcast expression when she told her mother what had happened. "Oh sweetie, that's terrible," Laurie said. "Poor Alicia." She gave Kate a hug. "Are you okay?" she asked.

"Sure," Kate said. She had to think for a moment to realize that Laurie was worried death might upset her. "Can we go see Alicia?" she asked. "Maybe I could cheer her up or something."

"Yes, of course. That's very kind. You're a good person, do you know that?"

They went that same evening, right after dinner. Kate tried to wear the yellow square around her neck, but it didn't look right, too small, so she tucked it in the pocket of her skirt. On the way, they bought some flowers. Mrs. Curran answered the door herself. She wore a dark blue shift dress. A gold cross hung down over the high neckline. "Oh, Kate," she said. "Hello. Did Alicia call you?"

"The teacher told them at school," Laurie said. "I'm Laurie Cohen, Kate's mother."

Mrs. Curran smiled weakly. "I'm Josephine Curran," she said, and held out her hand.

Kate hated to leave her mom in the living room with Mrs. Curran and some other people, sipping tea and talking about children. But she just had too much to do. She found Alicia sitting on her bed, curled up in the corner, looking at a sitcom on her small TV as if she was frightened of it. She didn't seem to notice Kate standing in her doorway. "Hi," Kate said. Alicia didn't answer. "I brought you flowers." Kate stepped into the room and held out the bunch she'd chosen.

Alicia turned her head to stare at the flowers. "They're the wrong kind," she said. "Those are roses. You're supposed to bring lilies when somebody dies."

Kate put down the roses. "I thought maybe I could talk to you. About your dad. And what happens to people."

"I don't want you to. I don't want to hear your weird ideas."

"They're not weird. You've got to trust me, Alicia. I know all about—about death."

Alicia stood up and folded her arms across her still-flat chest. "Oh, you know all about death," she said sarcastically. Suddenly her eyes narrowed. She swiped at the yellow silk poking out of Kate's pocket, just missing it as Kate jumped back. "Why are you wearing that?" Alicia demanded.

Confused, Kate said, "You gave it to me. I wanted to wear it to show you—"

"How dare you wear that? You were my *knight.* You were supposed to protect me." She was shouting.

"That's what I'm trying to do," Kate pleaded. "Protect you."

Suddenly Laurie and Mrs. Curran were in the room. Mrs. Curran said, "Alicia, darling, please. Kate just came because she cares about you. She feels sorry that your father died."

"She does not," Alicia said.

"Of course she does." Kate feared she would blush. If only she could just tell them all. Alicia said loudly, "I don't want her here." When Mrs. Curran tried to touch her, she flailed her arms, forcing her mother to back off. With a hand on her chest, Mrs. Curran said to Laurie, "I'm really sorry."

Laurie took Kate's hand. "That's okay," she said. "She's just upset. We better go."

Josephine Curran said, "I really am sorry, Kate. I'm sure in a couple of days Alicia will calm down. And then I'm sure she'll appreciate your being here." She looked more scared than her daughter.

In the street, Laurie tried to reassure Kate that everything would turn out all right. Kate only marched on ahead, with her eyes fixed on the street. She just had too much to do to take time to act normal for her mother.

It wasn't until the next day that Kate found the chance to do what needed to be done. She thought of doing it at night, after her mother had gone to sleep. But Laurie stayed up notoriously late, and besides, the sounds might wake her. And she thought of doing it at lunchtime, while Alicia's acolytes were squeaking and whispering together. But she wasn't sure how long it all might take, and she wanted to be there with Alicia when it happened. So she waited until after school, with Laurie still at work, when she could get rid of her books at home, change to a dark red dress, and head for the small park near her apartment building.

She found a wide rock to stand on and for nearly a minute she did only that, stand there, waiting for a woman walking a dog and a man on a bicycle to move out of sight. She held her whistle in the palm of her hand and stared at it. It was really cute, she thought, a silver tube about an inch and a half long, with the labyrinth design marked into the metal on the side. Maybe she shouldn't do it. Maybe she should just run home before Laurie could catch her all dressed up. But then she thought of poor Alicia, and how she alone of all the people in the world could help her. She blew on the whistle as hard as she could.

She realized she was expecting a crack of thunder when it didn't happen. In the silence, she turned around and saw Mother Night walking toward her across the grass, with Cara and Lillian close behind. Kate jumped off the rock and ran to put her arms around her godmother. "You're late," she said. "I mean, I thought you'd come right away."

"My apologies, Kate," Mother Night said. "I will try to do better next time." She wore a knee-length dress of layers of thin silk, green and blue and gold, all shining through each other like a series of screens. Her circular hat shone a dark red, the same color as Kate's dress.

"I need your help," Kate said. She told her about Alicia, her fear of dying and her "stupid weird ideas," and how Kate tried to tell her the truth but she just got angry, and even when her father died she just wouldn't listen.

Mother Night said, "I will speak to her if you choose, Kate, but she will not believe me any more than she believed you."

Kate shook her head. "No, it's not that." She noticed Lillian staring at her.

"Are you saying you want me to take her to see him? I definitely would not recommend that. It would upset her more than it would please her."

"*No,*" Kate said. "I want you to bring him back."

Lillian smiled slightly. Cara rolled her eyes. Mother Night said, "Back?"

"You know, back. Back from the dead. Alive."

Mother Night shook her head, very slowly. The sun, directly behind her, lit first one side of her face, then the other. "No."

"No?" Kate repeated. "What do you mean?"

"I mean that I cannot do that."

"You *can.*"

"No."

"You're lying. It's not true. You just don't want to help me. This is the only time I've ever asked you for anything."

"I do not lie, Kate."

Cara put her hand on Kate's shoulder. "Believe her, kid. I've known her for a long time, and she always means what she says."

Kate twisted away. "I don't care." To Mother Night she said, "You're my godmother. You're supposed to help me." Mother Night didn't answer. "You've got all your . . . your cars and motorcycles and balloons and everything, but you won't even help me keep my friend. You're just a fake!" She turned and ran along the path toward the street.

Lillian called, "Kate?" and took a step, but Cara grabbed hold of her wrist. Lillian turned. "Uh-uh," Cara said and shook her head. Lillian shrugged and stepped back.

At home, Kate frantically removed her dress. She grunted as she worked the gold chain with the whistle off her neck. "Stupid, stupid," she said, and threw it at the wall. She glanced at the clock, making sure Laurie wasn't due home for half an hour. Then she began to cry. She cried in big gulps, adding occasional high-pitched screams. "You're supposed to help me!" she cried to the air. "You're my *godmother.* You're supposed to do what I say!"

When Laurie got home, she found Kate in the living room, reading a girls' mystery story. Though Kate didn't look up, she could feel her mother appraising her. *Please*, Kate thought, *just go away. I don't want to talk. I'm fine, I'm fine. Can't you see that?*

"Sweetheart?" Laurie said. Kate kept herself from rolling her eyes as she looked up. Laurie said, "Umm . . . what would you like for dinner?"

"I don't care. Spaghetti's okay." Laurie nodded and turned toward the door. "I'll help," Kate said, surprising herself.

Kate was cutting a cucumber when Laurie came over and stroked her shoulder in that tentative way she had, as if her daughter frightened her. "You know," she said, "you really are a good person. And good people—sometimes people don't understand good people. Or they use their goodness as a way to hurt them."

"I guess," Kate said.

"I think maybe your friend Alicia has some problems."

"You mean about her dad dying?"

"Well, I think she may have had them before that. And people with problems—sometimes it makes it hard for them to accept someone else's goodness."

Kate looked down modestly. "I know," she said.

Her mother stroked her shoulder again. "I'm sure you do. Maybe someday Alicia will understand that you just wanted to comfort her. But for now, I think you're going to have to leave her alone. I'm sure there are lots of other girls to be friends with." Kate nodded. And then, as if she realized that wasn't enough, she put her arms around her mother and laid her head on her mother's chest.

Looking down at the red waves of her daughter's hair, Laurie thought of Jaqe, and how proud she would have been of Kate, and of Laurie, who had worked so hard, given up so much, to make the child worthy of the mother who had given her life. And yet, barely noticeable, a queasiness pulsed through the love and the pride.

Kate had already made up her mind not to speak to Alicia, not ever again. When Alicia returned to school Kate did her best to consider the chair behind her empty, and when Alicia stood before the class to thank them for their "heartfelt caring" and to tell them of the "beauty and splendor" of her father's funeral, Kate just stared out the window.

She decided as well to ignore her godmother. She wrapped the chain around the whistle and laid it in the jewelry box, alongside Alicia's silk square. "The two people who have hurt me the most," Kate whispered to herself.

She did not see Mother Night for nearly a month, and when she did, it happened through no intent of hers. She and Laurie had traveled to Grandma and Grandpa Lang's for the weekend. After a Saturday of shopping trips and presents, and Laurie's reports of Kate's achievements, Kate had gone to sleep in Jaqe's old bedroom, with her mother in the room next door. She had gone to bed smiling, for Laurie had whispered to her the story of her and Jaqe's compromise with Mr. and Mrs. Lang's demand that Laurie not sleep in Jaqe's bed.

Sometime in the middle of the night Kate opened her eyes. Lying sideways, she stared at a blue darkness in the middle of the moonlit room. It reminded her of the sky around the dying star her godmother had shown her. Only when the darkness moved did she realize she was looking at fiber, a dress, a body. "Stand up," Mother Night said.

Kate's heart began to push against her chest as if it were trying to escape. Absurdly, she wished for a moment that she had kept her protective whistle. She got up and stood beside the bed.

Mother Night stood with her back to the window. She wore a long blue dress, old-fashioned and prim, with buttons up to the neck, and lace-up boots that disappeared under the hem of the dress. For once, she wore no hat. Her dark hair, its redness faintly visible in the moonlight, rolled down her back, much longer than Kate had ever suspected. Kate began to shiver. The thought of running moved her eyes to the door. She yelped when she saw Cara leaning against the wall. Cara nodded once, and cocked a finger at her.

"We are going out," Mother Night said. "Please put on your shoes and socks."

"Out?" Kate said. "It's the middle of the night." Her godmother said nothing. "I'm not allowed. What about my mom? She'll have a fit."

"We will return before she wakes up."

"But what if we wake her when we leave?"

"We will not wake her. Nor your grandparents."

"That's not fair," Kate said. "You can't just—just come and take me whenever you want and—and put a spell or something on my mom. It's not fair."

A slight smile pulled at Mother Night's mouth. "Nevertheless," she said, "I am doing it."

Kate pulled on her white socks and her running shoes. They looked dumb, she thought, under her flannel nightie. "Won't I get cold?" she asked.

"Cara will give you her jacket."

Walking down the stairs between her godmother and Cara, Kate wondered what would happen if she screamed. Instead, she stayed silent until they had left the house and were crossing the lawn to Mother Night's limousine parked at the edge of the grass. Kate fell back a little to whisper to Cara, "Is she going to punish me?"

"Punish you? For what? You haven't done anything."

"Then where are we going?"

"Mother wants to give you a gift."

They drove for hours, it seemed, to a woods at the edge of a housing development Kate had never seen. They left the car and quickly moved out of sight of the houses. The trees became dense and dark. If they left her there, Kate wondered, would she ever find her way back? Suddenly they came into a small meadow. Despite the lateness of the year, thick grass rose up around Kate's legs. Looking at the trees from the open air, they appeared even denser than when she was traveling through them. She wished she could have secretly left some trail behind her.

Her godmother said, "Kate, look at me." Kate turned her head as far to the side as it would go. "That will not do," Mother Night said. Her hand on Kate's cheek gently turned Kate's head to face her. She was squatting down with her long dress tucked under her knees. With a shock Kate saw that Mother Night's head was lower than hers. If Laurie bent down like that, it brought her and Kate to eye level. Kate had never realized how short Mother Night was.

"Now you must listen," Mother Night said. "I will show you how to become a healer."

"Healer?"

"Yes. Because of your concern for people's anguish about death." She grabbed hold of some weeds growing beside them. "Do you see these plants?" Kate stared at them. They were tall, about five feet high, with a thin stalk and small branches holding clumps of purple berries. When Kate looked up, she noticed that these plants grew all through the meadow. Her godmother said, "Remember the look of them. When you get older you will come to this place and harvest them, several at a time."

"How will I find it?" Kate asked. "I mean, the place."

"When the time approaches, Cara will show you the path in the daytime, and you must memorize it. For the harvest you must come at night, during the full moon, for the moon will increase the plant's potency."

"Potency?"

Mother Night slowly pulled the plants in her hands loose from the ground. She shook them slightly to loosen the dirt from the roots. "This is what concerns you," she said. "The root. You will take the roots and clean them and cut them in pieces and soak the pieces in alcohol for six weeks. When you have removed the pieces, this will create a solution called a tincture."

Kate glanced at Cara, who told her, "Don't worry, it's easy."

"When someone becomes very ill you will go to his or her bed. You will look for me in the room. If you do not see me anywhere, then the illness is minor and you can suggest ordinary healing to the person. But if I appear in the room, you must look where I stand."

"Where you stand?"

"Yes. Now remember this carefully. If you see me by the foot of the bed, you will tell people that you, and you alone, can heal them. Then you will give them the tincture. Three drops in water three times a day for three days, and they will become better. But if you see me by the head of the bed, then you must tell them nothing can be done and they should prepare for death. You will sit beside them, and speak to them of dying. And they will believe you and find peace. Do you understand?"

"I think so," Kate said. "Do I *have* to do all these things?"

Mother Night stood up. Smiling, she stroked Kate's cheek. "No, Kate darling, I do not compel you to do anything. I give you this knowledge as a gift, a companion to the knowledge you already possess as my goddaughter. You may use it as you wish. But I must tell you—as with Alicia, people's fear of death will call to you. Their yearning will seek you out."

Kate said, "I guess."

Mother Night laughed and hugged her. "Good. Then we will return. You do not need to think about these things for now, Kate. They will stay with you, and when you become an adult you may decide for yourself what to do with them." She put a hand on Kate's shoulder and guided her back toward the woods.

Just before they left the meadow, Kate turned and looked back. To her surprise, she saw small bright lights on many of the trees at the far side of the grass. At first, she thought the trees were on fire. Then she realized—candles. Each flame was a candle, perched on the branches and burning in the night. Kate was about to ask about them when her godmother moved her into the woods, and the fires vanished from sight.

Part Four

The Woman in the Boat

One

The Secret in the Brown Bottle

The sign read "Opening to the Great Mystery: Death as a Partner in Healing. A Workshop with Kate Cohen." Kate nodded her approval. They'd made the poster a good size, she thought, and given it a prominent place near the entrance, just where your eye would fall if you were standing and catching your breath after coming in from the cold.

"How do you like it?"

Kate turned her head to look at Eleanor Hofstra, programming director of the Open Circle Conference Center. Eleanor was tall, though still an inch or two shorter than Kate's five-foot-ten. She looked to be in her mid-thirties, pretty with a round face and tight black curls. She wore a short green sweater, embroidered with pink and yellow flowers, over a long gray woolen skirt and soft brown boots. Kate smiled at her. "It's great," she said. "I love it."

"I hope the graphics turned out okay."

"They're perfect. I'm really happy you were able to use them." Along with her bio material and press photo, and the publicity texts for her "performances" (a term she used only to herself), Kate always sent a small group of images taken from her collection of mythic representations of death.

"Oh, of course," Eleanor said. "They're so . . . so evocative. I must tell you, everyone here is so excited that you're doing this."

Thanking her yet again, Kate began to move toward the lounge and the ornate brass samovar filled with green tea. Why did she ever agree to teach in the Northeast in winter? She could be sitting in the tropical sun now if she'd just done a better job of scheduling. Or even Africa, or New Zealand in the middle of summer (except that none of the offers she'd gotten included enough money to make it worth the trip). At least, she thought, they did the place up right. Polished hardwood floors with Persian rugs in the workshop rooms, large potted plants in the dining room, food you actually could enjoy, a large stone fireplace in the lecture hall and a smaller one in the lounge, and a bedroom with a view over the tops of the pine trees to the mountains. No wonder people from the cities poured out here to spend $420 each on a weekend workshop. Enjoy life while you learn about death. Well, why not? Kate was glad she'd come early and could stay a day or two afterward if she wanted.

Sitting on one end of an overlong couch, Kate warmed her hands on a mug full of hot tea. She was wearing a long loose velour top, extra thick and soft, over cotton tights and heavy socks. Laurie had given her the velour top. She smiled as she thought of her mother, and the last time she'd seen her, standing up at a Lesbian Justice meeting, saying that lesbian mothers would die before giving up their children.

Afterward, Kate had told her what a great speech it was, and added, "Who would have thought we'd both end up as public speakers?" Laurie had laughed and said she was hardly in the same league as her famous daughter. "Maybe," Kate had said, "but what you speak about really matters." Laurie had looked startled, and then, as she so often did, changed the subject.

At the end of the couch, Eleanor leaned toward her. "I just have to ask you," she said. "Where did you get such wonderful hair?"

Kate laughed and moved her head slightly, rolling her hair against her shoulders. She said, "I'm afraid all the credit goes to some gene locked away in my chromosomes. And where *those* come from will have to remain a bigger mystery than what happens after we die." Actually, she thought, she could get the information if she wanted it. Laurie and Mark had offered her the sealed information when she was eighteen. She'd turned it down then and wasn't about to change her mind now.

"Oh," Eleanor said. "Oh, I'm sorry." She blushed again, forcing Kate to look away to keep from smiling. Kate's family history, or lack of it, was well known—her anonymous father (though she allowed people to think the sperm came from a "bank," a term which always made it so much more respectable), her mother who'd died before Kate could know her. A television journalist had suggested once that Kate's exploration and acceptance of death had come from the need to understand the loss of her mother. Kate had contradicted her—gently, of course—and spoke of the love and dedication she'd learned from Laurie.

"You don't have to apologize," Kate said to Eleanor. "I'm very happy with my genes. Whatever their source." She leaned back and took a sip of tea. "Mmm, it's really lovely here. Do you live here full-time?"

Eleanor shook her head. "No, I still keep my place in the city. But I'm here more and more. To be honest, Kate, since Jesse and I broke up I've simply thrown myself into this work. I love it here, all the great teachers, the people who come for the workshops, the warmth and the sincerity of their quest. It's really sustained me."

Kate nodded. Jesse, she thought. Was that a he or a she? She said, "How long has it been since the breakup?"

"Oh God, who knows? Yesterday? Ten years ago?"

Before Kate could pin it down any further, Rob, who ran the front desk, came into the lounge. "Excuse me, Kate," he said, "there's somebody here who'd like to see you. I told him you were resting and weren't giving any consultations, but he kind of insisted."

"It's okay," Kate said, and put her mug down on the pinewood coffee table. She leaned over to touch Eleanor's shoulder. "Sorry. We'll talk more later."

"Sure," Eleanor said. "I'd love to."

The middle-aged man waiting in the office looked out of place in the Open Circle, with its huge quartz crystal in the center of the desk. Unlike Rob, who wore a slightly shabby sweater and loose jeans, the visitor wore a gray suit and striped tie. The suit looked like a tailor had made it just for him, though anxiety had rumpled it as if he'd just woken up in it. His hair looked like he'd left the marines about three weeks ago.

"Carl Harmon," he said, and held out his hand. He shook hands like a salesman, Kate thought, with practical firmness. Just like her.

"Glad to meet you," she said. "I'm Kate Cohen."

"Yes. Yes, we—my wife and I—we saw your picture in the *Gazette*. That's our paper. Actually, Alice saw it first."

"How can I help you, Mr. Harmon?"

"Right. Sorry. I'm usually pretty focused." He took a breath. "Look. I'm sorry to bother you. I'm sure you have to prepare for your conference."

"It's all right," Kate said. "Really. We don't start for hours."

"Well, I better explain then." If she'd wanted, Kate might have saved him the time. Alice Harmon was sick, of course. Very sick. In fact, her doctors had sent her home from the hospital, secretly urging Carl to avoid any heroic intervention. She might last six weeks, they said, or six months, but she almost certainly would die. Of course, when Carl talked about the article, he dutifully spoke of Kate's help for people preparing for death. Kate always stressed that aspect, bringing the interviewers back to it. But he really came—of course—for the other thing. Hope. Maybe Alice Harmon would fall into that special group: the ones Kate Cohen could bring back.

The *Gazette* interviewer, like so many others, had tried to press Kate on what made the difference. "There's no category," she'd said. "No special criteria."

"But aren't you setting yourself up—and please excuse me here—"

Kate had waved a hand. "As a kind of God? Deciding who gets to live and who doesn't?"

"Not at all. I don't make any decisions. I simply observe what happens. All I have done is allow intuition to return to its rightful place in our encounters with death. Do you realize that most of the people I see have already been written off by the doctors? I would not fault their doctors; believe me, the more I learn of the medical profession the more I respect it. But it's the doctors who decide nothing can be done. And they do so on the basis of objective criteria. The same rules for everybody. By trying to save everybody, in the same way, they end up writing off a few people who might not have to die."

"Wait a second," the interviewer said. "If you've got some magic potion, why not give it to everybody, and see who gets better and who doesn't?"

"If I did have a magic potion, I would agree with you. But I don't. All I do is admit that some people will die, no matter what we do. And because I'm willing to treat death as a friend, death will sometimes tell me who does not have to die."

"*Death* will tell you? Are you describing death as a person?"

"No, no, of course not. But death *is* a power. And if we allow ourselves to become intimate with death, that power becomes our ally."

Alice Harmon had read all that. She'd shown it to Carl, who'd come running, hoping that Kate Cohen's alliance with death would save his wife from that undesired intimacy. He said, "I'll be honest with you. I usually don't hold much with that New Age stuff—" he didn't notice Rob wince—"but if you can help us, either way, I don't know how we could thank you."

Kate smiled. "I'll get my things." In her room at the back of the center, Kate picked up her small black doctor's bag. She touched the polished leather. Louise had seen it in a nostalgia catalogue and had given it to Kate a year ago, partly as a joke, partly as a tribute. Show it to a modern doctor, Louise had said, and he'd probably wonder how to open it. Kate had loved it from the moment she saw it, though she'd joked that carrying it might get her arrested. When she'd seen Laurie's worried look, she'd laughed and said, "Mom, it's okay. If the cops come after me for carrying a doctor's bag without a license, I'll just tell them I carry my shrunken heads in it."

Leaving the Open Circle now, she noticed Carl Harmon's slight nod of approval at the bag. She smiled. Maybe the cops could make a case after all. They drove in Harmon's blue Mercedes. On the way, he began the recitation of his wife's medical history. He'd gotten as far as the word "pancreatic" when Kate stopped him.

"Please, Carl," she said. "I don't want to know any of that. Not the diagnosis, not the treatment, not anything." Harmon's anxiety level leaped enough to make the car lurch. "First of all," Kate said, "I'm not a doctor. Not only will the words mean very little to me, I can end up in jail if I even pretend to do anything with them. Or if anyone just *thinks* I'm doing something with them."

The Harmons lived in a three-story wooden house on a rural road about three miles from the Open Circle. The master bedroom may have been upstairs, but Alice Harmon lay now in what looked like a guest room, except that the original bed had been replaced by an electrical hospital bed. Ribbons, a trio of dried corncobs, some sort of tribal doll tied on by its hair, and a handmade get-well card with a child's lettering all helped to decorate the bed's metal frame. Kate wondered if Mrs. Harmon might be less alien to the New Age than her husband believed. A walker stood beside the bed. The half-open door of a night table revealed a bedpan. A pill lay on a saucer next to a prescription bottle. Kate glanced at it, and then at Mrs. Harmon's relaxed face. Demerol, she thought, or maybe even the hard stuff.

Carl wavered between pointing to Kate and his wife, as if he couldn't remember his etiquette lesson on whose name to speak first in an introduction. Finally he said, "Alice, this is, umm, Kathryn Cohen."

"Kate," Kate corrected him.

"I'm so glad to meet you," Alice Harmon said. "When I read that article—in the *Gazette?*—I was so excited. You just said all the things I've been thinking about, and trying to say, to all those *doctors*—" she made the word sound like a curse—"for months now."

Kate glanced quickly at Carl, who looked down at the pale pink carpet as if his wife had embarrassed herself. Kate thought how she liked Alice Harmon. And hated her work.

Alice went on, "Anyway, I told Carl I just had to meet you. Even if—well, you know." Kate nodded. She knew indeed. Alice laughed, a harsh wheezing noise. "I'm afraid I just sent him off to fetch you. I do that sometimes. Take advantage of him. He's so sweet."

Kate sat down in a wooden chair alongside the bed. "I'm sure it's okay," she said. "I think Carl probably likes doing things for you." She took Alice's hand, causing Alice to open her eyes a little in surprise. So few people touched the dying. Kate wondered if they feared getting stuck, as if the dead would pull them in after them. Alice's hand felt doughy, inflated with some kind of lifeless paste. The skin was yellow, the fingernails almost white. Alice said, "Are you going to read my palm? I'm afraid that's just what poor Carl was scared would happen. I made him read that article and he said it sounded like you told fortunes or something."

"Alice," Carl said, "that's not fair. You know I wanted—"

Still holding Alice's hand, Kate turned her head. "It's okay," she told Carl. "She won't shock me. People have accused me of casting Tarot cards and seeing if the card of Death shows up." She turned back to Alice. "I've been shocking people for years. It's fun, isn't it?"

Alice moved her head on the pillow. The muted light from the lamp beside her accented the yellow skin, the dark layers around the eyes. "I guess," she said, and Kate cursed herself for trying to feed Alice straight lines.

She said, "Do you mind if I look you over a little?"

"You're the doctor."

Kate laughed. "Don't say that. You'll get me in trouble." She looked at Alice's eyes, and the flesh around her eyes. She examined the tongue and stroked her neck, she rubbed her feet and worked the joints in her elbows and knees. Almost as a distraction, she noticed the various signs of decay, the colors and textures of a dying body. Kate had first started these routines as a way to help people accept her judgments by letting them see her doing something. Some of it she'd learned in weekend courses on alternative medicine; other parts she'd made up herself. And yet she'd begun to notice things. Patterns, colors, signs. Sometimes she wondered if she could do it all on her own, without waiting for her godmother.

When she'd finished her routine, she smiled at Carl and said, "Do you mind leaving us for a minute?"

"Oh," Carl said. "No. Of course not." He backed out reluctantly.

"You see?" Kate said in a low voice. "That proves I'm not a doctor. I send people out of the room *after* I've done the examination."

"Better yet," Alice said, "you speak directly to the patient and not to the family." Though her voice sounded tired, she added, "I suspect that's why they call you a 'patient.' You have to wait until someone decides to tell you what everyone already knows."

"Right," Kate said. "Maybe we should change it to 'impatient' and shake things up a little." Without a pause she said, "Alice, what do you think of life?"

Alice said nothing for several seconds, then, "To tell you the truth, Kate, I find it very strange."

"And your own life?"

She sighed. "Oh, I don't know. I feel like . . . I feel like I wished I'd known how strange it all was when I was younger. Does that make any sense?" Kate said nothing. "I truly thought that you were supposed to plan everything. That's what my mother taught me. Marriage, children, money. Vacations, pleasure. If you made the right plans, and they came true, then you had a good life. And if you made the wrong ones, or they didn't happen, well, then you might find yourself bitter, or unhappy. But you would know why. Just like in the movies. But now—" She sighed, then moaned slightly, tired or in pain. Kate suspected that she moaned without noticing it. Probably scared poor Carl without knowing she was doing it. "Now it all seems so very strange. And it's not just, you know, the sickness. Please don't think being ill has unsettled my brain. Even before . . . Sometimes I would just *stare* at things. The furniture. The lawn. Even Carl, sitting in his chair watching television. And think to myself, *What is this?*" Her attempt at a laugh changed to a wheeze and then a groan. "Tell me something. Do you think I made myself sick in some way? I worry sometimes that I turned against life."

Kate shook her head. "No," she said. "Death goes where it wants and does what it wants. Think, Alice, who are we to believe we can summon death or send it away?" Eyes closed partly, Alice nodded. Kate said, "None of us have been in the world for more than, oh, one hundred years at the most. I know many people say we've lived many times, but I'm talking about who we are this time around. And death—death has been traveling this planet for hundreds of millions of years." Now Alice closed her eyes completely and smiled.

When she opened them again she said, "I thought—oh, I don't know—that maybe I just gave up or something."

"Do you really think that?"

Alice smiled. "No, I . . . Secretly, Kate, I think maybe I've seen through it all. All the things my mother told me. And everybody else. And maybe that's why I'm dying."

Kate held Alice's hand between both of hers. "Dear Alice," she said. "Let me tell you something that happens to some people. Sometimes we know where we're heading. We know before we know. If we stop seeing death as the great enemy, then sometimes it will talk to us. Teach us."

"So I'm going to die?"

"I don't know. I haven't looked at that yet."

"Looked?"

Instead of answering, Kate closed her eyes. She took several deep breaths, turning herself inward to the darkness deep inside her, inside the world. She didn't need to detach herself like this. She could look for her godmother whenever she wanted. It just made it easier. Easier to tell the truth.

Kate wasn't sure how much time had passed before she opened her eyes. She loved the darkness, the temptation to dissolve herself, to let go of all her secrets.

The first time Kate had looked for her godmother by someone's bed she'd expected to see her the way she'd always seen her, as a friendly middle-aged woman in bright clothes and an outlandish hat. Instead, Mother Night had appeared as a tracing in the air, something that didn't go away but wasn't really there. Like a hologram, Kate thought, like the beautiful princess in that old space movie.

Now, when Kate didn't see Mother Night at the head of Alice Harmon's bed Kate thought something had gone wrong. For just a moment, she thought her godmother had taken away the gift, and now she really would have to do it on her own. And then she remembered, and turned her head.

The moment she saw her godmother standing at the foot of the bed, anger jolted Kate. She'd been so sure of this one, so confident. Relief followed the anger. Alice, lovely Alice, was going to live. To stand in front of the mirror and stare at her healthy body with all the amazement she'd found in the furniture, or the grass, or her husband's boredom. And yet, the anger remained as well, or something like it. For the ones who died, Kate actually did something. For the others—she was a messenger.

The messenger became aware that Alice was looking at her. Kate gave it her best payoff smile. As she did so, some of the old excitement flooded her. She said, "I have something to tell you, Alice." Alice seemed to be frowning at her. "My sense of this—what death has told me—is that I can help you."

"Help?"

"You don't have to die, Alice. Not now. Not from this illness."

"You mean I can last longer?"

"No, no. I mean you can recover."

"Is this—this isn't—you're not just trying to make me feel better?" Kate shook her head. "Did Carl ask you to do this? Tell me this . . . this fairy tale so I will suffer less?"

Kate sighed. She called out, "Carl? Will you come in here, please?"

Carl took a step into the room and waited. The sight of his wife's agitation rippled his own face with fear. Kate reached into her black bag and took out two small brown dropper bottles. She said, "I want both of you to listen to me. Carl, I have told Alice that it's my deep belief that she will live, and recover."

Carl whispered, "Oh my God."

Kate said, "Right now, she is afraid to believe me." She turned to look directly at Alice. "But Alice—and Carl—it actually does not matter if you believe me or not. It doesn't matter what I say." She held up the bottles. "This is what matters. Three drops in water. Three times a day. Three days. And then you will know. You will know by how you feel. Just three days. Will you do that for me?"

Carl took one of the bottles and held it up to the light as if he could analyze it. "But what is it?"

"Nothing but simple herbs boiled down to a liquid."

"Then how—"

"Just three days. That's all I ask."

Carl said, "Does she have to stop her regular treatments?"

"No. But when she starts to feel better she may want to start tapering them off."

There was a long silence, and then Carl said, "This is—God, I can't—I don't know what to say." But he did, for a moment later he added, "How—what are we supposed to pay you?"

"Nothing," Kate said.

"What?"

Kate glanced at Alice, who lay back with her eyes closed. She was smiling. Kate took a card from the bag and gave it to Carl, who frowned at it. "Wait six months. Three days to turn the illness around, the rest of the time to believe that it really happened. Then, if you want, you can send a check to the Godmother Foundation. Or me, personally, if that seems more straightforward to you. You can also ask me to send you a bill, if the other way makes you nervous. But not before six months. One day early and we send it back. And Carl—if you and Alice decide to send nothing at all, that's all right. I know you think I'm working you on this, but I'm not. I like money. I like it a lot. But I also like doing this work more." She stopped, tired suddenly. Glancing toward the empty spot at the foot of the bed, she wished Mother Night, or her phantom, would stick around, just once, for all the tedious stuff that came afterward.

Carl thrust the card in his pocket and reached over to pick up one of the bottles. Stepping over to his wife, he placed it in her hands. He whispered to her, "What do you say, Halo? Shall we give it a try?" Kate left the room without waiting for Alice's answer.

Writing quickly, she left a note for Carl. "I've decided to walk back. It helps me prepare for my lecture. Lots of luck to you and Alice. Kate Cohen." Once out of the house, she worried about her dismissive tone. Would Carl drive around looking for her to apologize? Maybe she should look for a side street.

It was late afternoon, about three hours before her lecture, and almost entirely dark. Kate was beginning to wonder if she should look for a store where she could call the center and ask for someone to pick her up when she heard the rumble of a motorcycle rolling up slowly behind her. A voice she hadn't heard in months drawled, "Kind of cold to be out walking, isn't it, kid?"

Kate stopped as Cara pulled up alongside her. They looked at each other, then Kate said, "Don't call me kid."

Cara laughed. "Whatever you say."

"Did she send you after me? Was she worried I'd get sick?"

"Mother's always looking out for you. Don't you know that?"

"Yes. I'm sure she is." Kate began walking again.

Rolling alongside her, Cara said, "Want a lift?"

"No, thanks."

They continued that way down the quiet street for nearly a minute before Cara said, "She misses you."

"She knows where to find me. She knows where to find everybody."

"Yeah, of course. But c'mon, Kate, she's not going to push herself on you."

"She pushes herself on everybody else, why not me?"

"Mother doesn't interfere with people. She does her job. And if she didn't, you couldn't do yours."

"Believe me," Kate said, "I know that very well. I might have to find some honest work."

"Is that what this is about? No one's forcing you to do what you do. If you resent it so much, do something else."

Kate stopped. Sighing, she turned to look at Cara, so young and strong, so exactly the same as the very first time Kate ever saw her. "I don't resent my work," she said. "I don't even mind that she handed it to me as a gift. I really don't. I think I've made something—something that helps people. And maybe the core of it came from her, but it's still me."

"Then what the hell is wrong? She loves you."

Kate sighed again. To be loved by Mother Night. "I don't know," she said. "I don't know what's wrong."

They stayed that way for a while, then Cara said, "You sure I can't give you a ride?" Kate nodded. Gently, Cara urged the black beast down the street. Watching it, Kate thought of all the times she'd ridden on it as a child, holding on to Cara's waist, tracing the letters on the back of the jacket, even falling asleep with her face pressed against the leather.

She said softly, "Cara?" The motorcycle turned sideways and stopped. Kate thought how Laurie would never have heard her at that distance. When Cara turned to look at her, Kate said, "Will you give her a message for me? Thank her. For Alice Harmon." Cara nodded. Tears began to form around the edge of Kate's eyes. A sharp, cold breeze dispelled them. "Cara?" she said again. "Can I still have that ride?"

The performance began with slides and sound effects. Double projectors allowed the pictures to merge into each other, overlapping while the sounds rose and fell. First came the images of death, the decayed bodies, the gunshot victims, the ethereal old people and the children burning in napalm. A mixture of terror and beauty accompanied by a mix of voices, some shouting or screaming, some whispering, all but isolated phrases incomprehensible. Underneath it all, barely noticeable, ran the deep bass of a heartbeat (not a human heart;

after weeks of experimentation, Kate had found that an elephant heart worked best). Slowly the pictures and the sounds began to change. The slides became darker, more abstract, until the bodies and blood merged into an image of a tunnel, dark dark red, leading to a pinpoint of light. The sounds moved from human cries to animal howls to wind and the crashing of rocks.

A steady switching of the slides created the illusion of the tunnel reaching toward the audience or, rather, of each watcher flying through the tunnel while the light became larger and brighter. The elephant heart began to thump louder and faster, becoming a boom agitating their bodies. While the tunnel and the light disturbed them, Kate knew they would cling to the idea of light. Virtually every one of them had read the comforting accounts of white light, beloved relatives, and angels reported by those who'd medically died and come back again.

Kate never spoke for the first minutes, preferring to let the agony of the dying crash through the audience's complacency. Now, as the tunnel neared its end and the heartbeat shook their bodies, Kate spoke into the microphone. "However slowly death approaches, however varied it comes to us, it always arrives the same. In a flash." The entire room exploded with light—light and a sharp crack like a mountain splitting apart. The light came from the screen, but also from flashbulbs Kate and Eleanor had concealed, at irregular intervals, all about the walls, the ceiling, even under the seats. Though Eleanor had worked on it with her, Kate was sure she heard Eleanor's voice among the screams.

Now that she had them, she began to treat them more gently. When they could see again, they found the screen moving through images of color and dance—concentric circles pulsing with hundreds of bright dots; masked dancers, part human, part animal, sexual and ferocious; cave walls covered in red handprints; ruined temples shaped in the form of a woman's body, with huge hips and breasts. The sounds became softer as well—whistling noises, both wind and human; bird songs; very distant sounds that might have been laughter or the shriek of some animal.

Kate began to talk about death. Death comes all at once, she said. It takes us across the boundary between everything we know and everything we do not know. Death is a thief, stealing our souls from our bodies, our very selves from the physical world we accept as reality. Death steals our souls and leaves behind memories. Illusions of love and anger. Simplifications of our lives.

And yet, if death steals us, it does not keep us. As a thief, death is a kind of Robin Hood, recklessly giving away everything it has taken. Death gives us away—to what? With images ranging from classical friezes to multicolored spirals, to a ray of light from the winter sunrise penetrating a stone mound, to a roomful of people on mats talking about their previous lives (the tape played all the voices at once), to children in skull headdresses and flowered necklaces polishing their great-grandparents' bones before a picnic, Kate catalogued the many claims made for our fate after death. And all of it fantasies, she said. The dreams of the living. We know one thing, and one thing only, about death. Whether we want it or not, it enters our bodies. Lover or rapist, death will fill us and then it will empty us out.

Now, as she began to talk about allowing ourselves intimacy with death, Kate brought up the lights in the room, just enough for the audience to see her as she moved closer to them. Kate had asked Eleanor to seat people on cushions and low benches so that she could squat down with them, using her own posture and voice to suggest a shadow of death's intimacy.

Though she'd done this set piece more times than she could recall, Kate still sweated and had trouble breathing an hour or so before starting. What if this time it didn't work? What if she couldn't crack open their comfort? Couldn't shock them or pull them out of their world and into hers? And then, a few minutes into it, all her doubts would break apart as she herself followed the trail of the sounds and pictures. When she started this work, she needed to wait for the lights to come up and show her the faces before she would trust that she had them. Now she could feel their bond with her long before she saw it. Soon the questions would come, another kind of closeness. By the time the exercises began the next morning, they would sit down all primed to allow death into the room, into their fears and memories, into their bodies.

But this time as the lights rose, something about the room startled Kate, so that she missed a beat and almost broke the web of concentration holding her and her listeners together. Something—the room looked more crowded. They'd drawn about forty people for the weekend, but as Kate scanned the audience she guessed that another fifteen or so had slipped in during the slide show. She didn't like that. First of all, Eleanor should have told her if they were opening the lecture, and second, they still should have closed the doors once the actual performance began. The newcomers all stayed in the back, where Kate couldn't see their faces, something else she didn't like.

Setting her annoyance into a pocket where she could retrieve it later, she went on speaking. Now she talked about dying stars, how they exploded gloriously, sending out fused molecules and dust which later would form into younger stars and planets, and even living creatures. Like us, she said, all of us, formed from the light of exploding stars.

The newcomers all looked so shabby, she thought. Their clothes didn't fit right or were torn, they looked like they hadn't eaten in . . . *Oh God*, she realized, *the dead.* They were all dead. The dead had come to hear her speak.

She did this, Kate thought. *She set them up to this.* They all just sat there, some with their arms folded, some leaning against the back wall, just sitting there and staring at her.

Kate clenched her fists. Focus, she ordered herself. Concentrate. She realized that some of the living, the non-dead, were looking at her a little oddly. Deliberately, she returned her attention to them. It doesn't matter, she told herself. What the dead think makes no difference, none. She wasn't doing this for them. Intimacy with death, Kate thought, belongs to the living.

Much later, Kate was gently kissing Eleanor Hofstra's shoulder when Eleanor said, "Tell me about your first love."

Kate moved the kiss down to the top of Eleanor's breast before she lay back and said, "Do you mean my first sexual partner?"

Eleanor touched a fingertip and then her tongue, briefly, to Kate's nipple. Kate gasped and Eleanor laughed a little. They'd first lain down two hours ago. "Not sex," Eleanor said. "Just the first person you loved. The one you had your first crush on."

"When I was ten," Kate said, "I spent all my time with a boy named Jimmy. Probably neither of us would have thought of it as a crush, but that's really what it was. I didn't want any other friends."

Eleanor stroked her cheek. "That's so sweet. Did the two of you, you know, experiment?"

"We tried kissing. I don't think much else even occurred to us."

"Funny. I can hardly imagine you with a boy." Kate raised her eyebrows. Blushing, Eleanor said, "Oh, I don't mean that you're so overly butch, or dykey or anything. It's just—just that you're so good with a woman. This woman, anyway."

"Thank you," Kate said. She stroked Eleanor's hair, then kissed her eyes. When she leaned back again, she said, "Actually, Jimmy was not your average boy. He wore dresses almost all the time. Our favorite game was dress-up."

"Wow. Now that's kinky. What did his parents say about it?"

"Nothing, I'm afraid. They were dead."

"Oh. I'm sorry. That's so sad. What happened to him? Did you keep in touch?"

Kate shook her head. "No. Unfortunately, Jimmy himself died just a couple of years after I met him."

Eleanor lifted herself up slightly to touch Kate's cheek. "You poor thing," she said. "What a shock."

"Yes," Kate said. "It was."

"Do you suppose that's why you became so involved in death issues? Because you lost your friend Jimmy?"

Kate lay silent for a few minutes. Finally she said, "Maybe. Losing Jimmy—like that—shocked me very deeply." She rolled onto her side and took Eleanor into her arms.

"Shouldn't you get some sleep?" Eleanor said. "You've got to teach in six hours."

"This is better than sleep," Kate said, and began a slow kiss, softly pressing her lips to Eleanor's mouth. Her fingernails traveled up the inside of Eleanor's leg.

Two

The Spinning Bed

The summons came through the Godmother Foundation's managing director, Hilda Mantero. Kate had just finished the Easter Extravaganza, her private term for her annual Spring Festival of mythic death and resurrection. The festival, which had grown to include theater, dance, puppet shows, and all-night performances as well as the original lectures and workshops, always exhausted Kate. Sometimes she traveled afterward, moving anonymously among the living. This year, however, she'd hardly seen her mother, and so she'd gone home and was sitting in the kitchen with Laurie, Louise, and Aggie, Louise's lover, when Hilda called.

"Do you know who William Reed Evans is?" Hilda asked her.

"Of course. The painter. Willie Reed."

Hilda laughed. "That's right. I forgot they called him that. Well, his secretary just called, a man named Jason Haverwell. Evans is very sick. Haverwell tried to tell me what, but of course I stopped him. Though I wouldn't be surprised if it has something to do with alcohol. The man's a famous drunk."

"If it helped him paint *The Railroad at Dawn*," Kate said, "it's worth it."

There was a pause, and Kate could hear Hilda's surprise over the phone. "I'm sure you're right," Hilda said finally. "Though right now Mr. Evans himself might not agree. They seem to have waited rather long to call you."

"Don't they all?"

"Yes, but in this case it really is the last minute. Haverwell says Evans can drop any day now. If you agree, they want to messenger you plane tickets for Friday."

Kate glanced at her mother. Laurie was studiously looking at Louise and Aggie, but Kate could feel her worry. Phone calls from Hilda always frightened Laurie. Two days, Kate thought. She'd only arrived the day before. She said, "What do you think, Hilda?"

"I *think* that if you could help *Willie Reed* it would kick your work up a whole other level. Rich artists get rich by spreading their work in very rich circles. But I also think it could backfire. *And* I think he sounds like a goner."

Kate smiled. Despite Hilda's brilliance as a businesswoman, Kate valued her most for her cynicism. My conscience, Kate called her. She said, "Give me a recommendation."

"Throw it on me, huh? Okay. If you want to take the gamble, I would go for it. We certainly didn't make it this far by not taking chances."

Kate nodded. With all her cynicism, Hilda never doubted Kate's powers. They rarely spoke about it, and she never asked *how*, but she never doubted. Kate trusted her more than any living person she knew. "All right," she said. "Tell him to send the tickets here, to my mother's house."

"Got it. Good luck, Kate."

"Thanks."

Kate hung up the phone and went over to touch her mother's shoulder. She could feel the stiffness through the denim blazer. She said, "It's looks like I'm going to have to go away for a couple of days. An emergency call. I'm really sorry."

Laurie reached an arm around Kate's waist. "You don't have to apologize. It's the kind of work you do." She added, "Anyway, I promised Marcie I'd help her put up bookshelves. She's moved again."

Kate nodded. Marcie was one of her mother's ex-girlfriends. Every couple of years Laurie would meet someone and they would date for a while, maybe go beyond that, and then decide—after six months, a year—that it wasn't going anywhere and they would just do better as friends. Louise had told Kate once that she was the only one of Laurie's friends who hadn't had to serve an apprenticeship. She couldn't decide, Louise said, if that was an honor or an insult.

"Thanks," Kate said, and bent down further to put both arms around her mother for a hug. "I'll come right back. I promise."

The next afternoon Kate went downtown to a museum that housed a permanent collection of the works of William Reed Evans. From room to room she followed the forty years of his career—the early work, with lumps of black paint smeared over a brown canvas; the so-called Rage paintings, chaotic bursts of color struggling with darkness; the red canvases torn by machine-gun fire from across his studio. These various experiments gave way to the painting that had made him an international celebrity. *The Railroad at Dawn* occupied an entire wall in a room all by itself. The basic canvas mingled abstract shapes and lumps of paint with partial images that suggested decayed columns in a building, broken benches, train tracks penetrating a room like an act of rape. All of these somehow called forth both an old railroad station and a human body cut open and rotting. Overlaid on this basic image were more definite forms, both actual photographs and faces and scenes painted in photographic realism. Isolated from one another, they each depicted one of the many organized slaughters that had punctuated Kate's terrible century. Ovens to cook human beings, dead peasants piled high in a rice field, a burning child. The very center of the canvas contained a small white square, the subject of endless speculations as critics argued for hope, nihilism, peace, horror, madness, salvation . . . Evans had once told an interviewer (Evans was drunk at the time) that he'd included "that fucking square" to "give the masturbators something to do."

Kate had seen the painting many times, the first when she was thirteen. Louise, who'd taken her to the museum, had tried to urge her away, but Kate had refused to move. She thought then, and she still thought, that *The Railroad at Dawn* was the second most terrifying thing she'd ever seen. It also was the most exciting, a fact which disturbed her for weeks until Mark said that we build our lives on terror, so what could possibly touch us more deeply?

On this day before meeting the painter himself (or what was left of him), Kate spent only ten minutes looking at the famous work. A class had assembled around it, and the teacher's glib analysis annoyed her. Besides, she wanted to see the later pieces. In the past fifteen years, Evans had shocked his followers by painting literal scenes from children's stories. Though many critics at first dismissed them as "illustrations," the Familiars, as Evans called them, emerged as a major force in his work. With adults drawn as squat and ugly, and dark trees that groped at children "like a blind child molester" (as one critic put it), the paintings portrayed Evans's horror at both history and human desire. Kate stayed longest by a painting of a deformed woman pushing a child at an oven that stood all alone in a dark woods. Unlike the gnarled quality of the characters and the trees, the oven looked factory tooled of smooth iron. Glimpses of barbed wire among the trees turned the woods into a camp. A yellow star lit up the child's arm.

After a couple of hours Kate went and sat in the museum café, where she stared out at the people enjoying early spring in the sculpture garden. Why did she never paint? she wondered. Or even just write about painting? She could have done that. She knew from the criticism she'd read that she saw things other people missed or ignored. Maybe, she thought, maybe it was just too easy to take what Mother Night offered. With the gift, Kate could do what nobody else in the world could do. And she could become famous, not to mention rich. She'd just never asked herself if it was what she wanted.

William Reed Evans lived—lay dying—in a house overlooking the sea on the other side of the turtle from Kate's home. Built one hundred and fifty years ago, which made it old for that part of the world, the wooden house included towers and steeples, curved window bays, and scallops, all of which gave it a look somewhere between stone and gingerbread. The long white car that had picked Kate up at the airport drove through a security check and up a curving driveway past a series of statues, some modern, some very old.

Jason Haverwell was waiting for Kate in front of the house. Did she want to rest? he asked her after he'd introduced himself. The driver of the car had already begun to carry her bags into the house, all but the black leather, which Kate held by her side. No, she told Haverwell, she wanted to see Mr. Evans immediately.

The night before, when she'd returned from the museum to find the tickets waiting on Laurie's kitchen table, she'd sat for a while, then called Jason Haverwell. She wanted him to know, she said, that the chances of her actually curing Evans hardly existed, and probably she couldn't do any more than ease his dying, maybe not even that. No matter, Haverwell had told her, no matter. Mr. Evans had asked for her. At least they could try.

They walked down a long corridor lined with paintings, none of them by Evans. At the end of the hall a large oak door opened and a woman stepped out to stand in front of it, arms folded like a barrier. About Kate's age, the woman was tall, possibly taller than Kate, and very thin. She wore an austere white blouse buttoned up to the neck, and a pleated green skirt of heavy silk that came down to a few inches above her soft brown shoes. She had pulled her brown hair back in a tight bun. Her face carried a detached beauty, only enhanced by the iciness of her stare. It looked like the work of an artist dedicated to aesthetic perfection. "Is this the faith healer?" she said. "Where are her snakes and juju charms?"

"Melissa," Haverwell said, "please. We agreed to try this."

"I agreed to nothing of the sort."

Haverwell sighed. Turning to Kate, he said, "Ms. Cohen, this is Melissa Evans, Mr. Evans's daughter."

Kate didn't bother putting out a hand. "I'm Kate Cohen," she said. "I'm sorry to meet you in such troubled circumstances."

"I'll bet you are."

"Ms. Evans," Kate said, "I didn't ask to come here. I did not push myself on you and your family. Mr. Haverwell called me. Until then I did not even know that your father was sick."

"And I'm sure you resisted the idea of coming here."

"Yes, as a matter of fact, I did. From the very little I've heard, it frankly does not sound as if anyone could do anything at this stage, let alone me. What I do is really very narrow."

"And just what *do* you do?"

"I listen to death," Kate said. "I try to understand what death wants with each person. Sometimes, if death will let the person go, I can help him or her get stronger. That's all. No miracles. No faith healing."

Melissa nodded. "No miracles," she repeated sarcastically. She turned her furious body toward Haverwell. "For God's sake, Jason, how could you do this? This insults my father's death. Can't he at least die with some dignity?"

Haverwell told Kate, "Ms. Evans has been overseeing Mr. Evans's treatment. She's a biochemist."

To Melissa Evans, Kate said, "I have no desire to interfere in your father's dying. If you wish, I can return right now to the airport and take the next plane home. I won't see your father or disturb him in any way."

"But you will send a fee. For your professional services. I'm sure of that."

"No fee."

Haverwell burst in, "This is simply too much. To have her come all the way to the door to Willie's room—and then turn around? No—I won't have it. You know very well that your father asked to see this woman."

Melissa rolled her eyes. "Jason, you've worked for my father all these years and you still can't recognize when he's making fun of you?"

"I'll take that chance. I say we let Ms. Cohen do whatever it is she does. What harm can it cause? She's already said she won't interfere with his treatment. And even if she did, what difference could it make? What harm could she do to him?"

Melissa said, "She can harm his dignity. That's all he has left."

"And to save his dignity you would block any last spark of hope? I'm ashamed for you, Melissa. You're better than that. Much better."

There was a long pause. Kate wondered what she wanted, go home or stay. She looked at Melissa Evans's narrowed eyes in that beautiful face and thought how much she would like to show her up.

Shaking her head, as if to contradict herself, Melissa said, "All right. But I go with her. I want to see whatever she does."

"Of course," Kate said.

Whatever the original function of the room where Willie Reed lay, its transformation into a hospital had obliterated its history far more than in Alice Harmon's family room. The oversize hospital bed, empty of any cards or totems or any other decoration, dominated the bare room. No paintings hung on the walls, though Kate saw enough faint outlines of frames to guess that the room may once have served as a gallery. She wondered if Evans had ordered them removed, wanting no competition for the display of his illness. Machines lined up alongside the bed—tracking devices for heart, lungs, and brain, IV lines and oxygen tanks—all of them unused, unplugged. Only one device remained in use, a morphine drip attached to the railing and seeping relief directly into Evans's veins.

Evans lay propped up against a trio of pillows. The sun burning through the wide windows lit up the yellow of his skin, his fingernails, even the sclera of his eyes. He looked plump and rounded, but Kate recognized the bloat of poison taking the place of meat and fat. Alongside the bed a chromium stand contained a glass of orange juice and a plate of baby food, both untouched. On a lower level of the stand Kate saw a pair of shiny clean bedpans, and next to them an open box of incontinence underwear—diapers for adults. A slight smell of excrement hung in the air. Either Evans needed a changing or else he'd leaked into the sheets and his attendants hadn't gotten around to replacing them. The thought of Melissa guarding her father's dignity stung Kate's throat, and she had to clench her fists not to cry.

A young man in a white uniform and an older man in a suit stood up from wooden chairs when Kate and the others entered the room. Haverwell introduced them as Evans's nurse and doctor. As soon as he had shaken hands with Kate, the doctor excused himself, stopping only to look sharply at the nurse, as if to say, "I can't stay in the room for this. You watch our patient." For once, Kate wished she wasn't holding her black bag.

Though Evans stared at her, Kate couldn't tell how much he understood. His puffy eyes gave him a quizzical look, accented by his half-open mouth. If indeed he had asked for Kate as a joke, either on his doctors or his own dying, he probably had forgotten the point.

Melissa smoothed his thin unruly hair with her fingers. "Willie," she said, "this is Kate Cohen. The—the healer. She's going to examine you." Evans gave no sign of having heard her.

Kate shook her head. What should she do? Go through her routine, check the eyes and the tongue? She probably would blush if she even tried it. In her mind she brought up the image of the paintings she'd seen the day before. Could this yellow sack of skin, these limp hands and staring eyes really have painted *The Railroad at Dawn*? Where do we go? she thought. Where do we go before we die, when we run from our bodies?

She realized that Melissa was watching her. All of them were waiting, expecting her to do something. She closed her eyes. No good. That dark refuge inside of her had closed up for today. Nothing inside but invasions of light. When she opened her eyes she saw—of course—her godmother at the head of the bed. The phantom image appeared embedded in the wall, as if it had stood there forever, as if they'd built the whole house around it.

Kate wondered why she'd come. Because of the career move, as Hilda thought? Or because it was Willie Reed? A waste, she thought. A waste of time, a waste of hope.

And then something happened. Maybe Melissa's hostility did it. Or maybe Mother Night, with her implacable ownership. Or maybe Evans himself, lying so helpless in the grip of an invisible woman. "Turn the bed around," Kate said.

Melissa said, "What?"

"Turn it around. So the feet face the wall. *Now.*" She began to tug at a corner of the metal frame. Haverwell and the nurse hovered nearby, unsure of what to do.

"This is ridiculous," Melissa said. "This is even worse than I thought."

"Help me," Kate said to Haverwell. He began to push at the opposite end of the bed.

"Stop it," Melissa demanded. "Stop it right now."

In a voice harsher than ice scraped against a brick wall, William Reed Evans said, "No. Do what she says."

Twice Melissa opened her mouth then closed it, while Kate, still pushing the heavy bed, wondered if Willie Reed considered it all part of the joke. Then one long step took Melissa to the side of the bed, where she flipped a switch to release the brake on the wheels and the bed swung easily around. While Melissa steadied the morphine drip, Kate and Haverwell and the nurse finished aligning the foot of the bed perpendicular to the wall.

Kate didn't realize she was holding her breath until she forced herself to look at the cream-colored plaster. There stood her godmother, still stuck in the wall, only inches away now from the small hill of Evans's feet under the blanket. The phantom image darkened, becoming denser, then abruptly vanished. Kate turned quickly to look by Evans's head, and then all about the room. Empty. No one but her three helpers and Willie Reed, who lay back with his eyes closed and a slight smile turning up his yellow lips.

Exhausted, Kate managed somehow to go through the routine with the two brown bottles. Melissa sniffed the potion and announced she wanted to do a chemical analysis, but otherwise allowed Kate to explain the dosage and, finally, blessedly, to leave the room.

Haverwell, too, said nothing as he led Kate upstairs to her own room. They no longer all dined together, he told her, but she could call down to the kitchen whenever she wanted, and the cook would send something up or, if she liked, set a place in the dining room. He went on to give her more bits of information, including his and Melissa's extensions, but when he saw she wasn't listening, he promised to write it all down, and then left her alone.

The room was large and as filled with sunshine as the sickroom on the ground floor. In other circumstances, Kate would have loved it here, the queen-size wooden bed, the cherrywood desk, the view of a terraced formal garden behind the house. Right now, all she cared about was the private bathroom and the pile of fresh towels. She thought at first to take a long bath, but she knew she lacked the strength to do anything more than wash her face. What the hell had she done, she thought, as she splashed hot water on her closed eyes. Either she would make a total fool of herself and blow her infallible reputation, or else—what? Don't think, she decided. Sleep. She dried her face and left the bathroom—

And Mother Night was there, standing in front of the window, blocking the sun despite her small size. She was dressed in the kind of outfit Kate remembered from her childhood—a long blue dress, sparkling blue shoes, and a wide floppy hat, amber colored, with what looked like tiny golden faces embedded in the folds.

"Godmother," Kate whispered.

Mother Night turned and stared at her. For several seconds, neither of them moved, and then Kate's godmother turned her head from side to side. "Don't you ever do that again," she said, and marched past Kate to the door. For several seconds Kate stood with her hand against the top of her chest, breathing rapidly. And then somehow the fear washed out of her, and she realized how much she missed this terrifying old woman. She dashed out to the landing. Mother Night was already down the stairs and halfway to the front door. Softly, afraid to shout, she called, "Godmother? I'm sorry. Please. I just didn't know what to do. I'm really sorry." Mother Night left the house without turning around.

Several times over the next couple of days Kate thought of leaving. She didn't think anyone would stop her. No one called for her, or spoke to her, or left her any messages. Maybe they were waiting for her to come check on her patient. She knew she should do that, of course. Hilda would have ordered her right down to the sickroom. Somehow, Kate couldn't make herself go there. She'd already done everything she knew how to do. If she went to see Evans, she would be going for nothing but her own curiosity. And besides, she'd promised her mother she'd come right back.

On the third day, she was sitting up in bed, looking at a book of Evans's early drawings, when someone knocked at the door. "Come in," she said, and before Kate had even put down the book, Melissa strode into the room. She was wearing a loose-knit white cotton sweater with a round neck and wide sleeves over narrow black jeans and no-nonsense sandals. She had pulled back her hair again, but not as tightly as the other day, so that it lay in a dense circular weave against the back of her head. Kate thought how it was a pleasure to look at her.

Melissa held up one of the bottles at almost arm's length. "Do you know what this is?" she said.

"A plant," Kate told her. "Tinctured in alcohol for six weeks. Vodka, to be precise."

"*Phytolacca Americana.* That's your plant's proper name. Did you know that it's fatal in large doses?"

A sick feeling jumped in Kate's stomach. Godmother, she thought. Her godmother had set her up. She'd let Kate think . . . Kate said, "I never give it in large doses."

"No, I'm sure you don't. In small doses, like the amount in your '*prescription*,' *Phytolacca Americana* shouldn't do much at all. Not for someone like my father. It gives the immune system a boost. My father needs a whole immune transplant. Not to mention several new organs."

"I'm sorry," Kate said.

Melissa burst out, "Do you know what he did today? He sat up. All by himself. And he ate. He ate a banana and a plate of mashed vegetables and a cup of broth. All by himself. And then he made fun of Jason." She looked at the brown bottle like she wanted to throw it against the wall but didn't dare. "How could this stuff *do* that?"

All the usual words came into Kate's mind—how she listens to death, how the tincture floats death's wishes. Instead, she said only, "I am very glad to hear that your father is feeling better."

Melissa's anger changed suddenly to tears. "What's going to happen? Will this genuinely last? Or are you just giving us a little magic? A dropkick to the immune system, and then as soon as you vanish he'll go right back to disintegrating."

"All I can tell you," Kate said, "is that everyone else who's tried this has gotten better. But if you want a guarantee, I'm sorry."

Melissa nodded. She looked at the bottle and nodded again before she turned to leave. At the door she stopped and turned. She kept her face blank, but Kate could see it wanting to smile. "By the way, Martin—that's Dr. Hovin—he's having a fit."

Kate saw no one for the next couple of days. Shadow people left food for her on trays outside the door or by her bed if she'd gone out, and then the trays vanished, taking even the crumbs she'd dropped on the floor. Now she really did want to go see Evans. Ten, twenty times she thought of marching into the sickroom to exult over the results of her experiment. Only, what had she actually done? Wasn't it just another trick? Kate wondered if she was finally sick of it, if maybe the time had come to stop playacting and shut the whole thing down. Maybe Willie Reed would be her farewell performance.

She called her mother, late, and got the answering machine. Wondering if Laurie and Marcie had progressed beyond the bookshelves, Kate left a message that she had to stay a little longer. Monitor the recovery, she said. She would get home as soon as possible.

She took to walking through the grounds, spending hours moving among the garden, a small woods on the other side of the house, and the paths along the cliff overlooking the sea. The drop wasn't really a cliff; the slope down to the water contained scrub brush, wildflowers, and even some wind-stunted trees. Kate probably could have made it down and up again if she really wanted, but she was just as happy to sit on the grass above and watch the light move on the water.

She was sitting there, watching a hawk ride the currents above a layer of gulls, when Melissa came and joined her on the fifth day after Kate's first and only visit with William Reed Evans—the Man Who Didn't Die, as she'd begun to think of him. Melissa leaned forward with her hands on her thighs, and said, "Is it okay if I join you?" Kate smiled at her, suddenly glad that she'd washed her hair that morning, and that the wind wasn't blowing it across her face. And glad too that she'd worn her long silk shirt, oversize and with the sleeves rolled up, over leggings and bare feet. Melissa wore another long skirt, but this time with a pale yellow T-shirt instead of a blouse.

"Have you heard the news?" Melissa asked. Kate didn't answer. "No, I suppose not. My father got out of bed today."

"I'm glad," Kate said. "To be honest, I really didn't know if what I did—the tincture—if it would help at all."

"That's not all," Melissa said. "He got out of bed and started drawing."

"Drawing?"

Melissa laughed. "All over the wall. Poor Jason. Willie—my father—sent him off to get crayons. *Crayons.* Not art crayons, but the sort that children use at school. I think Jason had to send someone into town. And then once he had the box of Crayolas—and of course they brought him the deluxe set—Willie got out of bed and started drawing pornographic graffiti all over the wall. That long one, you know, opposite the windows." Kate closed her eyes a moment to recall the room, and then she nodded. Melissa said, "You'll have to come look at the new pictures. I'm not sure if Jason was more upset by my father flaunting his condition, or the defaced wall, or just the embarassing crudity. I'm afraid Jason is quite a snob." Before Kate could say anything, Melissa added, "Why haven't you visited him? I would think you would want to . . . inspect your handiwork."

"I don't know. I guess because I really don't believe I did anything. I just suspected that he might not have to die. The tincture did the rest."

"But it's your tincture." Kate said nothing. "Tell me something. Do all your . . . patients experience such miraculous recoveries?"
"No. Most of the people I see die."
"Ah. Of course. But you don't treat those."
"No."
"You see, I've done my homework. And the ones you do treat?"
"They've all recovered, but usually not as quickly as your father seems to be doing."
Melissa stared at Kate, who did her best not to look away. Finally Melissa said, "Why did you do that? That thing with the bed."
Kate thought how she knew it was coming. She said, "What I do—when I see someone—it depends on waking up intuition. So I can sense what death wants from the person. When I do odd things, I do them more for my own sake, just to help something click. Inside of me."
While Melissa continued to stare at her Kate thought—again—how beautiful this woman was. Not just the perfection of the face, but the changing light of the eyes. And her body—usually Kate didn't like thin women, but Melissa made it seem almost a prerequisite for movement. And stillness. She sat very straight but with no rigidity, the straightness of a young tree. A tree with skin, Kate thought, and imagined moving her fingers along that sparkling neck and down between her breasts.
Melissa said, "You sound a little like a lecture."
Kate laughed. "I guess I've done too many interviews."
"And do you often spin bodies around?"
"First time," Kate said. She held up a hand. "I swear it."
"Uh-huh. Somehow I wouldn't have thought of you as a Girl Scout."
"No," Kate said, "I'm sure they don't give merit badges for death journeys."
"Or snake charming." Melissa stood up. "Will you walk back with me? Willie does want to see you."
"Of course," Kate said. She did her best to get up gracefully. Before turning toward the house, she looked out once more at the water. The sunlight on the moving sea looked like ships, a fleet of fiery boats moving gently together in some secret migration. Between the waves hitting the shore and the back-and-forth cries of the gulls, she imagined she could hear voices calling to each other across the water. She

said, "Do you ever look at the ocean so long you think you can see things?"

Melissa turned to stare silently at the water. After a few moments she said, "Candles. The bits of light look like endless candles."

In Kate's mind the boats vanished, replaced by flickering flames. "Yes," she said. "Yes, I think you're right."

Melissa laughed. "Come on."

Evans was sitting in a high-backed wooden chair when Kate and Melissa came into the room. He wore only a nightshirt and sat with his legs apart, like a child daring anyone to bend down and look. Though he appeared to sit up without difficulty, Kate noticed that he held tightly to the chair arms. He looked thinner, she saw, and paler, emptied of most of the poison his broken liver had pumped through his body. His real form had begun to emerge, as if released from a spell, and Kate noticed now the hook of his nose, the folds of his chin, the long blunt fingers.

His eyes fixed on her as she came near him. "At last," he said. "My miracle worker returns to the field of her triumph."

Kate inclined her head toward him. "I'm Kate Cohen, Mr. Evans. I'm delighted to meet you."

He looked startled a moment, then laughed. "Huh. I like that. Our last encounter wasn't much of a meeting, was it? You can't meet a dead person."

"You weren't dead. You just thought you were."

"Why not? Everyone told me so. I must be getting old, believing what people tell me. But you didn't believe them, did you?"

"No."

Evans pointed a finger across the room to where his doctor stood by the bed, alongside Jason and the nurse. "Have you met Martin, my doctor? No?" He lowered his voice to a stage whisper. "*You* may be delighted to meet *him*, but he sure as hell ain't delighted to meet you."

Dr. Hovin said, "What I'm delighted about, Willie, is that you're recovering."

Evans said, "Oh? You're sure about that? I'll tell you what, Martin. I don't want to ruin your professional reputation, so if anyone asks I'll tell them I died."

"Don't worry," the doctor said, "I'm sure my reputation will survive your survival."

Kate crossed the room to shake Hovin's hand. "You've got the hard job, Doctor. I just gave him a boost. You've got to treat him."

Hovin said, "I don't know what the hell you did, Ms. Cohen, but yes, I'm delighted you did it." He shook his head. "Melissa's told me what that—that medicine of yours contains. I don't understand it, but I'm happy it happened."

"Tell me something," Kate said. "Do you know why people get sick?"

Hovin thought a moment. "I suppose I could describe the breakdown of cells or the actions of parasites. But I know that's not what you mean. So no. Ultimately I suppose I don't."

"Then why worry if you don't know why someone gets better?"

Hovin shrugged. "Why indeed?"

Loudly, as if calling across a chasm, Evans said, "Hey, witch doctor." Kate turned. "I've got more gratitude to shower on you. You didn't just march in here and save my life, you even got me back to work." He lifted a hand to wave it at the wall of drawings. "What do you think of my finger painting? See? You've given me a new life, so I figure I better start all over again."

Kate stood opposite the wall and looked from side to side. The drawings, cartoons actually, in red, yellow, and green, ranged from a few inches high to nearly two feet. Full of energy, they moved between pornography and violence, showing a man who was little more than a matchstick extension of his giant penis performing various acts with an equally skinny woman whose sharp pointed breasts and buttocks turned her body into a weapon. Kate wondered if the woman was meant to be Melissa. Mingled with the parade of sex, Evans had sketched in bulls and horses. Though they appeared simple, little more than a few curved lines, they conveyed a rush of movement, and even realism, as if Evans had spent years watching and sketching animals in motion.

"Come on," he prodded Kate. "What do you think?"

"I think everyone should have a chance to see this," Kate said.

Evans grunted. "There. Do you see, Jason? The witch doctor knows art." To Kate he said, "You don't mind"—he paused, as if she would expect him to say "the obscenity"—"the chaos?"

Kate studied the wall again. The pictures appeared in no particular order. Here and there, Evans had run them together, or superimposed one over another. And yet, the more she looked at them, the more they seemed to move together, even prod each other into life. She said, "There's nothing chaotic about it." Turning to face him she said, "How did you do all this? In what, a few hours?"

Evans stared at her for a moment until suddenly he sank back, closing his eyes. "The actual work doesn't take all that long. Not with crayons. It's the thinking, the planning." He sighed. "I had a lot of time to plan. When you're dying, people leave you alone." He paused, then added, "And you can go places. And see things."

For a few seconds no one moved, and then Dr. Hovin glanced at the nurse, who went over and helped Evans get to his feet. Dr. Hovin said, "Miracle cure or not, you've got to rest, Willie." The nurse moved Evans into bed.

Melissa touched Kate's arm. "Come on," she said.

In the hall Melissa said, "So. Now you've met the real Willie Reed. At least one version of him."

"Are there many?"

"Oh yes, Kate," she said. "I'm sorry he didn't—show more appreciation."

"He doesn't need to."

"He does, but he won't. You know, I think you surprised him. About the picture. He expected to shock you, but got shocked back in return."

Kate said, "I've admired his work for years."

"Be careful. My father—he's a little bit like a drug, I'm afraid. A poisonous addiction." She sighed. Kate found herself wanting to reach out and stroke Melissa's face. Melissa said, "I gather you haven't left the grounds since you got here. Would you like to go have dinner with me tonight? My treat."

"That sounds wonderful," Kate said.

Melissa took her to a small town up the coast where the single street contained only two businesses, a real estate agency and a restaurant. They left early so that they could enjoy the afternoon sun as they sat on a wooden deck at the edge of sand dunes and pine trees. As they sat and talked, Kate marveled at how much her mood could change in just a couple of days. Melissa in a white dress and with her hair falling free looked brighter than the sun. They drank locally brewed beer and ate salad with pieces of various creatures who lived in water, and vegetables grilled on long skewers, and chocolate cheesecake, followed by coffee that tasted of walnuts. They talked about their work, their adventures with colleagues or clients. They were both teachers, they realized. Kate described the centers where she taught and the kind of people she encountered, while Melissa told her of the traps laid for women in the land of biochemistry.

As they drank their coffee, Melissa looked silently down at her mug. Here it comes, Kate thought, the questions, the weirdness. She thought of leaping in to change the mood but said nothing, partly because Melissa quiet looked even more wonderful than Melissa laughing. When Melissa spoke, she surprised Kate by saying nothing about Kate's healing techniques. "It feels almost strange," she said. "To get my father back. I'd worked so hard to accept his death." She looked up at Kate. "Does that sound heartless?"

"You know it doesn't."

"Yes. It's funny, though. I think the time I had him most was when he was sick. At least until the sickness took over completely. Now I'm sure he'll go back to being Willie Reed."

"I think I got a taste of that today."

"A taste, yes. Can you imagine growing up with it? Such a huge presence. And never really there. Did you know that the name 'Melissa' means bee?"

"Yes," Kate said. "The Greeks worshipped bees. They thought that bees carried the souls of dead people."

"When I was a child I used to wish I could turn into a bee. I wanted to buzz all around my father, and when he would try to swat me I would sting him, smack, right on that big nose of his." She paused, and Kate reached out a hand to stroke, lightly, the side of Melissa's hair. Melissa smiled and held Kate's hand for a moment. She said, "The funny thing is, I can't remember if I wanted to punish him or just get his attention."

"He must have been middle-aged when you were born."

"Forty-eight. My mother was twenty-four. His second wife. Willie always liked them young."

"Where was your mother when you were growing up?"

"My father bought her out."

"Bought her?"

"When she couldn't stand his screwing around anymore, he simply made it clear to her that she could divorce him, with a superb settlement, so long as I stayed behind."

"And you didn't see her? What about visitation?"

Melissa shrugged. "Oh, she tried. She really did. Once a month for a while. Then holidays. But she'd moved away, you see. I used to believe he'd bribed her for that too. But now I suspect it was just . . . easier for her. She'd remarried, of course. I have two half brothers whom I see, oh, once a year."

"I'm sorry," Kate said. "What about your father? Didn't he remarry?"

Melissa laughed. "Did he ever. Four times. I had a whole line of stepmothers, like one of those sad little girls in the stories. Except that my stepmothers weren't wicked. I still get cards from one of them. It's just that they didn't last long. They couldn't, you see. Willie would just steamroller over them."

"So you're an only child? I mean, your father's only child?"

"Yes."

"Me too. Funny," Kate said, "I guess in a way I also was raised by a stepmother. My mother died just a few months after I was born. Her girlfriend raised me. She adopted me when I was two. That's kind of like a stepmother. Though if anyone ever says something about my 'real' mother I always tell them that Jaqe may have given birth to me, but my real mother is Laurie."

"And your father?"

"Anonymous. A donation in a cup. When I was little I used to make up stories about him. Not all the time, just now and then. He was a cowboy, or an astronaut, or a prince, off on some great adventure. But to tell you the truth, I'm not sure I ever wanted him to return." Of course not, she thought to herself. However grand her fantasy father might have been, how could he have competed with her godmother? She wished she could tell Melissa some of the things she'd done, and seen, with Mother Night.

"Maybe sometimes the story is better."

There was still an hour of sun remaining when they left the restaurant, and Melissa suggested they drive up a mountain whose winding road began just past the village. The ride took half an hour to the top, with the sea and the sun continuously on their left, and tangled bushes and trees on the right. Kate loved the sea, especially high up like this and at sunset, when the light already had begun to turn the sky orange. Now, however, if she looked toward the water she did so primarily as an excuse to watch Melissa. She watched the slight tilt of her head, the different parts of her face lit by the sun as the car moved around the curves, the way her fingers rested on the gear stick just before shifting. She imagined those fingers against her cheek, moving on her breast, her hip . . . She imagined kissing that bare shoulder, that bend of the elbow.

Kate felt like a child, confused about what to do and what was going to happen. She had grown so used to knowing how to make it start, when and where to touch the other person, how to lure that person to touch her. She wanted to kiss Melissa's cheek, the back of her neck. If she closed her own eyes, she knew, she could conjure exactly the sensation of Melissa's body pressed against hers. But was that what she wanted? *Why not?* she told herself. And yet, like a twelve-year-old, she wanted perfection and feared that everything she did, or failed to do, might scratch it.

At the top, Melissa parked in a small pullover protected from the cliff's edge by a log fence. One other car sat there, a purple van, with no owner in sight. Kate guessed that the van owner probably had followed a dirt trail that headed steeply down the slope into a thick woods. "Shall we step out?" Melissa said. "There are some benches a little way down where we can say goodbye to the sun."

"You won't be cold?" Kate could feel the wind against the car.

"If we get cold we'll scurry back."

"Or warm each other," Kate said.

"Or warm each other."

The wind hit them as soon as they stepped outside, roaring into their faces and whipping their hair back. Their clothes pressed into the front of their bodies and billowed out behind them. Melissa said loudly, over the noise, "It's a lot gentler by the benches. Come on." She started down the path.

About fifty yards along, the path forked, with a smaller trail leading to a wooden bench where a natural hollow in the rock gave shelter from the wind. "Wow," Kate said when they'd sat down and could breathe again. "You forget how strong air can be."

"I love it," Melissa said. "It's so free."

The bench faced the water, where the red sun hung seemingly a few inches above the sea. The disk, and the tendrils trailing out around it, reminded Kate of her godmother. Pushing the thought away, she smiled at Melissa. "Is my hair as tangled as yours?"

"It looks wonderful. It goes with the sunset."

Kate reached out spread fingers toward the side of Melissa's head. "Let me untangle you," she said. She moved her hands gently back and down, shaking the fingers to work loose the knots.

Melissa closed her eyes. "I love that. My nanny used to do that for me when I was little." She opened her eyes to look at Kate. "I think I like this version even more."

Kate settled the hair onto Melissa's shoulders, stroking outwards, then she returned her fingertips to the face, beginning just at the side of the mouth and stroking upward, across the cheeks to just over the ears. Twice she did this, marveling at the depths in such smooth skin.

It was Melissa who first kissed Kate. She opened her eyes and looked at Kate for several seconds, until Kate became frightened she'd offended her. And then Melissa moved her hands up to press against Kate's cheeks. A moment later her mouth followed, touching Kate's lips softly at first, then fully.

Kate's body turned liquid, and only a secret miracle kept her upright. They kissed without tongues, holding the sensation of melting lips. When they separated they looked at each other, then pressed their bodies tightly together. Apart once more, Kate saw that Melissa was crying. Kate brushed the wetness with the tips of her fingers, then moved her fingers down the cheeks, the sides of the neck, the shoulders—those wonderful shoulders, chilled by the evening—and around the outside of the breasts and under them, tracing their form. When Kate pressed her palms against the nipples, Melissa gasped so loudly they both laughed and hugged each other again. Another kiss, more forceful, and at the end of it, Melissa's fingers slid down Kate's back to press sharply on either side of the spine, a couple of inches above the waist. Kate's back arched, shot through with electricity. Melissa said, "Why don't we go back to the car?"

They spent twenty minutes in the car, kissing and necking like teenagers as they slid their hands under each other's clothes, stroking and digging their fingers into each other's skin. They might have stayed longer if they hadn't heard the van owner, whistling as he came up the path. Hours later, Kate wondered if he had seen them from below and was giving them a warning. "Are you sure you can drive?" Kate asked as Melissa lurched the car onto the road.

"I'll make frequent stops," Melissa said, and set off down the mountain.

When they'd passed the security gate, Melissa asked if they could go to Kate's room. Hers was right above her father's, she said, and she didn't want to worry about making noise. "I don't mind if he knows," she said. "I just don't like the idea of him listening."

"Do you think he would he try to listen?" Kate asked.

"Of course."

Kate found flowers in the room when she entered, a mix of shapes and colors, as if someone had chosen them at random walking in a field. Kate said, "They're gorgeous. The flowers, I mean. Thank you."

"Yes, they are," Melissa said, and then, "Oh. Did you think I put them there? I thought you had. I wonder if my father ordered them. It would be like him to know what we were going to do before we did. And make sure he took part in some way."

Kate wished she could tell Melissa not to worry, tell her how these flowers came from someone else, who knew them, and Willie Reed for that matter, better than they knew themselves. She said nothing, only stroked Melissa's hair, her cheeks, her lips, and down her neck to her breasts. They looked at each other until they could no longer tell where one face ended and the other began, and then they began to kiss—the lips, the cheeks and the chin, a tongue curling along an eyebrow, the neck, that long soft road to the body. They pulled each other's clothes off so that they could rub all around and up and down each other, their nipples touching like flashes of explosions, their legs riding up each other's thighs to press and slide against the electric wetness of their groins.

Melissa lay on the bed for Kate to scrape her fingernails down the chest to the hard vibrating nipples, following her fingers with flicks of her tongue before she moved her face down to its home between Melissa's legs.

Kate discovered that day how there are many different kinds of orgasms, some which pulse steadily, arching the back over and over, and others which flood the body and the air around it. She discovered the intensity of following the orgasm in her lover's body, gasping and moving with every wave and leap, and the orgasm in her own body that starts all by itself and never stops, an orgasm that will go on forever after, humming gently under the surface of her life.

Hours later, the birds began their excited discovery of the coming dawn, a signal, Kate and Melissa decided, that they could trust themselves to sleep and start again when they awoke. Instead of closing her eyes, however, Melissa reached over Kate for something Kate had taken off and laid on the night table. "What's this?"

Kate half uncurled herself from Melissa's breast and belly and thighs. "A whistle," she said.

Melissa laughed. "A whistle? You wear a whistle around your neck?" Kate said nothing. "It's beautiful, actually. Mmm. It's even got a kind of little labyrinth inscribed on it. Can I blow it?" She lifted it toward her mouth.

"No!" Kate said, and grabbed it out of Melissa's hand.

"What's wrong? What is it? I wasn't going to blow it very loud."

Tell her, Kate thought. Tell her all of it—Mother Night, the MGs, Dead Jimmy, the healings . . . Melissa's father . . . "Sorry," she said. "It's a . . . kind of a lucky charm. I got it when I was a child, and scared."

"Scared of what?"

"I don't know, everything. The world. Life. I remember I prayed one night for God to help me, and then the next day my . . . my mother gave me the whistle. I told myself that if things ever got really desperate I could blow the whistle and God would help me. Since then I've never blown it. I guess I sort of convinced myself that as long as I don't blow it everything is okay. That must sound really crazy."

"No, it's not," Melissa said. "It's sweet." She took the whistle back and held it before her. "I promise never to blow it. Ever. After all, how bad can things get? I've got my snake charmer." She set down the whistle and a moment later fell asleep.

Kate stared at the flowers, whose colors were slowly returning in the morning light. It's when things become really good that they become desperate, she thought. She thought of going outside and blowing the whistle into the clamor of the birds. She wanted to tell her godmother, "Protect us. Give us more than human shortness. Give us forever." But moving, she told herself, would only wake Melissa, whose rolling breaths sounded sweeter than joy. Kate held Melissa tighter and closed her eyes.

Three

Bee Sting and Snake Girl

They stayed together for two weeks, traveling along the coast, stopping early and staying late between the dark whispers of trees, the steadiness of water, the secret restlessness of yellow cliffs. They traveled to uncover each other in different places. And they traveled to avoid Melissa's father, whose eyes and ears filled his house, as if his paintings had inserted him directly into the walls behind them. "The witch doctor's potions work again," he said. And "Do witch doctors only doctor witches? What do they do for sad little princesses?" So they left, and moved along the edge of the sea.

It was Melissa who broke the spell and returned them to the world. Kate would have canceled everything (she'd already canceled a board meeting of the Godmother Foundation), but Melissa said that she had let her life wither to take care of her father, and now that Kate had given that life back to her she didn't want to belittle the gift by ignoring it. So they flew toward the sun and their separate lives, plotting the times and places they would join together.

With a couple of days before her next obligation, Kate decided to visit her mother. Maybe, she thought, she could make up a little for leaving so abruptly and not returning when she said she would. Kate believed, had believed for years as a staple of her life, that she treated her mother terribly, even betrayed her, all the time. She didn't see her enough, she didn't speak to her enough, she didn't tell her enough about her life. Over and over Kate vowed she would spend more time with Laurie, or talk more deeply with her. But nothing ever changed. Like the dead, Kate once thought. Like Dead Jimmy.

Laurie never complained. She would just say how proud she was of Kate's success, as if her daughter's career explained everything. But she never asked much about what Kate did. Or how she did it. She'd never even come to a workshop.

As soon as she left Melissa, Kate wondered if she should have told her mother over the phone about what had happened. She'd told Laurie about Willie Reed and how the cure had worked. She'd talked about the crayon drawing, about Evans's sarcasm, and she'd even told her how she'd become "close" with Willie's daughter, and how they were traveling together up the coast. But her real feelings for Melissa she wanted to describe in person. At least that was what she assured herself.

When she walked in the door, Kate found Laurie and Louise sitting on the couch, drinking coffee. While Kate talked with her mother about the flight she noticed that Louise was watching her, staring at Kate over the top of her mug. Kate noticed the picture on the mug—stick-figure women dancing over the tops of mountains. Kate was thinking how she and Melissa could do that, exactly that, dance from peak to peak, when Louise began laughing.

"Louise—" Laurie said. "Watch it."

Kate said, "What's going on?"

"I can't help it," Louise said. "Kate Cohen in love. I just never thought I'd see it."

Laurie said, "Damn it, Louise." To Kate she said, "Honey, I swear I didn't say a word to her. No. No, I've got to be honest. I told her you were seeing someone. But that's all."

Kate bent down to put her arms around her mother's shoulders. "It's okay," she said. "Really." She turned toward Louise. "It's that obvious?"

"Well, with all those little lights popping all over your face, I would have to say yes. Not to mention your great skin tone."

Laurie said, "Louise, you're a middle-aged lady. Don't you think it's time you learned some decorum?"

"Nah," Louise said. "I've got time to do that when I die. You can arrange my body as decorously as you like. What's her name, Kate? See? You can trust your mother. Didn't even tell me the woman's name."

"Melissa," Kate said. "Melissa Serenity Evans."

Laurie said, "Serenity. What a wonderful name."

"Not exactly," Kate said. "Her father chose it. He's a lifelong drunk. When Melissa's mother got pregnant she insisted that Willie—Melissa's father—go to a support group. Apparently they talked about serenity a great deal. Melissa thinks he pushed the name as a sarcastic joke."

"Wait a minute," Louise said. "Willie? William Evans?" Kate nodded.

While Laurie looked down, embarrassed, Louise said, "You know, I always suspected your work would bring groupies." She held a hand up against Laurie's objections. "I'm glad it's brought something decent as well."

Laurie got up. "Kate, come on in the kitchen while I make you some coffee. Then we can all sit down and you can tell us everything."

Louise added, "Well, almost everything. We are middle-aged, you know."

In the kitchen Laurie said, "Honey, what Louise said about

groupies. I didn't want to talk about this on the phone, but are you sure that Melissa—that she really cares about you, and not just . . . what you've done for her?"

"Absolutely."

"That was an awfully quick answer."

"It's the only answer."

There was a pause, and Kate wondered if her mother was going to warn her to wait, or be careful, or cover herself against getting hurt. Instead, Laurie said, "Let me tell you something I've always admired about you. From the time you were a little girl, if you said you knew something you knew it." She hugged Kate for a long time. "Congratulations. I can't tell you how much I've waited for this." She hesitated. "The love your mother and I—"

"You're my mother."

"Jaqe and I—the love we had, most people never know anything like that. Sometimes they find something they think is everything they could want, but deep down—and I really believe this—they know there's something missing. Something just doesn't fit right."

"What about Marcie? And Rebecca? And the others?" *Shit*, she thought to herself. Why did she have to do that?

She began to apologize, but Laurie waved it away. For a while, Laurie said nothing. Then she turned her head slightly, and her eyes a little more. Kate followed her mother's gaze to find herself looking at the old vinyl-covered chair that had stood in the corner of the kitchen through most of her childhood. "Do you see that chair?" Laurie said. Kate nodded. "That's the chair I found your—I found Jaqe in. The day she died. I came in the kitchen and she was just sitting there. Bent over, with—with everything vanished. Just the body left. Her beautiful body was there, but she was gone."

"Oh, Mom," Kate said. With all of her knowledge of death, she thought, she still could fall so deeply into the sadness of life. She said, "So that's why you kept it. To remind you of her."

"Um-hum. And something else. Around that time—when we got the new chairs—" Laurie paused and made a face. "I started thinking I was going to lose my mind if I could never—never be with anyone again. Do you know what I mean?"

"Of course."

"But I didn't know what to *do*. I couldn't stand the thought of betraying Jaqe."

"Mom," Kate said, "she'd been dead ten years."

"I knew that. And you know something else? I knew that Jaqe would want me to—have lovers—find someone. But I couldn't just—just throw her out."

"Ah," Kate said. "So you didn't."

"Uh-uh. When it came time to get rid of the old furniture—you remember that, don't you?—I kept that chair. Right there. So I knew she was with me. Sometimes I sat in it. I could almost feel her. Touching me, holding me. Telling me it was all right." She reached out and touched her daughter's cheek. "Sounds pretty spooky, huh? Either that or just plain nuts."

Kate didn't answer for a moment. Finally she said, "Mom. Melissa and I—we're like you and Jaqe."

"I believe you," Laurie said. "I should never have worried. Not with you."

That night Kate talked to Melissa for two hours from the phone in her bedroom, telling her about Laurie and listening to Melissa's description of traps laid for her by her department chairman. "The evil dragon," she called him. "Whenever his snideness got too bad, I thought of my good witch, and how I had you and he didn't. With such magic to protect me, what could he possibly do to me?"

When Kate finally hung up the phone and went into the kitchen she found her mother sitting at the table reading a magazine. "I'm sorry," Kate said.

"Sorry?"

"For tying up the phone so long."

Laurie put down her magazine. "Let me tell you a secret," she said. "When you were a teenager I used to worry like hell because you didn't talk on the phone for hours. That's why I got you that phone in the first place."

Kate laughed. "That's no secret. You used to ask me didn't I want to call anybody. I think you weren't sure if I should be calling boys or girls, but you knew it should be someone."

"Well see? That telephone owes you hours of service."

"Thanks." About to leave the kitchen, Kate said, "Can I ask you something?"

"Of course," Laurie said. She looked nervous.

Kate waited a long time. Finally she said, "It's about secrets, actually. Did you ever keep secrets? I mean, real ones."

"Real?"

"You know, things you couldn't tell Jaqe. Couldn't tell anyone."

"What secrets are you keeping?"

"Nothing. I was just wondering."

"Are you sure? There's nothing you need to tell me?"

"Of course not."

Laurie sighed. "Secrets," she said. "Secrets—growing up with secrets, living with a secret—it can kill you. It can become your instinct. Your first response. Whether it's necessary or not."

"What if it's something you just can't tell? Maybe something no one would believe?"

"I don't know. I know that sometimes if you don't do it when you have a chance, it can become much harder when you have no choice. Does that make any sense?"

"I guess," Kate said. "I mean yes. Yes, of course. I just don't know."

"Do you know that you can always talk to me?"

Can I? Kate thought. *Or do you just say that because you're my mother and that's what you're supposed to say? If I tell you about my godmother will you tell me why you hate her? Will you tell me what you hid from Jaqe?* But how could she tell Laurie about Mother Night? She'd have to tell her how she'd lied to her, year after year. Silently, in her mind, she said to Mother Night, *It's not right. You shouldn't have made me do that.* And to Laurie—silently—*You're right. Secrets can become an instinct.* Out loud she said, "Yes, of course I know that."

The next day Kate rented a car and drove to the place where her plants grew, Thorny Woods, it was called. Though she didn't need any fresh tincture at the moment she also did not expect to get back to the area for at least a couple of months. And the *Phytolacca* would be just right now. Quickly she made her way through the woods, using a stick she found to push aside the thorn branches. It must have rained, for the path had gotten muddy and slippery with leaves, making Kate wish she'd borrowed Louise's rubber boots before setting out. At least, she thought, the *Phytolacca* would yank out of the ground easily.

She had almost filled her canvas bags when she noticed something strange near the base of one of the trees. It looked like a bone sticking out of the mud. Already filthy, she bent down and began digging with her hands and the stick. There was a whole cache of bones, she saw, bunched together in a narrow hole which someone must have dug—when? Last night? Last year? Last century? The rain had washed away so much dirt it made it hard to tell how deep the hole had been originally.

Now that she'd found them, what should she do with them? She did her best to wipe the dirt off one of the larger ones. If only she could tell how old it was. But she didn't know anything about bones. She squinted at it. Could it be from a person? Maybe a child. She made a face at the thought. If it was a child she should report it. But if she did that, wouldn't they come and dig up the whole meadow? What would happen to the plants?

She was still wondering about it when she heard a noise. Crying, she realized. The steady wail of a child crying somewhere in the woods. She put back the bone and stood up. The sound bouncing off the trees could be coming from anywhere. "Hello?" she called. "Where are you? Are you all right? Tell me where I can find you." The crying went on. Several more times Kate called out, standing at different points along the ring of trees. No answer.

And then as suddenly as it started, the crying stopped. "Hello?" Kate called again. "Is anyone there?" She thought of going to look for the child, but without even the sound she would have no idea where to start. Probably, she thought, the child's mother had come for it. Again she considered speaking to the police, not just about the bones now, but the child as well. But wouldn't they just answer politely and ignore her? "I was in the woods, officer, and I heard a child crying like it was lost, but then it stopped." "Thank you, ma'am. If the crying stopped, then it probably wasn't lost anymore." The same with the bones. "I was in the woods and I saw a pile of bones uncovered by the rain." "There's no law against bones, ma'am. Probably a dog buried them. And what were you doing in the woods, ma'am?" "Well, I was pulling up plants." "There is a law against that, ma'am." Kate took a last look around, and when she couldn't see any trace of the child, she left.

That night she thought of telling Melissa about the child and the bones. But what if Melissa got upset with her? And more, what if Melissa asked why she had to go to that one place to get her plants? Melissa probably knew better than Kate that *Phytolacca Americana* grew all about the Northeast. How far could Kate push intuition as an answer? So instead, Kate talked about Grandma and Grandpa Lang, who had recently amazed Kate, and especially Laurie, by joining an organization called "Grandparents of Lesbians and Gays."

"That's so sweet," Melissa said.

"Well, it's certainly better late than never."

"Do they call it GLAG? It sounds like someone choking." Melissa laughed, the sound Kate loved most in the world. "I can't imagine Willie joining a parents' group. He will never condemn anything, whether I go with men or women. But support? Actually, I must say he seems to like you very much."

"Really?" Kate said.

"Oh, he'll never come out and say so, but I've noticed a certain affectionate tinge to his sarcasm. Oddly, I don't think it's because you saved his life."

"I'm not sure I'd agree with that description."

"How could you argue it? But I suspect it's too big a thing for him to think about. If I'm reading him correctly, what he really likes about you, besides your good taste in art, of course, is your nerve."

"Well, thanks," Kate said. "And how about his daughter? Is that what you like about me? My nerve?"

"I like all your nerves. And your arteries and your capillaries and your follicles and your cartilage—" Kate laughed. "And especially your gorgeous heart's blood flowing through all of it."

Kate found her next workshop difficult to sustain. She would lose her concentration or even want to joke just when she needed to bear down on their fears or expectations. She herself feared only one thing during the weekend, that someone might ask her to do a healing and she would have to descend from the light of Melissa into the black hole of some stranger's death. Finally, the workshop ended and Kate could flee her students' devotion and fly to the town where Melissa lived, a place Kate thought she would think of always as the Heavenly City.

Melissa lived in an apartment converted from the top floor of a former mansion across the river from the college where she taught. From the living room, they could look out at stone buildings designed to look hundreds of years older than the people who built them. With all the students and teachers safely hidden by distance and trees, the college looked both elegant and cold, like a cemetery for rich people.

As they came up to her door, Melissa told Kate, "I wanted to carry you over the threshold, but I'm afraid you just didn't give me enough time to lift weights in the gym."

Despite the building's former grandeur, the rooms surprised Kate with their smallness. "Rich people were smaller then," Melissa told her. "Or perhaps our lives have gotten so big nothing can contain us." Kate admired the contrasts of Melissa's decorating style, the single extravagance of a green velvet settee with gilded legs set against the clear lines and grained wood of country furniture, her lumpy gray teapot and brilliantly glazed cups, her three paintings by three different artists. The one by her father showed a girl in a room with scarred walls and a black stove, shaking a lifesize doll with a human head about to topple off its shoulders. "Willie's choice" she said when she saw Kate admiring it. "He gave it to me as a housewarming present."

"A hell of a present."

"That's my father."

"No, I mean it. It's so strong. I'm just wondering what it's like to share a house with it."

"You'll notice," Melissa said, "that I don't keep it in the bedroom."

Late that night, lying naked in a bed set into a wall of books (mostly textbooks, a fact that made Melissa blush), Melissa showed Kate photos of her childhood. Kate loved the seriousness on the child's face as she composed herself with great consciousness for the camera. "I wish I could go back and visit you then," she said.

"I doubt that you would like me. I hardly even spoke very much."

Kate's favorite photo, the one she threatened to sneak away when Melissa was sleeping, showed Melissa at ten, in a long white dress with more ruffles and lace trim than Kate could count. "Oh God," she said when she first saw it. "Were you a bridesmaid?"

Melissa shook her head. "Uh-uh. First communion."

"You're kidding. Don't tell me Willie is Catholic. Catholic upbringing maybe, but not practicing."

"Oh, I don't know. I think it might appeal to him. Actually, it was Joanna's idea. Stepmother number two. I suspect that she decided to save me when she couldn't save my father."

Kate held the book up for a closer look. "Did you feel swept away in religious rapture?"

"Hardly. I convinced myself it was a bridal dress and any minute a prince in a top hat and tails would lift me into his arms."

"I thought princes wore armor."

"Not my prince. Do you have any idea how much it hurts being hugged by someone in armor?"

Kate kissed her, holding her with one hand and sliding the other down Melissa's back to rub the roundness of her small soft ass. She said, "If you'll settle for a commoner I'll go rent the tux right now."

"Too late," Melissa said. "When Joanna left I got so angry I made Billie—the gardener—tear up the dress and burn it."

Kate said, "I guess that means a naked wedding."

"Guess so."

At the back of the album Kate noticed a group of older photos, some in black and white, of people posing in the more formal style of earlier decades, when people considered photographs similar to painted portraits. "What are these?" she asked Melissa.

"Just some old pictures I found in my father's office. I think some are from my mother's family, but I've never been able to persuade him to identify them for me. Oh, here's one I know." She pointed to a photo of a man with slicked-back hair standing next to a woman in a beaded dress. "These two are the family's claim to fame before Willie."

Sickness twisted Kate's insides. "Who are they?" she managed to say.

"I never actually knew them because they died when I was a baby, but they were Willie's aunt and uncle. Abel and Marguerite. They were performers. Dancers. They even appeared in a couple of movies."

Kate knew she had to get by herself. Speaking and moving as naturally as she could, she told Melissa she needed to go to the bathroom. Inside, with the door safely closed, she bent over, holding her belly while she willed the nausea to subside. Abel and Marguerite. Maybe Melissa had never known them, but Kate had. She'd even seen them perform. Mother Night had taken her to a party and she was fooling with Jimmy when suddenly someone started playing the piano and then a couple came out and did a dance with so many swirls and swoops that she and Jimmy had giggled helplessly in the corner. *Shit*, Kate thought. *Goddamn it. It's all wrong.*

The nausea came under control just as Melissa called, "Kate? Are you all right?" Going back to her lover, Kate thought how earlier that day Melissa had described Kate's relationship with Laurie as "idyllic."

"It almost seems as if you never needed to rebel, she was always so supportive." Now Kate thought how much her godmother had pushed Laurie to the background, and how difficult it was to rebel against Mother Night. In her mind she told Melissa, *Ah honey, you think Willie Reed is tough?*

Their time ended on a bright Wednesday, good flying weather as Melissa said. All Tuesday Kate had insisted she still could cancel her television taping, the same one she'd canceled earlier to extend her stay in Melissa's father's house. Melissa refused to listen. "I don't want to be the death of your career," she said.

Kate laughed. "Death *is* my career. And to tell you the truth, I think I wouldn't mind letting it die."

"Well, I would mind. I want you to go on doing for others what you did for my father. And I want to see the awe in people's faces when I tell them, *My* lover is Kate Cohen, the Mistress of Death."

On the plane, trying not to cry, Kate thought of the son and daughter of an acquaintance of hers. Kate had visited the family on a day when the boy, six years old, had suddenly acquired his own room with the departure for college of a big brother. His very own room, the boy told Kate. No longer would he have to share bunk beds with his four-year-old sister. And yet when the time came to sleep, he looked wistfully at his new kingdom but lay down on his old bunk, just so he could tie a red string from his sister's ankle to his own, so that when morning came, if she happened to wake up before him, her movement would yank the string and let him know the moment had come to resume playing. *That's us*, Kate thought. She and Melissa, with an infinite string tied around their feet.

That night, in the hotel room provided by the television station, Kate took a long time getting to sleep. As soon as she hung up the phone from speaking with Melissa, she just wanted to call her again. But Melissa had to grade papers that night, and Kate didn't want her going to sleep too late. She didn't want Melissa to suffer because of her.

Without the weight and the sounds of Melissa's body to enrapture her, Kate dreamt for the first time in days. She and Melissa were walking along the river, watching a rowing team perfect their silent glide. The coxswain seemed to be shouting the stroke, but Kate could hear nothing. She looked up to discover birds performing some complicated dance. How do they make all those arrangements, she wondered. What do they say to each other?

One of the birds began to descend, a huge thing of no species Kate had ever seen, all ragged feathers and a sharp yellow beak, dropping feet first, with its wings unfurled and its talons arched, ready to strike. Melissa stared up at it, smiling, and Kate knew that if she didn't warn Melissa to get out of the way the bird would slash open her face.

She was still trying to get the words out when the dream shifted and she was lying on a tar and gravel roof. Though she was naked, her skin and even her muscles and organs had turned to a dark mud which clogged her mouth and ears. Near her, on a wooden rack, stood nine bottles of *Phytolacca* and vodka. The Good Stuff, as Melissa had taken to calling it. Only, eight of the bottles had broken so that the tincture had leaked away into the dirt, and the ninth just sat there, farther away than the birds. The birds, she thought. If she could just get them to come down and tear away the mud then she could get to the bottle. If she could just call them—if she could just—

She woke up slowly, confused as to where she was and what she was doing. Sunlight filled the room. Nine o'clock, she saw, when she picked up her miniature alarm clock, a sunny nine A.M. in a hotel room much too far from Melissa's body. Sadness filled her at the sight of the unused pillow beside her on the bed. She reached for the phone. Still sleepy, she needed two tries before she could dial all the numbers right. When the phone finally rang she knew even before the fourth ring that she would have to settle for the sound of Melissa's voice on the tape. "Hello. This is the answering machine of Melissa Serenity Evans, the happiest woman on Earth. When you hear the beep, please leave your message about biochemistry, snake charming, or anything in between."

"Hello, my darling," Kate said. "This is your reptile lady, in agony of missing you. I tried cuddling the python last night, but it just wasn't the same." She rambled on about the interview coming up, their plans to get together again, and whatever else she could think of until the beep of the machine cut her off. She called the college next, only to have the secretary in the chemistry department tell her that Dr. Evans hadn't come in yet. Feeling about to cry, Kate put down the phone and padded into the bathroom to start getting ready for the taping.

Throughout the interview Kate kept losing her concentration. Her ankle itched, and just as the interviewer would launch some hard-hitting question ("Have you ever done follow-up on the people you rescue from death?" or "Why have you refused to license this wonderful elixir of yours?") Kate would bend over to scratch her leg or, worse, smile at the thought that it was Melissa, pulling on the red string. Luckily she'd heard the questions many times before and could plug in the suitable answers without having to think much. She even managed to hold up her twin bottles of cure-all with the right element of drama and flair.

Kate had finished the interview and was leaving the station, half annoyed with her lack of professionalism and half thinking of retirement, when the assistant producer who'd herded her through makeup and lighting checks came up to her. "Ms. Cohen? There's a message for you." Kate grinned, thinking Melissa had felt the string tug and was calling to wish her well, or maybe apologize for distracting her. The producer handed Kate a card. "A Mr. Haverwell called for you. He asked if you could call him as soon as possible."

"Where?" Kate asked.

"The number's right there. I wrote it—"

"*No.* Where the goddamn hell is a phone?" Startled by Kate's rudeness even more than her alarm, the producer took her to a small office where he silently cued the phone for an outside line. Kate had punched in the number even before he left.

Haverwell answered on the second ring, saying only "Yes?" Kate could hear the sound of an engine and she thought he must be in a car until she realized the sound was too large and was more likely a plane. Why would Jason Haverwell call her from a plane?

She said, "Jason, this is Kate Cohen."

"Oh, Ms. Cohen. Thank God."

"What is it? Is it Will—Has Mr. Evans suffered a setback?"

"No. No, Mr. Evans is fine. He's right here with me. We're calling—you've called us on a plane. I'm afraid—I'm afraid I have some bad news." *No*, Kate thought, *I don't want to hear this.* Jason said, "There's been an accident. Ms. Evans—Melissa's car apparently skidded off the road this morning. Apparently, it crashed into a bridge post."

Apparently, apparently, Kate thought. "Is she—how is she?"

"In critical condition." Kate's breath exploded out of her. *She wasn't dead. They hadn't come for her. No redheaded bikers disguised as paramedics were zipping up her body bag.* Haverwell said, "The doctors won't say what her chances are, just that she's in grave danger."

"I have to get there."

"Of course. According to the police, Ms. Evans stayed conscious long enough to give them first your phone number and then Mr. Evans's. Apparently she gave them your number over and over until she passed out."

If I'd been home, Kate thought, *I would have heard right away.* She said, "I need plane tickets."

"It's already arranged. You have shuttle reservations for three o'clock, four o'clock, and five o'clock, whichever one you can reach. If you call us from the airport or the plane, we'll make sure a driver is waiting for you when you land."

"Thank you. Give me the hospital number as well." She wrote it down alongside Evans's cellular number on the paper the producer had given her. "Thank you," she said again. "I'm on my way." Before she hung up she added, "Oh, and thank Mr. Evans for me. We'll speak at the hospital."

"Of course. Thank *you*, Ms. Cohen. I . . . I've known Melissa all her life and—" Kate could hear him swallow tears. "I hope you get there in time," he said.

She called the hospital twice from the plane, with no news either time. For the rest of the flight she just sat there, unable to read or to eat or drink any of the food or liquids the stewardess kept putting in front of her. Toward the end she found herself looking around at the other passengers. A man was swaying in his seat as he read from a small leather-bound book. Another man had closed his eyes and was moving his lips as he fingered a set of beads. A woman was turning cards over on the tray in front of her, three rows of three, and then she would shuffle them and do it all again.

They were all praying, Kate realized, for protection or help or just peace. That's what she should do. If ever there was a time . . . But how? Kate could hardly think about prayer, let alone work out how to do it. Talking to some invisible god had never made any sense to her when all she had to do was blow a whistle and Mother Night would come stand in front of her.

She took the whistle out from under her blouse and rubbed it between her fingers. What would she say? Beg her to spare Melissa? What if she refused, the way she'd refused to help Alicia Curran so many years ago? Maybe, Kate thought, she could just get Mother Night talking and refuse to let her go. Any time Godmother tried to go, Kate could just blow the whistle and summon her again. But suppose Mother Night took back the whistle? Anyway, as long as the MGs remained outside Kate's control, holding Mother Night wouldn't make any difference at all. She would see her godmother soon enough, Kate thought. At the head or the foot of Melissa's hospital bed.

In the car from the airport Kate thought of her plan never to die. All she had to do was ask her godmother, she'd believed, and her godmother would save her from everything. Now all she cared about was this one case. Melissa. Just save Melissa.

Though Willie hadn't arrived yet, he'd given word to the hospital to send Kate up immediately. "Usually we only allow immediate family—" the woman at the desk tried to tell her, but Kate didn't wait to hear it. In the elevator it struck her that intensive care units often put people in open beds so that the specialized nursing staff could watch over everyone at once and call for help as soon as someone hit a crisis. She didn't like that. She wanted to do whatever she needed to do behind closed doors. When she reached the floor, however, she discovered that the hospital maintained a VIP intensive care room, specially set up with a private nurse for anyone willing to pay for it. The power of money, Kate thought. The power of art.

It took all of Kate's will to stop herself from screaming the moment she saw Melissa. Beautiful Melissa, serene Melissa. Cut, and battered, burned, and smashed, all wrapped up in wires and tubes and tape. No screaming, Kate thought. No screaming. She had work to do.

And the first thing she needed to do was get rid of the nurse who stood watching Kate as if she'd come to steal the body. The nurse said, "You can only stay a couple of minutes, I'm afraid. If you like, you can come look again in half an hour. There's a family waiting room at the end of the hall."

"Leave," Kate said.

"What?"

"I need a few minutes alone with her."

The woman smirked. "That's hardly possible. Perhaps you don't understand, but this woman is in extremely critical condition. She needs twenty-four-hour monitoring."

"I will let you know if I need you."

"If you need me—" She glanced down at Kate's black bag. "Are you a doctor? Because if you are it makes no difference. I am not leaving my patient."

"I'm better than a doctor."

The nurse rolled her eyes. "Yes, and I'm sure you're better than God too. Nevertheless, Ms.—" She made it a question.

"Cohen. Kate Cohen."

The woman's mouth fell open. Just like in the stories. "Oh my God," she said finally. "Oh, my God. I can't believe it. I'm Caroline Mayberry." Kate only looked at her. "Marsha Mayberry's granddaughter?"

Kate nodded. Marsha Mayberry. She was one of the first, Kate remembered. When the power—the trick—still amazed her even more than it did her clients. She said, "Ms. Mayberry—"

"Caroline."

"Caroline. Please. I need to—"

"Of course," the nurse said. "Of course." To Kate's surprise the woman hugged her. "Good luck," she said. At the door, she looked back nervously. "If anything—if you need me—"

"I promise I'll call you the moment anything happens."

Caroline Mayberry nodded. She looked about to cry as she closed the door.

Finally, Kate thought, as she rushed over to the metal chair beside the bed. She should get right to it, she knew, find out the worst right away. But she couldn't bear to take her eyes off Melissa. Very carefully, she took Melissa's hand. One of the few places without even a bruise, its soft delicacy looked unreal attached to such a ruined body. Melissa stroked the palm with her fingertips. "Hi, bee stinger," she said. "It's me. I love you, Melissa."

The puffed cut eyes opened a crack. In a drugged whisper, Melissa said, "Did you bring the snakes? I think I need them." And then the eyes closed again and the hand went limp.

“Melissa!” Kate said. About to scream, she looked at the monitors and saw that nothing had changed. It was just the dope, she told herself. That’s all. From experience, Kate knew that an accident, with all its blood and broken pieces, could look a lot worse than it really was. So she could still allow herself to hope as she closed her eyes in preparation for the terrible moment of looking.

She didn’t want to open her eyes ever again, but she did so only a second after closing them. “Godmother,” she said, and the absence of any resonance of hope flattened her voice.

“Hello, Kate.” She hadn’t come as a phantom this time. Instead, she stood in her body in the small space between the wall and the head of the bed, with her hands resting on the bright steel railing. She wore a fitted jacket of lavender silk over a long flounced skirt. Like the night she’d given Kate the gift, she wore no hat, but allowed her red hair, so much finer than Kate’s, to spread across her shoulders. “I’m very sorry,” she said.

Kate didn’t try to answer. Instead, she started yanking and dragging at the corner of the bed. If she could just turn it around quickly enough . . . But it was no use. Mother Night reached her in two steps and before Kate could even move the bed a few degrees out of line, her godmother had taken hold of her hand in a grip impossible to break even though Kate’s whole body shook with the effort. “That won’t help,” Mother Night said. “All you will do is tear her loose from her life support. I don’t think you want to do that.”

“Life support?” Kate said. “What the goddamn hell is that going to do?” But even as she stood up, it occurred to her that the necessity of stopping her had moved Mother Night to the foot of the bed.

Some smirk of satisfaction must have shown on her face because her godmother shook her head, saying, “Kate, darling Kate, do you really think it makes a difference where you position me?”

“But you said—”

“I gave you a way of knowing. A way to speak for me to people I service.”

Service, Kate thought. *Is that what you call it?* But she only said, “You’re lying. What about Willie? What about her father? If it doesn’t make any difference, why did it work for him? Why won’t you do the same thing for her that you did for her bastard of a father?”

“Sweet Kate—”

"Don't you call me that."

"I changed Mr. Evans because of you. Because you wanted it so desperately."

"And I don't want this? I don't want this? *This is Melissa.*" She took a step backward as a thought struck fire in her. "If it doesn't work, why did you tell me not to do it again?"

Kate's godmother looked at her so sadly that Kate would have slapped her if she could have imagined such a thing was possible. "That wasn't just a command. It was a warning. Did you think you could change the way something is meant to happen without pulling on the possibilities for something else? Did you think you could open a locked door without the wind slamming shut another door in return?"

Kate shook her head. "Wait a minute. No. No, you're not saying what I think you're saying." Mother Night didn't answer. "Goddamn it! Don't you tell me that *I* made this happen." Again no answer. Kate wanted to grab her godmother and slam her back against the wall. She took a breath. No. No, no, no. She had to think, to *think*. Even if she could do such a thing, if she could attack Mother Night, what would it accomplish? This was about Melissa, she told herself. Melissa. Not Kate's anger, or her fear, or the trick her godmother had played on her, all the tricks, on her and everyone Kate had loved throughout all of her life. This was about Melissa. Fight, she thought. She had to fight for Melissa in any way she possibly could.

"Take someone else," she said. "If someone's door has to slam shut, slam someone else's."

"I'm sorry. That is not the way it works."

"The way it works! *You're* the way it works. If it weren't for you, none of us would have to go through this at all. Don't you think I know that?"

Her godmother tried to reach out and touch her face, but Kate snapped her head away. "Poor Kate," Mother Night said. "You think you understand it all, but you do not. Do you really believe that I invented death? Why, Kate? Why would I do that?" Now it was Kate's turn to say nothing. Her godmother said, "The mysteries of the body, of each person's body and the body of the world, will not give way as easily as you think. Not to me any more than to you. I have not come here to hurt you, Kate. Not you. Not ever. I only do what needs to be done. There are purposes which no one can break. No one, Kate, least of all me. And lines which no one can cut."

"Goddamn it, then take back Willie. Do you think I care about him? If something has to crash, why can't you crash his plane?"

"And all the other people on board? What about them?"

"Then give him a heart attack. Or crash the plane and make everyone else have a miraculous escape. Let the newspapers write it up as a sad irony. Daughter recovers from crash, famous father dies on way to see her. I don't care. I don't care. I just want Melissa."

"I'm sorry. When you pushed me to spare her father you took a step that cannot be withdrawn."

"That's not fair," Kate said. You didn't tell me. You didn't warn me. You're making me pay a price I never knew existed."

"I have no more choice in all of this than you do."

"Why? Why? Because the rules are the goddamn rules? *Change* the rules. I'm your goddaughter."

Mother Night shook her head. "Darling Kate. Even for you I cannot change what cannot be changed."

"I don't believe you. What are these lines you can't cut? Bloodlines? Lines between relatives? Then why does it have to be a daughter? What about a brother or a sister? And if you spared Willie by taking his daughter, why can't you spare Melissa by taking her mother?" Mother Night didn't answer. "Do you know what I think? I think you're punishing me. Because I defied you. Or because I didn't show enough appreciation. I was your pet meat and I forgot to sit up and hold out my fucking paws. You set this whole thing up just to put me in my place."

Suddenly angry, Mother Night took a step toward Kate, who needed all her nerve not to jump back. "Your place? Your *place?* I gave you a place wider than any living being walking upon this Earth. I showed you how to see, and to understand. Do you take that as worthless? Do you consider my gifts empty? You above all women should know the truth of what we do and what we cannot do."

"I know that I want Melissa. I know *that* more than I've ever known anything in my life. Why won't you listen to me? How the hell else can I say it?"

With her eyes fixed on Kate, Mother Night stretched out an arm to point a finger at Melissa. "No!" Kate shouted, and would have leaped at the arm to knock it down, except that when she looked at

Melissa her lover was sleeping peacefully, with all her circle of machine mothers whispering the reports of her continued existence.

"This woman," Mother Night said. "She means more to you than everything I've given you?"

"Yes," Kate said immediately. And then, "Wait a minute. Is that what this is about? Jealousy? Are you . . . You're so jealous of my love for Melissa—for someone else—goddamn it. I don't *believe* this. You can't just push her aside, can you? Like you did with Laurie. That won't work anymore. You can't lure me away with all your glorious spectacles. You can't just keep me isolated from everyone who isn't dead. Finally I've found someone who matters more to me than my magnificent godmother. And you can't stand it. So you're just going to take her. Just like that. Because I had the nerve to love somebody else, some weak pathetic human, more than I loved you."

Without moving, Mother Night said, "My motives and desires do not matter now. Nor do yours. I have asked you a question and you must answer me. Think. Words have power. *Do you value Melissa more than the gifts I have given and promised you?*"

"Yes."

"Kate, I am not just talking about my benevolence. I swore an oath to protect you and teach you. Do you consider my promises meaningless that you would give them up so easily?"

"There's nothing easy about it. If you want to help me, then give me Melissa."

"I ask you one more time: You will choose her above everything else? Think."

Kate said, "I don't need to think. I know."

Mother Night lowered her arm. For a long moment she simply stared at Kate, who did her best not to look away. All at once, sadness filled Kate's godmother, driving everything else out of her body. Kate thought how she could see in Mother Night's eyes all of the pain she must have witnessed in her incalculably long life. For just a moment, Kate wanted to get down on her knees and wrap her arms around her godmother's waist.

"Good," Mother Night said. "Come with me." She began to move toward the door.

"What?" Kate said. "Wait a minute. I can't leave. I'm staying here with Melissa."

"Oh, Kate," Mother Night said. "Shall I take you by the hand and pull you after me? Or do you think you could resist that as well?" Feeling like a child refusing to go with Mommy, Kate folded her arms. Mother Night said, "Come. Leave the bottles of tincture and come with me."

The shock of hope almost knocked Kate to the floor. *Leave the bottles? It was going to work.* Godmother had given Melissa back to her. Without thinking, she walked over to the bed. Not sitting down, she touched the side of Melissa's face. "Stinger?" she said. "I've got to go for a little bit. I'll be back as soon as I can. And Willie and Jason should be here soon. It's going to be all right, darling. It's really going to be okay." Stepping back, she watched Melissa breathe. The professional in her noticed the easier movement of the chest and she thought how already Melissa was starting to change. She turned her head to look at her godmother. "Thank you," she said. Mother Night nodded. "Okay," Kate said. "Let's go."

When they left the room they found Caroline Mayberry nervously hovering by the door. When she saw Mother Night she shook her head in amazement. "Kate?" she said. "Ms. Cohen? Who is—I didn't see anyone go in. I was standing right here."

Kate said, "Caroline Mayberry, this is Mother Night. She's the person who saved your grandmother."

Caroline squinted at Mother Night, who inclined her head toward her. Looking at Kate again, Caroline said, "I don't understand. Is she your partner?"

Kate said, "No. Melissa Evans is my partner. Caroline, I need you to do something for me. Inside, you'll find two brown bottles containing an herbal tincture. Ms. Evans—your patient—needs to take three drops of this tincture, three times a day, in water, for three days. Three days, three drops, three times a day. Have you got that?"

Caroline glanced down the hall, as if afraid someone might be listening. "I'm not sure," she said. "I don't think—I'm not allowed to give anything unless a doctor prescribes it. Not even an aspirin."

Kate sighed. "Of course. Then will you do something for me? Ms. Evans's father—William Evans—will arrive soon, along with a man named Jason Haverwell. If I don't get back before they get here, will you make sure they get the brown bottles? If you can, give them to Jason. Do you understand?" Caroline nodded. "Good. I knew I could count on you." Kate took a deep breath against the tears trying to take over her body.

Once more she looked at the door to her lover's room. It was all she could do to keep herself from running in and trying to barricade the door shut behind her. "Goodbye," she whispered. "I really love you."

She and Mother Night walked down the hall.

The Candle That Burned through the Day

Instead of taking the elevator, Mother Night led Kate to a narrow stairway at the end of the floor. Neither of them spoke as they marched down, floor after floor. Beyond the stairwell, Kate could hear the murmur of voices, the thump of doors slamming shut, the chimes of doctors' codes on the loud-speakers.

At the bottom of the stairs they came to a street door. Even before Mother Night held it open for her, Kate felt a blast of heat strong enough to give a red tinge to the gray metal. And even though Kate held herself back when the door opened, the dry heat fastened itself to her chest, making it hard to breathe. "Come," Mother Night said, holding the door for her. "It's just candles." Kate held back for a moment, then stepped into the sunlight.

She found herself standing at the edge of a parking lot behind the hospital. Filled with cars and even buses, the lot seemed to go on and on, with every spot taken, as if everyone had come for visiting hours all at once. Beyond the cars on one side rose a round hill with old trees, forming a sort of small park, but everywhere else the lot continued as far as Kate could see. And everywhere, on the roofs and the hoods of the cars and buses and ambulances, on the branches of the trees, on the blacktop lanes and the sidewalks, on the dividing lines between the cars, on the reserved signs for doctors and disabled people, everywhere Kate looked she saw candles. Some burned on plates or small clay holders, others dripped their wax into glasses or directly onto the roofs of the cars. They were all sizes and colors, some long and thin, burning with a tight elegant flame, others shorter but thicker and sloppier, burning hotly and dripping lips of wax all over their bodies. There were candles as ephemeral as the birthday candles of little children, and others that looked strong enough to burn for weeks. At any particular moment, candles, hundreds of them, would flicker out, while at the same time others seemed to ignite all by themselves, so that in the midst of this great field of fire, individual flames appeared to leap from one place to the next.

"Do you know what these are?" Mother Night said.

Kate was holding her hands up in front of her face. She didn't want to answer. She didn't want to know. She wanted to run back inside and hold Melissa in her arms. But even if she thought she could move fast enough, she knew she would find the door locked. And something else. After all this time, she discovered a pride at being Mother Night's goddaughter. She didn't want her godmother to think she hadn't learned anything.

"Yes," she said. "I think I do. They're lives, aren't they? They're people's lives."

Her godmother nodded. "Each one burns for the length of somebody's moment between birth and death. Look." She pointed to the nearest car, a blue hatchback whose entire roof and hood was filled with candles, all of different sizes. "Do you see the short ones, already beginning to sputter out? These are the old and the sick." Even as Kate watched, a flame in the middle of a lake of wax flickered once, twice, then vanished, leaving only a faint plume of gray smoke that dissolved into the fiery air.

"And do you see the others?" Mother Night said. "The long bright ones? They burn for the young, who believe that their fire will go on forever. But look." She pointed to one of the little candles, with only enough wax to burn for a few minutes. "These are the ones born in sickness. And these—" She pointed to a line on the blacktop where a whole row of candles had tipped over and spilled their wax, which had grown cold and hard. "These are the people lost in violence."

Now Mother Night swept wide her arm. "Do you see them all, Kate? Do you see how they go on and on? How the new candles burn out of the wax of the old?"

"Melissa," Kate said. "I want to see Melissa's candle. Show it to me."

Mother Night pointed to a small red car. Unlike the others, it supported only one candle, a blue one set into an ornate silver holder perched in the center of the roof. The candle stood straight and fresh, brand new and burning brightly in the sun. "Oh God," Kate breathed, "thank you." Now she truly wanted to rush back to Melissa, so they could celebrate. And so she could escape the brutal vision of all these lives pushing against each other, and all the thousands snapping out of existence wherever she looked. But she knew she had no choice. She had to ask the other question. "Godmother," she said, "show me my candle."

Instead of answering, Mother Night began walking down the aisle between the nearest cars. Kate followed her gingerly, nervous that she might brush up against someone's candle and either knock it over or burn her leg with someone else's life. Her godmother stopped at the crossroads of two aisles. All around, candles burned in no particular pattern, but in the center of the intersection Kate saw a plain white candle pressed in its own wax on a small plate. Melted wax nearly covered the plate, and even ran over the edge onto the blacktop, for the candle had nearly burned out, with only a stub remaining. Already the flame had begun to flicker.

"*No,*" Kate said. "Don't do this." Mother Night said nothing. "How could you let all those others burn and not mine? I'm your goddaughter. I'm the one that's supposed to matter to you." Again no answer. "How could you give me back Melissa and then take me away from her? Give me another candle." She glanced back at the stub. The flame had begun to leap up sporadically in its last moments before going out. "*Hurry,*" Kate said. "*Give me another candle.*"

Quietly, Mother Night said, "The only way I can do that is if I give you a candle from somebody else."

"Then do it. Do it right now."

Mother Night pointed to a fresh green candle burning on the hood of a car. "How about this one?"

"Yes." Mother Night's hand reached out. "No, wait," Kate said. The old woman's hand stayed suspended in the air. Laurie, Kate thought. What if that was Laurie's candle? Or Mark's, or Louise's? "I don't want that one," she said. "I want—I want the candle of someone I don't know. Someone I've never met."

While Mother Night looked around, Kate watched her own struggling light. "Here," Mother Night said, and Kate had to turn her head to see a thick, partly burned candle on the roof of a station wagon. "Will this do? It belongs to a poet. He has been working for many years on a poem concerning the secret history of creation. If I give you his candle he will never finish. Is that what you want?"

"Hurry," Kate said. "There's not much time."

"Then I better bring your candle to the strong one." Mother Night took a step back to the crossroads. As she bent down, however, she seemed to trip slightly. The forward motion of her body brought her toe against the candle, and before she could grab it, the stub, almost all liquid wax now, spilled out onto the parking lot.

Kate ran. Without a scream or a shout, she simply turned and dodged and leapt over people's candles until she came to the wall of the hospital, where she didn't bother to try the door but headed for the nearest corner. She only made a noise when she turned into cool air, and found herself in front of the building, twenty yards or so from the main entrance. Then she let a grunt explode out of her as she paused a moment to bend over and catch her breath. But only a moment, for even if she could no longer see the candles or feel their heat, she knew that her godmother—or the Motorcycle Girls—could come up and grab her at any moment. Longing to see Melissa cut through her. She knew she didn't dare. Wouldn't that be the first place they'd look? And so she ran away from the hospital, and when she reached the nearby streets she began making turns at random, trying to keep her mind blank of any plans or scheme.

She stopped several times, listening for motorcycles, before she finally allowed herself to slow down to a walk. She was in some kind of suburban neighborhood, she saw, with large lawns and big white houses with black shutters, and no one in sight, not in the windows or the driveways or walking or bicycling along the streets. Despite the clear wealth of the neighborhood everything looked dilapidated, the houses in need of paint, the lawns half taken over by weeds. Though the weather had turned warm several weeks ago the trees here hadn't sprouted, so that the bare branches stuck out over the lawns like gawking skeletons.

She kept walking, block after block, until the blocks disappeared, and then the houses themselves, and she found herself on a narrow road walking past fields that may have been farms except that no one had woken up the ground after winter. She looked at the brown and lumpy fields, with their leavings of yellow stalks and shriveled-up blades of—something, some plant no one could recognize without its normal shape and color. For all she knew, the whole field could have contained her friend, *Phytolacca Americana*, and she never would have recognized it. Anyway, she thought, what good would it do her without the vodka to cure it in? And who would give it to her? Who would turn her bed around?

She stopped suddenly. On a cone-shaped hill across a field she saw what looked like a group of animals, cows or sheep, grazing together. The sight of them excited her and made her want to cry in some way she didn't understand. She wanted to run over and—and pet them or something, whatever you did to the animals who gave us our food, day after day, life after life. But when she looked again she couldn't tell for sure if they were animals or just rocks.

She tilted back her head to survey the sky, looking for birds. At first it all looked as empty as the dirt, but then she spotted a pair of birds flying high. Blackbirds, she thought, crows. She remembered that time in the balloon with Mother Night, rising so high they could stare down at the birds. And she remembered how she'd tried to tell her friend about it, and just ended up lying when she'd tried to tell the truth. Lying can become your basic instinct. When no one will ever believe you, what else can you do? Kate began to cry.

Stop, she told herself. She could cry later, when—when she'd figured out what to do. She found a tissue in her pocket and wiped her eyes. Laurie. She missed Laurie so much. She needed a phone. She would call Melissa, and then she would call her mother. And they would talk, and cry, and tell all their secrets.

She took a deep breath and looked around once more. The damn road just went on and on and on. Maybe if she cut across the fields she'd come to a farmhouse. She made a face. Better not, she thought. She was still wearing her interview clothes. Suppose she fell and got mud all over her linen pants, or tore her blazer? She could just imagine what some farmer would do if a disheveled woman banged on his door and asked to use the phone. Probably summon Mother Night with a blast of his shotgun. Just keep walking, she thought. Just keep moving.

Night came. She'd hardly even noticed it getting dark when suddenly there it was, all around her. With no streetlights or stores or houses, and only a sliver of moon, she could hardly see the ground or her own feet, let alone anything in front of her. If only she'd smoked cigarettes, she would have had some matches. She didn't want to stop, but at least the darkness would hide her. She walked to the side with her arms out until some branches brushed her face. Reaching down, she found the roots and followed them back to the trunk. With a sigh, she sat down on the dirt and settled herself with her back against the tree.

Sleep. Sleep would give her strength for tomorrow. She closed her eyes, only to open them a few seconds later. She just didn't feel tired, even after all those hours of walking. And what if they came for her? If she stayed awake she could see the headlights. Try to hide. And suppose they could track her by her dreams? She imagined her dreams broadcasting through the darkness, like radio waves. Maybe her godmother could tune her car radio to Kate's dreams. Or maybe Cara, or Lillian, or all of them, had tracking devices mounted on the handlebars of their bikes.

She would just have to wait. How long before it got light? Five o'clock? Maybe by four it would be light enough for walking. She pressed back against the tree and rotated her shoulders. She'd never done so much walking in her life. An image came to her, sharp as a photo. She and Melissa, eighty years old, walking on a beach. She smiled, happy for the first time since—since . . . She couldn't seem to calculate time very clearly. No matter. She just thought about Melissa at eighty, her face written all over with delicate lines, like a manuscript of all their years together.

What must it be like, she thought, to lose someone after so many years? She could hardly imagine an agony more acute than the thought that Mother Night had almost taken Melissa that same day. But suppose time had allowed them to grow into each other, slowly becoming one body? How could you exist with half your body torn out? She thought about the old story of the first woman taken from the rib of the first man. It had always struck her as absurd, but maybe instead of the woman's creation, the story described her death. Torn out of his side after their hundreds of years making babies to people the Earth. She imagined the woman eating some poisoned fruit, an apple from the Tree of Death. And then it occurred to her that she better not eat anything here in the woods. She knew so little about plants, how to recognize the good from the evil. Hell, she thought, she knew so little about anything. Just death, and loving Melissa.

The sky brightened, and she stood up, dusted herself off, and began walking again.

Hours later, the road began to widen, with fewer trees, and soon she came around a corner, and there stood a gas station, and outside the door of the small concrete building a shiny pay telephone. She took off running, but when she got within twenty feet she stopped. What could be more dangerous than a gas station? All they had to do was come rolling in for a tankful and there she'd be. But after ten minutes of standing there, unable to make up her mind, she knew she had no choice. She couldn't bear not speaking to Melissa. She could keep an eye on the road, and if she saw them she could run behind the building, or hide in the ladies' room. Shaking with excitement, she got to the phone—and discovered she couldn't remember the number. She searched through her pockets until she found the piece of paper with the message from Jason. There were the numbers, but which one was the hospital? She felt like slamming the phone down against the box. Why couldn't she think? She took a deep breath. Okay. Do it slowly, she told herself. She was just tired from staying up all night. Vaguely she remembered something about a group of people confused by the telephone, but when it wouldn't come clearly she left the thought behind. She stared at the paper. The number on the top—that had to be Jason, right? Because she was supposed to call Jason first? In fact, the other number—that was her own handwriting, wasn't it? Jason himself had given it to her.

A simple task. Transfer the numbers on the page to the buttons on the box. Slowly, with one false start after another, she hunted down the numbers one by one, all the while thinking of a man she'd known, a friend of Mark's, who'd suffered a stroke and could never seem to find the right words for the thoughts jamming together in his head. Finally she'd done it and the phone began ringing on the other end. Nervously, she scanned the road. No cars or motorcycles. She'd done it. She was going to speak to Melissa. But instead of the hospital she just heard a machine voice asking for forty-five cents, repeating it over and over, and before Kate could get the change from her pocket and figure out the coins, the voice had given up on her and removed itself, returning her to the flat buzz of the dial tone.

Once more she traveled down the river of numbers, this time with her coins all laid out on top of the box. After she'd put in her money a voice came on. A voice and a horrible scratching, so loud it made it impossible for Kate to hear whatever it was the voice was saying. "Melissa Evans," she half shouted into the phone. The voice said something else. The number, Kate thought. It needs the extension. Or the room number. She searched the memo paper, while all the time the scratching got louder and the voice farther and farther away. Finally, she heard a click, and though Kate shouted, "Don't hang up!" she knew she had missed her chance.

Forcing herself not to cry, she marched into the building, where a gaunt boy about seventeen sat behind a counter stacked with newspapers, doughnuts, and lottery cards. "I need a phone," Kate said. "The one outside is broken."

"Right out past the air pump."

"I just told you. That one is broken."

The boy shrugged, and Kate wanted to strangle him. "Sorry," he said, " 's only one."

Kate asked, "What do you do if someone robs you? What do you do if they shoot you and you've got to call for an ambulance?" He shrugged. Kate might have screamed at him if she hadn't heard a car pull into the lot, followed by the ping of a bell summoning the boy to service.

Kate spun around. It was okay. Just a station wagon, a long white thing with rust spots over the front wheel. A man in a suit sat behind the wheel. Safe or not, Kate decided she couldn't stay there any longer, not even if this boy getting up meant she could search for his hidden telephone.

Twice more that day, as she passed through small towns, Kate tried to call the hospital. She tried from a pay phone but kept getting the wrong numbers, and she even asked a woman in an insurance office to dial it for her, saying she had arthritis. When that, too, failed, reaping nothing but busy signals, Kate knew the phone system had beaten her.

Everywhere she went along the town's single shopping street she heard people talking about death. "Can you believe it? He jogged five miles a day. Skinny as Mickey Mouse and didn't even drink coffee, and then a fucking blood clot smacks him in the brain." "Sorry about the dinner. Michael's brother died and we couldn't reach everybody in time." "The really sad thing is, we found that dog half starved. We had to give it saucers of milk like a kitten. Just so a brat in his father's car can come and wipe it away." "She was supposed to go speak at that gender rebels conference, the one they showed on TV? And then her lover starts spewing blood onto the bathroom mirror and the next morning she's dead." "I still can't believe it. He got through the operation. It was just a simple cut. I can't believe it." "They're calling it an accident. Yeah, right. In the back of the head?"

Kate wished she could protect herself. Maybe she could stain her clothes with blood. Or wear flowers around her neck. Or stuff her pockets with fingernail clippings. She remembered Alicia, sad Alicia, who'd tried to protect herself from death and the punishment she imagined would come after it. Avoiding cars and restaurants and high winds, only to have her own father surrender to the enemy.

The night found her out in the country again, this time by fields instead of hills. Just before the darkness settled on her, she spotted a trio of large rocks set in a semicircle and took a chance on crossing the field so that she could sit down with her back against the middle stone.

She dreamed that night, though she couldn't remember feeling tired, or even closing her eyes. In the dream, Melissa came and sat in front of her, there in the field. She wore a dress of thick braids, every braid a different color. The material rippled against her body like an everlasting waterfall. Pictures fell from the sky. At first Kate thought they were rain but as they slid down Melissa's face, Kate could see them more clearly—spirals and stars, and dancing sticks, and blue circles radiating light. Melissa touched Kate's cheeks and shoulders, and stroked her eyebrows and the side of her neck, but when Melissa tried to kiss her, Kate turned her face away. Please, she told her lover. Listen. Nothing was more important now than listening.

She told Melissa about her godmother, and the Motorcycle Girls, about all the secret trips they took, and Dead Jimmy and the street-market, and Alicia Curran. She told her about Laurie, and how Kate had lied to Laurie all her life. "I don't want to lie to you too," she said. "Please don't let me do that. I want you to know." Throughout the telling she held Melissa's hands in each of hers, and when she finished she still held them, even though she leaned forward to kiss Melissa's lips. "When you wake up," she said finally, "promise me you'll remember. Will you promise me that? Will you remember?"

"Yes," Melissa said. "I promise."

When morning came Kate got up, shook herself slightly, and once more started walking.

She had no idea how long she'd been going when she came to the edge of the woods. She recognized it, of course. She knew Thorny Woods better than anyone. Almost anyone. Better keep away, she thought. Wasn't that the first place they would look for her? Maybe they were already waiting. She better run.

She had already turned and was trying to remember which way to go when she heard the crying. Sirenlike, it rose and fell, cutting through the trees. Kate looked all around, and when she saw no one she called out "Hello?" first stiffly, then louder. She glanced down the street, thinking maybe someone would hear, and wondering if she could bang on someone's door. The street looked so deserted. Even the one car she could see in someone's driveway looked all rusty and flat, as if it had stood there for years.

When she turned toward the woods again, the crying rose in volume and speed. "I can't go in there," she shouted. Even raising her voice like that made her nervous. She wanted to say "I'm sorry you're hurt, or whatever it is, but I can't go in there. I've got to keep moving. Can't you understand that?" The crying rolled on and on. "Damn!" she said, and began running through the trees.

Kate didn't worry about the tree branches, or even tracking the sound. She just headed for the clearing. Just before she got there the crying suddenly stopped, and when she burst into the small meadow she had to look around for a few seconds before she spotted the child crouched down tightly at the edge of the trees. "Hey, it's all right," Kate said. "It's okay." She patted the air, as if the waves would reach the child and soothe her terrified body.

The girl looked about seven years old, though her crumpled face and posture made it hard to tell. She wore a red T-shirt and bright yellow overalls, stained all over with dirt and grass and some kind of purple berries. Her blond hair, all tangled up and half in her face, shone brighter than her clothes in the dull cloud-harried light. She looked like she'd been hiding in the woods for days.

Moving very slowly toward the girl, Kate said, "It's okay. I'm here to help you." As the child uncurled her body, Kate saw that she was clutching some bundle, wrapped in a blue cloth. Even before she knelt down beside the child and gently tugged at the corners of the cloth she knew what it was. The bones. The same bones she'd seen—weeks ago?—when she'd come for her supply of *Phytolacca.* The bones gleamed, and Kate wondered if the girl had washed them in a stream, or maybe licked away the dirt.

"They're really precious to you, aren't they?" Kate said.

"They're my brother's."

"Oh God," Kate whispered. She closed her eyes for just a moment and saw a terrible vision of a screaming child being hacked to pieces. When she opened her eyes again she discovered she was crying. She pulled the child close to her.

She was still holding her when she heard a growl behind her. The girl began to yell and struggle, but Kate held on tightly to her. "What is it?" she said. "What is it?" The growling got louder and Kate realized it was coming from behind her. Shit, she thought, it must be a dog or a wildcat or even a bear. But when she turned around she saw something so strange she cried out and pulled the girl even more closely against her. A woman stood there. A woman of medium height, wearing an old-fashioned dress, tight at the bodice and flaring out stiffly, like metal flanges, from the waist. Her hair—she seemed to have wound her hair into tight coils on either side of her head. Her face—but Kate couldn't see her face, just as she couldn't see her neck or her arms, or even really her hair. For wherever her body should have shown there was only the outline of a form, and within that form a darkness. It was the darkness that terrified children each night as they lay down in their beds. An infinite darkness filled with monsters.

There was nothing of the refuge that Kate had discovered when she would close her eyes before looking for her godmother by the beds of sick people. Instead, waves of rage and hunger battered her, and with each wave an undertow tried to suck her in, clawing away her skin, her face, everything that kept her human and safe. The child's crying had changed to screams that vibrated through Kate's body so that all her bones were screaming. "Keep away from her," she managed to say. "You can't have her. I won't let you."

The moment she said them, the words struck her as ludicrous. The monster would leap at her, sink its invisible teeth into her face . . . But instead, the creature changed. Instead of the darkness, Kate saw the normal skin and eyes and teeth of a woman hardly older than Kate herself. Like her clothes, there was something old-fashioned, even sweet, about her. She looked like a picture of an ideal mother from some storybook hundreds of years old. She said, "Oh, thank you for taking care of my daughter. I've been so worried about her."

The girl had fallen silent now, and as Kate loosened her grip, the child looked from Kate to—her mother?—and back again. Kate concentrated, trying to remember the woman's other form, and what it was that had frightened her so much.

The woman said, "She's been so much trouble since her poor sweet brother died. Poor little thing. I'll take her now." She stepped forward.

"I don't know," Kate said.

"Here," the woman said. "Let me take her. The poor darling is so scared. I've been looking everywhere for her."

Kate looked down at the ground. The bones lay there, glowing, as if a fire of rage burned inside them. Flashes of vision sparked in Kate's mind—a child slashed and cut to pieces, a small body boiled in a red pot while the bones shrieked in an agony that went on for thousands of years. When Kate looked up again the kind face of the woman still smiled at her, but inside it, underneath the skin, she could just make out that dark ocean of destruction. "No," she said, and her own voice sounded chalky to her. "No, you can't have her."

"Don't be ridiculous," the woman said. "What do you think you could do against me? Give me my daughter."

Kate's whole body was shaking, but she held on to the girl. The woman opened her mouth. Deep inside, Kate could hear a churning noise, the sound of all life being torn apart over and over. *Why?* Kate thought. Why didn't the creature just devour the child, and Kate as well. And then she realized. The woman had lied. There was in fact something very powerful that Kate could do. Except that it would mean the final surrender of hope.

"Give me my daughter," the woman told her, "and I will let you go. Wouldn't you like to return to your love? I will help you. And *my* help will never turn against you."

Kate tried to think. She could almost see Melissa in front of her, even feel Melissa's body pressed against her. Once again she saw that vision of the two of them, old women walking together along the edge of the water. She started to smile and her grip loosened around the little girl. Only, in the vision, the girl was walking with them. She held Kate's hand, and as the foam of the waves rushed over her feet they cut her so that her blood drained away in the undertow . . . She heard the child whisper "Please. She's not really my mother. She says she is and I believed her. But she's not, she's not."

Kate focused her eyes to see the woman's hand only inches away from her face. Weeping, she reached into her blouse and brought out the silver whistle that still hung, as it had for so many years, on the line of gold circling her neck. She blew into it, first softly then louder, and the trill rolled in the air. Even when Kate dropped the whistle the notes continued, changing, it seemed, to the call of a bird somewhere high above the trees.

The woman half stumbled backward. She beat her hands against her ears, as if to crack the drums and keep out the sound. And then another sound joined the lilting whistle. Hands. Five sets of hands clapping in unison, slowly, over and over, as they kept time with the trill.

From all sides of the circle of trees they came, forming the five points of a star. Cara and Lillian and Ester and Amy and Gloria, driving the false mother into the open where the light of the sun pushed through the clouds to touch her with fire. She tried to run, first one way, then another, and each time the clapping hands drove her back to the center. Except the last time. One hole remained in the circle, the sixth point of the star. The creature turned around and around until she saw them, her two intended victims crouched together in the dirt. Still holding her ears she ran at them with her mouth open, silently roaring.

Kate couldn't seem to move. The creature's face and neck had begun to shred, bringing back the darkness. Inside the mouth, Kate could see flashes of lightning. Kate managed to let go of the girl and hold up her hands. She couldn't do it, she knew. She would get the beat wrong, she would destroy their rhythm. "Kate!" Lillian shouted at her. "The bones!"

Kate dropped down to the blue cloth and grabbed a large bone in each hand. Just before the woman could grab her she banged the bones together, striking them at the same moment as the hands of the Motorcycle Girls. A shock of fire jolted her backward but she kept hold of the bones, kept striking them together.

The creature, all darkness now inside its ancient dress, ran back to the center, where it spun around. Spokes of darkness, lit by flashes of pain, shot out from it in all directions. It began to spin, and spinning rose from the ground, slowly at first then faster, until Kate found herself staring at it several feet above her head. It was going to escape, she thought. Whatever they could do just wasn't strong enough to hold it.

From the side, Kate saw a flash of motion. A short woman in a dress of many colors ran past her, swooped down to the ground for a handful of dirt and in the same motion flung it at the spiked and whirling beast. The creature fell with a thud, still spinning, still shooting out spikes of rage. Already the dirt was spinning off it, freeing it once more to escape.

Mother Night yanked a single hair from her head and held it out to Kate. "Take hold of the end," she said. "Hurry." Kate dropped the bones and reached for the end of the hair. It came alive in her fingers, like an electric snake, when Mother Night let go of it. "Throw it," Mother Night told her. Kate held it in front of her. "Now."

With a flick of her wrist Kate flung the hair at the false mother. It wrapped itself around and around the spiked darkness, and the more the thing struggled the tighter the coils pulled. As Kate watched, it began to come apart, first slowly, then faster and faster, while the Motorcycle Girls speeded up their rhythm. The spikes disintegrated, the mass lost its form then broke up into blocks, then jagged lumps, and finally pearls of darkness which hung briefly in the air until a puff of wind blew them away. With a great sigh Cara and the others dropped their hands. Mother Night looked at Kate and nodded. "Good," she said.

Too weak to stand, Kate got down on her knees and took hold of the girl. She hugged her so tightly she almost thought she could absorb the child directly into her body. When she looked up they were all standing around her. "That thing—" Kate said. "Is it gone? Did we kill it?"

Mother Night said, "Yes. Others like it will come, but this one is gone. I am very proud of you, Kate."

"Thank you," Kate whispered. Then louder she said, "I have to go with you, don't I?"

"Yes."

"I can't see Melissa?"

"Not now."

Once more Kate hugged the child and then she stood up. When she turned to her godmother she saw something she never would have thought possible. Mother Night looked nervous. "Kate—" she said, and hesitated. "I must tell you something. If I have harmed you in any way—if I have come between you and your mother—I am sorry. I have not taken a godchild in many years. Perhaps I acted wrongly. Cara believes so. I am sorry."

Kate nodded. "Thank you," she said. She turned to the girl. "Will you be all right?"

The child said, "Sure. I like these people. Aren't they great?"

"Yes," Kate said. "They are."

"But you're the best. You're even kinder than the other lady."

"Other lady?"

"She helped me bury the bones. She was kind, but you're kinder." She reached into the pocket of her overalls. "Here," she said, holding her fist out to Kate. When Kate put out her hand the girl dropped a stone into it. "The other lady gave me this, so now I'll give it to you."

Kate held it up to the sun. She recognized it immediately, of course. It was the stone Dead Jimmy had thrown at her. The one she'd tried to give to Laurie. But when she looked at the stone closely, it seemed to have changed. Or maybe she was just seeing it more clearly. For there were faces in it. On the side with the tree she saw her own face, very small but clearly her, there among the branches. And on the boat side, the stick figure poling the boat along the river also had a face. A young woman with curly hair and round eager expression. At first, Kate tried to tell herself she didn't know who it was, but a moment later she gave way to the knowledge. "Jaqe," she whispered. She could feel Mother Night touch her shoulder, but she paid no attention. Instead, she held up the stone for the sun to light the face. "*Jaqe.*"

Five

The Laughing Women

Everyone at the funeral agreed they had never seen anything like it. Louise, who had taken charge of the arrangements, had expected a "decent-sized turnout" as she'd put it, but nothing unusual. After all, Kate had traveled so much she'd never stayed in one place long enough to spin a real net of friends. So when Mark told Louise to rent a hall rather than depend on the chapel in the funeral home, Louise had simply stared at him. "Trust me on this," Mark said. "Rent the biggest place you can find."

From all over the country they came, and even across the sea. Laurie could only stare in amazement as the hall filled up, row after row after row. Melissa, who had come off a hospital bed only days before, said that most of the people would have had to start traveling the moment they'd read the news in the paper or heard it on the radio. After the rabbi had offered her formal prayers, and Louise and Mark had given eulogies, with Laurie nodding and Melissa's bruised face coated in silent tears, the others began to speak. One by one, they told how Kate Cohen had saved their lives, bringing them back to land, when everyone else had set them adrift down the river of death. And more, they described the spells Kate cast over them, so that when they found themselves brought back to the world they also found themselves different. Able to accomplish the things that had always slipped away, or to replace bitterness with love. A woman named Alice Harmon said nothing about whatever destruction Kate had saved her from, but talked only of her constant amazement at the weight of the air on her skin, or the way her husband's face moved when he spoke to her. Kate Cohen had understood such things, she said, and that understanding had taken away fear, leaving only the purity of surprise.

Toward the end of the service (which ended only because the funeral director pleaded with the crowd to allow the body to go to the cemetery), a whole new group of people came into the hall. Laurie wondered if they belonged to some sort of cult where Kate had taught a workshop, for they all arrived together, about twenty or thirty of them, and even though they dressed differently from each other, some in very old-fashioned styles, their clothes all looked a little shabby, as if the cult leader forbade them to wear anything new. Laurie's suspicions increased when the group began to make a low whistling noise, hardly more than a sigh except that it went on and on. Laurie might have asked them to leave if the funeral hadn't ended just then. Luckily, the strange group didn't go to the cemetery. Maybe, Laurie thought, the cult forbade them such direct contact with death.

After the burial, when they'd returned to the apartment, Laurie told everyone, even Melissa, that she wanted a few hours alone. The night before, Louise and Mark had stayed with her and Melissa at the funeral home until eleven, and then Laurie and Melissa had stayed up another three hours, telling their very different stories of Kate. Melissa would have stayed up all night, but Laurie insisted she sleep. Now Laurie told Melissa, "I just want to sit by myself and think. Try to take in some of the things all those people said—I still can't believe it. I never had any idea. You don't mind, do you?"

"Of course not. Miracle cure or not, I should go rest. And I do need to change my clothes at some point." Though she'd rented a hotel room, Melissa had slept in Laurie's old room, wearing to the funeral the same clothes she'd traveled in the day before. They all agreed to meet at six, Melissa, Mark, Louise and Aggie, and Kate's grandparents, Allan and Marsha Lang. And then suddenly Laurie was alone for the first time in days, the first time in over thirty years. For a while she just stood there, shaking her head, but then she sighed and went to the kitchen to make herself a cup of black tea. Holding the cup before her like some stone of power, she sat down in the living room to stare at the two huge plants guarding the window. All those people, she thought. How modest Kate had been. Never a word, and if Laurie had tried to ask about the strange (and frightening) fact that Kate actually healed people who were dying, Kate had always waved the questions away.

Like Melissa, Laurie thought. Two-thirds dead only a week ago. *Oh Kate*, she said to herself, *if you could do that, why couldn't you have rescued yourself?* All those people.

I should have got up there and joined them, Laurie thought. *She saved my life too.* If Kate hadn't been there when Jaqe died, Laurie knew she would have drifted into some place emptier than death. She got up and moved to her bedroom, where she had collected in a lacquered bowl the few items found with Kate's body. Everything, even the two coins found in her pocket, seemed to glow, as if Kate's last breath had refused to leave the world but instead had taken refuge in these random objects. Laurie fiddled with Kate's emerald stud earrings and her onyx ring. And then she picked up the odd thing, the small silver whistle on its golden chain. According to the police report it had lain alongside Kate's body, as if she'd been holding it when she died. Laurie held it up to the light. Kate had worn this thing for years, since she was a child in fact. Laurie couldn't even remember where Kate had gotten it. Maybe Mark had given it to her. It looked like his kind of thing, a silver tube with a precise labyrinth inscribed on the side.

She should give it to Melissa, she thought. Melissa would like that. She put the whistle in her pocket.

In the living room again, she finished her tea, and then, for no reason at all, she turned on the radio. Listlessly, she turned the dial in search of some peaceful music, but all she could find was raucous commercials and even more raucous talk shows. She was about to give up when she caught a station, very faint and crackling, with seemingly nothing on but two women talking and laughing together. What a strange program, she thought, but the sound relaxed her, so she sat back in the chair, smiling, with her eyes closed.

"Jaqe!" she shouted suddenly, and jolted forward in her seat. *That was Jaqe's voice.* She couldn't make out the words, but she would know that laugh forever. And—and—Kate. The other voice belonged to her daughter, she was sure of it. Out loud Laurie said, "Oh shit, I'm losing my mind." But she knew she didn't care. Crazy or not, she just wanted to hold on tightly to that gorgeous duet.

She had no idea how long it lasted. A minute, five minutes— She rolled in it, swam in it, even though she could only catch one word, repeated several times during the conversation. "Laurie." She laughed and clapped her hands at the thought that they were talking about her.

When the voices began to fade into static she leaped forward to try and bring it back, though she knew it was hopeless. Within seconds, the static had swallowed the last shreds of their voices. Laurie turned down the sound, leaving it on just in case they returned. For a while she stayed there, bent forward slightly. Funny, she thought. Kate was older now. Older than Jaqe. Only when she noticed that she couldn't hear the static did she realize she was moaning, rocking back and forth and moaning so loudly she became scared someone would come banging on the door or even call the police. She pressed her lips together and clenched her fists. When she felt she could sit up without shaking she turned off the radio.

She got up and walked over to the coat closet, where for no reason she could think of she took out her old black leather jacket. She held it up in front of her, amazed that it hadn't just crumbled after so many years on the hanger. She put it on, laughing to herself at how much it weighed. She was about to take it off when she shrugged and snatched her keys from the table.

Down in the street she walked quickly, with her hands pushed into her pockets. She felt much too old to go walking around in black leather. After a while she found herself at the old bridge crossing the narrow river between the two boroughs. She hesitated, then strode onto the footpath. Halfway across she stopped and leaned over the railing. Below her, the river moved sluggishly, smeared with oil and chemicals. She could see no sign of anything alive down there. Nothing moved along the bank, and even the scraggly bushes looked lifeless and broken, surrounded by bricks and scrap metal and old beer cans. Go home, she told herself. Go home and go to sleep.

But how could she sleep in such an empty world? How did she sleep, or eat, or do anything before she met Jaqe? Before Kate was born? How could she go back to that?

She began to cry, and searched in her pocket for a tissue. But instead of soft scrunched paper she found something small and hard. She took it out and stared at it. Kate's whistle. It sparkled so sharply in the sun that Laurie wondered if Kate had polished it just before her death. Laurie held it for a moment, then blew into the delicate mouthpiece. A birdlike trill floated in front of her. She blew it once more, trying to imagine Kate with birds around her.

From a few feet away on the bridge a voice came. Though Laurie had not heard it in thirty years, and had tried to forget it ever existed, she knew it from the first syllable. "Hello, Laurie," Mother Night said.

Laurie's first thought was to run. Her body stiffened, even lurched sideways, but then she sagged, and let her breath out. Where? Where could she run that Mother Night couldn't get there ahead of her? Hadn't she learned that lesson thirty years ago? And besides, there was nothing to run to. Nothing left.

So she stood there, silently. But when Mother Night reached out to touch her, Laurie jumped back. "You do not need to fear me," Mother Night said. "I have not come to take you. This is not your time."

Now Laurie turned to look at her. Mother Night wore a long patchwork velvet dress and a multilayered hat, with each layer a little smaller than the one below. "Goddamn you," Laurie said. Then louder: "Goddamn you! It wasn't Kate's time either. And Jaqe. *And Jaqe.* It wasn't Jaqe's time thirty fucking years ago!"

"You are wrong. I know your anger. Believe me, I know it better than anyone. But I do not control these things. I do not control nearly as much as you and Kate have thought."

Deep inside Laurie, lights were flashing and a voice was shouting,

Don't get her angry. You know who she is. But Laurie no longer cared. "Don't tell me your goddamn lies," she said. "You control everything."

"No." Mother Night turned away a moment, glancing at the water. When she looked back at Laurie her face had softened. She said, "Kate says that I have hurt you. That I came between you and her."

For a moment, wonder pushed aside Laurie's rage. "You talk to her?"

"Of course. She is my goddaughter, after all."

"And Jaqe? Do you talk to Jaqe?"

"Jaqe is with me always."

All of Laurie's anger came rushing back. "She should be with me! What right did you have to just take her like that? So she could be with you always. You didn't need her. *I* did." Mother Night said nothing. "And Kate. Kate needed me, not you. You took her from me all her life."

Mother Night shook her head. "No. Possibly I tried to do too much with Kate. As I told her, I have not had a godchild in many years. If so, I apologize to you, Laurie. And perhaps I inhabited her childhood more widely than I should have. But if I ever sought to take her from you, or replace you in any way, then I most certainly failed.

"Please listen to me, Laurie. I know that you believe that you failed your daughter. But I tell you this, and I tell it to you because it is the truth: despite your fears and confusions, you were as fine a mother as any child has ever had."

For a long time, Laurie just stood there, facing the old woman, not sure whether to thank her or scream at her. Finally she said, "You should never have done it. I don't care whether it worked or not. You should never even have tried. To separate us like that. Do you understand?"

Mother Night bowed her head, very slightly. "Yes. I am sorry."

Another pause, and then Laurie said, "Will you tell her—tell *them*—that I love them? Very, very much?"

"Yes. I promise you."

Once again, Mother Night glanced at the water, and this time Laurie turned and looked over the bridge railing. Something was moving down there— A turtle? A large turtle was slowly paddling through the greasy water. Despite everything, Laurie stared at it in amazement.

The lines etched into its shell seemed to form patterns, some kind of design she couldn't quite make out . . .

She jerked her head around. Mother Night was gone. "No!" Laurie shouted. She turned all about, searching up and down the bridge. "Come back here! I'm not done." The bridge stayed empty.

"Damn!" Laurie shouted, and hit her fist against her leg. She began to cry, wildly, holding on tightly to the bridge railing, as if the force of her tears might lift her over the side. There was so much more she wanted to say, so many messages she wanted to give them.

She had no idea how much time had passed, but the wild sobbing had dwindled to a stream of tears as steady as the river when she felt a tug on the sleeve of her jacket. Laurie jumped, only to feel foolish when she turned and saw a little girl, about five years old, looking up at her. The girl wore yellow overalls and a blue T-shirt, and her blond hair looked freshly combed. She was holding up a red cotton scarf. "Here," the child said. "Do you want to use this? You can blow your nose."

Laurie smiled and dug into her pockets until she found a couple of tissues. "It's okay," she said. "Thanks." When she'd cleaned up her face as best as she could, she asked, "Where did you come from?"

The girl tilted her head. "Over there," she said vaguely.

"Are you lost?"

"I don't think so."

Laurie crouched down. "Where's your mommy?"

"She's gone," the child said, and Laurie wondered if the girl's mother had run away or died or simply left for the day. Whatever had happened, the girl didn't seem bothered by it. Not nearly as bothered as Laurie, who found herself furious that such a young child could be wandering around by herself for whatever reason.

"I'm hungry," the girl said. "Can you give me something to eat?"

Laurie stood up. "I'll tell you what. How about I get you some food somewhere, and then we figure out where you belong?"

"Okay." She took Laurie's hand and they began walking off the bridge. "You're nice," she said.

"Thank you."

As they reached the land, the girl looked up at Laurie. She said, "Can we all live happily ever after now?"

Laurie laughed. "Sure," she said. "That sounds like a great idea."